St □□□□□□□□□□□□□□□ a First
I □□□□□□□□□□□□□□□ ntest,
ar □□□□□□□□□□□□□□□ e than
a □□□□□□□□□□□□□□□ es as
The Magazine of Fantasy & Science Fiction, Weird

Also by Stephen Woodworth:

Through Violet Eyes
With Red Hands
In Golden Blood

From Black Rooms

Stephen Woodworth

piatkus

PIATKUS

First published in the US in 2006 by Bantam Dell,
A division of Random House, Inc., New York, New York
First published in Great Britain as a paperback original in 2010
by Piatkus

A CIP catalogue record for this book
is available from the British Library.

ISBN 978-0-7499-4142-0

Typeset in Palatino by Action Publishing Technology Ltd
Printed and bound in Great Britain by CPI Mackays, Chatham, ME5 8TD

Papers used by Piatkus are natural, renewable and recyclable
products sourced from well-managed forests and certified
in accordance with the rules of the Forest Stewardship Council.

Piatkus
An imprint of
Little, Brown Book Group
100 Victoria Embankment
London EC4Y 0DY

An Hachette UK Company
www.hachette.co.uk

www.piatkus.co.uk

This book is dedicated to the many close friends
whose unswerving encouragement and support
have sustained me throughout my writing career:
David and Diana Whiting, Amy and David Trotti,
David Rickel and Edward Wheat, Jason Yee,
and so many others.
Most of all, I owe this novel
to the best friend I could ever have,
my wife and colleague, Kelly Dunn.

Acknowledgements

I relied on many information sources in the writing of this novel and owe a particular debt of gratitude to *The Rescue Artist* by Edward Dolnick for inspiration.

I would also like to thank the following individuals for their unflagging support, patience, and assistance: my steadfast editor Anne Lesley Groell and the whole crew at Bantam Dell; my previous agent, Jimmy Vines; my present agent, Danny Baror; my family and friends; and, ever and always, my beloved wife and colleague, Kelly Dunn.

To the Reader

All of the paintings described in this book are real
artworks that were actually stolen from the places
mentioned and in the manner described. As yet,
none of them have been returned, and no one
knows who has them or where they are ...

Disease, insanity and death were the angels which attended my cradle, and since then have followed me throughout my life. I learned early about the misery and dangers of life, and about the afterlife, about the eternal punishment which awaited the children of sin in hell.

—*Edvard Munch*

1

The Children of Dr. Wax

On the day Bartholomew Wax had selected to kill himself, he called in sick at work to spend the entire day saying goodbye to his children. He would enjoy their company as he ate his last meal.

With the strains of a Vivaldi violin concerto issuing from the speakers of his home's built-in sound system, Wax uncorked his finest bottle of burgundy and prepared himself a plate of brie, foie gras, cracked wheat and rye crackers, and fresh grapes. Once the wine had had a chance to breathe, he placed it on a sterling-silver tray along with the platter of food and a cut-crystal goblet, and carried it from the kitchen to a door in the hallway. Setting the tray on the adjacent mahogany side table, he punched in a seven-digit combination on the door's digital keypad, and the carbon-steel bolts slid back into the jamb with the *shuck* of shells pumped into a shotgun barrel.

Wax pulled the door open, revealing the foot-thick depth of insulation and metal behind its wooden façade. The walls of the basement had been similarly reinforced. The plaster and drywall hid tungsten-carbide plates and sandwiched layers of concrete, steel, and Sheetrock, making the shelter impervious to fire, drills, and explosives. The vault had cost his employers at the North American Afterlife Communications Corps a couple million dollars to build, but no price was too great to pay for his children's safety.

They glowed in welcome as he descended the cellar steps with the silver tray. Sensors detected his heat signature and switched on the lamps that illuminated his family. Warm yellow light bloomed in patches in the darkness of the black-walled room. Basking in their individual spotlights, the children smiled at him—as precious to him as if he'd given birth to them himself. Wax had positioned the spots to light each canvas to best effect, precisely calibrating the intensity so as not to fade the colors. Although a blistering New Mexico heat broiled the exterior of the house, climate-control systems kept the cellar at a constant seventy degrees, with just enough humidity to keep the paintings from cracking.

An office chair and a small table in the center of the floor provided the chamber's only furnishings. As the vault door automatically sealed him inside, Wax set the tray on the table, unwound the bread-bag twist-tie he'd used to hold back his hair, and shook out the ponytail until it fell down around his shoulders in a gray mane. Popping a grape in his mouth, he seated himself in the chair, which he could swivel to view the artwork hanging on any of the cellar walls. There, with forced air and piped music swathing him in a cool swirl of Vivaldi strings, he spent his last hour with the only real family he had ever known.

As an only child, Bartholomew Wax had virtually grown up among paintings. His divorced mother couldn't afford a babysitter during summer vacation, so every morning she would drop him off at the Isabella Stewart Gardner Museum while she went to work the day shift at a Dunkin' Donuts shop in downtown Boston. Back in the seventies, when parents were still naïve about pedophilia and when day care was considered a luxury, Bartholomew's mother told herself that it would do the boy good to spend his days surrounded by high culture rather than at home watching television.

A withdrawn and frail boy with an autistic's love of routine, little Barty came to cherish his hours in the dim galleries of the Italian-style palazzo. The docents all knew him by name, and he would eat his sack lunch among the white lilies and Greco-Roman statuary in the peaceful courtyard, alone with his thoughts. But what he loved most were the paintings, each of which remained exactly where Mrs. Gardner had decreed it should stay forever. Masterpieces of different sizes and themes jammed some walls so closely that their frames butted against one another, resembling a patchwork of postage stamps on an enormous envelope. Each one silently whispered its story, and when no one else was in the room, he would talk to each in turn, telling them all his secrets and his grand plans for the future. They were his family, after all.

Several members of that family now hung before him in this vault. Munching a cracker spread with brie, Wax basked in the delicate glow of *The Concert* — one of only thirty-five Vermeers in existence. The artist's muted use of light gave a preternatural tranquillity to the scene of a seventeenth-century Dutch family playing musical instruments; Wax could actually hear the quiet harmony of the clavichord and guitar calming the frenzy of thoughts in his mind.

Next to the Vermeer, *Storm on the Sea of Galilee* churned in an endless, frozen tempest. Rembrandt's only seascape, it depicted Jesus' disciples clinging to a sailboat that cresting white water threatened to overturn. Golden sunlight touched the wave-tossed boat as a hole of blue sky opened in the coal-smoke clouds, the promise of God's salvation for the faithful. Now more than ever, Bartholomew Wax needed the possibility of peace and redemption.

His meal finished, he rose from his chair and strolled past the remainder of his collection, sipping wine from his goblet. Here were the other siblings from the Gardner—a tiny Rembrandt self-portrait, *Chez Tortoni* by Manet, *La Sortie de Pesage* by Degas, and more. Alas, those barbarians from the Corps had savagely cut the pictures from their frames, and Wax himself had had to remount the canvases on stretchers and find suitable replacement frames. He also made sure that the NAACC took greater care the next time they procured children for him to adopt.

Wax had always dreamed of having such a family. Reproductions would not do, for even the finest lithographs could not capture the play of light upon the actual brushwork, the depth and textures of the swirls and ridges, the translucence of the glazes. As a boy, he decided that he would have to become very rich so that he, too, could buy a mansion full of artworks like Mrs. Gardner's. His need for money drove him into medicine, for weren't all doctors well-to-do? Yet as he matured and learned more about the rarified world of art auctions, Wax discovered that even works painted by the artists after their deaths—the posthumous "collaborations" created by the government's violet-eyed conduits for the dead—sold for millions of dollars each. And these were not the works he wanted. He considered starting his own biotechnology company to make his fortune in the stock market, but soon realized that even the wealth of Bill Gates could not purchase the works he truly wanted—the priceless treasures that hung in the Gardner and other museums around the world. And that was when he made his bargain with the North American Afterlife Communications Corps, offering his services in exchange for their promise to accumulate the unattainable collection he craved.

Wax lingered before each item in the gallery as he made his way around the vault attempting to delay the inevitable. After more than fifteen years of effort, his work for the Corps was near an end, which meant that so was he. Ironically, success rather than failure spelled his doom. As soon as the NAACC obtained what it wanted, it would take his family away and eliminate him to protect its secrets.

He paused in front of da Vinci's *Madonna of the Yarnwinder*, raised the goblet to his lips, but found only a dribble of wine left. Once again, he toyed with the idea of sealing himself up with his treasures like a pharaoh in his tomb. But Wax knew better than anyone that you could take nothing into the afterlife. The Corps would no doubt breach the vault sooner or later, and Wax could not bear to think of his children ending up in the hands of a ghoul like Carl Pancrit.

He contemplated Leonardo's rendition of Mary and the Christ child, which had once adorned the home of the Duke of Buccleuch in Scotland. In the painting, the baby gazed at the T-shaped wooden spindle in his hands, a symbol of the cross that awaited him—the end prefigured in the beginning. Mary's right hand hovered uncertainly over the infant, as if she longed to hold her son back from his destiny yet knew she could not. Certain sacrifices had to be made.

Wax approached the final and most recent acquisition in his collection with reluctance. His time was almost up, but that was not why he dawdled. The last picture frightened him. Although he had seen countless copies and parodies of *The Scream*, none had prepared him for the terror portrayed in the original, brought here all the way from the Munch Museum in Oslo. Beneath a sky as red and fluid as an arterial hemorrhage, a solitary androgynous figure shivered on a bleak seaside boardwalk, its eyes and mouth gaping, its grotesque, distended hands pressed to its temples.

Most people who saw the picture did not realize that it was not the humanoid figure screaming. No, Wax mused, the mutant being was struck dumb with fear as it vainly covered its ears to shut out the eternal, cosmic wail of the universe—"a loud, unend-

6

ing scream piercing nature," as Edvard Munch had put it.

With its indigo eyes and bald, skull-like head, the figure might have been a Violet, its scalp shaved to accommodate the electrodes of a SoulScan device.

The resemblance filled Bartholomew Wax with both revulsion and a renewed sense of urgency. What would it be like to hear that awful shriek of transcendental agony ... and never be able to shut it out? What if everyone could hear it? Would the human race be able to withstand the constant sound of its own inescapable mortality?

The questions preyed on Dr. Wax, hastening him into action. Tying his hair back into its ponytail with the twist-tie, he did not take the trouble to clean up the remains of his last meal, but left the cheese and pâté to rot on the silver tray beside the wine. His remaining time was too valuable, and he would never return to this place, anyway.

Instead, he began taking the paintings off the wall one at a time, meticulously packing them into the special reinforced shipping crates he'd accumulated in the cellar for that purpose. Custom-cut Styrofoam brackets held each frame motionless within its box, ensuring that nothing touched the surface of the canvas, while wood inserts prevented the cardboard sides from being crushed or punctured. The crates all bore shipping labels with the name "Arthur Maven" and a false return address as well as the packages' destinations: the Munch Museum in Norway, Drumlanrig Castle in Scotland, and, of course, the Gardner, among many others.

Wax actually smiled as he imagined the astonishment on the recipients' faces when they opened the boxes and discovered their long-lost pictures inside. The thought made him happy. Unlike human beings, artworks had no afterlife in which to perpetuate their existence. A painting that no one saw ceased to be, and his children deserved to live.

The CD changer on his stereo system switched from Vivaldi to Mahler's Ninth. Opening the vault door, Wax began the laborious task of carrying the crates up the stairs and out to his Ford Explorer. He left the engine running and the air conditioner on full-blast while loading the SUV which barely contained his collection. At last ready to depart, he grabbed the antique black doctor's bag that usually carried only his lunch.

The afternoon sun cast the vertical ridges of the Organ Mountains in sharp relief, the craggy gray range resembling the pipes of a church organ as its name implied. Dr. Wax lived in a desert housing development a few miles outside Las Cruces, and had to hurry to make it to the shipping office before the cutoff time for overnight delivery.

"You want more than fifty bucks' insurance on any of these?" the thick-fingered clerk asked him when she weighed in the packages.

Wax smiled at the folly of assigning a dollar value to an irreplaceable work of genius. "No, that'll do."

With the members of his adopted family safely on their way back to their original owners, Dr. Wax drove his SUV back onto U.S. 70 headed east. He now had to attend to his other progeny—the misbegotten ones.

Dusk tanned the chaparral along the road a dirty orange, and the scattered houses at the city's edge grew more infrequent. Wax wound his way through the deepening shadows of a cleft in the mountains until he passed the turnoff for Route 213 South, which brown-and-white signs indicated would lead to White Sands National Monument. He turned instead on the restricted road that served as entrance to the missile range, pausing at the guardhouse to display his I.D. badge to the soldier on duty. The G.I., a crew-cut beanpole of a boy whose face still broke out in zits, waved him on with barely a glance. He knew mousy Dr. Wax. Everyone here did.

A herd of oryx grazed along the road toward the military base, adding a surreal touch to an already alien landscape. Distinguished by the black-and-white coloration on their heads and their long, straight horns, these African antelope had been imported here as part of a program to introduce exotic game into the region, and they had thrived in the New Mexican desert. The animals scattered as Wax veered down an unmarked offshoot of the main road.

Before long, the desert gave way to an even more desolate landscape: stark dunes of granular gypsum, as white and coarse as ground bones. In places, the windswept mounds of sand had crept over the fringe of the pavement, attempting to reclaim the path and bury it. The SUV's tires bounced over and crunched through the occasional hillocks, which the Army would plow aside like drifting snow. At last, Wax arrived at a large, windowless gray building that resembled military barracks. No sign identified the structure; only those who already knew its purpose were allowed inside.

Wax parked in the adjacent asphalt lot amongst a few civilian and military vehicles and carried his black bag up to the structure's only door, which required him to slide his I.D. into a slot and press his thumb on a touch pad for authorization.

"Dr. Wax!" The corporal on duty at the front desk smiled as the scientist entered the foyer. "We weren't expecting you today. How are you feeling?"

"Much better, thanks." He smiled back, embarrassed that, although he saw her practically every day, he'd never bothered to remember the corporal's name. "Just came by to check on the subjects."

"Sure thing. You want me to call an orderly?" She nodded toward the building's auxiliary wing, where the staff lounge, offices, and laboratory were located.

"No, that won't be necessary," he replied, although he could have used the help. He'd never had to deal with the patients alone before.

"Whatever you say." The corporal tapped in a code on her computer keyboard, and the door behind her buzzed. Wax opened it and passed through into a corridor lined with identical gray doors, each with a round glass portal at eye level.

The doctor donned the white lab coat that hung on a rack to his left, but waited until the security door swung shut behind him and the buzzing ceased before opening his black bag. Instead of his usual bagel, lox, and cream cheese, it held a pneumatic vaccine gun and dozens of glass vials filled with clear liquid.

Wax drew a deep breath and set the bag on the floor. *Do no harm*, he thought. But it was far too late for Hippocrates now.

He took the first vial and inserted it top-down into the circular tube on the vaccine gun. It was the same device he'd used to inject the carrier virus into the subjects to commence their gene therapy. He hoped the gun's familiarity would keep it from spooking the patients. The doctor wouldn't be strong enough to deal with them alone otherwise.

With the gun loaded, Wax went to a wall panel beside the corridor's entrance and turned on the preprogrammed classical music he used to calm the patients during his visits. The hall filled with the sonic balm of Pachelbel's Canon in D. Although Wax himself detested the piece, he found it had the soporific effect of elevator music upon the test subjects.

Holding the gun behind his back, Dr. Wax approached the first room and peered through the porthole. When he'd satisfied himself that the occupant was not waiting to attack him, Wax entered the security code on the door's keypad to unlock it. The music was not quite loud enough to drown out the scream that burst forth as the door opened.

"Get away from me! Leave me alone!"

Dr. Wax knew that the patient was not shrieking at him. The plump man lay curled in the far corner of the room between the mattress and the toilet and did not even seem to register the doctor's presence. But Wax could not help fretting that the subject knew what he had come to do.

"Hello, Harold. How are you today?" Although he knew perfectly well how Harold was, Wax employed his usual bedside patter to avoid upsetting the patient as he advanced, the gun concealed behind him.

Harold pounded on his head with his fists, which were bound in padded cotton mittens. Scabs and scars still streaked his face and shaved scalp where he'd clawed the skin with his fingernails. "GO AWAY! *ALL* OF YOU!"

Fecal matter smeared the back of his loose hospital smock as he squirmed against the vinyl upholstery of the walls and floor. Unlike a true Violet, Harold could neither allow a dead soul to inhabit his body nor shut out the souls who tried. He lived, therefore, in a gray zone between this life and the next, constantly bombarded by spirits that knocked and knocked and knocked.

"Easy, Harold." Wax knelt and brought his arm from behind his back. "I can make them go away."

He jammed the point of the gun into Harold's upper arm and pulled the trigger. With a spitting sound, the needle shot the fluid under the skin, and Harold's eyes snapped open to stare at Wax.

"*You.*" His pupils, flecked with both violet and robin's-egg blue, became an electric shade of lavender. "*You* did this to me. I'll—"

Wax stumbled back as Harold lunged for him. But

the convulsions dropped Harold onto his belly, where he quivered like a salted slug. Not one to take chances, Bartholomew Wax had put almost ten times the lethal dosage of procaine in the vaccine gun's solution.

The doctor returned to his bag and replaced the empty poison vial with a fresh one before proceeding to the next room. Through the door's circular window, he could see a young Hispanic girl pacing the tiny cell and hugging herself. Her scalp, like Harold's, had been shaved and tattooed with the twenty node points that showed where to attach the SoulScan electrodes.

Her resemblance to the figure in *The Scream* eased his conscience over what he was about to do. It was for the best—for her, and the whole world.

When Wax entered the room, the patient darted her eyes toward him. One was violet, the other brown, like mismatched marbles. "Hello? Who are you? Where am I?"

"Don't worry. Everything's going to be all right." With the vaccine gun hidden behind him, Wax edged toward her, waiting for some indication of how dangerous the soul that inhabited her might be.

The girl swiveled her head to take in her surroundings. "Is this a hospital? I remember being in an accident." She looked down at the smooth brown skin of her arms. "What's *happened* to me?"

"You'll be fine," Wax assured her. "I'm a doctor."

The problem in handling Marisa was that the person she had been no longer existed. The quantum connection in Marisa's brain that had once moored the electromagnetic energy of her soul inside her body had eroded away, leaving her an empty receptacle for any dead soul to inhabit. Another spirit might displace the current one at any moment, but if Wax could keep the present soul at bay long enough for the injection ...

"You've got to call my husband," she beseeched him. "You've got to tell him where I am."

"Of course. But, first, let me give you something to help you relax."

Before he could administer the poison, Marisa's body jerked right as if yanked. She waggled her head, her face twisted by tics, and when the fit passed, she stood with her feet spread apart, fists clenched at her sides, her brows lowered in a glare. *"So help me, I'll kill you, Wax."*

Marisa launched herself at him, seizing his throat. Strangulation starbursts blurred his vision, and he stabbed the gun's needle blindly into her torso and pulled the trigger. Only when her hands fell away from his neck and she collapsed to the floor did he look down to see that he'd pierced the thin cloth of her hospital gown, injecting her right over the heart.

Harold, he thought, rasping to restore his breath. Wax hadn't counted on the poison working so quickly, although he'd heard that procaine in sufficient quantities could cause cardiac arrest. He couldn't risk having the patients he'd killed inhabit the other subjects; he'd have to work faster.

Hurrying back to the doctor's bag, Wax transferred

all the remaining poison vials to the deep pockets of his white coat. He paused only long enough between rooms to put a new dose in his gun. Each victim added bites, bruises, or bleeding scratches to his wounds, yet he kept on. He saw Edvard Munch's pitiful, haunted creature in each skull-like countenance, and he was determined to silence once and for all the scream they heard.

The last one, a skinny black man named Ezra, survived long enough to pursue Wax into the corridor. The doctor stumbled and crawled across the hall, hyperventilating as the dying man threatened to topple on him. When Ezra slumped halfway through the door instead, Bartholomew Wax sprang up and reloaded his gun, swapping the vials as if changing the clip in an automatic weapon. Then he cast a sheepish glance to his right.

The corporal from the front desk stood only a couple of yards away, her .45 pistol drawn and aimed at his head. She wasn't smiling.

A tall, stocky man in a navy-blue suit stood beside her. Silver threads filigreed his dark hair and thick black eyebrows, and the furrows in his face gave him a fatherly beneficence.

He tipped his head in greeting. "Dr. Wax."

'*Mr.* Pancrit." The title was a deliberate slight. Wax knew that Carl Pancrit was a doctor, too, in the technical if not the ethical sense. "I didn't expect to see you here at this hour."

"Obviously not," his colleague observed, nodding toward the man sprawled in the doorway. "But I've been expecting you. For some time now, I've

15

suspected that your heart isn't quite in this project."

Wax tightened his finger on the vaccine gun's trigger. "Take a look around you, Carl. The experiment is a failure."

"Not if it prompts further research. Yet you haven't submitted a new proposal in months, and that makes me think you're holding out on us. You wouldn't do that, would you, Barty?"

Pancrit advanced, arms spread as if to embrace him in a paternal hug, but Wax swung the gun toward him. "I'm done, Carl."

The corporal cocked her pistol.

Pancrit raised his hands to placate both of them. "Please! Let's be sensible about this." He motioned for the soldier to lower her weapon, then gave Wax a sympathetic look. "I can't blame you for putting the poor devils out of their misery. I would have done the same thing myself—"

"I'm sure you would have." Wax kept the vaccine gun level with Pancrit's chest.

"—but you still owe us for those pictures of yours. We went to a lot of trouble to get them for you. Do you want us to send 'em right back where they came from?"

Wax gave a wan smile. "That won't be necessary."

He drove the needle of his gun into his own carotid artery and pulled the trigger.

As he crumpled to the floor, the corporal rushed forward, brandishing her pistol in case Wax was playing some kind of trick.

He wasn't.

*

Carl Pancrit sighed as he watched Bartholomew Wax twitch in his death throes. "Don't think you can get away from me that easily," he muttered.

2

A Slave to the Masters

Natalie Lindstrom could not help feeling a stab of envy when she arrived at Hector Espinoza's house in Laguna Beach. Working in the Corps's Art Division had made Hector rich enough to buy this white Art Deco palace by the sea, while she and her daughter and father all had to squeeze into a two-bedroom condo in Fullerton.

Just be glad he's willing to see you, she reminded herself as she saw the sign beside the front door's buzzer. DO NOT DISTURB! it shouted. MEETINGS BY APPOINTMENT ONLY.

Natalie had phoned to arrange such a meeting a week ago, but when she pressed the buzzer button three times without a response, she began to wonder if Hector had changed his mind.

Finally, a heavy Latino man in a baggy black tank top and board shorts opened the door. His tattooed scalp had been shaved more cleanly than his face, and his violet eyes were bleary and red as he scratched crumbs of sleep dust from their corners. "Yeah?"

He apparently wasn't awake enough to recognize her in the black pageboy wig and green contacts she wore to evade the Corps Security agents who tailed her. Natalie, too, kept her head shaved, for some of

18

her fussier clients insisted upon having a SoulScan confirm that she actually summoned the dead artists she claimed to work with.

"It's me, Hector," she prompted.

"Boo? Holy crap, is it noon already?"

"Quarter-past, actually. I'm fashionably late."

"Sorry ... I spaced." He stood to one side and waved her forward. "Come on in. And pardon the freakin' mess."

He led her through several rooms that managed to look both cluttered and barren at the same time. The dining room contained a card table covered with unopened mail and one metal folding chair. The den had a flat-panel plasma TV, a black leather couch, and a shelf unit stuffed with art books, sketchbooks, and files of loose papers and drawings. Stacked pizza boxes and balled-up burger wrappers littered the hardwood floors, and empty beer bottles lay scattered like bowling pins. That was all the furnishing Hector had use for—indeed, all he had room for. The rest of the house he surrendered to the paintings.

Finished canvases leaned against the walls and armrests of the sofa, some stacked five-deep with sheets of cardboard in between. Works in progress rested on easels erected with the careless arrangement of highway roadwork signs: here a Monet, the vibrant purples and reds of its water lilies still sticky and shiny with damp paint; there a crucifixion by Raphael, awaiting its fifth glazing. The styles ranged from the dark Baroque palette of Velázquez to the drop-cloth paint spatter of Jackson Pollock's Abstract Expressionism. The place might have been a warehouse for the world's great museums, yet only one artist's work actually hung on the plain white walls—Hector's.

"These some of your latest?" Natalie recognized his signature style: spray-painted scenes of L.A. urban life with the exaggerated cartoon figures of graffiti art "I like them."

He shrugged. "Eh! I thought, hell, if no one else wants 'em, I'll put 'em up myself."

His offhand tone couldn't quite disguise his bitterness. Natalie knew that serving as a Violet in the Corps's Art Division was rather like being the lead singer in a cover band. The audience didn't care about your originals, only other people's hits.

"Hope you won't mind if I help myself to some breakfast," Hector said as they entered the kitchen. Teetering piles of dirty dishes shared counter space with jars of paintbrushes that bathed in blackened fluid while waiting to be cleaned. The heavy, refried-bean scent of microwaved burritos mellowed the sharp odors of turpentine and stale Heineken that saturated the air. Hector snatched a bottle opener from among the chaos and took a beer from the fridge. "How about it, Boo? Want to join me?"

"No. And I told you not to call me that," she said, referring to her old nickname. When she was a kid, all the Violets who went to the Iris Semple Conduit Academy with her called her "Boo," since everything seemed to scare her. She still displayed a hypochondriac's concern for her health, which was why she didn't drink alcohol—a fact Hector knew well.

"Suit yourself." He popped the cap off the bottle

with a grin and sucked up the geyser of foam that gushed from it.

"I thought you gave up drinking."

"I did."

He downed half the beer in the time it took for them to climb the stairs to his studio. As always, Natalie suppressed a sigh when she saw the size of the room, with its enormous picture windows providing a panoramic view overlooking the stippled waves of the Pacific Ocean. She usually had to paint on her condo's narrow balcony, or sometimes in the kitchen.

Still more paintings crowded the studio, most of them barely beyond the pencil-sketch stage. Beside one easel, a tall wooden bar stool supported a stained palette and an assortment of what looked like multicolored toothpaste tubes, which had been gnarled and kneaded and rolled up to squeeze the last gob of oil paint from them. A Soul Leash dangled from a nail driven into one leg of the stool. Worn like a pair of stereo headphones, it served the same emergency function as the Panic Button on a SoulScan device. If the inhabiting soul attempted to take the Violet's body out of the room, the Leash would deliver an electric shock to the brain, thereby driving out the electromagnetic spirit and restoring control to the Violet. A conduit like Hector who worked alone with unpredictable souls could not afford to take chances.

On the ledge of the easel, a pair of thick, round-rimmed eyeglasses rested against the nearly blank canvas. Natalie recognized those glasses from the last time she had come to ask Hector for a favor. They had once belonged to Claude Monet, who near the end of his life had worn them to compensate for the cataracts that progressively dimmed the vision that had once helped to begin the Impressionist movement.

A glass-fronted cabinet opposite the picture windows contained an eclectic assortment of such memento mori. Touchstones—personal effects of the deceased that still bore a quantum link to the electromagnetic energy of their souls. Keys that could unlock the afterlife and summon the dead from the black rooms that confined them. Natalie knew a few of these items. A pathetic, yellowed letter from Vincent van Gogh to his brother, Theo, begging for more money. A plaster bust of Caligula from the personal collection of Rembrandt van Rijn, who had to sell it along with most of his other possessions when he declared bankruptcy in 1656. The Corps had used three-hundred-and-fifty-year-old auction records to track down the sculpture. There were at least two dozen other antiques in the case as well, but Natalie could only guess at the identities of the artists who had once possessed them.

Although the NAACC could have arranged for a Corps Violet like Hector to use a dead artist's painting as a touchstone, the government generally favored using more mundane objects. Picasso's shaving brush was a lot easier to obtain and transport than *Guernica*. Since Natalie did not have the luxury of access to either the artists' masterpieces *or* their toiletry gear, she had to rely on her connection with Hector. A decade older than she, he had been like a big brother to her back in their days at the School.

Hector squatted beside the glass case, scanning the contents as if selecting a doughnut from a bakery display. "So you really want to mess with the crazy Norwegian, eh?"

"It's what the client asked for." Natalie crossed her arms in a manner she hoped was nonchalant rather than defensive. "Ever since *The Scream* disappeared, Munch's become trendy."

Hector chuckled. "Yeah, that's the way it goes. Any artist worth stealing is worth owning. You and me, we couldn't *pay* thieves to take our stuff."

The remark nettled her, mainly because it was true. She'd offered her original work for sale in several of the local coffeehouses at prices less than what most collectors paid for prints. Nothing.

Hector swigged more beer. "I just hope you know what you're getting into."

"I summoned Vincent without shooting myself in a wheat field," she pointed out.

"Munch's different. He's got ... *issues* with women."

Natalie bristled. "Gender mismatch" had been the primary reason the Corps cited when it denied her application to the NAACC's Art Division. According to some of the Corps's psychologists, deceased artists who inhabited a Violet of the opposite gender might find the experience too jarring, making them uncooperative. Since most of the artists in demand happened to be Dead White Guys, the Corps told Natalie, male Violets were more suited for the job. They had no problem, however, with allowing her late friend Lucy Kamei to work with Mozart and

Beethoven, so Natalie suspected the rationale was merely the Corps's excuse for shunting her into the Crime unit, where they were short on conduits.

"I can handle Munch," she muttered.

"Yeah … that's what *I* thought." Hector's lips moved as he opened one of the case's glass doors, and Natalie knew that he was already reciting his protective mantra. That way, the soul couldn't knock when he made contact with the touchstone.

"I have to do this," she said, as if he'd asked for a reason. "I have a family to support."

"I know. I wouldn't have let you come otherwise." Nudging aside a couple of objects on one shelf, he took a scuffed, spattered paintbrush with coarse bristles from the cabinet. Hector twirled it around his fingers like a baton before offering it to Natalie handle-first. "Bring it back when you're done."

Natalie hesitated. Before taking the brush, she began repeating her own protective mantra in her mind: *The Lord is my shepherd: I shall not want. He maketh me to lie down in green pastures …*

"Sure you don't want a beer, Boo? If you're hanging with Munch, you might need it." Hector downed the dregs from his bottle. "I did."

She avoided the unblinking gravity of his gaze. "Thanks, but no thanks."

… He leadeth me beside the still waters, she continued, until she had placed the brush deep within her canvas tote bag.

As she drove back home to Fullerton, Natalie's self-confidence slid into uncertainty. Although she hadn't

24

dared to admit as much to Hector, she actually shared his misgivings about working with Edvard Munch. The Norwegian really *was* crazy—an agoraphobic subject to paralyzing panic attacks and nervous breakdowns—and he really *did* have issues with women. Handsome yet shy and morbidly sensitive during his youth, he endured a string of disastrous affairs, as duplicitous beauties seduced and manipulated him. One of his lovers, Tulla Larsen, threatened to shoot herself to keep Munch from leaving her. When he tried to wrest the pistol from her, the gun fired, taking off the tip of Munch's left middle finger.

He depicted another paramour, the statuesque violinist Eva Mudocci, as Salome, smiling in satisfaction as she posed with a likeness of the artist's severed head. Given such a history, it was not surprising that in *Vampire* Munch painted a man curled in fetal helplessness upon a woman's lap while she pressed her mouth to his neck, either kissing or feeding, as her long red hair drizzled over him like stolen blood.

How would a man who portrayed females as carnal, castrating creatures—vixens and murderesses—feel about inhabiting one of the very beings he so mistrusted and feared? Natalie had no way of knowing. She would have to rely on the psychological skills she'd developed during her years of summoning murder victims for the NAACC in order to keep Edvard Munch calm, controlled, and focused. Unlike Hector, Natalie did not have a Soul Leash that could banish the artist's spirit if anything went wrong.

"Hey, kiddo," Wade Lindstrom called out the

moment she stepped through the connecting door from the condo's garage. "Did you get it?"

Natalie made a face. She didn't really feel like discussing the Munch project with anyone right now, but her dad pressed her for details of all her Violet gigs, as if they were now the family business. "Yeah. Hector wasn't happy about it, but he gave me the touchstone, anyway."

"Great! Come here—I want to show you something."

She detoured into the kitchen, where Wade sat at the breakfast table in front of a stack of open textbooks and a portable CD player. Although forced into retirement he dressed as if he were still traveling the country selling climate control systems. Without the weight he'd lost since his bypass surgery, the sport coat and slacks sagged like tent canvas around the poles of his limbs, but he'd refused her repeated offers to buy him new clothes. Natalie had invited him to move in with her and Callie following the operation, for he had little to lose by abandoning the former family home in New Hampshire, given that serial killer Vincent Thresher had murdered Wade's second wife, Sheila Lindstrom, there.

Wattles bunched at the open collar of Wade's dress shirt as he bent his head over one of the books. He raised a hand when Natalie approached. "Just give me a sec ... "

Out of habit, she glanced at the calendar pillbox on the kitchen counter and noted that the week's TUES compartment was still shut. "Dad, you didn't take your meds."

He fluttered a hand in annoyance. "I know, honey—in a minute. First, listen to this." Rising from his chair, he tugged his lapels taut and cleared his throat. *"Hei. Mitt navn er* Wade Lindstrom." He smiled and gave a diplomatic bow. *"Det er en fornoyelse mote De."*

Natalie's mouth opened before she knew quite what to say. "Come again?"

"It's Norwegian! 'Hello. My name is Wade Lindstrom. It's a pleasure to meet you.'" He spread his arms with a *ta-da!* flourish.

Though she already suspected what he was thinking, Natalie hoped she was wrong. "Uh ... you planning a trip to Scandinavia?"

"No, silly! I want to help you with Munch."

Her frozen smile melted. *"Help* me?"

"Sure. Like this: *Herr Munch, hva vil De liker* ... oh, heck—" He shut his eyes a second, then peeked at one of the language texts on the table. "Oh, yeah. *Herr Munch, hva vil De liker male i dag?"*

"Translation?"

"'Herr Munch, what would you like to paint today?'" Wade beamed like a boy who's just learned to ride his first bike. "I figured you could do the summoning and I could do the talking."

Natalie rubbed her forehead, trying to think of a way to let him down easy. "Um ... that's really sweet of you, Dad, but I was actually going to speak French with Munch."

Wade's face fell. "He speaks French?"

"Yeah. He spent several years in Paris when he was young, and since I brushed up on French for

Monet and van Gogh ..." She finished the thought with a shrug.

Her father cast a crestfallen glance at all the books and language CDs he'd accumulated. "But wouldn't it help to have someone with you while you're ... you know ... *occupied?*"

The desperate eagerness etched in his expression tied a knot in Natalie's throat, and for a moment she couldn't reply. Ever since her mother, Nora, went insane from her work as a Corps conduit, Wade Lindstrom had wanted nothing to do with Violets. He had hardly visited Natalie during her years of training at the School, and had divorced Nora to start a new life with Sheila, a woman of exemplary normality. For him to volunteer to assist Natalie with her current work indicated how far he had come in conquering his past fears—and how much he loved her and Callie.

Still, the thought of having Wade watch her inhabited by another person's soul was akin to allowing her dad to videotape her having sex. Natalie didn't want him to see her like that.

"I wish you could help me," she told him truthfully. "But dead people can get touchy, and I have to handle them very carefully."

Wade shook his head, his blue eyes becoming rheumy with the water welling in them. "There must be *something* I can do. I feel awful just sponging off you."

"Dad, you're *not* sponging."

"How can you say that? I invade your house, eat your food, kick you out of your own bed—"

"It was my idea to take the couch. I'm fine with it,

really." She felt that offering Wade the master bedroom was the least she could do, since he had been forced to sell his business in large part because the government had blacklisted him when Natalie left the Corps.

As always, Wade refused her consolation. "I'd like to help you make a living."

"Believe me, Dad—what you save me in day care alone more than pays your room and board."

The wisp of a smile returned to his face. "That's not work, and you know it."

"I know. But I also know it means a ton to Callie to have you here." She crossed the room and folded her arms around him. "To me, too."

"Thanks, kiddo." He started to hug her back, but abruptly pulled away and looked at his watch. "Oh, shoot! Speaking of Callie, she must be about done at Dr. Steinmetz's office. I'd better run."

Natalie tried to stop him as he hurried out of the kitchen. "Relax, Dad, I can get her."

"No, no—not a problem. See you in a few." He rushed past her and waved a cheery good-bye.

Natalie snatched the pillbox off the counter and went after him. "Well, at least take your meds—"

The front door slammed.

Natalie sighed, the hand with the pillbox dropping to her side. She had moved to return it to the kitchen counter when the front door opened again and Wade leaned inside.

"Hey, kiddo! There's a guy out here to see you." He cupped a hand around his mouth and lowered his voice. "Looks like another client."

Wade winked and flashed her a thumbs-up, then left again.

"Wait! Your pills." Medication in hand, Natalie opened the door to catch him, but found a man with salt-and-pepper hair waiting on the front step.

He paused with his thick index finger only an inch from the doorbell, chuckled, and put out his hand. "Didn't even have to ring it! Ms. Lindstrom, I presume?"

Dressed in a dark, double-breasted suit, he stood a head taller than she, and she had to perch on tiptoes to peek past his broad shoulders at Wade, who strolled down the front walk toward his Camry. Noting her gaze, the man on the doorstep indicated her father with his thumb. "Your associate said you were available. Is this a bad time?"

As her dad got in his car, Natalie gave up on trying to nag him; she'd force the pills down him when he got home. She turned her attention to the stranger. "I'm sorry. What can I do for you, Mr. ....?"

"Amis. Carleton Amis. I understand you've been commissioned to work with Edvard Munch."

"I've been commissioned to do a painting *in the style* of Edvard Munch," she corrected him. Since she was no longer a registered member of the NAACC, Natalie could not legally claim her paintings were the products of deceased artists. That was why her works sold for thousands of dollars, while pieces by Corps artists like Hector fetched millions at auction.

Amis held up a hand, as if to stop her from repeating a speech he'd already heard. "There's no need to mince words with me, Ms. Lindstrom. The collectors who buy your work know they're getting the genuine artide. And I'm prepared to pay a great deal more for what they've been getting on the cheap."

She eyed Amis, from his smug expression down to his Italian leather shoes, to decide whether he was a legitimate client or a Corps Security stooge sent to set her up. "Oh? You want a Munch original?"

"Not exactly. My needs are much more specific than that." He smiled. "I want you to persuade Mr. Munch to create an exact replica of *The Scream*."

3

The Crazy Norwegian

Oh, brother, not another one, Natalie thought. *What do you bet he wants a* Mona Lisa, *too?* Still, she tried to exert some professional courtesy. It always paid to be polite to people of wealth—as Carleton Amis seemed to be—no matter how clueless they might be.

"I'm sorry," she said. "I'd like to help you, but I'm fully booked at the moment." That wasn't really true, but she hoped Amis would buy the excuse and save her the trouble of explaining her real reasons for turning down the assignment.

No such luck. Amis didn't budge from the doorstep.

"I understand how busy you must be, but I assure you I can make it worth your while." He gestured toward the interior of the condo. "Might I come inside to discuss the project with you?"

Natalie shifted to block his view of the living room, where she'd left her sofa bed unmade that morning. "I'm afraid it's a bit of a mess right now ..."

Amis chuckled. "Understood. And I didn't mean to put you on the spot. I only wanted the chance to clarify the full scope of my offer." He took a piece of paper from the inside pocket of his blazer and unfolded it. "You see, *The Scream* is only one of many paintings we'd like you to do."

The typed sheet he handed her listed the titles and artists of more than two dozen masterpieces. *The Concert* by Vermeer, *Storm on the Sea of Galilee* by Rembrandt, *Madonna of the Yarnwinder* by da Vinci, *Chez Tortoni* by Manet ...

Natalie scowled and passed the page back to Amis. "These are all the Maven paintings."

His smile broadened. "Precisely. I'm a producer for Persephone Productions, and we want to make a movie about the artworks' theft and mysterious reappearance."

"Ahh! I get it." Natalie could easily see Hollywood exploiting the art world's latest sensation. Stolen over a period of fifteen years, the paintings had, without warning, resurfaced a month ago at the museums from which they'd been taken. Police around the globe still had no clues as to the identity of the thief, who had puckishly named himself "Arthur Maven," or his motive for returning the priceless works without claiming any reward or ransom.

"We were very impressed with the work you did for *The Thomas Crown Affair* remake," Amis said, referring to a few Impressionist canvases she'd done for the film's museum-set dressing. "We'd be willing to pay handsomely for that kind of authenticity."

Natalie shook her head. "That's very kind of you, but I'm afraid—"

"Half a million."

The dollar amount stopped her like a pair of oncoming headlights. Natalie had pursued the underground Violet art trade as a way to remain independent of the Corps while avoiding the illegal and often dangerous freelance conduit gigs that had once sustained her. Although she was glad to make a living using her skills as a painter, the business had been a constant hustle and hardly lucrative. A thousand here, two thousand there. She hadn't heard a figure with more than four zeroes since . . .

Since that nutcase Nathan Azure suckered you into going to the godforsaken Andes, she reminded herself. The English tycoon had promised her four hundred grand for her help on a Peruvian archaeological dig, only to threaten and starve her in order to force her to find a fortune in Incan gold.

"That's a very generous offer," Natalie told Carleton Amis, "but I can't oblige you."

The severity of Amis's gaze belied the warmth of his smile. "Ms. Lindstrom, without these paintings as props, we have no movie."

"I understand that, but I think you'd be better off using an ordinary reproduction artist—"

"Absolutely not. We're going to be doing close-ups of all these canvases. If they can't withstand the most minute scrutiny, the whole film falls apart. That kind of accuracy requires the touch that only the original artists can provide."

"Of course. That would be ideal." Natalie drew a long breath, sagging against the door frame. Apparently, she'd have to give him the long explanation, after all. "What you don't understand is that the original artists *don't want* to paint works they've already done."

Natalie had learned this fact the hard way when

one of her first art customers had requested an exact copy of van Gogh's *The Starry Night*. Vincent became so enraged at the crass demand that Natalie was afraid he would cut *her* ear off, and she had to evict him with her protective mantra until his temper cooled.

For the first time, her refusal seemed to disconcert Amis. "But your *Thomas Crown* works—"

"Were all originals. The director didn't need copies of existing paintings, merely pictures that *looked* like they were done by Renoir and Monet."

"Look, I know for a fact that Munch produced at least four copies of *The Scream* during his lifetime. Surely you could persuade him to do one more." Amis's tone lilted upward, cajoling her.

Natalie allowed him to hear her sigh, hoping he would take the hint. "Even if I could talk these artists into repeating themselves, you wouldn't end up with exact copies. The paintings on your list have all aged, some for hundreds of years. You'd need someone who could artificially reproduce the fading, the darkening, the cracking."

"Couldn't you do that? I'd compensate you for the extra trouble."

Natalie shifted her weight from one foot to another, uncomfortable discussing forgery on her front doorstep. She tried to glance past Amis to see if Sanjay Prashad, the Corps Security agent on duty, was witnessing their conversation, but the visitor's monolithic frame filled her view. "I'm sorry," she began, "I really—"

"Eight hundred thousand."

Natalie put a hand to her forehead. "The number of paintings you want done would take months."

"*Nine.*"

"I appreciate your generosity, but—"

"*One million.*"

The elevation of the price shortened her breath, and for a moment she couldn't speak. She'd refinanced the condo to pay down her credit cards, and Dad had chipped in to make the monthly payments, but they weren't rich by any measure. Wade still owed money for his heart bypass and wouldn't qualify for Medicare for another three years, while Callie continued to rack up thousands of dollars in therapy with Dr. Steinmetz. A million dollars was more cash than Natalie had earned in her entire life. They could pay off the mortgage, have decent health care, send Callie to college, maybe even travel …

In lieu of a cold shower, Natalie forced herself to remember slogging through the Peruvian mud, pursued on horseback by a posse of Nathan Azure's murderous henchmen. She'd made the mistake of thinking with her wallet one too many times before.

"I wish I could help you," she told. Amis, and stepped back from the door to shut it.

He barricaded the door with one beefy hand. "Name your price."

Natalie could barely think over the ringing of the warning bells in her head. She decided to dispense with the professional courtesy. "I'm afraid I'll have to ask you to leave."

His smile shifted from genial to shrewd. "I have some influence with the Corps. If you won't take money, perhaps I could interest you in, shall we say, preferential treatment?"

She saw all pretense of being a movie producer run from his face like melted greasepaint. "Who *are* you?"

"Someone who could help you a great deal, Ms. Lindstrom. You and your family."

The calm self-assurance in his tone told Natalie that he spoke the truth. It also told her that the job might cost her far more than a few months' work.

"I'm not interested." She glowered at the arm that braced the door open. "Now, if you'll excuse me, I'm very busy."

Amis took his hand from the door and backed away, a pitying condescension in his demeanor. "Very well. But when I'm gone, so is my offer. You'll never have this opportunity again."

"I'll take that chance." She hardened her expression, refusing to blink lest he sense her weakening resolve.

Amis chuckled and shook his head, then turned and strode down the front walk without looking back.

Natalie shut and locked the front door, but hurried to the living-room window to watch him leave.

Nudging aside the curtain, she saw Amis approach a gold BMW parked across the street. Behind it crouched Sanjay Prashad's black Mitsubishi Eclipse. Of the three Corps Security agents assigned to intimidate Natalie with round-the-clock surveillance, Prashad was the only one whose name she knew and the one who worried her the most. The others were paycheck drones who put in their eight hours and went home, but Prashad exhibited the enthusiasm of naked ambition, sitting behind the wheel of his car with the erect posture of a corporate-ladder climber toiling in his office. When he made eye contact with Amis, however, the agent waved and gave an ingratiating grin—a peon currying favor with the boss.

As Amis drove off in the BMW, Natalie let the curtain fall back into place, a queasy feeling in her stomach. Amis had said he could use his influence with the Corps to benefit Natalie and her family if she agreed to provide his paintings. He never said what he would do if she refused.

To bury her concerns about Amis and his offer, Natalie swept into preparations for her Munch assignment—despite the fact that she hadn't intended to begin until the following day. For a mild-mannered Impressionist like Monet, she might have set up her easel on the condo's balcony or even driven to the local university's arboretum to work outdoors, but Munch's unpredictability made her want a more secure, controlled environment. She therefore moved her decrepit Volvo out to the street and assembled her art supplies in the condo's attached garage. Its connecting door had a dead bolt that she could lock to keep herself in, and her dad and Callie out, if things got hairy.

Even when she had readied everything she could think of, Natalie gnawed at her thumb in uncertainty as she surveyed the makeshift studio she'd created. On the concrete floor, she'd unrolled an old nylon sleeping bag to give herself someplace soft to lie down in case the inhabitation was ... uncomfortable. Beside her easel, she'd clamped a couple of articulated drafting lamps to the garage's workbench to provide sufficient lighting. In addition to her usual assortment of canvases and paints, she'd laid out a variety of pastel chalks, colored pencils, sketch pads, sheets of cardboard, even woodblocks and chisels, since Edvard Munch had worked in several different media and became as famous for his drawings and engravings as for his oils.

Providing the raw materials was the easy part. The challenge for a Violet who collaborated with a famous artist was to provide inspiration that sparked the individual's unique creativity. Hector, for instance, had caused a sensation in the art world by showing Munch a posthumous photograph of his body laid out on its deathbed, a bouquet of flowers on its chest. Obsessed with death even while alive, the painter found the picture perversely funny. It tickled him to look back upon the event he'd so feared from the detachment of Eternity—to see his own funeral not as an existential cataclysm but as the transitory, rather tawdry affair that it was. The painting that resulted from this epiphany, *Self-Portrait as a Corpse*, depicted Munch in an upright casket, his eyes shut in beatific repose, his face aglow with the flush of a mortician's makeup, arms folded across his chest like a mummified pharaoh. Bouquets of roses, baby's breath, and fern fronds embraced the coffin in bursts of red, white, and green.

Behind and to the right of this vibrant tableau, a

dull brown door stood open, the rectangle of its frame leading into darkness. Submerged in the ebony were the wispy gray outlines of an old man with stooped shoulders and thinning hair—the weary wraith of Edvard Munch's soul, trapped at Life's threshold and observing the aftermath of his passing with the resignation of the helpless and hopeless. Many art critics viewed the painting as Munch's wry commentary on the irony of his current popularity: Munch, the dead artist, embalmed and enshrined in his final gaudy glory, was more alive to the world than Munch the immortal spirit.

But the picture resonated more personally for Natalie. It reminded her of her early Violet training, when she was only five years old. *Death is like a big black room,* her mentor, Arthur McCord, had told her. *You're feeling your way around in the dark, and you're not sure where to go. The things you touched while you were alive, the places you went, the people you knew—all of these are like closed doors leading out of that room. When a Violet touches one of these things, she throws open one of those doors, and your soul runs toward the light.*

To Natalie, Edvard Munch had perfectly captured the desperation of the dead.

Whatever the source of the painting's fascination, *Self-Portrait as a Corpse* had sold at a Christie's auction for twenty-two million dollars—a record amount for a Violet painting. Posthumous collaborations generally fetched lower prices than works produced during the deceased artist's lifetime, which investors considered rarer and more valuable since there would always be a fixed number of them.

Natalie could not hope to make that kind of money without the Corps's seal of approval, but a Newport Beach real-estate broker with pretensions of being an art connoisseur had offered her a flat fifty grand for an original (if unofficial) Munch, which was more than she'd made in the last six months. Unfortunately, as with so many of her assignments, the client paid a mere fraction of the fee up front; he would only cough up the rest if he liked the finished product.

Reluctantly trying to put herself in Edvard Munch's morbid mind-set, Natalie had accumulated a half-dozen books on the Holocaust, which she now spread out on the workbench next to the easel. Munch had died in 1944, before the full scope of the Nazi atrocities came to light, and she thought the artist would find the horrors of Auschwitz and Dachau the ultimate confirmation of his bleak views of humanity and its self-imposed suffering. Natalie became queasy as she glanced again at the photos of corn-husk corpses being bulldozed into unhallowed landfills, and she tried to quash the feeling that she was exploiting both Edvard Munch and the tragedy of history for her own material gain.

When she had everything in place, Natalie consulted her watch. It was now half-past three. On the days Wade picked Callie up at Dr. Steinmetz's office, he usually took her to a local playground for an hour or so and sometimes treated her to ice cream, despite Natalie's strict orders not to spoil her daughter with sweets. With any luck, Natalie would have an uninterrupted hour with Munch before they got back. She'd need to summon the artist for several more sessions to produce a finished painting, of course, but at least she could dispense with the awkwardness of the mutual introductions, which always felt like a cross between applying for a bank loan and meeting one's in-laws for the first time.

Before she started, however, she scrawled a MOMMY AT WORK! sign on a sheet of sketchbook paper and taped it to the condo side of the connecting door, then locked herself in the garage. Natalie could not predict what Edvard Munch might do while in her body, but no matter what it was, she didn't want her father or daughter to see it.

With the door secure, she grabbed her canvas tote bag from the workbench and lowered herself into a cross-legged position on the sleeping bag spread in the center of the garage. Before retrieving the touch-stone Hector had given her, she spent several minutes practicing her yoga breathing. She did this not only to focus her mind for the inhabitation to come, but also to remind herself that she was the absolute master of her mind and body—that if anything went wrong at any time, she could switch to her protective mantra and cast Edvard Munch's soul right back into its black room.

With a calm but wary confidence, Natalie began to recite her spectator mantra—a simple child's verse that would keep her consciousness in a state of stasis yet permit her to supervise the thoughts and actions of the artist while he resided within her:

> *Row, row, row your boat,*
> *Gently down the stream.*

She reached into the tote bag until her fingers brushed the grainy wood handle of the old paintbrush.

> *Merrily, merrily, merrily, merrily!*
> *Life is but a dream ...*

The pricking sensation began in her fingertips, as if the brush's handle had sprouted a thousand tiny slivers. The knocking soul's electromagnetic energy seeped into her skin like a transdermal drug, raising speckles of gooseflesh as it traveled up her arms, across her shoulders, and up the nape of her neck to stiffen the stubble under her wig.

Something did not feel right. Natalie's body rippled, but not with the epileptic palsy that usually convulsed her during an inhabitation. Instead, the sharp fingernails of a shiver clawed down her torso, and her stomach shriveled as if freeze-dried. The garage seemed to have swelled to gargantuan size around her, and the lamps appeared to swing toward her, bearing down on her as if for an interrogation.

Natalie lost the thread of her mantra and contracted into a shrimplike curl on the bedroll. *Wrong. This is wrong wrong wrong.*

The lights seared her with brightness as the walls of the room receded farther into the periphery. Panic pressed her flat on the floor. The roof sped away from her as though she were plunging into a chasm, shrinking to insignificance. The articulated lamps descended like the necks of thirsting cranes, the lights threatening to swallow the speck she'd become.

Natalie's measured breaths stuttered, stuck in her throat. She shut her eyes and wrapped her arms around her head to blot out the cavernous room, the carnivorous lights. *This isn't real!* Natalie shouted in her head. *It's just a dream.*

The words brought the mantra's refrain back to her. *Life is but a dream! Row, row, row your boat . . .*

As Natalie resumed the mantra, the solidity of the garage condensed around her. With it came the lucidity she needed to realize what was happening. During her research, she had read that in addition to bouts of depression, Edvard Munch had been plagued by fits of agoraphobia. Open, empty spaces seemed to exacerbate his existential fears of meaninglessness and mortality. Indeed, *The Scream* was inspired by one such panic attack, in which the artist froze in place against the railing of a dreary boardwalk near Oslo, paralyzed by the overwhelming sight of the bloodred sunset. The old vertiginous anxiety must have seized Edvard Munch, now that Natalie had yanked him from the narrow cloister of his tomb into the wide world of the living again.

As she quelled the fear they shared, the soul that cohabited her body sat up and surveyed the strange environment of the garage with the weariness of a prisoner dragged from his cell to a torture chamber. *"Hvem er jeg nå?"* she heard her voice mutter in a glottal Nordic accent.

Unlike her dad, Natalie had not brushed up on Norwegian before summoning Edvard Munch, but she could easily guess the painter's question by the way he clutched at her throat—as if the softness and higher pitch of her voice were due to a bout of laryngitis. *Who am I now?*

When summoned, most souls remained disoriented for a bit, not realizing that they resided in the body of another person. But Edvard Munch had been ripped from limbo dozens, perhaps hundreds, of times since his death, by Hector and other Violet artists around the globe, and he touched Natalie's smooth cheeks and delicate hands to ascertain the identity of his present receptacle.

Bienvenue, Monsieur Munch, Natalie murmured to him in the mind they shared. *C'est un honneur de faire votre connaissance.* With chagrin, she realized that she'd used the same stilted icebreaker in French that her dad had come up with in Norwegian.

Munch rubbed the soft skin of her forearms like an obsessive-compulsive with a rash. "Are we in France?" he replied aloud, his French fluent but guttural.

Relieved that the artist was willing to converse in the secondary language, Natalie continued. *No, this is the United States. I am a friend of Hector Espinoza and a great admirer of your—*

"You are a woman." The statement had an accusatory emphasis.

Uh-oh. Here comes the misogyny. Natalie reverted to English in case Munch overheard the thought. She switched back to even, fluid French to pacify him. *Yes. My name is Natalie Lindstrom, and I hope we can work well together despite—*

"*A mirror.*" Munch stood with Natalie's arms held

45

out from her torso, as if they were drenched in muck that he did not want to smear on the man's dress shirt she wore. *"Give me a mirror."*

If she had had control of her lungs, Natalie would have sighed. *Monsieur Munch, I really don't think—*

"A mirror! Now!" Her voice grew shrill with his eagerness, his dread.

Natalie weighed her options. She had deliberately avoided including any reflective surfaces when outfitting the makeshift studio, in hopes that she could delay the shock her gender might have on the artist. To fetch the mirror Munch demanded, she would have to permit him to leave the locked garage. If Dad and Callie came home while the crazy Norwegian was wandering the house in her body ...

It's still early yet, she told herself even though it was actually quite late. Natalie knew that if she alienated Munch he might refuse to collaborate with her, and she couldn't afford to lose this commission.

All right, monsieur, she said in French. *Please do as I say ...*

She instructed Munch on how to find the dead-bolt key, which she'd hidden beneath a coffee can filled with paintbrushes on the workbench. When he'd unlocked the door, Natalie guided him out of the garage and up the condo's stairs to the master bedroom, which had a full-length mirror mounted on the closet door. She hoped that being upstairs might also give her a couple of minutes to get rid of the painter if she heard her father and daughter come through the front door.

As part of her effort to minimize the impact of her

appearance, Natalie had dressed androgynously in an untucked white business shirt she'd borrowed from her dad and a pair of baggy gray slacks. Although she'd switched back to her shoulder-length, dusty-blond wig—the one she always wore at home, because it was the closest to her natural color—she'd tied it back into a bun to make it feel less feminine. But judging from Edvard Munch's husky breathing as he switched on the bedroom light and advanced toward her reflection, she might as well have been wearing a French maid outfit. It occurred to Natalie that, since he'd only been permitted to work with male Violets, she was probably the first live woman he'd seen since his passing.

Oh, swell, she thought. *He's gonna lose it.*

In the mirror, Natalie saw her eyes and mouth widen with his fascination. Her hands trembled as he raised them to the level of her chest, the palms hovering a few inches away from her slight bosom as if held at bay by repulsive magnetic force. "P-pardon me, mademoiselle," he stammered. "M-may I ...?"

Her fingers quivered over the buttons of the shirt she wore.

Natalie tensed. The last thing she wanted was a dead perv groping her to get his jollies. *The Lord is my shepherd*, she began instinctively. *I shall not want—*

As his control began to slip, Munch raised her hands, struggling to speak with lips that were growing numb. "N-n-no! Puh-puh-please ... I m-mean no offense. I-I-I w-want to draw you."

The promise of new artwork made Natalie break

off the protective mantra. Wouldn't it be worth giving the crazy Norwegian a cheap thrill just to get a picture out of him? It *was* fifty grand, after all.

You're thinking with your pocketbook again, she groaned to herself, but resumed her spectator mantra.

Her violet eyes became half-lidded as Edvard Munch watched in the silvered glass while he undid the shirt's top buttons with her thin fingers. Natalie had considered leaving her bra off because of its unmasculine constriction, but was glad she'd chosen to wear it, particularly when she heard the ragged sigh Munch exhaled as he exposed the cleft of her décolletage.

Quivering, Munch grazed the swell of one breast with her fingertip, a demure gesture that triggered a flood of associations that nearly subsumed Natalie in their tide. She cowered with him in humiliation at the Parisian prostitute who laughed at the adolescent ineptitude of his lovemaking, shook with his rage at the cruel dismissal of Eva Mudocci's insouciant smile, shared the claustrophobic revulsion as Tulla Larsen wrapped him in her desperate, clinging embrace. His lust for the female form he saw in the mirror only incited memories of how such objects of desire had betrayed him in the past.

Yet beneath Munch's loathing lurked tenderness and longing. The somber cast of Natalie's sculpted, oval face reminded him of both his sister Laura, who went mad and died in a sanitarium, and their sibling Inger—an attractive but severe-looking woman who remained his confidante throughout his life. He also saw in Natalie the ghost of his older sister, Sophie—the almost translucent pallor of her skin, the fragility of her wasting frame as she withered from consumption. Even the specter of a mother Edvard could not remember because she died when he was only five resurfaced in the maternal figure frozen in the glass before him. The pathologically shy and sensitive painter yearned for the love of women—for the completion that femininity could give his crippled psyche—but it remained forever unattainable and alien to him.

Natalie could feel adoration and contempt colliding inside him. Afraid the artist might explode into violence, she almost launched into her protective mantra again—when her brow suddenly smoothed to newborn blankness. Munch slowly turned her head from one profile to the other, waved her hand, undid the bun of her hair, gawping like a monkey in wonder that the reflection mimicked his every movement. For the first time, he viewed the image in the mirror not as an object to be coveted, but as himself. Thinking out loud, he whispered something in Norwegian that Natalie did not understand.

Pardon me, monsieur—what did you say? she asked in French.

"There is no difference," he repeated in kind for her benefit, his tone still dreamy with disbelief. "There never was."

It took Natalie a moment to comprehend the enormity of his revelation. The gulf that Edvard Munch had always imagined between the sexes had ceased to exist. Stripped of their anatomy and the attendant societal baggage, the souls of men and women were kindred spirits, each gender ascribing its own vanities and faults, neediness and selfishness, to the other. Just as dying had cured him of his dread of death, Munch needed to become a woman to realize that the creature he'd feared was not a vampire or vixen but a projection of his own insecurities.

"Quickly ... the easel! I must have the easel here, now!" Munch gesticulated as if he could summon the item by will alone, for he seemed reluctant to tear his gaze from the reflection.

Natalie 'hesitated. What time was it? She'd lost track. Seized by obsession, Munch could spend all night working on a painting once he'd started. Dad and Callie might come back at any minute, and the master bedroom did not have a lock to keep them out.

Why don't we make a sketch today while the picture is fresh in your mind? she suggested, hoping Munch did not take offense. *Then we can refine it over the next few days.*

He swept the air with her hand in impatience. "Yes, yes! But we must start *now*."

Without waiting for her consent, he hastened back to the garage and lugged the easel up the stairs along with the sketchbook and a rack of pastels. Natalie barely managed to get him to shut the bedroom door before he commenced attacking a blank sheet of paper with charcoal slashes of chalk.

Munch darted her eyes between the mirror's

reflection and the image forming on the sketch pad, posing her head and shoulders in three-quarter profile and comparing the tonalities and chiaroscuro of the subject and its portrait. Natalie had no choice but to watch in uneasy fascination as the picture darkened with detail, its features rendered with the expressionist's deliberate harshness and surreal distortion. Of all the artists with whom she'd worked, Munch was the only one who'd ever drawn her. Except the woman in the picture *wasn't* her. The face was hers, as was the unbuttoned man's shirt, but the grim set of the mouth and the cold incandescence of the eyes belonged to Edvard Munch. The woman in the portrait curled a hand around the left lapel of the shirt in an ambiguous gesture. Was the artist peeling back his male veneer to reveal to the viewer the femininity beneath, or was he hastening to hide the female heart he had unintentionally exposed to the world's derision?

Natalie was so transfixed at watching the master at work that the sketch was nearly complete before she noted the reflection of the bedroom door in the mirror. She had made sure that Munch shut the door when they came in, but it now stood ajar, with two inches of darkness between it and the jamb.

I think that's good enough for today, don't you? she interjected, now acutely aware that she stood there with her bra bared for all to see.

Munch spat some Nordic curse from her lips and slapped the chalk back in the rack. "It is not even close to being finished!" the notorious perfectionist grumbled in French. "We must complete the sketch tomorrow, then begin the painting immediately thereafter."

Of course, monsieur. Tomorrow. The bedroom door hovered at the periphery of her vision, and Natalie monitored it with apprehension as she recited the Twenty-third Psalm.

The second the protective mantra had swept Edvard Munch from her mind, she held her shirt-front closed with one hand and rushed to yank open the door. The gasp and scuttling footsteps in the hall she heard confirmed her worst suspicions.

"Callie!"

Her nine-year-old had made it as far as the top of the stairs and teetered on the top step as if debating whether to pretend that she hadn't heard her mother's call. She evidently decided that bolting would only get her in more trouble, so she faced Natalie with her most winsome expression. "Grandpa sent me up here to look for you," she said quickly, brushing brown bangs out of her violet eyes. "I'll tell him you're busy—"

"Wait." Before her daughter could escape, Natalie stalked down the hall, fumbling to button enough of the shirt to keep herself decent. She knelt until she was eye level with Callie. "How long were you watching?"

"I just got here." Her gaze strayed.

Natalie grew stern with her. "Tell the truth. How long?"

Her daughter's mouth wriggled. "Only a couple of minutes. Jeez."

"What did you see?"

A worry worse than getting in trouble aged Callie's small, round face. "You were drawing a picture . . ."

Natalie felt the stone in her stomach grow heavier. "And?"

"A Who was inside you." This time, Callie peered straight at her mother, eyes bright with anxiety. "It sounded like a bad Who."

Natalie nodded, her head drooping in guilt. Callie's favorite storybook had always been Dr. Seuss's *Horton Hears a Who!* about the elephant who could talk with tiny people no one else could see. Callie thought of Horton as a Violet like herself, and the Whos were like the souls who knocked and sometimes inhabited her.

Not all of the Whos were nice. Some, like Vincent Thresher, were very bad indeed. The serial killer had only possessed Callie on a couple of occasions, but the taint of horror and perversion that he'd left in her mind had driven the girl into counseling with Dr. Steinmetz. Her therapy had lasted three years so far, with no end in sight.

Natalie groped for a way to explain the difference between Vincent Thresher and Edvard Munch. "It was a Who," she began, "but not a bad one."

"Was it someone you know?" Callie's face brightened with misplaced hope. "Someone like Grandma Nora?"

"Not exactly." Natalie heaved a sigh. She had gone out of her way to keep her little girl from witnessing her work, hoping that Callie might grow up to enjoy a relatively normal existence—one that did not require her to lasso ghosts for a living. In training her

53

daughter to cope with her Violet abilities, Natalie avoided teaching her about spectator mantras and summoning. Callie herself had figured out how to call her dead father and grandmother back from limbo, a practice Natalie had permitted but did not encourage except in cases of emergency. Since Dan had gone to the Place Beyond four years ago, Grandma Nora had been the only soul Callie allowed inside her head. After forbidding her daughter to summon strangers, how could Natalie explain why she did so herself?

"Sometimes, honey, people who lived in the past have knowledge or skills that we want to ... bring back," she said. "I make money to pay for our house and food by letting those Whos into my mind so I can talk with them and work with them."

Callie's voice became very small. "Couldn't you make money some other way?"

Natalie grimaced. When she quit the Corps, the government had blackballed her in retaliation, making it nearly impossible for her to get regular employment. "Maybe, honey, but it's very hard to make enough money, and people pay more when you have a special skill—"

"But you *like* it. That's why you do it, isn't it?"

Though her mouth opened to answer "No," Natalie found she couldn't muster the denial. *Like* being a freak? *Like* having dead souls invade her head like poor relations moving in? Don't be ridiculous. It was horrendous to relive the final agonies of the deceased. Any sensible person could see that a Violet's life was tragic, nightmarish, pitiable ... or so

Natalie had believed since childhood.

Yet, only a few minutes ago, hadn't she watched, enthusiastic and enthralled, while Edvard Munch used her as an instrument to create a new masterpiece more than fifty years after his death? Even when the Corps condemned her to the bleak, gut-wrenching toil of homicide investigations—the daily devastation of sharing murder victims' anguish—hadn't the work gratified her need for purpose? Didn't she get a surreptitious thrill when she solved a case only she could solve? When she caught a killer only she could catch?

Did she *like* summoning the dead? Perhaps not. But it was the thing that made her unique, that shaped her life and gave it meaning. To say that she hated being a Violet was tantamount to saying she hated herself.

"What made you say that?" she inquired rather than answering Callie's question. "Why did you ask if I like it?"

The child's violet gaze shone with something that disturbed Natalie more than accusation: excitement. "'Cause sometimes I miss it," she admitted softly.

"What do you mean?"

Callie took a sudden interest in the carpet, the walls, the stairs. "I don't know. I feel so … empty sometimes. In here." She put her hands on her small chest. "I keep out the bad Whos, but no one else comes in, except Grandma Nora sometimes. It's not like when Daddy used to come."

Natalie nodded, unable to speak. Even ten years later, the memory of Dan could still tighten her throat.

Callie never knew Dan Atwater while he was alive. An F.B.I. profiler, he died in the line of duty while saving Natalie from the Violet Killer. Yet Callie had enjoyed a closer relationship with her father than any ordinary child could ever hope to know in this life. All through her babyhood, she could fill herself with his love and comfort whenever she wished. Natalie, too, had been able to draw Dan into her mind and body, achieving the total unity of being that most lovers could only dream of.

Then Dan went to the Place Beyond, a region from which even conduits could not summon the dead. Left alone with her grief, Natalie began to comprehend what life was like for normal people, all locked into their separate flesh, never knowing the incomparable joy of merging completely with a kindred spirit. It was appropriate that the body consisted of cells, Natalie mused, for it imprisoned the soul in solitary confinement.

"It's just me," Callie said, echoing her thoughts. "All the time. That's why I wanted to know if you liked having the Whos inside you. If they made you feel the way Dad did."

Natalie hugged her. "No, baby girl. Not like your dad."

"But you like it, right? If you do, maybe I would, too." Callie's voice became brittle, verged on cracking. "Would you teach me?"

Natalie tightened the embrace, in part to keep from quivering with her own misgivings. "We'll see."

Despite the noncommittal response, Natalie knew she would relent, for she could no longer deny the truth. Her daughter would never be merely a girl with violet eyes. She would always be a Violet.

4

Inmate X

The headquarters of the North American Afterlife Communications Corps featured four aboveground stories, each ornamented with the Greco-Roman columns and pilasters characteristic of the other self-important government buildings in Washington, D.C. In addition to numbers for each of the floors, the control panels of the building's elevators included a B button for the basement. But there was another level below that for which there was no button, only an unmarked slot. To reach that level, one had to possess both the knowledge of the subbasement's existence and the security card to insert in the control panel's slot.

Dr. Carl Pancrit owned such a card and knew how to use it. When the elevator shuddered to a stop at the base of its shaft and parted its doors, he pulled the card from the slot and stepped into a small foyer, where a pair of uniformed guards flanked the entrance to the world's smallest and most specialized prison, which had been meticulously tailored for its sole inmate. Each guard carried only two nonlethal weapons—a stun gun and a tranquilizer pistol—for the prisoner they watched was Evan Markham, the Violet Killer, and he was far more dangerous dead than alive. If his spirit ever got loose, he could potentially inhabit any living Violet.

One of the two officers rose from her desk to check Pancrit's I.D. Her lank brown hair was pulled in a tight ponytail, and she had the chapped lips and husk-dry voice of a chain-smoker. The engraved name tag pinned to her shirt said RYAN. "Please remove anything that could be used as weapon or a means of suicide, Mr. Pancrit."

She held out a large plastic tray. He emptied his pockets into the receptacle—coins, keys, wallet, a Montblanc pen. "That's *Dr.* Pancrit."

"Yes, sir. The coat, belt, and tie, too, please."

He peeled off his blazer and accessories with a wry look. "You sure you don't want my Jockeys, as well? I've heard some cons hang themselves with their underwear."

If the sarcasm offended Ryan, she didn't let it show. "Sorry, sir. Regulations."

The second guard folded the clothes and set them on the desk beside the tray and a half-eaten lunch of burger and fries that Pancrit had interrupted with his arrival. Ryan then indicated the flat-screen, full-color monitor on the wall behind her. "I'll get him secured before we let you in."

On the monitor, Pancrit surveyed the four split-screen shots of the cell's security cameras. They included an overhead view of the room, which resembled those for the patients at the White Sands facility in its absolute simplicity and innocuousness. Not a single sharp edge or hard surface existed in the enclosure of soft vinyl and contoured plastic. Even the spigots for shower and basin were smooth, featureless bumps that lacked valves to turn them off and on. The prisoner washed himself only when his captors allowed.

The only furnishing aside from the toilet and a mattress pad was a vinyl-upholstered chair in the center of the floor. One might have mistaken it for an ordinary recliner if not for the padded manacles on its foot- and armrests, claws open like the pincers of a crab.

A figure in bright red pajamas stained the cell's sterile white interior like a blood spot seeping through a bandage. The uniform—the only clothing the prisoner was permitted to wear—bore no number or any other form of identification; everyone here knew who he was. Crouched on all fours between the chair and the bed, the man performed push-ups with manic rapidity. Pancrit could not see the prisoner's face in any of the camera angles, only the long, scraggly black hair that brushed the floor every time his chest dipped to touch the vinyl padding.

Her eyes intent upon the inmate, Ryan craned the gooseneck microphone mounted beside the monitor toward her mouth and thumbed the TALK switch on it. "Markham! You got company."

Although the speaker system blasted her voice into the room, the cell's occupant did not heed her. If anything, he only quickened the pace of his exercise.

Ryan obviously expected his recalcitrance, for she kept hold of the mic and cranked up its volume. *"Take a seat, Markham!* Before we come in and *put* you there."

The prisoner got to his feet and stared straight into

one of the dark plastic bubbles that covered the cell's camera lenses. The shadows that accumulated beneath the overhang of his heavy brows made his eyes appear bottomless and empty. For the first time, Pancrit wondered about the wisdom of striking a deal with this nutcase. If Simon McCord hadn't commanded such loyalty from the rank-and-file of the NAACC's membership, Pancrit could have used a Corps conduit for his purposes. But McCord, a messianic mentor to his fellow Violets, was a religious fanatic who believed only God could create conduits, and he would use all his power and influence to stop Project Persephone if he ever learned its purpose. Carl Pancrit needed a conduit who had been excommunicated from McCord's Violet enclave. An outcast, a pariah.

Like the Violet Killer.

According to the staff hired to maintain a round-the-clock suicide watch on the prisoner, Markham had only spoken one word during the ten years of his incarceration: *Boo*. After considerable research, Pancrit learned that this was Markham's pet name for his former flame, Natalie Lindstrom. Therein lay Pancrit's principal bargaining chip. While Lindstrom had rebuffed his offer of employment, she might yet prove of use to him, for she had once been Evan Markham's lover. Of his ten victims, Lindstrom was the only Violet he could not bring himself to kill—the one he had permitted to capture him and turn him over to the police. Pancrit counted on both the love and the hate Markham had for Lindstrom in his negotiations with the madman.

As the Violet Killer peered into the camera, he scratched at the foot-long beard he'd grown in the years since the guards had refused to take the risk of shaving him. With a languid, unhurried air, he sank into the cell's chair and placed his bare ankles and wrists in the open manacles. The cuffs snapped shut, and on the electronic panel beside the monitor, a red light winked off as a green one came on.

Stepping back from the microphone, Ryan nodded to her heavyset male partner, whose name badge identified him as WILLIS. He hefted himself off his folding chair, pulled out a round key on a chain attached to his belt, and stuck it into a circular hole in a metal plate on the wall beside him. When Willis signaled his readiness, Ryan inserted her own key into a wall plate on the opposite side of the room. The system required them to turn their keys simultaneously—an extra security measure that prevented a single individual from opening the cell's entrance.

Ryan pointed to the corridor's metal portal as it slid open. "The inner door won't open till this one closes. The cell will shut automatically twenty seconds after you've entered the room." She paused to give him the obligatory disclaimer. "Containment is our first priority. If anything goes wrong, we might not be able to get you out."

Pancrit stiffened in apprehension. "I know."

He did not permit himself to consider all the implications of dying inside this prison as he proceeded into the brief passageway that served as a buffer zone between the cell and the reception area. Pancrit knew that the sleek white plastic of the walls hid layer upon layer of metal and insulation, designed to keep the electromagnetic energy of Markham's soul from escaping the facility in the event he should ever succeed in killing himself. Indeed, the threat of spending eternity ricocheting off the walls of this soul cage was probably the only reason Markham hadn't simply starved himself long ago.

Or perhaps he still has some unfinished business in the outside world, Pancrit mused as the door behind him hissed closed with the suction of an airtight seal.

A moment later, the door ahead of him slid away to reveal the red figure clamped into the chair at the cell's center. The prisoner did not move, and the depth of shadow in the man's eye sockets made it impossible for Pancrit to tell whether Markham even noticed him. Only when he entered the room and heard the door whoosh shut behind him did Pancrit see that the inmate's violet irises tracked his every motion with feline intensity.

"Good morning, Evan." Pancrit put his hands on his knees and squatted until they were face-to-face, looking for signs of comprehension. "I'm Dr. Pancrit. I want to help you. I want us to help each other."

Blanched by lack of sunlight, Markham's pallid complexion became almost translucent beneath the cold fluorescent lights, blue veins showing through the thin skin of his forehead. He might have been mistaken for a cunning waxwork if not for the glow of those narrowed eyes.

Pancrit straightened and cast a casual glance around the cell. "Are they treating you well? The food leaves something to be desired, I'm sure."

He nodded toward a plastic tray that sat by the door, upon which rested a pair of plastic bowls filmed with the residue of dried tomato soup and chocolate pudding. Markham, he knew, had once attempted to pierce his own jugular vein with the tine of a plastic fork. When his jailers stopped giving him forks, he tried to choke himself with the bowl of a plastic spoon. Now they had ceased giving him utensils altogether, forcing him to eat with his fingers.

The prisoner failed to respond to Pancrit. If anything, the visitor's presence seemed to bore him.

So much for small talk, Pancrit decided. "I know you want to get out of here, Evan. I can make it happen."

Markham's expression did not change, but his violet gaze followed Pancrit as the doctor idly paced the room.

"I know you're not a sociopath, Evan. The mutilation, the disembowelments, the eyes ripped from their sockets—that was all for show, to throw the police off your trail. You *wanted* the cops to believe it was the work of a sadist, because then they wouldn't suspect your true motive. Those Violets were your friends, and you wanted to end their pain. Isn't that so?"

He circled around behind the chair. Although Markham's head didn't move, Pancrit imagined the Violet's eyeballs twisting backward like owls' heads, as if to stare at the doctor through the back of his skull.

Pancrit glanced at the clamps on Markham's wrists to make sure they were secure, then squeezed the prisoner's shoulders in fraternity. "Like you, I've devoted my life to giving people peace. That's why I need you. If my work succeeds, you and your friends will never have to suffer again. Wouldn't you like that, Evan?" Here, he bent close to Markham's ear, observing his reaction. "Wouldn't you like to end Natalie's suffering?"

The inmate peered at him, unblinking and seemingly unmoved, but beneath his hand, Pancrit felt Markham's shoulder muscles tense.

The doctor smiled and sauntered back around in front of the chair, still gauging the effect of his words. "I visited Ms. Lindstrom a few weeks ago, actually. Or should I call her 'Boo'? Very pretty. So's her daughter, from what I hear—" Pancrit smacked his temple in mock consternation. "Gosh, that's right! You probably haven't heard. She had a kid with that FBI guy ... what was his name? You know it better than I do."

Markham's nostrils flared, and the blue Y of a vein rose on his forehead.

"Oh, yeah! Atwater, wasn't it? Not like it matters now—he's out of the picture. Natalie and her girl are on their own now." The doctor shook his head. "A shame, really. Won't be long before they're both slaves to the Corps, like the rest of your kind. But that's what you get for having such a rare and valuable gift, eh?" Pancrit bent until his forehead nearly touched Markham's, until he stared straight into the killer's eyes. "Of course, if *everyone* had that gift they wouldn't need you, would they? You could go off and do whatever you wanted, truly free for the first

65

time in your life. How's that for a trade, Evan? You give me your gift. I give you your freedom." He paused, cocked his head for a reply. "Do we have a deal?"

From the thicket of his beard, Markham's tongue flicked out to moisten the cracked dryness of his full lips, and his voice rasped from years of disuse. *I want to see her.*

Pancrit grimaced at the killer's demand, but nodded.

Markham bared his teeth in a death's-head grin and wiggled the fingers of his manacled hands. "How about getting me out of these things? As a sign of good faith ..."

A staring contest ensued between them as Pancrit assessed the risk of freeing the prisoner before the guards came in to back him up. Still ... he needed to assert his dominance and win Markham's trust in order for them to work together on the project.

"If you cross me," he warned, "you'll rot in this box forever."

"Think I don't know that? That's the only reason I bothered to speak to you." Markham waved his shackled hands again. "Well?"

Pancrit quashed his misgivings and turned toward the ceiling cameras, raising his voice so that the adjacent speakers would receive his instruction. "Release him."

A click came from the speakers, followed by Ryan's voice. "You sure about that, sir?"

"Yes. I have things under control."

He heard the hydraulic hiss as the clamps on

66

Markham's wrists and ankles opened, and half turned toward the prisoner. Now—"

He did not have time to say anything more before the Violet lunged forward to seize him in a headlock.

"I could twist your head off your neck before they ever got in here," Markham murmured. "And it wouldn't make a damned bit of difference to my future."

Pancrit bobbed his mouth for the breath to cry out, but the crook of Markham's elbow squeezed his windpipe like a nutcracker. Though he wriggled and tugged at the killer's arm, the doctor failed to break free.

"Let go of him, Markham," Ryan said from the speakers, a nervous quaver undercutting the authority in her voice. "You'll only make it worse for yourself if you don't."

Yet neither she nor Willis made any attempt to enter the cell to save Pancrit. *Containment is our first priority,* he heard her repeat in his mind as his lungs throbbed with trapped air and his vision dimmed from oxygen depletion.

Markham practically kissed his earlobe as he spoke. "Get this straight: I don't care about you or your little pipe dreams. I don't care about the Corps or the Violets or this cell or my own accursed life. All I want is Boo. And you'd better let me have her. Understand?"

As far as he was able to, Pancrit nodded.

"We're giving you ten seconds to back away from him," Ryan announced through the intercom. "Then we're coming in."

"No need," Markham replied, unhooking his arm from Pancrit's throat. "Everything's fine. In fact, the doc and I are partners. Isn't that right?"

The Violet Killer clapped a hand on Carl Pancrit's shoulder in filial camaraderie, but pinched the muscle as a reminder of the penalty for betraying their alliance.

Pancrit massaged his neck, telling himself, *It's only for the project. After that I can get rid of him.*

"Open the cell," he croaked to the guards. "We're coming out."

5

Familiar Faces

At the time, Natalie could not say why she took note of the man who loitered outside the Ralph's supermarket when she and Callie emerged from their weekly shopping expedition. He seemed to take no notice of them as they wheeled out a cartload of groceries; in fact, he had his back turned to them, so that Natalie could see only his frizzy, shoulder-length black hair and the long, dark overcoat that looked too heavy for the September afternoon's warmth. He might easily have been one of the homeless vagrants who sometimes hung around outside Fullerton's shopping centers, but something about his posture—hunched shoulders, hands shoved into pockets like concealed weapons—evoked a subconscious recognition that verged on déjà vu.

With sudden trepidation, she kept glancing over her shoulder at him as she rolled her rattling cart over to the Volvo and began loading the bags into the station wagon's rear cargo area. Strangely, it did not console her when the man failed to turn around and glower at her. If she had seen his face, Natalie could have convinced herself that he was merely some poor mental case the state didn't have the funding to treat. But the way he steadfastly refused to face her made it seem as if he didn't *need* to view her directly, as if he could watch her through the back of his head. His stance suggested a suppressed violence, like that of a disgruntled employee about to open fire on a crowd of postal customers.

Callie glanced up from the *Disney Adventures* magazine she'd bugged Natalie to buy for her in the checkout line. "What is it, Mom?" she asked, turning to gape at the stranger.

Natalie pivoted her daughter back toward the car. "No, honey. It's not nice to stare."

Etiquette did not keep her from peering at the transient, however, thinking *Turn around turn around turn around!* Was he one of Corps Security's new stooges? The NAACC had such high turnover nowadays that Natalie could hardly keep track of who was assigned to spy on her at any given time so she always watched for strangers who seemed to take more than a passing interest in her. Paranoia became a habit when people were actually following you.

As Natalie herded Callie into the Volvo's backseat, the derelict finally fulfilled her silent wish, for he spun around, flicked a half-smoked cigarette to the cement, and ground the butt beneath his boot before stalking into the supermarket and out of view. He did not appear to notice her, and the brief view she caught of his face dispelled the impression of familiarity she'd had when his back was turned. The thick black brows over recessed brown eyes, the long tangles of the Rasputin-like beard ... they didn't match anyone she knew.

Callie had ignored her admonition not to stare. "Do you know that man?"

Natalie shook her head, but without conviction. "No, honey. I've never seen him before."

Yet something about the vagrant continued to nag her as she and Callie got in the car. She didn't figure out what it was, though, until they were almost home.

Homeless indigents *never* leave a cigarette half smoked.

The vague menace of the man outside the supermarket continued to bother Natalie like a loose tooth, but she forgot all about him when she saw the black woman inclined against the condo's front door, dressed in a chic pantsuit belted at the waist. Even before Natalie could see the features of the polished-mahogany face, she recognized the devil-may-care poise with which the visitor crossed her arms and ankles, the relaxed pose belying the spring-loaded power of her wiry limbs.

"Serena!" In her excitement, Natalie braked the Volvo at the curb and rushed out to greet her old friend without collecting either Callie or the groceries in the back of the car.

Serena Mfume sauntered to meet her halfway down the front walk. "Hey, girlfriend!"

Though she wore a short, kinky-haired wig to cover her shaved head, she otherwise looked the same as the day she'd introduced herself ten years ago—the day she'd saved Natalie from being dissected by the Violet Killer. Yet a certain tiredness dimmed the twinkle of Serena's violet eyes and the white lightning of her grin lacked its usual voltage.

Natalie chose to ignore these ominous signs, instead embracing her friend as if welcoming her to Thanksgiving dinner. "It's so good to see you! How go things at the ranch? Is our Uncle Simon in good health?"

Serena laughed, some of the old mischief resurfacing on her face. "Oh, you know Simon. He's so stubborn, he'll outlive us all—and won't *that* be ironic!"

Natalie laughed. Like his late brother Arthur, Simon McCord had been an instructor during her training at the School. Simon believed the ability to summon the dead was a gift from God, and so he pressed all Violets to do their duty with fanatical devotion. He was so obsessed with keeping this world in touch with the next that Natalie could easily see him living forever through sheer obstinance, never moving on to the noncorporeal existence he extolled as the "True Life." Simon now spent much of his time on a large ranch in New Mexico, serving as mentor and religious guru to a group of handpicked disciples, of which Serena was his star acolyte.

"By the way, congrats about the Munch," she said. "I hear it went for five million at Christie's."

"Oh ... yeah. Thanks." Natalie repressed a groan. The real-estate agent who'd paid her fifty grand for the finished version of Munch's *Self-Portrait as a Woman* had turned around and auctioned it off last week for a hundred times what he'd paid for it—an astounding sum, considering that the painting lacked the Corps's imprimatur of authenticity. "Too bad I don't get either the money or the credit," she said to Serena.

"I knew it was you in that picture the moment I saw it in *Newsweek*," her friend assured her. "And I knew Munch couldn't have done it without you."

"That and three-fifty will buy me a cappuccino. Speaking of which, you wanna come inside for some coffee?" Natalie indicated the condo. "I'm such a caffeine fiend now, I even bought an espresso maker—"

Serena shook her head. "I can't stay. I just needed to talk to you."

"Business or pleasure?"

"You know it's always a pleasure, girlfriend." Serena's smile faded. "But I'm afraid it's business, too. I found out—"

"Mom?" Callie had opened a door of the Volvo and leaned out to call to her. "Can I see Serena, too?"

"Oh! Sure, sweetheart." Eager to postpone any bad news, Natalie motioned to Callie, who bounded out of the car and practically tackled Serena with a hug around the waist.

The visitor laughed and ruffled the girl's hair. "How's my favorite goddaughter? Still remember those moves I showed you?"

Serena held up her open palms, which Callie rabbit-punched in playful sparring. She finished by jabbing one foot sideways toward the target in a somewhat clumsy kickboxing maneuver.

Serena whistled and clapped. "That's my girl! Why don't you go inside and take those shoes off while I talk to your mom, and then we can practice a few minutes on the living-room carpet?"

Callie beamed. "All right! But you better watch out!"

Serena struck a defensive pose. "I'm ready for you."

Callie jabbed the air a few more times and ran on into the condo.

Serena shook her head and chuckled. "I swear that kid's a foot taller than the last time I saw her."

"That's what happens when you only show up once every two years." Natalie folded her arms, bracing herself for the news. "So why *are* you here?"

The gravity of Serena's expression deepened the lines of her face. "It's Evan. He's gone."

Evan. The vagrant outside the supermarket: his face drawn long with simmering resentment, his shoulders hunched as if to shelter the match flame of his life from the high wind of the world. The realization collapsed on Natalie with the suddenness of a cave-in, and she nearly dropped to the ground beneath its weight. "I saw him," she breathed.

Serena stiffened, tensing as if for fight or flight. "You *what?*"

"Just now ... at the grocery store. I saw someone I thought—" She tried to shake the idea from her head. "Are you sure? I thought the Corps had sealed him up for good, dead or alive."

"They did. But you know Uncle Simon. He trusts the N-double-A-C-C even less than they trust him. He didn't think the bureaucrats could handle a Violet who kills other Violets, so he paid informants at Corps headquarters to keep tabs on Evan. A few days ago, they sent Simon these."

Serena took some papers from the inside pocket of her jacket and unfolded them. The accordion-creased pages bore computer-printed stills taken from security videos of what appeared to be a high-tech prison cell. The pictures' resolution was not the greatest but Natalie had no trouble identifying the warlock-bearded madman clamped to his restraining chair. She had just seen him pretend to smoke a cigarette outside a Ralph's grocery store, feigning disinterest, always watching yet never looking. His face had gone feral, and if Natalie had not known his mannerisms since childhood, she would never have guessed he was once the sixteen-year-old boy with whom she had first tasted an infatuation that she mistook for love.

Seeing Evan so horribly changed and confirming that he was again loose in her world brought no immediate fear, only the gloomy acceptance of a pessimist who's been proven correct. What she did not expect was the familiarity of the other man shown in the photos from Evan's prison cell: a broad-shouldered stranger in a dark suit, with graying temples and the beneficent demeanor of a father-confessor. A man who, six weeks before, had introduced himself to her as Carleton Amis.

6

The Seventh Madonna

A claustrophobic apprehension closed in around Natalie as she sensed an as-yet-unseen conspiracy coiling around her. "I know this man," she said, indicating Amis.

Serena shot her a look of surprise that bordered on suspicion. "You're one up on me if you do. Who the hell is he?"

"I was hoping you could tell me." Natalie recounted how Carleton Amis had represented himself as a movie producer who wanted her to paint reproductions of famous pictures for an art-heist film. "When I turned him down, though, he claimed to have some pull with the Corps. You don't recognize him?"

"Nope."

"Well, *he* did." Natalie nodded toward Sanjay Prashad, who was parked at the curb in his black Mitsubishi. As he often did, the Corps Security agent sat in the car's front passenger seat with the window rolled down, the better to needle her with his ferret's stare. Whenever she made the mistake of making eye contact with him, he flashed her the grin of a card player flush with hidden aces.

A glare from Serena managed to scrub the smugness from his face, however. "Thought I'd seen every snake in the N-double-A-C-C," she muttered. "Guess they turned over some more rocks. Did this Amis give you any way to contact him?"

"No. When I refused the offer, he said I wouldn't have another chance at it. At the time, that was fine with me." Natalie now felt stupid that she hadn't gleaned more information about the stranger that she could share. She frowned at the photos of Carleton Amis again before handing them back to Serena. "I don't get it. If he's in bed with the Corps, why didn't he have one of the Art Division's Violets paint his pictures for him?"

"The Corps does lots of things it doesn't want its members to know about—like releasing the Violet Killer, for instance. If Amis used any Corps conduits for his dirty work, they'd be sure to tell Uncle Simon, who could put a stop to it." Serena stashed the photos in her coat. "These paintings he asked you to do ... how many artists are capable of that kind of work? Who could Amis go to after you turned down the job?"

Natalie considered a moment but shook her head. "I have no idea. But I think I know who could tell us."

As the phone at the other end of the line started to ring, Natalie plugged her free ear with a finger to shut out the karate shouts while Callie sparred with Serena in the living room. A brusque recording answered: "You know who you are. I don't. Leave a message."

"I know you're there, Hector," Natalie shot back after the beep. "Pick up."

"Only for you, Boo," the reclusive artist grumbled when he finally deigned to reply. "What d'you want?"

"You can stop calling me 'Boo,' for a start."

"Well, excuuuuuuuuuse me, Princess Natalie. How may I serve your ladyship?"

She laughed, imagining him dipping his bulk in a mock curtsey, plump fingers daintily lifting the folds of an invisible skirt. "That's more like it, peasant. Remember your place."

"At your feet, as always. So what's up, Boo? *Natalie*, I mean."

"I need your help—"

"With Munch? You gave back the brush, so I thought you guys were good chums by now. That *Self-Portrait* was rad, by the way."

"Thanks." Natalie exhaled annoyance, reminded again of all the money she *hadn't* made from the masterpiece she'd helped to inspire and create. "But this isn't about Munch. At least, not directly."

She described her meeting with Carleton Amis, but omitted any mention of his connection to the Violet Killer. "The cops think this guy might have something to do with the stolen paintings that suddenly resurfaced," she said to avoid having to explain about Serena and Evan Markham. "They've asked if I know anyone else who could copy all those paintings he wanted. What do you think? You familiar with any Violets who might take on a project on the sly?"

"Nope. Even if they wanted to risk pissing off the Corps, I doubt they'd have the know-how to age the fakes accurately. For that, you need a pro. A forger."

"And who might that be?"

"Let's see ... you say *Madonna of the Yarnwinder* was on the dude's shopping list, right?"

"Yeah."

"In that case, I'd start with Calvin Criswell. He's already painted six of them."

Natalie shifted the cordless receiver to her other ear, glancing through the kitchen door into the living room to make sure Serena was keeping Callie busy. "Whoa! Back up. This Calvin guy's painted six *what*?"

"Madonnas." Hector chuckled. "Pretty good scam, I have to admit After the real *Yarnwinder* disappeared, Criswell did six copies of it. Pretending to be a fence for the real thieves, he sold five of the forgeries to private collectors, none of whom could report him to the cops without revealing that they'd tried to purchase art on the black market. Unfortunately for Criswell, he tried to sell the sixth fake to an undercover detective for Scotland Yard."

"What happened to him?"

"He copped a plea and served two years. But no one in the art world will touch him now, so he lives somewhere in Silver Lake and paints kids and puppies for eighty bucks a pop."

Natalie made a face. "Honesty doesn't pay. You have an address for this guy?"

"Sorry. You'd have to get that from his parole officer. I doubt he even uses his real name anymore."

"That's okay. We can track him down."

Hector's jocular tone turned wary. "We?"

Natalie peeked into the living room again. Still poised for hand-to-hand combat with Callie, Serena gave her a quizzical look.

Natalie nodded to her, thanked Hector, and hung up.

Serena did, in fact, learn Calvin Criswell's present whereabouts from his parole officer, but she had to wait on hold through several long phone calls until she got access to the address. She suggested that Callie could stay home with Wade while they went to question the artist, but Natalie refused to leave either her father or daughter alone while Evan was on the loose. Serena had only her black Harley motorcycle for transportation, so all four of them piled into the Volvo and headed up the I-5 toward LA.

The late-afternoon traffic thickened like tar on the freeway, and Callie complained the whole way, making them exit twice so she could go to the bathroom at the nearest gas station or fast-food place. She finally settled down when Natalie bribed her with a McDonald's Happy Meal, and they reached the apartment house in Silver Lake near dusk.

The two-story Mediterranean Revival building bore the weary vanity of a faded screen star—cracked plaster splotched with white patches like a botched Botox job, tear streaks of rust trailing from its terra-cotta drainpipes. Like its neighbors, it served primarily as a shelter for Hollywood actors either on their way up or on their way down. The aura of gloom deepened once Serena convinced the apartment manager to let them inside, for the landlord had evidently decided to save electricity by refusing to illuminate the foyer until after nightfall. Natalie could barely see the toes of her Doc Martens as she and Serena clumped up the narrow wooden staircase to the door of one of the second-floor apartments.

Despite the catacomb darkness in the hallway, the young man who answered their knock greeted them wearing sunglasses. No, not sunglasses—*smoked* glasses with old-fashioned, nearly opaque rectangular lenses. Exceptionally tall and scarecrow skinny, he nearly filled the narrow space he opened between the door and the jamb. "Yes, miss? Can I help you?"

Must be our man, Natalie thought, seeing his black jeans and T-shirt freckled with paint spatters, drizzles, and smears. A lamb's-wool tuft of sandy-brown hair sprouted from his chin, a bohemian affectation Natalie had always loathed. She wondered if the glasses were supposed to hide eyes bloodshot from pot-smoking, but the only telltale aroma that seeped from the apartment was the stale pine scent of turpentine. "Mr. Criswell?"

He shook his head. "Sorry. The name's Turner. Fred Turner."

He receded from the door, but Serena stopped him from closing it. "No need to playact, Calvin. We know all about you."

Criswell sagged back against the doorjamb with a sigh. "Wish I could say the same. Who are you people?"

"Art lovers," Serena snapped before Natalie could introduce herself. "We admire your past work and want to know if you're doing anything new lately."

He chuckled but was clearly not amused. "You're kidding, right?" He cocked his head to glance down the hall. "Is this an episode of *Cops*? 'Cause I'm not gonna bite."

"You're not in trouble," Serena assured him. "Or should I say, you *won't* be if you answer our questions."

"We only want to know if anyone has approached you about copying some old masterpieces," Natalie added. "Rembrandt, Vermeer, Manet, Munch—"

"You mean *forgeries*. I went to prison for doing forgeries. I dont *do* forgeries anymore. So you can take your Munch and—Hey, wait a minute." Brows frowning over the lenses of his glasses, Criswell motioned toward Natalie's right. "Turn this way."

"Huh?"

"Turn! Three-quarter profile."

Scowling at him, she angled herself to the right until he raised his hand.

"There." He grinned and jabbed an index finger at her. "You're the girl in the Munch *Self-Portrait*. The one that just sold."

"Umm ... yeah." Natalie felt herself flush as if Criswell had found her in the centerfold of a men's magazine. She imagined those hidden eyes of his lingering on the portrait's half-concealed bosom.

"You know, that was a fantastic picture. I'd give my right arm to work with Munch. What was he like?"

Natalie opened her mouth, unsure how to respond, but Serena saved her the trouble.

"We'd love to talk shop," she said dryly, "but we're in kind of a hurry." She dug one of the photos of Carleton Amis out of her jacket and presented it to Criswell. "You seen this guy 'round here?"

Criswell did not betray any anxiety when he saw Amis. He was a convicted criminal, after all, used to keeping his cool in dangerous and suspicious company. But Natalie thought she could discern the ghostlike flutter of his eyelids behind the one-way glass of his shades.

"Nope. Never seen him."

Serena huffed and returned the photo to her pocket.

"Mind if we come in?"

Criswell laughed and shook his head. "Ah, ladies! If only you'd called ahead, I would have tidied up the place."

"Could you show us some of your recent pieces?" Natalie asked. Past his shoulder, she could see one corner of a canvas on an easel, lacquered with the dark glazing of the Dutch masters.

He moved to block her view. "You mean *Dogs Playing Canasta?* I think we can skip it. Sorry I can't help you, but I've been reduced to catering to the bourgeoisie. Call me the next time you want a candlelit country village."

He waved good-bye.

"We'll be back, Mr. Criswell," Serena said.

"Good. Bring a cop or a search warrant. Preferably both." He shut the door, turning the dead bolt slowly as if to make sure they could hear it lock.

"Lying dog," Serena muttered as she and Natalie descended the stairs on their way out.

Wade Lindstrom waited patiently for them in the Volvo, his lanky frame folded into the backseat. When Natalie and Serena got into the car, his head nearly brushed the ceiling as he sat forward, his face anxious in the rear-view mirror. "Well? You find out anything?"

"We found out you can't trust a crook," Serena groused. "That's about it."

Callie wilted against the armrest of her door in an agony of boredom. "You mean we came all this way for *nothing*?"

"Maybe. Maybe not." Natalie peered through the windshield at one of the apartment building's upstairs windows. An old drop cloth spotted with rainbow dots of paint served as a haphazard curtain. As she watched, a hand nudged one corner of the cloth aside, exposing a triangle of blackness as dark and deep as Calvin Criswell's smoked glasses.

Gazing down at the Volvo that lingered, engine running, on the street below, Cal could feel the Violets staring back at him. Although he couldn't distinguish the color of their eyes through his dark glasses, he knew who they were—*what* they were. Particularly the girl from the Munch portrait.

He didn't care if they saw him watching. Indeed, he'd been tempted to invite them in for espresso and half hoped they would come back to harass him some more. He could use their advice.

They did not return, however. When the car at last drove off, Cal let the paint-dappled curtain fall back into place, cutting off the waning light of dusk. Fortunately, one didn't need natural light for forgery. A bright halogen lamp illuminated the work-in-progress on the easel: Rembrandt's *Storm on the Sea of Galilee*. Beside it, a drafting table bore a half-dozen spread-eagled art books and four different posters of the original painting. Carleton Amis wanted the copy by the end of the month—an impossible deadline—and Cal intended to pull another all-nighter in a vain attempt to get it done on time. It was a hellish job, and the Rembrandt was only the beginning.

But the reward would be worth it.

To motivate himself, he shuffled into the apartment's closet-size bathroom, flicked on the fluorescent light, and took off his dark glasses. Leaning close to the medicine-cabinet mirror, he spread the lids from his right eye with his fingers, as if searching for a stray lash. Yes, he could see the flecks of violet forming among the green of its iris.

Worth it, he told himself again. The queasy flutter in his gut made him wonder if that were true, however.

"I can give you something far more valuable than money, Mr. Criswell," Carleton Amis had purred when Cal had refused to create the forgeries he wanted. "I can give you the masters themselves."

Cal gave a crooked smile. "I don't deal in stolen art, either." He indicated the shabby studio apartment around them. "It may not look it, but this place is bigger than a prison cell, and I'd like to stay here."

Amis chuckled and shook his head. "You misunderstand me, my friend. I'm not offering you a few measly paintings. I'm going to give you the artists who created them. All of them, whenever you wish."

For an instant, Cal froze, as if someone had strolled over his future grave. Then he laughed, sharing the joke, wagging his finger at the older man. "You know, dude ... you're nuts."

Amis clucked his tongue. "Oh, come now, Calvin. You can't tell me the thought—the idle wish—hasn't crossed your mind." He crossed to the drafting table, shoved aside a pile of Cal's sketches, and set his briefcase there. "You've spent the better part of your career aping the giants of your profession." He patted the lid of the leather case. "Why settle for imitations when you can have the real thing?"

Cal maintained a smile to emphasize that he was not taking any of this seriously. "Well, Carleton— since we're apparently on a first-name basis now— perhaps you can explain what the hell you're talking about."

"Of course! I wouldn't expect a good businessman like yourself to take such an offer on faith." Amis opened the case, which contained three objects set into custom-carved niches in the foam-rubber interior: an unwieldy, oddly shaped gun; a glass vial of algae-green liquid; and a small notebook computer.

He flipped up the laptop screen and punched in a pre-programmed video presentation entitled *PROJECT PERSEPHONE: An Overview*, which began with an arcane lecture on DNA sequencing and gene therapy, most of which went over Cal's head. A series of video clips followed, before-and-after shots of test subjects. Men and women with brown and blue and hazel and green eyes whose irises each turned various shades of violet. Electrode wires suckling on their shaved heads like leeches, the transformed subjects each became inhabited by deceased personalities, the presence of the dead entities registered by the seismic scratching of a SoulScan readout that scrolled up the left side of the screen. Calvin's mouth went dry as he watched the footage in dumb fascination, but it was the silent promise of those other two items in the briefcase—the weird pistol and the liqueurlike drug—that convinced him that Amis could actually bestow the miracle he promised.

When he recovered his voice, Cal felt as if he, too, had been inhabited, that the words he spoke were not his, for they emanated from a locked room within him, the existence of which he had never before acknowledged. "How soon would you need the paintings?"

Amis did not seem surprised, merely pleased. "The sooner, the better, but no later than the end of the month."

The rational part of Cal's mind rejoiced. He could never complete the job, so he needn't regret turning it down. But the sealed black chamber in his psyche still bled forbidden yearning.

"There's no way," he said, as much to himself as to Amis. "That many canvases—and they all have to be artificially aged ..."

"The scope of the assignment is somewhat daunting," Amis conceded. "I understand."

"I don't think you do." Cal crossed the room and hitched a painting off the wall—a faux Rubens he'd nearly finished at the time he was arrested. "You say you want these fakes to fool an expert, right?"

Amis nodded. "A man intimately acquainted with the originals, yes."

Cal turned the painting over so that his guest could see the rectangle of worn wood to which the canvas had been tacked. "Then you need stretchers from the appropriate period. That means buying a work by one of the artist's obscure contemporaries, stripping it, and painting over the canvas. That'll set you back at least a couple hundred thousand. Afraid that's out of my budget these days." Cal pointed out the knots and wormholes in the stretcher's wood. "And see here? Curators keep precise records of defects like these for authentication purposes."

"We can accommodate you on the canvases," Pancrit assured him. "And you don't need to concern yourself about the authenticity of the wood. Several of the paintings in question were cut from their original stretchers and mounted on brand-new ones."

"Unfortunately, that's not the only detail you need to worry about." Calvin flipped the picture again, angled it so the light reflected off the glazed sheen of the paint. "See this pattern of hairline cracks in the varnish? Chaos theory in action—like snowflakes and fingerprints, no two alike. Museums digitally map them these days, and they're impossible to reproduce."

Amis grew impatient with his quibbles. "The expert who'll see these forgeries won't have the opportunity to examine them that closely."

Cal tossed the cloned Rubens on his thrift-store sofa, still ranting. "And even if I could make an identical copy—who the heck would I fool? Everyone in the world's heard about the return of those stolen paintings."

"Let's just say the man in question doesn't get out much."

"He must live under a rock. What if he goes to the Feds?"

Amis smiled, cheeks dimpling. "Mr. Criswell, I am the Feds. Not only can I assure you that you won't go to prison—I can promise you a permanent, salaried position in the N-double-A-C-C's Art Division. Once your treatment is complete, of course."

Cal's gaze flicked toward the bottle of sickly green liquid in the briefcase, and he moistened his lips. "And how soon could I begin this ... treatment?"

"How soon can you deliver the paintings?"

Cal waggled his head as if to dispel the temptation. "No way. That many canvases would take months—"

"Then you can do one at a time," Amis suggested. "When can I expect the first one?"

Don't do it, dude, the rational part of Cal's mind warned him. *This guy's bad news. Tell him you want to sleep on it.*

But the inarticulate, needy howl from the dark chamber of his subconscious proved more persuasive. For his entire career, he'd been nothing more than a parasite of artistic genius, a flea feeding on titans. Could he now pass up his one chance to join the pantheon of masters he worshipped?

Studio, living room, kitchen, and bedroom melted into one another in the shoebox-size apartment, and a few paces took Cal to his bed, where he crouched and slid a battered old suitcase out from under the bed frame. Drawing breath as if about to plunge into the ocean, he unfastened the latches and lifted the lid to reveal the secret he'd never shared with another soul: his seventh copy of da Vinci's *Madonna of the Yarnwinder.* It was the best work he'd ever done, and he'd decided to keep it when he sold the other six. At the time the cops raided his apartment following his arrest, the *Madonna* was sitting in a safe-deposit box that he'd reserved under an assumed name, which was the only reason he still possessed the painting. Given all they'd survived together, could he bear to part with it now?

He stared down at the baby Jesus, who grasped the yarnwinder's wooden cross with his pudgy hands in fatalistic fascination. Some sacrifices were inevitable.

"Will this do for a start?" Cal asked, lifting the small canvas from the suitcase and carrying it to his new boss.

Amis took hold of the picture by its gilt frame, exulting.

"Flawless! I knew you were the right man for the job, Calvin."

"And the treatment . . . ?"

"Can begin immediately." He set the phony *Madonna* carefully on the drafting table, resting the top edge against the wall, and took the gun and vial from their notches in the briefcase. Amis slid the bottle into a vertical tube above the device's trigger, where it locked in place with a hiss of released pressure. He turned to Calvin, brandishing the gun. "Would you kindly roll up your sleeve?"

Cal had seen neither Amis nor his *Madonna* since that night. He doubted that he would ever see the painting again, and Amis would not return until he came to reward Cal for completing another canvas ... by giving him another injection.

Gazing in glum despair at the unfinished mess of his *Storm on the Sea of Galilee*, he wished that he had already undergone the whole "treatment," that he could call upon Rembrandt himself to do this infernal job. Like that Violet girl did with Edvard Munch.

Soon, he thought, licking his lips. Until then, he was on his own.

Cal set aside his brush and rubbed his eyes, which had begun to smart from the strain of the fine brushwork the Rembrandt required—or, perhaps, from whatever biochemical magic had begun to change the shade of his irises.

To keep himself from imagining nasty side effects and to get a second wind for the long night of work ahead, he went to the countertop that served as his kitchen, dumped the grounds from his espresso machine's filter, and prepped a fresh brew. As he steamed the coffee into a chipped Dilbert mug, Calvin Criswell wistfully wondered where his *Madonna* was now, and whether its intended audience appreciated his ultimate sham.

7

A Private Exhibition

With nothing better to occupy his attention, the man known to some as Carleton Amis fussed with the satin cloth that hung from the painting's gilt frame like a curtain over a proscenium arch. Intimidation depended on dramatic impact, and he did not want any portion of the picture revealed until the appropriate moment. He then inventoried the items arrayed on the table next to the easel: the amber flask of sulfuric acid; the can of lighter fluid; the blowtorch; the knives, ice picks, and box cutters all laid out with the precision of a surgeon's tray. Special tools for a special torture.

Carl Pancrit had always considered himself an extraordinarily patient man, but patience had its limits. Saboteur by suicide, Bartholomew Wax had already caused him an intolerable delay. Then Markham insisted that Pancrit move the entire project from the laboratory at White Sands to this abandoned convalescent home in Pasadena, just so the madman could pine after his former sweetheart. Now, when Pancrit was at last ready to persuade Wax to cooperate, the Violet Killer dared to keep him waiting while he stalked Natalie Lindstrom all over Creation.

An hour after the appointed time, Markham finally sauntered into the rest home's former dayroom, flanked by two hulking Corps Security agents dressed as orderlies. With his face clean-shaven and his hair trimmed and dyed blond, Evan would have been unrecognizable were it not for the sullen intensity of his gaze, which even his brown contact lenses could not dull.

"That's a new look for you," Pancrit commented. "Did it impress your girlfriend?"

Evan brushed off the sarcasm. "She didn't see me."

"She *will*."

"That's my problem, isn't it?"

"It's *our* problem until the project's complete."

"You don't want me to see her? Fine. I can go back to Corps headquarters." He turned as if to leave.

Pancrit laughed and made a *tsk-tsk* sound. "Ah, the pangs of despised love! Well, if you're not too heartbroken, could we get started? I'd like to speak to the dead before I join them."

"Sure. I see you've saved a place for me ..." Markham crossed to an old wheelchair positioned before the easel in the center of the room and dropped onto its cracked Naugahyde seat. He stomped his sneakers onto the metal footplates and spread his hands as if to say, *What are you waiting for?*

Pancrit frowned but nodded to the Corps agents. The larger of the two, known only by the nickname "Block," was a seven-foot black man whose sumo-wrestler bulk barely fit into his orderly costume. He waited by the door, his stun gun drawn, while his partner, a tattooed, bearded ex-Marine with red hair and freckles, fittingly dubbed "Tackle," drew up behind the wheelchair. When Markham made no sudden moves, Tackle sidled around to strap the Violet Killer's wrists to the chair's arms with ratcheted plastic bands. Evan submitted his forearms for restraint with passive repose, as if receiving a manicure. Tackle then bound Markham's ankles to the metal rods of the footplates, checked the wheelchair's brake to make sure it was locked, and scuttled backward to his post at the door, never turning his back on the Violet.

Evan flexed his hands, tapped his toes. "Pretty snug. Feel safer now?"

After the unpleasantness in the cell at Corps headquarters, Carl Pancrit considered the question seriously. He didn't know who he should fear more—the unpredictable madman or the unknowable Bartholomew Wax. Pancrit would not have thought the docile Dr. Wax capable of squashing an ant, much less cold-bloodedly euthanizing more than a dozen of his patients. What would he do when he found himself with the spring-loaded power of the Violet's taut musculature?

"I have things under control," he murmured—less a statement of fact than an assertion of will.

"Sure you don't want a SoulScan?" Evan's tone lilted with amusement, taunting him.

"I'll know if I'm talking to the good doctor. And if he causes any trouble ... well, we're prepared." Pancrit tipped his head toward the Corps Security guards, both now armed with stun guns. "Are you ready?"

"Always." Lizard eyes unblinking, Markham beckoned with his right hand. "Lay it on me."

Pancrit advanced to within a foot of the wheelchair and drew a folded business envelope from the inside pocket of his blue blazer. He thumbed back the flap and poured the envelope's sole item into Markham's open palm: the green bread-bag twist-tie Pancrit had taken from the hair of Bartholomew Wax's corpse.

Evan curled his fingers over the laminated wire and shut his eyes, his lips fluttering with soundless syllables. His speech did not become audible until he raised his voice several minutes later.

"... *sodium, magnesium, aluminum, silicon, phosphorus, sulfur ...*"

Belted to the wheelchair by the plastic bands, Markham continued to list the chemical elements of the Periodic Table in order, dipping his head forward then jerking upright again, like a deep-sea angler straining to reel in a sailfish. The volume of his spectator mantra rose with the ferocity of his bobbing trance.

"... *THORIUM, PROTACTINIUM, URANIUM, NEPTUNIUM, PLUTONIUM—*"

He snapped up, board-stiff, and the back-and-forth swaying gave way to a lateral jitter, causing the wheels of the chair to rock and squeak. Evan's expression roiled, as if another face fought to escape his skin. The wheelchair wobbled sideways, on the verge of tipping over, and the Corps Security guards started forward, but Pancrit raised his hand to stop them. When the Violet's eyes flicked open, the soul behind them quickly took in the surroundings and did not seem in the least surprised when it saw Carl Pancrit wave in greeting.

"Welcome back, Barty. Hope you enjoyed your little vacation."

Markham's face lengthened with the weariness of Bartholomew Wax. "Carl. I should have known you were the Devil."

"Yes, actually, I am. And I have a lien on your soul." Pancrit smiled. "You may recall that we had a business arrangement ..."

"To my lasting regret, yes."

"I delivered on my part of the bargain. Our Corps agents took significant risks filching your pretty pictures for you, but you welched on payment for services rendered." He wagged a finger. "Nobody likes a quitter, Barty. That's why you're going to finish the project, even if I have to bring you back a hundred times to do it."

Wax tried to lift Markham's hands but could not twist them free. He let the Violet's head droop instead. "I can't. Not if you bring me back a hundred thousand times."

"There! You see? Negative thinking—that's your problem."

"Carl, you *saw* what happened to those people!" It was the first time Pancrit had ever heard the soft-spoken Dr. Wax shout. "Get it through your head: *the treatment doesn't work.*"

Pancrit shook his head. "Seems to me the only thing that's not working is you, Barty. But that's about to change." He returned to the easel, hooked his thumb and forefinger around one corner of the satin that covered the painting. "I know we don't see eye to eye on many things, Dr. Wax, but I have to admit I like your taste in women. Particularly this one."

He yanked the cloth away with a flourish, unveiling Calvin Criswell's rendition of Leonardo's *Madonna of the Yarnwinder*. If Pancrit had any remaining doubts about the superlative accuracy of the forger's work, they disappeared when he saw Bartholomew Wax gape at the picture in strangled, openmouthed shock.

"No," he croaked. "I—I sent it back. I sent all of them back. How did you ...?"

"The same way we did the last time. Plucked it right off the wall of Drumlanrig Castle." Actually, the genuine *Madonna* still hung in its home, safe and sound, but Wax had no way of knowing that Pancrit hadn't wanted to take either the time or risk required to steal Wax's "children" back from their respective museums, so he counted on Criswell's forgeries to persuade the dead scientist to cooperate.

"Beautiful, isn't she?" he said, admiring the *Madonna*. Criswell really was a gifted artist in his own right; it was rather a shame that he would suffer the same fate as the other subjects of the failed gene therapy. Still, he would last long enough for Pancrit's purposes.

"Leonardo's work is truly unmatched." Pancrit selected the flask of yellow fluid from the table of torture implements. "One might even say ... *irreplaceable.*"

Wax squirmed in the wheelchair, gaze darting

between the painting and the bottle. "What are you doing?"

"Seeing how much of an art lover you really are." Pancrit loosened the eyedropper that served as the flask's stopper, filled its glass tube with amber liquid. He held the dropper above the picture and lightly squeezed its rubber bladder until a yellow tear dangled from the glass tip. "Now … perhaps you'll consider rejoining our little team?"

Wax panted as the amber drop quivered with surface tension. "I *can't*— "

"Oops!" With an insouciant twitch of his hand, Pancrit let the drop fall on the painting's frame. The sulfuric acid hit the ornate scrollwork with a sizzle, the golden paint bubbling to evaporate into gilded smoke.

The dead scientist wriggled and whimpered as if the acid had landed on his skin. "*Stop it!*"

"Ah-ah." Pancrit lowered the dropper over the canvas and coaxed another drip to its drooling tip. "Settle down now."

Wax froze, mewling as if afraid the vibrations of his movement might dislodge the acid droplet. "But you *can't*," he protested, like a child who hasn't yet learned that rules can be broken. "You and I—we don't matter. *This* matters."

"Does it? Destroying those test subjects at White Sands mattered more to you than this masterpiece. Avoiding your obligation to the project matters more to you than this triumph of the human imagination. Whatever happens to this painting will happen because you want it to. So let's see just how much it does matter to you.

"What should we do, Barty? Dissolve it?" Pancrit raised the acid flask, then indicated the other implements at his disposal. "Burn it? Slash it? Your pick."

Wax blubbered, his gaze fixed on the dropper of acid. "*I told* you, the treatment doesn't work! There's nothing I can do ..."

Pancrit sighed. "There's that negative thinking again."

He wiggled the dropper, and Wax shrieked as the acid on the tip shivered. "*All right! All right!* I'll try. Please ... *leave it alone.*"

Pancrit grinned. "We've readied a laboratory for you, Dr. Wax. I trust you can start immediately?"

The dead scientist jerked hard enough against the bonds that held him that the entire wheelchair rattled. "If I ever—"

The Corps Security agents moved to flank him, stun guns ready.

Pancrit swung the eyedropper back toward the painting. "You were saying?"

Wax seethed but remained still. "I am at your service, *Mr.* Pancrit."

"Now you sound like a team player." Pancrit placed the dropper back in the flask. "We'll call you when we need you."

Evan Markham's head snapped back, drawing breath as if for a sneeze. Block, the sumo-shaped orderly, leaned close, his stun gun held within an inch of the Violet's pulsing throat. Before it could spark, however, Evan exhaled and righted himself in the wheelchair, glaring at the Corps Security agent with his customary hostility.

"There a problem?" He cast a glance at the stun gun and the guard withdrew it. Evan waved his bound hands, and Wax's bread-bag hair tie fluttered from his unclenched fist to the floor. "You can take these things off anytime now."

The Security agents sought authorization from Pancrit, who nodded. Tackle grabbed a box cutter from among Pancrit's torture tools and sliced the plastic bands off Markham's wrists and ankles while Block kept his stun gun close by.

The Violet stood and shook the circulation back into his fingers. "You know Wax is holding out on you, right?"

Markham's idle comment excited Pancrit. "Why? Did his thoughts give anything away?"

"No. He was fighting hard *not* to think about the project, which is how I could tell he knows more than he's letting on."

Carl Pancrit smiled, his hunch confirmed. He stooped to retrieve the twist-tie. "We'll see whether the good doctor is more forthcoming in his work. If not, we'll have to stage a more dramatic showing of this painting."

"So, am I dismissed?" Markham made a move toward the door, only to have Block stand in his way.

"Not until I'm done with you," Pancrit said. "Needless to say, you'll have to summon our dear Dr. Wax on a regular basis until his research is complete. But I also require your services for the recruitment phase of our project."

"'Recruitment phase'?" The madman sounded more annoyed than curious.

"Yes. We need volunteers. Test subjects with a psychological predisposition to accept the results of our therapy. We've tried using unwilling subjects—prisoners and so forth—but the results were not ... satisfactory." Pancrit tapped a finger on his forehead to clarify his understatement. "They weren't prepared to have their perceptions opened in that way. We need people for whom the change would be welcome."

"You mean people who want to be Violets," Evan said.

Pancrit grinned. "Exactly."

The Violet Killer exuded icy confidence. "I know one."

8

A Prime Candidate

An autumnal mist submerged Seattle in gossamer gloom, dampening the khaki military fatigues of the hirsute man who lurched up University Boulevard, one dirt-darkened hand cradling a stain-streaked paper cup of coffee. Day after day, he rinsed out the same cup and took it back to the supermarket deli down the street, where they refilled it for free, assuming he was a homeless veteran. A decade after the Seattle police had shot him in the leg, Clement Everett Maddox still walked with a limp that slowed his gait and garnered him a disability check every month, which he tried to stretch as far as possible. Today, however, the misery of smarting joints and sopping clothes made him wish he'd simply paid the two bucks to get his java at the yuppie bistro across the street from his electronics shop.

A side street led Maddox to the entrance of Clem's Gadget Garage. The paper sign taped to the inside of its glass door once read TEMPORARILY CLOSED, but years of sun exposure had faded the penned letters to near invisibility. The front window display still offered a petrified edifice of black-and-white TVs, eight-track tape players, Beta videocassette machines, and other obsolete devices—not one of which had sold since the store's "temporary" closing. Luckily, the landlord didn't care about the state of the business as long as Clem's rent checks cleared each month.

A gifted electrician, Clem used to enjoy a lucrative career as a retailer and repairman, but that was before his wife, Amy, died of breast cancer. Before he became obsessed with tuning his radios and televisions to what he believed to be the frequency of her soul's electromagnetic energy, attempting to bring her back as a transcendental broadcast. Before the Violet Killer framed him for murder and the Seattle cops blew a hole in his femoral artery.

Shivering and cursing as he entered and relocked the door behind him, Clem swigged his coffee, which had already gone cold and bitter, then shrugged off his wet jacket. He tried to excite himself about the long night of work ahead, but the thrill of discovery had palled before the desperation of defeat. The cops had confiscated all the touchstones he'd collected from the Violet Killer's victims, leaving him with no way to study the souls of deceased Violets—the key to his theory of electronic communication with the afterlife.

Forced to rely on the knickknacks he'd accumulated from common dead folks, he spent fruitless hours scrutinizing the spattered blankness of snow-covered television screens, listening endlessly to the hissing interference of the radio frequencies between stations. The dreary lack of progress made him doubt his theory ... and even his sanity. Where before he saw the suggestion of faces in the flickering pixels, he now saw only the impenetrable fog of a cathode-ray tube; where he once sensed the whisper of insistent voices, he now heard only the meaningless fuzz of static.

While there was still a bleak gray dusk outside, it was already night in Clem's Gadget Garage. The rectangle of the doorway to the back room shone with the bluish pastel shimmer of the stacked television sets Maddox always left on, and he trudged toward the light, sneezing from the dust and mold that thickened the shop's cold air. Maybe he'd forget trying to talk to the dead for one night: just change the channel of one of his TVs to some dumb sitcom, nuke a dinner in the micro, and work up a good beer buzz until he passed out for the night. What the hell—sounded like a plan.

Clem passed through the doorway's arch, tossed his wet jacket on a pile of dirty clothes beside his cot, and squatted to open the small icebox in the corner. He swapped his cold coffee for a cold beer, placing the java in the fridge to reheat in the morning. Clem popped open the can and started to guzzle, but the sight of a silhouette next to his on the wall made him choke and spew.

"Welcome back, Mr. Maddox," a voice said from behind him. "I've been waiting."

Clem spun around to see a tall, well-dressed man outlined by the rows of speckled, glowing screens that lined the shelves at the opposite end of the room. "Who the hell are you? How'd you get in here?"

"You can call me Dr. Amis. Carleton Amis." The stranger squinted at one of the televisions as if peering into an aquarium. Like all the others, the set had a personal article from a deceased person—in this case, a Raggedy Ann doll—tied to its rabbit-ear antenna with a piece of wire. "And as for how I got in, well, as I like to say, there's no stopping good news."

"Get out. Get out before I call the cops."

Amis shook his head sadly. "Really, Mr. Maddox! I would think you'd have even less of an affinity for the police than I do."

"What do you know about it? Who told you about me?"

"A mutual friend." Bathed in the television's fluorescence, the stranger's face looked as rapturous as Clem's once did, when eyes stared back at him from the on-screen blizzard, when mouths gaped, yearning to scream their secrets. "You know, we have a lot in common," Amis observed. "We share a fascination with the tissue-thin barrier that separates our world from *theirs*—and we both want to penetrate that barrier."

Comprehension made Clem narrow his eyes. "You with the Corps?"

Amis laughed. "I am *with* the Corps but not *of* the Corps, if you get my meaning. The N-double-A-C-C wants to maintain its monopoly on postmortem contact, whereas you and I want to, shall we say, *democratize* the gift of necromancy." He indicated the TV nearest him. "It's a shame the Corps didn't back your research into electronic mediumship. I find it immensely interesting, if a bit clumsy." He ruffled the yarn hair of the Raggedy Ann touchstone, lashed to the antenna like the figurehead on the prow of a ship.

Despite the disillusionment Clem felt about his work, he bristled at the snub. "Look, you people had your chance. I ain't giving you my discoveries, so take your money and shove it."

"You misunderstand me, my friend. I didn't come here to demand. I came to give." Amis strolled over to the workbench and gestured to the corkboard where Maddox had pinned a crazy quilt of newspaper and magazine clippings about the exploits of famous Violets. "After all, would you rather see your late wife trapped behind the glass wall of a video monitor ... or feel her *inside* you, the way a real conduit does?"

Clem didn't realize he was shaking until he heard the sloshing of beer in the can he still held, forgotten, in his right hand. "What're you talking about?"

"Simple, Mr. Maddox. I can make you what you always wanted to be. Question is ... how badly do you want it?" Amis fingered the touchstone attached to the television on the workbench—the one given a place of honor, apart from the others. Nudged by his touch, the diamond on Amy's engagement ring twinkled in the electronic moonlight.

9

Unwelcome Roommates

Calvin Criswell compared the skin tone of the topless blond woman perched on the overturned milk crate with the pigments he'd mixed on his palette, blinked his aching eyes, and swore. *It's wrong, wrong, wrong,* he thought, daubing in more peach tone with his brush.

Lately, it was always wrong. As the shade of his irises shifted inexorably toward the violet end of the spectrum, so did their light absorption, continually changing his perception of color. It drove him nuts—especially when he was trying to reproduce the subtlety of the hues in *Storm on the Sea of Galilee.* Desperate to put aside the unfinished Rembrandt for a while, he decided to try his first original painting in years, but it was giving him just as much of a headache.

The woman on the milk crate posed in the fashion of a Greek goddess, her dark roots and metallic green toenails notwithstanding. Calvin had folded and tied a white bedsheet around her waist as a faux toga, turned her head to the left at a demure angle, and instructed her to lift one elbow over her head as if stroking her own hair. But now she twitched and fidgeted, shifting her thighs from graceful to bow-legged. "Are you almost done, Cal?" she carped. "My arm's tired."

He blinked again as the light in the apartment seemed to waver in intensity. The cheap green contact lenses he'd bought to hide his altered eyes didn't help, either. "Just hold still, Trank."

"You know I hate that! Use my whole name, for God's sake."

"I'm too embarrassed." Cal had met her at one of the countless art openings he attended for networking and free wine and cheese. She'd told him then that she was Tranquillity Moon, and had since refused to admit that it was not her real name. "Your parents must have been very cruel," he'd said at the time, and she'd giggled. At the time.

"Gee ... lighten up, Picasso!" She stiffened back into a statuesque posture. "I thought I was doing you a favor. It's not like I don't have better things to do on my day off than stand here for hours half naked—"

Calvin slammed his brush down on the edge of the easel and rubbed his temple. *"Hold still!* That means no talking. Is that too much to ask?"

Tranquillity dropped the Athenian demeanor and put her hands on her hips in her usual slouch. "You know what your problem is, Mr. Grouch? You need to forget about that picture and enjoy the real thing."

She sashayed off the crate, coming over to where he stood, in what she obviously intended to be a seductive manner. As she snuggled up against his shoulder and drew close to kiss his cheek, though, the partial portrait on the easel caught her eye.

"Holy crap! *Please* tell me my hips aren't that big ..." Tranquillity stepped away, glancing from her thighs to the painting and back again. "It's this stupid sheet. I *told* you it wouldn't look good on me."

Cal shoved his palette on the drafting table and held his head, groaning. It wasn't Tranquillity's fault, but he couldn't deal with her right now. He shouldn't have asked her out in the first place, but after seeing only men for two whole years during his stay in prison, any female company seemed welcome. As soon as he made parole, he'd picked the first woman who'd shown any interest in him. The more time they spent together, however, the more Calvin realized he had nothing in common with her, a fact that only made him more conscious of how truly alone he was in the world, how much he'd screwed up.

Cal steadied his temper with a long breath. "I'm sorry, Trank ... Tranquillity. I'm not feeling too good. Maybe we should call it a day."

"Just like that, huh?" She indicated her R-rated outfit. "I go through all this, and now I don't even get— Cal, what's wrong? Cal!"

Calvin sank onto his haunches, arms crossed over his skull as if afraid the roof were about to collapse. He'd never had a headache like this one. Maybe he'd pinched a nerve, for an electric prickling had spread out from behind his eyes to envelop his entire face and scalp.

Tranquillity crouched to put an arm around his shoulders. "Cal, what can I do? Should I call nine-one-one?"

The lights in the room seemed to flicker—especially the vintage fixture mounted directly overhead. Cal rolled his gaze up toward it, his vision blurring.

I'm done for. I'll never work in this town again.

The thought startled Cal, for although it certainly applied to him, it wasn't his. He slumped sideways as the prickling sensation infected his arms and legs, as if the blood to his limbs had been cut off. Pain constricted his throat until he gagged for breath, the fuzzy orb of the overhead light lowering over him like a desert sun.

The talkies won't have me. Even my agent says I sound like a frog ...

"Cal! What's wrong? Can you hear me?"

He could hear Tranquillity—dulled as if by depths of water—but he could no longer see her, could not feel her shaking him. Instead, he saw the studio apartment around him, only it wasn't his apartment anymore: a vanity with makeup and perfume bottles rested where his drafting table should have been. His perspective had changed, too. He no longer lay on the floor but instead stood on a wooden chair with his bare toes curled over the edge of the seat. The sleekness of a silk stocking caressed his throat, and the frilly hem of a woman's slip brushed his knees as he pushed the chair out from under himself.

For a drawn-out instant, he seemed to hover like a gull borne on a thermal updraft. Then his body plunged, the stocking pulled taut, and his swinging weight yanked the bolts of the light fixture out of the ceiling. Both the stocking and the cord of the lamp to which it was tied remained intact, however, and his feet fluttered about eight inches above the floor. Sparks crackled above him and the lamp flickered. His view of the room drifted to the right, then rotated back to the left as the stricture of the noose made him bob his mouth open for air.

This isn't me! Calvin screamed in his mind. *I didn't kill myself!* But the sense-memory of choking—of flailing and scissoring his legs in a vain effort to plant his feet on the floor—had the immediacy of firsthand experience.

"I ... m-made a ... m-mistake," he heard a man say. His confusion swelled when he realized the voice was his own.

"What, Cal?" Tranquillity again, from the far side of the ocean. "Did you say something?"

He hadn't said anything, yet his mouth repeated the phrase: "I m-made a m-mistake."

It's her, Cal realized. The woman he'd seen—the woman he *was* in the awful death-memory—was speaking through him. And she *had* made a hideous mistake. Not only had the washed-up silent-screen star chosen to hang herself, she hadn't considered that jumping from a chair would not give her enough gravitational acceleration to break her neck. Instead, she ended up twisting at the end of the stretched stocking for better than half an hour, head and heart welling with immediate regrets yet unable to save herself or cry for help as her collapsed windpipe starved her body of oxygen with agonizing slowness.

"I made a mistake," she said, more firmly than before. *"And I want to come back."*

Cal yelled to Tranquillity, but only became more frantic when he understood that she could not hear him. His last remaining perceptions of the outside world disappeared as if he'd been smothered by shovelfuls of dirt, buried alive in his own body.

Suddenly, a new variety of pain dredged him from the well of his subconscious like a winch. Relief flooded through him as he felt his cheek throb and saw Tranquillity standing before him, panting and livid, her arm still at full swing after belting him.

"You have a *lot* of nerve," she hissed, "talking to me that way while I'm phoning the paramedics to save your sorry hide!"

"My God." Cal discovered that he was now standing, though he could not remember rising from the floor. He put his hand to his face, testing whether he could both touch and feel. "Tranquillity ... what did I say?"

She sneered in disbelief. "You oughta know! Calling me a hussy and a whore and telling me to get out of your place—"

He hugged her. "Bless you, Trank. I'll make it up to you."

Another burst of tingling jolted his body, nearly paralyzing him. The studio's former tenant wanted to take up residence again.

Cal stumbled to the apartment's door and out into the hall. He had to leave this place—her place—before he lost himself again. He didn't know where to go, however. Only Carleton Amis knew what was happening to him, and Amis had refused to tell Cal where to find him, or how to contact him between their appointed meetings.

Tranquillity followed Cal as far as the doorway, crossing her arms to cover her exposed breasts and glancing toward the adjacent apartments with embarrassment. "What is *up* with you, anyway? You on drugs or something?"

"You could say that." He braced himself against the handrail as he stomped downstairs. That woman in the Munch painting—the Violet who'd come to see him. She would know how to help him ... if he could find her in time.

10

The Haves and the Have-nots

As far as the Internet was concerned, Carleton Amis did not exist. Seated in front of her laptop at the desk in her living room, Natalie Googled and Yahooed the name without learning the identity of the man who had asked her to counterfeit the world's most notorious stolen paintings—and who had somehow convinced the NAACC to release the Violet Killer.

Natalie had not seen Evan in the week since Serena arrived—at least, not that she knew of. She couldn't be sure, for the Corps had long ago taught Evan to disguise himself beyond recognition. But Natalie *felt* him everywhere, his presence as formless yet as palpable as the drop in air pressure that presaged a storm. If she stepped outside the condo, she sensed his covetous gaze piercing her like X-rays, exposing the scar tissue and dormant tumors of dead love. If she stayed inside, he lurked like Grendel outside her windows, awaiting the chance to extinguish the life and light inside her home. Even Corps Security had never made her feel so violated—or so vulnerable.

At Natalie's request, Serena had agreed to stay on as a bodyguard, the two of them sleeping in shifts as

114

they watched over Wade and Callie. Natalie only went out once, armed with a can of pepper spray, to buy food for the week. During the day, she surfed the Web, seeking some shred of information that would illuminate the connection between Evan and Carleton Amis.

"Can't we go to the pool, at least?" her daughter wheedled. After seven days of virtual house arrest, Callie was close to expiring from captivity. "You could sit there with me. I'll even stay in the shallow end."

"Not now, honey." Natalie entered another fruitless search in her Web browser, attempting to cross-reference Evan's and Amis's names with the titles of the stolen paintings. No results.

Hanging on the back of Natalie's chair, Callie pushed herself onto her tiptoes, raising her mouth to her mother's ear. *"Pleeeeeeease?"*

"I said *no.* It's too dangerous. Why don't you go play Monopoly with Grandpa Wade?"

"We've played Monopoly, like, a hundred times already. Even Grandpa's getting sick of it."

"Then why don't you play cards?"

"We're bored with that, too. We've played every game to death, practically. Can we *ever* go out again?"

"When we're sure the bad man out there won't hurt us, then we can go out. Not before."

Callie let go of the chair with a growl. "Who is this jerk, anyway?"

Natalie's lips twitched into a frown. "He's a bad man. That's all you need to know."

Shame more than parental discretion had kept Natalie from explaining that Evan Markham had not only been the Violet Killer but also her boyfriend. How could she admit to her daughter that an infatuation she'd had in her teens now threatened all their lives?

Serena saved Natalie from further debate with her daughter by entering the condo's front door. Callie bounded to meet her, grateful for any distraction. "You're back! Can we spar now?"

"Might as well. Got nothing better to do." Serena let the girl punch at her raised arm, but looked toward Natalie. "Hope you had better luck than I did."

Natalie stood and massaged the cramp in the small of her back. "Your Corps connections didn't have anything on Amis?"

"They didn't know or wouldn't say, which amounts to the same thing. You?"

"Nothing. I knew it was too much to hope that Carleton Amis was his real name, but I didn't have anything else to go on."

"And Evan?"

Natalie made an *ixnay-on-the-Evanay* face, but it was too late.

"Evan?" Callie said. "Is that the bad man's name?"

Natalie sighed in annoyance, and Serena shrugged an apology. "Sorry. Forgot."

"If you know who he is, why don't you just have the police arrest him?" Callie looked from her godmother to her mother, awaiting an explanation. "That's what Dad would do."

"We don't know where he is, honey," Natalie said,

adding for Serena, "but, as far as I can tell, he isn't killing anyone. Yet."

Her friend nodded. "So far, so good. But we can't stay cooped up in this place forever."

"You can say that again," Callie interjected.

"What you wanna do, Nat?" Serena asked. "We got no leads."

Natalie pursed her lips to keep from answering too quickly. She *had* an idea, but it was rash; drastic. If she gave the Corps any excuse to crack down on her ...

"One person knows who Amis is." Impatience got the best of her. She grabbed one of the photos strewn around her computer and strode toward the front door. "Let's ask him."

She was already headed down the front walk before Serena caught on, trying to catch her. "Whoa, girlfriend! You don't want to go there."

But Natalie did go there, right up to the passenger side of the black Mitsubishi parked at the curb, Serena a step behind her. Sanjay Prashad saw them coming and rolled down the electric window.

"Ms. Lindstrom!" An ivory grin split his nutshell face. "You have not favored me with your notice in months. Are you feeling quite well?"

"I'll feel better if you tell me who this is." She thrust the picture of Carleton Amis toward him.

He made a show of examining the photo before shaking his head. "I have never seen this man before."

"That's funny. You practically prostrated yourself in front of him when he came to see me back in August."

117

"Unlike you, Ms. Lindstrom, I strive to be pleasant to everyone." He bowed his head with an ingratiating smile to prove his point.

"He's with the N-double-A-C-C, isn't he? That's how you know him. That's how he got the Violet Killer out of Corps headquarters—"

Serena discreetly kicked her shin, and Natalie realized that she'd said too much. The Corps wasn't supposed to know that Simon McCord's informants had learned of Evan's release.

Sanjay Prashad appeared to suppress a snicker, as if he'd spotted a bit of spinach stuck in her teeth. "The Corps has the Violet Killer safely under its control. However, if you perceive some threat to you and your family, we would be happy to take you into protective custody."

Natalie knew from experience what *protective custody* meant in Corps-speak: indentured servitude.

"Forget it," she muttered. "I should've known talking to you was a waste of time."

"On the contrary, Ms. Lindstrom—you only waste time when you evade your duty to ..."

The Corps Security agent's diatribe dissipated like cigarette smoke, and for the first time, his smile lost its smugness. Natalie wished she could have taken credit for his dismay, but he peered past her right shoulder. She turned in that direction and saw a rust-freckled VW bus parked across the street. The driver emerged with his scarecrow arms clamped over his head like the jaws of a vise to hold his skull together. Dressed in black jeans and a Bauhaus concert T-shirt that years of washing had Swiss-cheesed with holes, he tottered toward them, flinching and lurching as if struck by unseen blows.

Natalie rushed forward as he faltered and dropped to his knees. Her eyes widened when Calvin Criswell lifted his face, his cheeks scarred by tear tracks.

"Please help me," he rasped.

Natalie and Serena buttressed Criswell as he shuffled into the condo. While Serena eased him down onto the living-room sofa, Natalie shut the drapes. Outside the window, she could see Sanjay Prashad seated in his car, having a heated conversation with someone on his cell phone.

The first few minutes they tried to question him, Criswell merely held his head and moaned. Natalie sat down beside him and touched his shoulder in sympathy. "What's wrong? How can we help?"

He jerked away from her hand as if it were a branding iron. "Make them stop!"

She withdrew to the opposite end of the couch. "Make *who* stop?"

"You know. The voices. The—the souls."

She traded a startled glance with Serena. "Whose souls are you hearing?"

"Just people. In my apartment, on the street. I don't even know who they are. *Please* . . . you guys are Violets. Tell me how you get rid of them."

Natalie remembered the dark glasses Criswell had worn the last time she'd talked with him and how she'd wondered if he might be on drugs. Perhaps he was suffering some kind of bad trip now. "Calvin, please don't take this the wrong way," she began, "but if you're hearing voices, maybe you should see a doctor. You're not a Violet."

"I am now." He put his fingers to his eyes, and for one awful instant, Natalie thought he was going to pull an Oedipus and pluck the balls from their sockets. Instead, he pinched the soft green contact lenses off his corneas, flicked them away with disgust, and stared at her with eyes unlike any she'd seen before: irises zigzagged with a corona of violet around the pupil yet speckled with green, like the inlaid surface of a Fabergé egg. "See?"

Natalie could not respond. A breach of Nature's laws, those misbegotten hybrid eyes filled her with the fascination and repugnance ordinarily reserved for sideshow abominations. She suddenly understood the revulsion Violets must inspire in ordinary people, a thought that further sickened her.

Serena lunged forward to grip Criswell by the jaw, tilting his head up and spreading one of his eyes wide to scrutinize the mutant flower of its iris. "It's a trick," she snapped. "Probably sent here by Carleton Amis himself."

Criswell let out a hysterical laugh. "Are you kidding? He'd kill me if he found out I was here."

His turn of phrase jarred Natalie, reminding her that, while they spoke, Sanjay Prashad sat right outside their door, squealing to Lord-knows-who on his cell phone. "What does Amis have to do with this?" she asked Criswell. "How did he do this to you?"

"Why don't you ask him?" he sassed back. "You guys were buds before he ever came to me."

Serena evidently didn't find any fakery in his eyes, for she released him with a shove. "Funny how you didn't know who Amis was the last time we met. Any other lost memories you'd care to recover?"

"I'll tell you anything! Just—make it *stop!*" Criswell clutched his temples and let out a yelp.

Natalie winced in empathy. He was acting exactly as she often had as a child, before her Violet training at the School. "Is someone knocking right now, Calvin?"

He sniveled. "Knocking?"

She clarified the conduit slang. "A soul. Is a soul bothering you right now?"

"*Yes!* Yes, already! Make it stop!"

Serena gave a derisive snort. "He's lying. *I* don't feel squat."

Natalie frowned. She didn't sense anyone knocking, either. Indeed, she'd bought this condo because it was brand-new at the time, so it could not serve as a touchstone for any deceased prior residents. Of course, the electromagnetic energy of certain souls constantly circulated through the atmosphere like a free-floating ether, but they seldom knocked unless a Violet established a quantum connection with them by making physical contact with some object the dead individuals had touched during their lifetime. If Criswell was somehow picking up those random entities, he was a far more sensitive Violet than either Natalie or Serena. Too incredible to believe, but ...

"I'll be back in a sec." Natalie rushed from the living room to the kitchen, where she snatched a roll of aluminum foil from one of the drawers beside the stove. Returning to her seat beside Criswell on the couch, she ripped off a large rectangle of the foil and handed it to him. "Wrap this around your head."

He looked at the sheet of metal in his hands with miserable chagrin. "You've *got* to be joking."

Natalie blushed, and even Serena regarded her as if she'd lost her mind. "It won't work as well as a full soul cage," she said by way of explanation, "but the metal should serve as a buffer to the souls' energy. Like driving under a bridge will fade out your radio reception."

Calvin Criswell sighed, then molded the foil over his cranium, pressing it down over his curly brown hair and crimping it to keep it in place, until his head looked like a Jiffy Pop bag. The fact that he was willing to endure such an indignity convinced Natalie that his desperation was real.

Crowned with aluminum, he tilted his head this way and that as if it were a satellite dish. His face brightened. "I think it's working!"

Serena folded her arms with sarcastic casualness. "Swell. Now, if the voices in your head are done talking, mind if we have a few words?"

Natalie scolded her with a glance and took on the role of good cop. "Calvin, if we're going to help you, we need to know how you got this way—and what Carleton Amis has to do with it."

He goggled at them, perplexed. "But I thought you guys knew all about it. You're in the Corps, aren't you?"

Natalie hesitated. "Um, that's kind of a long story—"

"Guilty," Serena cut in. "Mind telling me what I'm supposed to know?"

"Project Persephone." Criswell paused for a reaction and seemed surprised by the puzzlement he got in return. "That is the name, isn't it?"

"The name of *what*?" Serena demanded.

"Of this." He indicated his eyes. "It's some kind of DNA hocus-pocus that's supposed to make me like you."

Project Persephone, Natalie repeated silently, wondering why the name sounded so familiar. Then it came to her: the movie company Carleton Amis had claimed to work for. Persephone Productions.

She strained to dredge up what little she'd learned of Greek mythology in her English classes at the School. Persephone had been the beautiful daughter of Demeter, the goddess of grain and fertility. Determined to make Persephone his bride, Hades, god of the underworld, tricked her into eating part of an enchanted pomegranate, after which she was condemned to reside with him for a portion of every year, presiding over the dead as his queen. If what Calvin Criswell said was true, that's what Project Persephone intended to grant—mastery over the dead.

Natalie fought to quell her disquiet. She felt as if part of her birthright had been stolen from her, as if the Corps had cloned her without her knowledge. *It isn't possible*, she thought, but she could tell that even Serena's skepticism had begun to slip into fear.

"You say Amis did this to you. How?" Serena bent

123

until her own violet eyes peered into Criswell's two-toned ones. *"Why?"*

The artist took a long breath, either to calm himself or to stall for time to get his story straight. "Amis needed some paintings—"

"Some forgeries," Natalie amended.

Criswell bobbed his head, a tacit admission of guilt. "Given my record, he knew I wouldn't risk the job unless he had something ... *special* to offer."

"He offered to make you a Violet?" She shook her head. "Why on earth would you want to do that?"

"I was washed up. My career was over. Amis promised me a job with the Corps's Art Division." Criswell stated this rationale with rote concision, but the way he avoided her gaze made Natalie certain he hadn't revealed his true reasons. Before she could probe further, however, Serena continued to grill him.

"If Amis didn't send you, then how did you find us?"

"The art community is a small world ... and word gets around about someone who does a painting like *Self-Portrait as a Woman.*" He snuck another glance at Natalie. "I called a few of my connections."

"Then how do *we* find Amis?" Serena demanded.

"I don't know."

"What's his real name?"

"I don't know."

"Come on, Calvin! You're doing business with the man, aren't you? How do you set up your meetings?"

"He sets them up. I give him the painting, he gives

me the treatment—that's it. I don't even know his phone number."

A plan took shape in Natalie's mind, hazy as an unfocused telescope image. "When's your next rendezvous scheduled?"

Criswell's silvered head drooped. "Saturday. But there's no way—the picture isn't even close to being done."

"What if I could finish it for you? Do you think you're up to meeting Amis?"

He slapped his palms on his temples. "If I can keep these dorks out of my head."

Natalie nodded. "Can you bring us the painting?"

Criswell shook his head so hard he had to grab the foil to keep it from falling off. "No way. I can't go back there. A woman—she killed herself in that apartment ..."

He didn't need to go on.

"That's okay. I can get it," Natalie said. "But where are you going to stay?"

Calvin Criswell's eyes glazed over with the desolation of the suddenly homeless. "I don't know."

Natalie screwed her mouth shut, resolving not to be a pushover. But he reminded her so much of herself as a child, tossed and tugged by tidal forces she could barely comprehend, that she couldn't help feeling sorry for him.

"You could crash here, I guess."

He pounced on the invitation like a mouse on cheese. "You wouldn't even notice me, I swear. I'll even take the couch."

Natalie tightened her mouth again. "The couch is mine."

125

"The floor, then. Heck, I'll sleep in the closet if I have to. Please—let me stay."

"Whoa. Cut." Serena chopped her hands together like a movie clapboard. "You can't trust this guy, Nat. He's in league with Amis."

Natalie sized up Calvin Criswell. With his head capped in what looked like a toddler's space helmet, he seemed as harmless and helpless as a four-year-old.

"He needs to find Amis even more than we do," she decided.

Serena grunted grudging assent. "If you say so, girlfriend. But you ain't going to his place alone." She snapped her fingers at Criswell and opened her palm. "Gimme your keys."

He surrendered his key ring without objection. "The painting's on the drafting table next to the easel," he volunteered. *"Storm on the Sea of Galilee."*

Natalie knew an act of fraud shouldn't impress her, but it did. "You paint Rembrandt from scratch? Without his help?"

"Yep."

If it had been up to her, Natalie would have talked shop right then, pumping Criswell for details on his technique, but Callie pounded down the stairs, dragging her grandfather by the hand.

"My favorite girl suggested we get pizza." Wade took in the scene's interrupted tension, noticed the stranger with the ridiculous shiny wrap on his head. "This is a bad time, isn't it?"

Callie aimed an index finger at Calvin. "See? That's the weird guy who showed up this morning."

She turned her fearless face full on the artist. "Are you Evan?"

Natalie watched Criswell for any sign of recognition, but the name seemed to mean nothing to him.

"No," he said. "Sorry."

"Are you a bad man?" Callie asked.

He fidgeted before answering. "Depends who you ask, I guess," he replied, chuckling to make it sound like a joke.

Serena reached beneath her suit jacket to produce a stun gun, which she passed to Wade. "We've got to go. If he acts up while we're gone, zap him and call the cops."

Natalie's father clutched the weapon as if she'd handed him a live grenade. "I guess that's a negative on the pizza."

"Whatever. C'mon, Nat." Serena did not spare a glance at Calvin as she headed for the door.

Natalie, however, reached for his hand to comfort him, then recalled how he'd shied from her touch. It occurred to her that she could serve as a touchstone for any number of dead people. In his heightened state of sensitivity, Calvin might even feel Natalie's murdered mother knocking if she made contact with his bare skin.

She withdrew her arm. "You'll be safe here."

His eyes grew liquid again. "Thank you," he whispered.

She left him with a sympathetic smile, grabbed her canvas tote bag to fetch a change of clothes for him, and joined Serena outside.

"I guess we don't have to worry about being

tailed," her friend remarked dryly. It took Natalie a moment to catch her drift.

Sanjay Prashad's car was gone.

11

Unfinished Business

Natalie had grown so accustomed to the NAACC's round-the-clock surveillance that Prashad's sudden absence worried her far more than his usual intimidation. No change in her relationship with the Corps could be for the good, she thought, and she almost hoped that she'd see the Security agent's black Mitsubishi in the rear-view mirror as she and Serena drove to Silver Lake. When they pulled up in front of the mock Mediterranean villa, however, Prashad was still nowhere in sight.

"Want me to go with you?" Serena asked when Natalie opened the driver's-side door to get out. "Never know who might be up there."

Don't be silly—I'll only be a minute, Natalie was about to say, but another look at the apartment house's frowning façade made her reconsider. Maybe Sanjay Prashad hadn't tailed them in his car because he was already here, lying in wait for them. Perhaps he had called Carleton Amis to arrange an ambush, and the two of them stood inside, licking their lips in anticipation, with a half-dozen other Corps Security agents stationed in hiding around the building, ready to take her into "protective custody." Calvin had said Amis would kill him if he knew that the artist had leaked the secret of Project Persephone. No doubt he would do the same to anyone else who'd learned that secret.

"Yeah." Natalie looped the canvas handles of the tote bag over her shoulder. "Keep me company."

Serena nodded and accompanied her as she left the Volvo. When they entered the building, she took the lead, scanning the interior with the alertness of a soldier on point as they ascended the stairs to Calvin Criswell's apartment. She motioned for Natalie to stand back, out of sight of the peephole, and listened at the door, before unlocking it with the keys she'd borrowed from Calvin.

No one burst out to capture them when she pushed the door open. Serena leaned into the doorway, scanned the studio, then gave Natalie an *all-clear* nod. Letting out her pent-up breath, Natalie passed over the threshold and made a beeline for the drafting table where Calvin had said he'd left the Rembrandt-in-progress.

She didn't make it. Her skin crawled with the sting of sciatica, and she dropped to the lacquered pressed-wood floor with a smack, her limbs shivering in seizure.

Struck dumb, Natalie could no longer cry out, but her lips stammered for her. "I ... made ... a mistake."

She had, too. She'd been so worried about the obvious threats that might await her in this studio—Prashad, Amis, Evan—that she'd forgotten about the woman Calvin had felt knocking. The one who had killed herself here.

"I ... want ... to come ... back," the suicide insisted

with Natalie's voice, straining to solidify her mastery of the body she inhabited.

Serena shut the apartment door and rushed to straddle Natalie while she was still prone, pinning her to the floor before the inhabiting soul could get her body upright. "Give 'em the mantra, Nat. Kick the bastard out, whoever it is."

Her friend sounded muted and remote, but her coaching served as a Heimlich maneuver for Natalie's psyche. The suicide had stunned her with the surprise ambush, but now Natalie reverted to her lifetime of training as a Violet, reiterating her protective mantra with conditioned calm: *The Lord is my shepherd; I shall not want . . .*

The dead tenant's soul receded like a wave of nausea, leaving Natalie woozy but stable. She pushed herself into a sitting position, chanting the Twenty-third Psalm in her mind to prevent the suicide from capturing control again. Serena braced her as Natalie took shuddering breaths to clear her head. "Thanks for pulling me out of that one."

Her friend grinned. "Don't mention it. Been there plenty of times myself."

Natalie shook her head and chuckled. "Simon would've flunked me out of the School for letting a soul sucker-punch me like that."

"That's okay. To the Maestro, we're all amateurs." Serena stood and pulled Natalie to her feet. "Let's grab that picture and get out of this dump."

"Amen." Reorienting herself, Natalie turned toward the easel a few steps to her left. A life-study of a blond woman with a sheet wrapped about her

131

hips in neoclassic fashion, done in a rather bland modern style reminiscent of Modigliani, rested there. Another painting lay atop the drafting table beside the easel, as if tossed aside in impatience. Even viewed edge-on, the canvas was obviously old, its tacked fringe discolored and darkened from centuries of exposure to air and light.

The face of the canvas, however, still bore the sticky, honeyed shininess of fresh pigment, without the yellowing and spiderweb cracking in its lacquered surface wrought by the passage of time. The picture hadn't yet reached the stage where Calvin could age it artificially. A few of the disciples in the storm-tossed craft wore only pinkish smudges for faces, and the whitecaps of the waves lacked the undertones of black and green to give them the surge and swell of the original. But what Calvin *had* finished so astonished her that she nearly stopped reciting her protective mantra.

Natalie marveled at the brushwork, mouth ajar in awe. *This wasn't Rembrandt*, she thought. *Calvin did all this by himself*.

Were it not for the missing details and the painting's newness, however, even an art historian would have had difficulty distinguishing Calvin Criswell's virtuosity from that of the Dutch master. He hadn't merely rendered his own version of the original composition, as most artists would have done. As nearly as possible, he had replicated the painting stroke for stroke: the wispy wash of gold that created the dim shafts of sunlight penetrating the dark clouds of the background; the white streaks that became the mist of sea foam lashing the boat; and, seated in the stern, the unperturbed figure of Christ—the only point of peace in the seascape's swirling turbulence. With ultimate audacity, Calvin had even counterfeited Rembrandt's signature on the keel, exactly as it appeared on the original.

Serena cast a cursory glance at the picture while keeping watch on the apartment door. "Well? That it?"

"Oh, yeah. This is it, all right." Natalie picked up the canvas by its edges, angling it this way and that to appreciate the way the layered textures of paint and glaze caught the light. Despite his notoriety as a forger, Calvin seemed like such a slob that Natalie had underestimated his true skill as an artist. A tinge of envy tainted her admiration: his was the kind of technique that got you into the Corps's Art Division.

I can't finish this, she fretted, feeling like a bar-band singer forced to audition right after Pavarotti leaves the stage. Unless she summoned Rembrandt himself to help her, how could she hope to finish the fake well enough to fool Carleton Amis? Even assuming she obtained the dead Dutchman's help, Natalie knew nothing about how to make a fresh fraud look centuries old. Her whole plan suddenly seemed impossible, insane ...

She didn't have time for second-guessing, though, for Serena was already out the door and scouting the stairwell. Natalie hustled to the only dresser in view and snatched shirts, underwear, and socks by the fistful and shoved them into the tote bag for Calvin, then returned to the drafting table for the painting.

133

"Just grab the thing and come on," Serena barked.

"*Okay*, I'm coming." Natalie carried the picture out of the studio with the delicacy of a collector. "But you'll have to hold it on your lap while I drive and make sure nothing touches it."

Serena shook her head as she locked up the apartment and started down the stairs. "Just call me the Human Easel."

When the voices of the two women withdrew from the studio and the door's dead bolt sealed them out with a reassuring *shuck*, Tranquillity Moon inched her head out of the bathroom to make sure that she could safely emerge from her hiding place. After confirming that she was alone, she skittered on tiptoe to the front window, where she peeped through the gap between the dirty, speckled drop cloths that served as Calvin Criswell's curtains.

On the street below, Tranquillity saw two figures emerge from the apartment building and approach a maroon Volvo, its sheen dulled with oxidization. The redheaded woman in the T-shirt and jeans handed a painting to her companion, a short-haired black woman in a business suit, who balanced the canvas on her fingertips as she opened the passenger door.

There wasn't much time. Tranquillity scampered out of the apartment and down the stairs, pausing on the building's front doorstep until the red-haired woman swung behind the Volvo's steering wheel and started the car. As the station wagon made a U-turn and drove away, Tranquillity stepped out onto the sidewalk and read the car's license plate, repeating the alphanumeric combination under her breath as if it were her own mantra.

She had no idea who these people were or why they had the keys to Cal's place, but she meant to find out.

After Cal had freaked out and abandoned her in the studio, Tranquillity had stood shivering in his lame Greek getup, her arms folded over her bare torso, for nearly ten minutes, hoping he would calm down and come back with a decent explanation for his weirdness. When he didn't, she tore the stupid bedsheet from around her waist, swearing, and went to take a hot bath to warm up. To kill time, she stayed in the water until her fingers looked like raisins, then got out, did her hair and makeup, put on her purple peasant skirt and corset top. Tranquillity figured Cal *had* to return eventually, at which time she'd give him a nice, juicy piece of her mind.

Lucky for her, she was still preening in front of the bathroom mirror when she heard someone unlock the apartment door. Assuming Cal had finally slunk home, she was about to burst into the studio and give him a double-barreled lecture about acting like a psycho. But she stopped at the bathroom door when she heard *two* voices murmuring on the other side—both of them female. What they said made no sense, but she had a feeling Cal could clear up the mystery for her. And she had a feeling these women could tell her where Cal was.

Tranquillity hurried back upstairs to the apartment, where she looked up the number for the local police in Cal's dog-eared phone directory. She punched the number on her cell phone's keypad and waited, twirling a ringlet of her blond hair around her index finger.

"Yeah . . . somebody hit my car and drove off," she said when the operator answered. "But I got their license number. Any way you could tell me how to find them?"

12

Something You Believe In

Awkward.

That was the word that came to Calvin's mind as he slouched on Natalie Lindstrom's sofa, his head encased in Reynolds Wrap, and avoided the stare of the violet-eyed little girl and the silver-haired guy with the stun gun, seated in the chairs about three feet in front of him. Although they hadn't been introduced, Cal deduced from the old guy's resemblance to Natalie that he must be the family patriarch. Mr. Lindstrom seemed to think that lowering his weapon would be a dereliction of duty, so he ended up propping his elbows on his knees as his arms got tired of holding the gun aimed at Calvin's chest. Over an hour had snailed past since Natalie and her friend departed, and yet no one had worked up the nerve to say anything. The silence accumulated in the room like leaking gas that would ultimately suffocate them all.

Cal blew breath out through his lips with a braying sound and lightly snapped his fingers as he slapped his right palm against his left fist. Awkward as the Lindstrom family's silence was, he preferred it to the vying of disembodied voices in his head.

Staring at his hosts was not only rude but also

nerve-racking, so Cal allowed his attention to meander around the living room to learn whatever he could about Natalie Lindstrom. His gaze alighted on prints of works by Monet and Georgia O'Keeffe and framed posters from *Gigi* and *Singin' in the Rain*, which showed that she had good taste in movies as well as art. But there were other pictures hanging on the walls that he did not recognize—mostly stark black charcoals or soft pastels, and a few oils, as well.

The quality of the compositions made Cal wonder if these were some of the posthumous collaborations the Violet had done with her All-Star Team of past masters. The works displayed a unique vision and originality, however—something Cal easily recognized and envied, since he had none. Here was a massive red rose opening like a womb to reveal the profile of a human embryo in its heart. There was a character study of a homeless derelict dozing on a bus-stop bench while the Expressionistic cityscape of walls and street lamps curved over him as if they were waves about to break. And if Cal needed further proof that these were Lindstrom originals, there hung the most striking example of all: a portrait of the little girl as a toddler, her violet eyes both innocent and aged, as if she'd seen an entire lifetime's drama during her brief existence. In the bluish background behind the girl lurked another portrait—a transparent figure who shared the child's facial features yet had the body of an adult man. The male mirage enfolded the girl in arms of glass.

Calvin was speculating on the identity of the portrait's second subject when Mr. Lindstrom cleared his throat.

"Sorry about this." The old guy shifted the stun gun to his left hand so he could flex a cramp out of his right. "I plan to order some pizza as soon as my daughter gets back. You're welcome to join us."

Cal nodded at the man charged with blasting him if he made the wrong move, unsure how to take this peculiar combination of hostility and hospitality. "Um ... thanks."

Mr. Lindstrom smiled at the girl sitting cross-legged in the chair next to him. "Callie here likes pepperoni and olives, but we could get one with whatever you want."

Cal gave a sheepish grin. "Pepperoni and olives sounds great to me."

The girl pulled her legs up to rest her chin on her knees, peering at him with those violet irises, which now seemed enormous. "Your eyes are weird. Are you really a Violet?"

Her grandfather looked both shocked and amused. "Callie!"

She kept staring at Calvin. "Well?"

"Sort of. I guess." He smoothed the crinkled foil on his head, remembering the voices.

"My mom works with famous painters and she used to help the police catch murderers, too. What do you do?"

Cal suddenly missed the silence. "I'm an artist. And I guess you could say I've also ... been involved with law enforcement."

"Really?" The girl sat forward, allowing her feet to dangle over the edge of her chair. "Did you know my dad? His name's Dan Atwater. He was an F.B.I. agent."

Cal's gaze flicked to the translucent man in the portrait of Callie on the wall. "I can't say I did ..."

The girl's interest dimmed. "I didn't think so. He's been dead a long time. *I* can't even talk to him now that he's gone to the Place Beyond—"

Mr. Lindstrom returned the stun gun to his good hand. "Kiddo, I don't think you should bother Mr. ... I'm sorry, what was your name?"

"Criswell." Cal stifled a laugh, thinking it hilarious that his captor should be worried about offending him. "But feel free to call me 'Cal.' Everyone does. And she isn't bothering me, really."

"See?" Callie said to her grandfather with *told-you-so* satisfaction.

Mr. Lindstrom sighed. "Just like your mother."

Callie turned back to Cal and pointed at his head. "So, what's that thing?"

"Huh? Oh." Cal touched the foil, abashed. "It's supposed to keep the ..." The word did not come easily for him. "... souls out of my head."

The little girl swung her legs back and forth, staring at him as if he'd said he'd never learned to walk. "Don't you have a mantra?"

"A what?"

"A mantra." She waited for some inkling of comprehension from him. "You know—the words you say to keep out the bad Whos."

Cal looked to the only other adult in the room for a translation. "Whos?"

Mr. Lindstrom understood his confusion. "That's her word for souls. It's from a Dr. Seuss book."

"It's from *Horton.*" Callie stressed the title, empha-

140

sizing that it was not just *any* Dr. Seuss book. "He was an elephant who could hear the people no one else could."

Cal gave a sage nod. "I see."

"So you don't have a mantra to keep out the bad Whos?" she asked again.

With a cockeyed grin, Cal parodied a swami pose. "You mean, like *owah tagoo Siam*?"

Callie scowled. "Don't be stupid."

"*Callie!* Be polite." Apparently used to doting on his grandchild, Mr. Lindstrom seemed befuddled when he tried to be cross with her.

She went on despite him. "Your mantra has to be special," she told Cal. "Something you believe in. Like mine, for instance: I say, 'Now I lay me down to sleep. I pray the Lord my soul to keep.' And I keep saying it until the bad Whos go away." The girl put a hand to her mouth in sudden alarm, as if, for the first hme, she'd said the wrong thing. "That's a secret, by the way. You're never supposed to tell your mantra to anyone."

Cal smiled. "I won't tell a soul. Literally. I only wish *I* had a mantra."

Callie straightened herself with scholarly rectitude, obviously relishing her position of authority over an adult. "I know you'll find something that works. Just ask yourself, 'What do I believe in?'"

Cal opened his mouth for another clever quip, but the reply that came out was almost inaudible: "I don't know."

Without the safety net of sarcasm to stop him, Calvin plunged into introspection. His parents had

141

shelled out more than a hundred grand to send him to Columbia University, yet all his talent and education had earned him nothing more than a prison term and a felony record. His father disowned him after his conviction, leaving Cal with neither a career nor a family. Tranquillity Moon served as his latest attempt to pretend that he possessed some sort of connection to this world, but the truth was that he'd reached the age of thirty-five—life's fifty-yard line—without believing in anyone or anything. Heck, he didn't even believe in himself. Why else did he paint others' art, like a mirror reflecting the stars, pathetically congratulating himself on how well he aped their brilliance?

Natalie and her friend barged into the condo at that point, sparing Cal further self-analysis. "Got it," Natalie announced, displaying the fake Rembrandt he'd abandoned.

"Thank heavens!" Mr. Lindstrom stood and handed the stun gun back to Natalie's surly companion. "Serena, I believe this is yours. Can I order pizza now? I'm starved."

Callie hopped off her chair. "Me, too."

Natalie seemed distracted, her attention divided between her family and the painting. "Sure ... but bring some slices to me when it gets here—I need to get started on this now. Calvin, could you come with me?"

He started like a student unprepared for class. "Me? Where?"

"To my studio." She jerked her head in the direction of the kitchen. "Or at least one of the places I use as a studio. Try not to laugh."

"You want me with you, Nat?" the woman named Serena asked, eyeing Cal.

"No, we'll be fine. *Won't* we, Calvin?" Natalie smiled with saccharin sweetness.

"Scout's honor." He followed her, happy to be escaping Serena, if only temporarily.

Natalie led him through the kitchen and beyond a door into the condo's attached garage. She must have parked her car outside while she worked, for the concrete floor was bare except for an easel bridged across an oil spot. Art supplies shared shelf space with cans of Drano and Roach Pruf.

"It's not much," Natalie said by way of apology, "but my muse calls it home." She set aside the large drawing tablet that had been on the easel, so she could put his Rembrandt there.

Cal couldn't help peeking at the sketchbook, which lay open on the wooden workbench. He knew the subject, of course, as well as the bold, almost careless slashes of pastel chalk that composed the picture. "Is this a study for *Self-Portrait as a Woman?*"

His interest appeared to embarrass Natalie. "Oh ... no, we actually did that afterward. Munch's such a perfectionist, he just can't let it go." She turned to his forgery, putting her hands on top of her head as if being frisked by police. "Can you help me with this?"

Cal tapped the sketch. "If you can do this, you don't need my help."

"But I *can't* do that. And I can't do *this*, either." She shook her head, gazing at his phony *Storm*. "Not without a real artist to guide me."

143

"You *are* a real artist. I saw those drawings in your living room."

Natalie's pallor turned a fetching shade of pink, and she put a hand over her face. "Those aren't Rembrandt. And I've never worked with him, so I can't summon him. Can you *help* me?"

Cal hung his head. "Wish I could. It's this stupid treatment—it's screwed up my eyes. I can't get the colors right."

Natalie bit her thumb, her expression becoming increasingly glum as she considered the unfinished forgery. "I don't know how you do his style so perfectly. I don't think I could ever ..." The pinched anxiety in her face eased a bit and her gaze darted toward the Munch sketch on the workbench. "Amis had a whole list of paintings he wanted copied. Does the Rembrandt have to be the next one you give him?"

Cal scratched his goatee. "No, I don't see what difference it would make."

"What if we gave him *The Scream* instead?"

Her mischievous smile inspired his own. "You think Munch'd do it for you?"

"Why not? He did four copies of it when he was alive, not counting prints and woodcuts." She indicated the *Self-Portrait* sketch. "As I said, he's kind of obsessive-compulsive. Good thing for us, 'cause van Gogh wouldn't have the patience."

He stared at her as she took *Storm* off the easel and replaced it with a rectangle of cardboard. "You—you worked with van Gogh?"

"Did I ever! Every time, I swear I'll never deal with

the jerk again, but he's such a good seller, what can I do?"

"I hear that," Cal murmured. Van Gogh had been a mainstay of his forgery business, as well. It felt surreal to be discussing such things with a woman he barely knew—or anyone else, for that matter—but it felt good, too. Refreshing.

Natalie reached to a high shelf to grab some jars of tempera, and Cal couldn't help noticing how her T-shirt rose from the waist of her jeans to expose a glimpse of her ivory midriff and the shallow shadow at the small of her back. She was really very pretty, he thought. In fact, Munch's so-called *Self-Portrait* didn't begin to do her justice. And the more he became aware of her attractiveness, the sillier his own appearance seemed to him.

He covered the foil on his head with his hands under the pretense of holding it in place. "Uh ... is there anything I can do?"

She arranged the paint bottles beside her rack of pastel chalks on the workbench. "Tell you what, if you get us some pizza and make me some coffee, you can sleep on the couch instead of the floor tonight. I'm going to stay up and work, anyway."

Cal supposed he should have been grateful for the courtesy she offered. Instead, he slumped his shoulders like a kid left on the bench in Little League. "Would it be all right if I stayed and ... watched?"

He wondered if he turned as pink as she had, for Natalie's violet eyes sparkled with merriment. "You speak any French?" she asked with a saucy arch of her eyebrow.

Cal held his right thumb and forefinger about a quarter inch apart *"Un petit peu."*

"Good. Then you can help me handle the crazy Norwegian." She grabbed a pencil from a jar on the workbench and began to mutter something under her breath.

13

Prelude to a Scream

It took longer to persuade Edvard Munch to redo *The Scream* than Natalie anticipated. "*No, no, no!* I am done with that monstrosity," he complained aloud in French, her voice guttural with his accent. "It is the new *Self-Portrait* that requires effort. I must make changes—"

We will make the changes, Natalie promised him, speaking to him inside her skull. *But it is vital that we paint* The Scream *again.*

He threw up her hands in exasperation, shouting to the ceiling as if her admonition emanated from Heaven. "Why should I bother with old work when there is so much new work to be done?"

"Because *The Scream* is ... lost," Calvin answered, halting when he struggled to find the right French word. "Someone stole it. Without it, The Frieze of Life is incomplete."

He neglected to mention that the picture had since been returned.

Munch had all but ignored the scruffy young man beside him until then, but the news of the theft struck the painter as if it had been a death in his family. "Is this true?" he demanded.

"Yes." Calvin managed to keep his face solemn, regretful.

If she'd had control of her mouth, Natalie would have grinned at his cleverness. Munch had always been notoriously possessive of his paintings; indeed, he'd refused to sell the originals during his lifetime, but chose instead to leave his entire oeuvre to the city of Oslo upon his death. The Frieze of Life was the thematic series of artworks to which he'd devoted his entire career, and Calvin must have calculated that nothing would rankle a perfectionist like Munch more than knowing that a crucial piece of his masterwork was missing.

"This is intolerable," the painter muttered, kneading Natalie's hands together and pacing the garage floor. He stopped and jabbed a finger at Calvin. "You! You will see that my *Scream* returns to its family?"

Calvin bowed like a proper servant. "Of course, Monsieur Munch."

"Very well!" Munch snatched up the pencil Natalie had laid out for him on the lip of the easel and started sketching on the cardboard she'd cut to the proper dimensions. Ghostly outlines of the familiar composition appeared: the bleeding sky, the ominous boardwalk vanishing to infinity, and the asexual figure openmouthed in endless horror.

The artist worked with a manic speed driven by the irritation of one who feels his precious time is being wasted. Several times, Natalie had to restrain him from "improving upon" his original design, and he nearly quit in outrage when she dared to refer him to reproductions of the original in some art books she'd opened on the workbench.

"*I know* what it looks like!" he shouted, flinging a

piece of chalk onto the concrete floor so hard it shattered.

Forgive me, Monsieur Munch, she pleaded. *Please ... continue.*

While she coaxed and cajoled and subtly steered the brittle artist, Calvin sat on a stool nearby and watched in mute fascination. Natalie assumed he was starstruck to be in the presence of the Norwegian master, but he continued to stare at her when, at about five in the morning, she sent Edvard Munch back into the void and amended some of the finer details herself to make the forgery more accurate.

Calvin's scrutiny made her self-conscious, and she stepped back from the drawing, scanning it nervously.

"What? Is it bad? Am I screwing it up?"

He chuckled. "No. No, it's ... beautiful."

But he wasn't looking at the picture.

"Thanks." Natalie didn't know whether to take his flattery as a compliment or a pickup line, and she was too tired to think about it. Now that she'd retaken control of her body, she could feel how her legs and feet ached from standing in one place for hours, how fatigue weighed on her eyelids every time she blinked. She added a few more accents to the phony *Scream*—which she had sarcastically titled *The Whine*—then tossed the pastel she'd been using back in the rack, smearing her skin with indigo chalk dust as she rubbed her face. "Well? Think it'll fool Carleton Amis?"

Calvin nodded, tugging at his annoying goatee. "Close enough for government work ... so to speak."

"But it hasn't been weathered or distressed," Natalie groaned as she compared the forgery with reproductions of the original in her art books. Munch, she knew, was infamous for abusing his artworks, leaving them out in direct sunlight and rain, scratching them with tools, even flagellating them with a whip to "improve their character."

"Let me handle that," Calvin suggested. "It's my forte, after all." He got up from the stool. "Why don't you go get some rest?"

She gave him a weary smile. "But I promised you the sofa."

"I'll take the next shift."

"Okay. Maybe just a catnap." Natalie deflated as she exhaled the last of her caffeine-fueled energy. "Good night, Calvin. Or should I say 'good morning'?"

"Both." His joker's face turned serious. "Thanks for taking me in. For ... everything."

She bowed her head in acknowledgment. "You're helping me, too. More than you know."

And I hope you never find out, she added silently as she left the garage, thinking of Carleton Amis and Evan Markham and what they would do to Calvin if they ever discovered that he had helped her track them down.

When Natalie finally awoke from her "catnap," she rolled over on the unfolded sofa bed and found Serena glowering down at her.

"Good *afternoon*," her friend said.

The greeting jolted Natalie upright. It was later

than she thought; after keeping watch over the house during the night Serena usually dozed all morning in Wade's bed upstairs. With her fingers, Natalie combed out the tangles in the red wig she'd been too exhausted to remove before going to sleep that morning. "What time is it?"

"Three."

Natalie could hardly believe it. Residing in the living room usually precluded oversleeping, since her father and daughter would come stomping down the stairs in the morning on their way to breakfast in the kitchen. "Where is everyone?"

"Your dad didn't want to disturb you, so he decided to give Callie her lessons at the library today."

"And Calvin?"

Serena folded her arms, her sleeveless muscle-tee revealing hard brown biceps. "Since your pop's gone, I let him crash on the bed upstairs. He was still there when I checked on him ten minutes ago."

"Did he finish the picture?"

"Beats me. I know he didn't come outta that garage until past noon."

Natalie noted the puffiness around Serena's eyes, the lids at half-mast "How about you? You get any sleep?"

"Not since Mr. Criswell came. But I can take it. Went three days straight once when I did Black Ops with the Agency."

A strange disappointment descended on Natalie. "You still don't trust Calvin, do you?"

Serena pouted her lips in disapproval. "Put it this

151

way: I trust your friend *Calvin* about as much as I trust anyone right now."

"What about our plan? Can we count on him to lead us to Amis?"

"No, but I ain't got any better ideas, so let's go with it."

Still wearing her T-shirt and jeans from the night before, Natalie swung her bare feet onto the floor and stood to straighten the sheets on the sofa bed's mattress. "In that case, you oughta take your turn on this couch. We've got a busy day tomorrow."

Serena didn't move. "I'll doze, but on one condition."

"Which is?"

"You don't trust *Calvin* any more than I do."

Natalie resented the implication that Serena didn't trust *her*, either. With a touch of guilt, though, she had to admit that she'd let down her guard when it came to Calvin. Natalie had felt such a kinship working with him last night that it was far too easy for her to forget that she knew almost nothing about him ... other than the fact that he was a convicted felon.

"I'll keep an eye on him," she promised.

"See that you do, Nat."

Her friend lay down on the fold-out cot fully clothed and shut her eyes. Her body never fully relaxed its hair-trigger tension, however, and Natalie wondered if Serena ever slept deeply enough to dream.

True to her word, Natalie went up to the master bedroom and looked in on Calvin. Still in his black jeans and hole-ridden concert shirt, he snoozed flat on his back in her father's bed, a light snore escaping his open mouth. With his face smoothed to somnolent blankness, he appeared utterly guileless. But hard experience had taught Natalie to mistrust her own first impressions. Her first boyfriend, after all, had turned into the Violet Killer.

With the condo's only other occupants napping, Natalie yielded to the temptation to peek at the progress Calvin had made on their collaborative fraud. From the moment she entered the garage and flicked on the light, she stood stunned before the easel, because a transformation had taken place. Although the picture there resembled the one she and Munch had drawn during the long, feverish night, its colors had taken on a yellowish tinge, like newsprint left in the sun.

The cardboard appeared dirtier, its edges separating into layers of paper and its corners blunted as if banged by a clumsy curator. Battered and darkened with abuse, the picture's new pall only served to deepen the dreariness of its dismal theme.

The Whine had become *The Scream*.

Since Natalie hesitated to share the sofa bed with Calvin and Serena refused to sleep while Calvin was awake, they decided to take turns on the sofa bed that night so they would all be alert to confront Carleton Amis the following day. Despite their plan, they all looked bedraggled come Saturday morning. Natalie, for one, had spent most of her allotted rest time lying with her eyes wide open as mental movies of her past and future encounters with Evan

Markham played on the screen of the living-room ceiling.

Calvin was by far the worst off of them, however. Long after Natalie and Serena were up and dressed, he curled on the bed gibbering to unseen interlocutors. The aluminum foil on his head ripped as he pulled it down around his ears, like a small boy shutting out monsters with a bedsheet. When Natalie shook his shoulder to nudge him out of his nightmare, he cried out and sprang upright.

"They're back." He wrapped his arms around his skull, gasping. "Get some more foil—a lot of it. *Hurry.*"

Natalie ran to the kitchen and fetched a double-length sheet of Reynolds Wrap, which she folded in half before giving it to Calvin. He replaced the ripped foil with the new, flattening it on his forehead like a cold compress.

"You gonna be okay?" she asked when his panic subsided.

He nodded, but without conviction. "Knock on wood."

"If you aren't up to this, tell us now," Serena cautioned him. "Anything goes wrong, and we're all dead meat."

Calvin's ashen cheeks reddened. "I'll be fine."

Before he and Serena could get in an argument, Natalie pulled a baseball cap from a backpack of supplies she'd assembled for their mission. "Here. I thought you might want to wear this to cover the foil."

Calvin accepted the hat but knitted his brows when he saw its embroidered insignia. "San Diego?

You realize the Padres suck, don't you?"

"It's a disguise, not a lifestyle." Not knowing or caring anything about sports, Natalie had picked the hat because it was cheap. And although Calvin's attitude nettled her, she took it as a positive sign. He wouldn't be making smart remarks if some dead guy were trying to steal his body. Still . . . this latest attack worried her.

"Calvin, do you have some phrase that sticks in your mind?" She sat beside him on the bed. "Could be anything. A poem, a song, the Pledge of Allegiance even."

He chuckled. "You mean a mantra."

Natalie exchanged a glance with Serena, who acted impressed in spite of herself.

"You know about mantras?" Natalie asked.

"Your daughter gave me a crash course yesterday. But I don't know what would work for me, if anything."

"You won't know till you try. Next time the voices come, give it a shot. You might want to start with your ABC's—we call that the 'Alphabet Mantra,' and it's the first one most Violets learn when they're kids. Just keep repeating the alphabet over and over and don't think about anything else. Okay?"

"Sure," he said, though he sounded anything but.

Serena raised her voice like a drill sergeant. "All right, people. If we're done with Violet 101, let's get this show on the road."

Calvin grumbled and put on the Padres hat, molding it over the skullcap of foil and tugging the visor low over his eyes.

*

Their first job, of course, was to ditch Sanjay Prashad. Fortunately, the Corps Security agent had proven fairly easy to dupe in the past, and this time Natalie had help outwitting him.

In preparation, she had asked her dad to park his Camry in the garage the previous night. When they were ready to leave on Saturday morning, Natalie scrunched down in the space behind the car's front seats, out of view of the windows, so that Prashad would see her father behind the wheel and Callie in the passenger seat when the Camry rolled out onto the street. Since the agent could only tail one vehicle at a time, Natalie staggered their departures, forcing him to choose whether to follow Wade in his Camry, Serena on her Harley, or Calvin in his VW. Natalie hoped they would all be long gone by the time Prashad figured out that she was not going anywhere in her Volvo.

By prearrangement, they rendezvoused in the parking garage of a local mall. Wade dropped Natalie off there before taking Callie to the library for another school session. Natalie thought her father and daughter would be safer in public than back at the condo alone. When the Camry was gone, she put on her backpack and joined Serena and Calvin inside the VW bus.

"Any problems?" Natalie asked.

They shook their heads. Evidently, they'd given Sanjay the slip.

Natalie glanced at the portfolio case that lay on the carpeted floor beside Calvin, hoping that Carleton Amis found the forgery inside as convincing as she did. "Anyone have any questions?"

Calvin kept his gaze downcast, his hybrid eyes hidden below the bill of his cap. "When I give Amis the picture, he's going to offer to give me the next injection. If I don't take it, he'll be suspicious. What should I do?"

Serena sized him up with a hard stare. "Depends."

"On what?"

"On whether you really want to be one of us."

He tilted his head up to look into the two pairs of violet eyes that peered at him. "I do ... if you guys can teach me how to control it."

"We can teach you," Serena shot back, "but only you know whether you've got the will to do it. Do you?"

He didn't answer.

Natalie leaned, toward him and tucked in a crinkled tongue of foil that stuck out from beneath his cap. "If you have any doubts, Calvin, don't do it."

He nodded without signaling what his decision was, if he'd even made one.

His evasion obviously displeased Serena, but she dropped the interrogation. Instead, she held up a black motorcycle helmet. "Well, Nat ... ready to ride?"

Actually, Natalie doubted she'd *ever* be ready to ride with Serena. A decade had passed since Serena had rescued her from Evan with a bike just like this one, and Natalie had gotten over a lot of her phobias in the interim. She no longer refused to take elevators and could even fly in a plane without breaking into a cold sweat, but watching the 5 freeway zip beneath her like an asphalt conveyor belt still gave her palpitations.

Gripping the back of the Harley's seat with her thighs, she actually became nostalgic for the horses she'd been terrified to ride during her ill-fated trip to Peru. At least the plodding nags didn't go seventy miles an hour. At this speed, Natalie knew, the helmet and heavy leather jacket she wore served as little more than a fashion statement. They wouldn't keep her from getting squished like roadkill beneath the passing cars if she fell off the bike. As they zoomed north toward L.A., she bear-hugged Serena's midsection and shut her eyes. If they did wipe out, she didn't want to see it coming.

Natalie needn't have worried, for Serena got them safely to the place where Calvin had agreed to meet Carleton Amis—a bleak industrial district in the City of Commerce filled with beige buildings that resembled aircraft hangars. Although the tinted visors of their helmets hid their identity, Serena took an alternate route to the location so their arrival would not be observed. She killed the bike's motor while still several yards away from the chosen parking lot, had Natalie dismount, then pushed the cycle up to one side of the nearest warehouse. Raising their visors for an unobstructed view, they edged up to the corner of the building and angled their heads to peer around at Calvin, who already paced beside his VW bus, checking his watch every few seconds.

The exchange took place so quickly, it seemed anticlimactic. The gold BMW pulled up beside its poor

German cousin, and Carleton Amis got out and met Calvin in as jovial a manner as he had once greeted Natalie. She noticed that he carried a brown attaché case—most likely the same one Calvin had described ... the one that contained the gun for his injection.

The two men traded terse pleasantries before each climbed onto the VW's front seats. For a couple of minutes, only their silhouettes were visible through the bus's rear windshield. They emerged with much the same bland business expressions, only now Amis carried both the attaché case and the art portfolio. Calvin squeezed his upper right bicep as if it smarted, but covered the action by crossing his arms.

"That's it," Serena whispered. "If we tail Amis from here, it'll look too suspicious. I'll go 'round the block and come up behind him."

She lowered her visor and wheeled the Harley back the way they'd come. Natalie watched Amis set the case and portfolio in the Beemer before dropping her own windscreen and jogging after Serena.

Back on the bike, they circled around the warehouse complex to the thoroughfare that led to the freeway, rejoining it just moments before the BMW and VW bus turned onto the street in front of them. As they'd planned, Serena hung back until Calvin broke off to take the 5 South, back toward Natalie's condo. She then closed on the Beemer, trailing it up the on-ramp headed north. Although her nimble maneuvers made Natalie woozy, she proved adept at being inconspicuous, changing lanes and hiding behind other vehicles while always keeping Amis in view, even as he veered off onto the 10 East interchange in downtown L.A.

It was almost noon when Amis left the freeway, taking the last of several exits for Pasadena. Here, Serena's dance of surveillance grew even more delicate. The traffic thinned on the surface streets, and she allowed the BMW to get ahead of her by more than a block, risking that Amis could lose her at a red light yet disguising the deliberateness of her pursuit.

After several turns, the BMW finally came to rest in the parking lot of a drab, single-story institution, but Serena did not slow down. Natalie didn't get a good look at the place until they cruised a half mile past it, hung a U, and rode by it in the opposite direction at a lower speed. The facility masked its gracelessness with overgrown rosebushes that molted withered petals, yet the perfunctory beautification only accentuated the dreary architecture.

GREENER PASTURES ASSISTED LIVING, the sign out front proclaimed without a trace of irony.

Two men in white uniforms—one heavy, one lean—barricaded the entrance with their bodies. At their hips, they wore what appeared to be stun guns like Serena's. As Carleton Amis strode up, whistling and swinging the portfolio and attaché case, the larger of the two orderlies stepped to one side for him to pass through the automatic double doors.

Serena coasted until they were well out of sight of the hospice, then steered the Harley over to the curb and raised her windscreen. "Never seen an ol' folks homewith armed guards," she remarked. "Must be some feisty seniors."

Natalie lifted her own visor and adjusted the

straps of her backpack, which weighed on her trapezius muscles. "Yeah, I'd like to see who they've got in there. What would you say to some under-cover work? Can you play old?"

Serena gave an arid laugh. "Child, I *am* old. What do you have in mind?"

11

Greener Pastures

Although Natalie had brought some disguise elements in her backpack—basic makeup, colored contact lenses, an alternate wig, and a change of clothes for both her and Serena—she had not anticipated having to age her friend about thirty years. With neither the time nor the resources for a professional Hollywood makeover, they improvised. While Serena procured the components of her costume, Natalie looked up a geriatric supply outlet in the local Yellow Pages and called a cab to take her there.

"You ever deal with Greener Pastures?" she asked the store manager as he rang up her purchase.

Although she'd put in her pair of brown contacts, the way the manager stared at her made Natalie wonder if one of the lenses had slipped out. "Greener Pastures?" he asked, his tone incredulous. "The state shut that place down more than a year ago."

Natalie acted surprised, though she wasn't. Not a bit. "Oh! I guess we'll have to find Grandpa some other place. Thanks for the heads-up."

She slipped her debit card back in her pocketbook and scooted the secondhand wheelchair she'd bought out to the taxi. The driver had left his meter running while she shopped. Serena had promised to reimburse her for all of these costs out of her Corps expense account, but in the meantime it was fortunate that Natalie's checking account still contained some of the fifty grand in cash she'd received for the Munch *Self-Portrait*.

By arrangement, she ordered the cabbie to drop her off outside a convenience store about a block from the rest home. "'Bout time you got that cussed thing here, child!" an irate voice exclaimed as she pulled the collapsed wheelchair from the taxi's backseat and unfolded it. "Arthritis is paining me somethin' fierce today."

Natalie laughed as she saw the woman with the stooped posture and sour expression who hobbled toward her from the shade of the store's canopy. If she hadn't known that Serena had used the mini-market's lavatory as her dressing room, Natalie might not have recognized her. Serena's years with the C.I.A. had made her an expert at disguising herself with whatever materials came to hand. She'd frosted the short, frizzy hair of her wig with gray highlights from a spray can she'd found in the costume section of a local party store and shaded in the wrinkles and creases of her face with subtle applications of dark eyeshadow and grease from a black eyeliner pencil. To make her martial artist's physique appear feeble, she wore a frumpy dress two sizes too big for her and some scuffed penny loafers she'd bought at a Salvation Army store. She accessorized the outfit with support hose and a pair of flat-topped reading glasses from a pharmacy.

"You look great," Natalie said, lips twitching as she tried to keep a straight face.

Serena didn't break character, even to crack a grin. "Go 'head and laugh, missy. See how good *you* look when you get to be my age." She lowered herself into the chair with the strain of decrepitude and slapped the arms with impatience. "Let's get this train a-rollin'!"

Adopting her role as caregiver, Natalie began pushing Serena up the street toward Greener Pastures. "Where's the bike?" she asked when they were alone.

"Right over yonder, honey, in case we need to bail." Serena nodded in the direction of the Harley, which rested on its kickstand along the curb opposite the hospice.

The sight of a ready means of escape heartened Natalie enough to proceed to the rest home's entrance and its two hulking orderlies. She wheeled Serena up to the doors at a leisurely pace, cooing over every detail of the geriatric gulag as if it were Buckingham Palace.

"Just look at those roses! It's all so beautiful." She petted Serena's shoulder. "I know you're going to love it here."

Serena gave an unimpressed harrumph, and Natalie pushed her straight at the automatic double doors of the entrance. She stopped only when she was about to collide with the orderlies, acting surprised and insulted when they wouldn't make way for her.

"We're here for a *tour*," she said in the condescending tone of a prospective customer.

The larger of the two orderlies, a corpulent black

man, regarded her like a gnat he didn't consider worth the effort to swat. "Sorry, ma'am. This is a private facility."

"Damn well *better* be a private facility," Serena cut in. "What we're paying, I don't want no rugrats running 'round."

Natalie gave her an indulgent pat. "We think Mom will find a wonderful home here."

The orderly compared her pallor to Serena's rich mahogany complexion with evident skepticism. "She's your mother?"

"Mother-in-law, actually." Natalie bristled. "You don't have a *problem* with that, do you?"

Her political correctness tongue-tied him. Nonplussed, he looked to his partner for a response, but the freckled, redheaded orderly just shrugged with an *I'm-not-gonna-touch-this* grimace.

Serena arched her belly up in the wheelchair, moaning. "Oh, child, do I feel a BM coming on!"

"Oh, my!" Natalie fluttered in distress, then beseeched the first orderly. "Her Crohn's is acting up. Do you have a ladies' room, Mr. ... ?"

"Name's Block."

"Mr. Block?"

He rubbed his bald head and puzzled over the two women, struggling to keep up with the latest developments. "Ma'am, we aren't supposed to—"

"That's okay," Natalie said. "We can find it."

Serena wailed louder. *"Lord have mercy, I'm fit to explode!"*

Unnerved, the redheaded orderly backed up, and Natalie took advantage of the momentary opening between the two men to charge at the automatic doors. "Hang on, Mom!"

Block sidestepped to keep the wheelchair from running over his toes as Natalie and Serena barreled past him. "Wait! You can't—"

The automatic doors whooshed shut behind them, muffling the orderly's shout. Rather than slowing, though, Natalie leaned her paltry weight against the chair to hasten it to the intersection ahead, where the entry hall crossed another corridor. Orange carpet, grimed by decades of foot traffic and blotched by spills of either food or bodily fluids, whispered beneath the wheels. Eager to get out of the orderlies' view, she steered Serena around the corner to the left. Behind her, she heard the automatic doors sweep open again.

Natalie had become well acquainted with long-term care facilities during her late mother's lifetime battle with mental illness, and she could tell immediately that this place was no rest home. The giveaway was the smell—or rather, the lack of one. No bedpans, no disinfectant, only the mustiness of disuse.

Serena had fallen silent as she tuned her mongoose senses to the row of semiprivate rooms they passed. Judging by the ones whose doors stood ajar, they were all vacant.

Aware of the footsteps thumping fast upon her heels, Natalie bent close to Serena's ear. "Where to?"

From the end of the hall came the hammering of fists against glass, followed by a bottled yowl.

"Never mind," she said, and barrowed the wheelchair in that direction.

They came abreast of a lengthy window on their right that ran along what must have once been a dining or meeting room. It had only one occupant: a solitary patient in a shapeless hospital gown, who pressed up against the window and thudded his hairless head against it with the slow regularity of a funereal drumbeat. The glossy skin left a greasy smear on the glass. Natalie pushed Serena up for a closer look but froze when she saw the tattooed node points that specked the man's shaved scalp.

Evan?

As if in answer to her thought, the man slammed himself against the window, his yell muted by the barrier. Natalie recoiled, believing that it *was* Evan, that he had seen her and would lunge through crashing glass to tear open her throat and rip out her eyes . . .

The window shuddered but held, and when the man pressed his cheek against the glass, he did not look at Natalie. Rather, he cast his gaze upward, and the name he cried was another woman's.

"Amy!"

The man was not Evan, but Natalie blanched as if he were. Although they had never met, she knew him, his face stamped indelibly on her memory a decade ago by photos in dozens of newspapers and magazines after Evan framed him for the Violet Murders. But those eyes did not belong in his face, or in anyone else's. Each iris was two-toned, its ring an irregular crescent of blue completed with an arc of violet, giving the orb a bifurcated, reptilian repulsiveness. Even Serena gaped at him, aghast, over the tops of her reading glasses.

"I can't hear you, Amy!" The lizard eyes leaked tears as the man clutched his temples. The pose reminded Natalie of the way Calvin had tried to ward off the whispering voices that assailed him. "There's too many of them. They won't *let* me hear you."

He sagged against the glass, sniveling. Transfixed by the spectacle, Natalie forgot about the footsteps closing in on her until a hand clapped onto her upper arm. The redheaded orderly spun her around and jerked her forward until they were close enough to kiss.

"The bathroom is *this* way." He clenched his jaw, his mouth nearly buried in the rusty bush of his beard. "Use it and get out."

Serena hastily resumed her grunts of indigestion. "Yes, hurry, child, 'fore I have an accident!"

Natalie rotated the wheelchair and let the orderly herd her back down the hall, past the intersection, where Block waddled to catch up with them, and into the opposite corridor. They halted at a door with stylized plastic male and female logos mounted on it. The redheaded orderly opened it for the two women, not as an act of courtesy but as a reminder that he would be waiting right outside.

Serena kept puffing and moaning until Natalie had pushed her into the restroom. The moment the orderly shut the door behind them, however, she lowered her voice to a hiss. *"You wanna tell me what the hell Clem Maddox is doing here?"*

Relieved to hear Serena echo her own thoughts, Natalie didn't dare to speak above a breath's sigh. "You recognized him, too?"

"'Course I did. Simon has me monitor every Violet stalker nut-job in the country, and they all seem to be working for Carleton Amis. What gives?"

"I don't know." Natalie sifted her memory for what Dan had told her about Clement Maddox during the Violet Killer investigation. "He was obsessed with trying to contact his dead wife. Maybe Amis promised to make him a Violet too."

"Oh, great. Why doesn't he just open a drive-through? Violets 'R' Us!" Serena wagged an index finger at the toilet. "Do me a favor and flush that thing so I don't have to get out of this dang chair."

Once they had provided sufficient sound effects, Natalie braced the bathroom door open and nudged the wheelchair back into the hall. Serena favored the unsmiling orderlies there with a toothy grin.

"Bless you, boys! Made it in the nick o' time."

The orderlies made faces that said she'd already told them more than they wanted to know. The redheaded one motioned her on down the corridor. "That's swell, lady. Let's move along."

She stiffened with indignation. "Fine! Don't have to take sass from no young gangstas like you."

Natalie wheeled her back toward the entrance, the orderlies corralling them from behind. At intervals, they would hear another sob from Maddox reverberating along the hall. As they reached the intersection of the two corridors, however, the megaphone acoustics of the institution's concrete walls amplified other voices: two men in heated conversation. The discussion emanated from somewhere off to the right, but it was neither loud nor clear enough for

Natalie to make out what was said.

Filling her lungs with air for courage, she veered the wheelchair around the corner to the right, instead of left toward the exit.

"What the—*STOP!*" the redhead shouted.

Natalie hastened to keep a few paces ahead of him. If she could hear even a snatch of the conversation ... or tell who was speaking ...

A few yards ahead of her, one of a pair of double doors stood open. The declamation that oozed from the room could only have come from Carleton Amis.

"... this subject's going to end up like all the others. That is *not* satisfactory, Dr. Wax."

Dr. Wax. Natalie filed the name away for future reference.

"What did you expect, *Mr.* Pancrit?" came the peevish response. "I told you it wouldn't work."

Though she did not recognize the pedantic deliberation of the diction, Natalie had heard that voice too many times in her life to mistake it. Evan—he must be inhabited by this doctor named Wax. But why had he called Amis "Mr. Pancrit"?

"And I told *you* what would happen to your pretty pictures if you disappointed me," Amis intoned with an imitation of regret, "yet you insist on a demonstration."

Natalie didn't get to hear the rest of the dialogue, for the redheaded orderly skidded to bar the wheelchair from the open door. "I warned you."

She played the ingenue, flustered and flighty. "I— I'm sorry. I guess I got turned around. I'll go."

Before she could rotate the chair, he aimed his stun gun at her chest. "No. You'll *stay*."

"I don't know, Tackle," Block said behind her. "The boss says we're not supposed to attract attention."

"Oh, yeah? Let's ask him. *Hey, boss! We got a situation!*"

The escalating argument in the room ahead abruptly ceased. "What the devil?" Carleton Amis muttered as he emerged into the hallway.

Natalie jerked the handles of the wheelchair upward. Serena took the cue, hitching up her skirt and jumping out on her left foot as the chair tilted forward. Tackle adjusted his aim, but too late. With her right foot, Serena high-kicked the stun gun from his hand. His right hand injured, he shot out his left fist to clip her jaw, but she deflected the blow with her right forearm, balanced her stance, and catapulted the heel of her left palm into his throat. Gagging for breath through his injured windpipe, he caromed backward into Amis, throwing them both against the open door.

Natalie did not have time to appreciate the spectacle of watching Serena beat the crap out of Tackle while wearing a housedress and support hose. Block had his own stun gun aimed at Serena's back. Natalie pivoted the wheelchair and rammed him, crouching low and keeping her head down. She heard rather than saw the stun gun's darts whiz past an inch above her, felt their wires drop lightly onto her arched back like streamers from a popped party favor. Then the chair plowed into Block's sprawling stomach as if hitting a side of beef. He let out an *oof* and reached for her over the back of the chair. But as soon as his porterhouse hands encircled her neck, the fingers slackened their grip, jittering with the electricity coursing through them. He thumped onto the floor, his fat rippling, and Natalie stood to find Serena squatting a few feet behind her, holding the stun gun she'd scooped off the floor.

'Teach you to mind your elders, boy," she drawled, setting the gun's handle back on the floor so it could continue to pump its paralyzing current into the helpless Block.

Serena bunched her skirt in both hands and lifted the hem to her waist to sprint toward the automatic doors of the facility's entrance. Natalie followed her lead, risking only a brief glance back at Carleton Amis. The whole melee had happened so fast, he remained sandwiched between the door and Tackle, who gasped in his arms. With disgust, Amis threw his semiconscious goon to the floor and glared at Natalie, his face ripening to red fury.

Though she'd either ditched or lost her reading glasses in the fight, Serena made no attempt to remove the rest of her costume when they got outside, but saddled up on the Harley, support hose and all. Nor did she take time to put on either of the helmets that dangled from the handlebars by their chin straps. Instead, she cast both helmets off on the sidewalk like unwanted ballast and fired the bike's motor to life. Natalie barely had a chance to climb on the back before they zoomed off at motocross speed, but she couldn't complain. Although the ride home was even more terrifying without any protection for her head, the wind felt good on her face, for it meant she was still alive and free.

15

<u>Mr.</u> Pancrit Cleans Up the Mess

When the interlopers had absconded, the man known variously as Carl Pancrit and Carleton Amis smoothed the lapels of his blue blazer, surveyed the worthless Corps Security agents laid out like sausages before him, and debated what to do first. Tempting as it was to let Block and Tackle suffer the consequences of their own incompetence, there was too much work to do, and Pancrit himself had higher priorities to attend to.

Sighing, he stepped over Tackle, who clutched at his throat and made little gurgling noises, and went to pick up the stun gun that the black woman in the grandma getup had left on the floor. Pancrit gathered the gun's insulated wires in his fist and yanked on them to dislodge the electrode darts from Block's prostrate bulk. When the man stopped his gelatinous quivering and rolled his eyes open with a moan, Pancrit pointed to Tackle.

"Assuming he fails to die the way he fails at everything else, take him to the lab and start crating up the equipment. We're moving ... *again*." His irritation festered in the final word. "I'll listen to your excuses when you're coherent enough to give them."

Confident that Block would obey his commands,

he didn't wait for verbal agreement. Although the infiltrators who'd sandbagged Tackle and Block were a nuisance, Pancrit had a far more serious saboteur to punish.

He returned to the rec room, where Evan Markham still sat strapped into a wheelchair much like the one the interfering women had abandoned in the hallway. Markham's expression bore a trace of amusement, as if Bartholomew Wax could hardly restrain a smile at Pancrit's expense.

"Trouble, Carl?" Wax asked with mock concern.

"Nothing that need concern you." Pancrit strode to the two easels set up a few feet apart in front of the wheelchair. On the left one rested the *Madonna of the Yarnwinder*; on the right, *The Scream*, which he'd collected from Calvin Criswell that morning. "You have more important things to worry about, Dr. Wax."

He stroked one edge of the *Madonna's* frame.

The gesture wiped all mirth from Wax's manner. *"Don't."*

The exclamation doubled as a plea and a warning. Pancrit ignored both.

"What shall we use this time?" Like a chef selecting his ingredients, he picked the bottle of acid from the smorgasbord of torture paraphernalia arrayed on the table beside him, considered it. "Nah, we've *done* that. No, I think we need something with some more spark to it." He exchanged the bottle for a can of lighter fluid that he raised to Wax as if proposing a toast ... which in some ways he was. "Aha! That's more like it."

175

The Violet's visage paled. "I've *done* everything you asked."

"Who do you think you're fooling, Barty?" Pancrit uncapped the can. "You perfected the treatment months ago, and we both know it."

"I d-did not!" Wax babbled, hastening his speech as Pancrit moved the lighter fluid closer to the *Madonna's* canvas. "Please ... I'll try harder."

"Oh, you'll do better than try, Barty, or I'll bring each of your children here, one by one, and do *this.*"

The dead scientist began to scream even before Pancrit squirted the flammable liquid over the Virgin and child. With the pungent kerosene scent weighting the air, Pancrit took a box of matches from his pocket, struck one, and flicked it at the painting with the offhand sadism of a pyromaniac. A flower of blue-and-yellow flame blossomed from the point where the match head bounced off the picture, petals unfurling to curl around the frame. Through the waves of translucent fire that shimmered up over the canvas, the faces of Mary and Jesus melted and ran, bubbled and blistered.

Apoplectic with impotent rage, Bartholomew Wax hurled himself toward Pancrit, but the plastic cuffs held Evan Markham's powerful body fast to the wheelchair, which tilted forward and dropped back with a clatter. A shorn Samson, Wax stammered at falsetto pitch, his naive vocabulary unable to summon a sufficiently awful epithet for his oppressor. "You ... you ... *MONSTER!*"

Pancrit cast a wry look at the blackened canvas beneath its shroud of fire. "Shame about that one—it

176

was my favorite. I assume we'll see more promising results from your research in the near future, Dr. Wax?"

Wax grew ominously quiet, withholding tears, like a boy too proud to cry before a playground bully. "Yes, *Mr.* Pancrit."

"Good. Because if we don't—" He indicated the Munch on the right easel. "—you'll get to *hear* that picture scream."

The dead scientist sagged, drained of defiance. "When can I get back to work?"

"Soon. Once we've ironed out a few small problems."

Wax didn't nod so much as bowed the conduit's head in defeat. When the man in the wheelchair raised his face again, the violet gaze radiated Evan Markham's freezerburn coldness. He sniffed and blinked his watery eyes, Bartholomew Wax's anguish no more to him than an irritating allergy. "The doc seems more compliant now. You want me to go back to the lab and summon him to get started again?"

"No, I'm afraid there's been a bit of a delay." Pancrit took a box cutter from among his torture implements and cut the Violet loose from the chair. "Maddox is worthless now. I need you to recruit another test subject."

"Already on it." Markham stood and rubbed his wrists, his gaze flicking toward the unending wails that drifted through the building like inclement weather. His hands clenched and unclenched, hungering for work. "You want me to dispose of him?"

"No," Pancrit said, "I'm conducting a little experiment with Mt. Maddox. But there *is* something else you can do for me."

"And what would that be? Wash your car?" The Violet advanced on him, tensing with unrelieved aggression. "Maybe I don't like being your errand boy."

Pancrit took an instinctive step backward, aware that he did not have Tackle and Block to protect him. "I understand your impatience—I'm impatient, too. If that girlfriend of yours hadn't interfered—"

Markham stiffened at the mention of Lindstrom, the way he had in the cell at Corps headquarters. "What about Boo?"

"She and her friend came for a visit." Pancrit tightened his grip on the box cutter to defend himself if the Violet attacked. "They evidently bluffed their way past those two Einsteins out in the hall, with some amateur theatrics. I, however, recognized Ms. Lindstrom at once, having seen pictures of her in all manner of cheap wigs. I need you to find out why she was here."

The news appeared to disturb the Violet Killer, but he iced over any anxiety he may have felt. "You wouldn't have to worry about her if you'd just let me—"

"No. You can't have her yet." For his own safety, Pancrit decided to bluff. "I've left orders: if anything happens to either me or the project, she'll be killed. You'll never have her."

A frosty smirk rose on Markham's lips. "I've waited ten years. I can wait a little longer."

"I've waited longer than that, Mr. Markham. And I *can't* wait anymore." Pancrit pulled out the fire extinguisher he'd placed under the table and dowsed the crackling *Madonna* with carbon-dioxide fog. He didn't let the Violet Killer see how he quietly stashed the box cutter in his coat pocket for protection.

After Markham departed, Carl Pancrit went to the makeshift lab they had established in what had once been the rest home's kitchen. Anyone expecting the sparking Tesla coils and bubbling beakers of a mad scientist's lair would have found the accoutrements disappointing: mostly electronic devices paneled in beige plastic like so much office equipment. Fluorescent gene sequencers, thermal cyclers for "amplifying" or replicating desired DNA strands, and scores of other automated analyzers, as well as assorted centrifuges, microscopes, and desktop computers. Block and Tackle listlessly shuffled around the room, packing the delicate devices in plastic crates and cushioning them in molded foam rubber. Block seemed to have recovered somewhat from the stun gun's electroshock, but Tackle still rasped and hacked, a huge oval bruise blooming over his Adam's apple.

"Leave this one out," Pancrit instructed them as he set a battery-operated SoulScan unit onto a pushcart along with a roll of surgical tape. With its green monitor and tangle of electrode cables, one could easily mistake the SoulScan for an electroencephalograph, were it not for the large and ominous red button on its control panel. Violets had charmingly nicknamed this the "Panic Button" for its capacity to eject an inhabiting soul from a conduit's body with a short, sharp shock of electricity. Not a pleasant experience, but often preferable to possession by a dangerous dead person.

Pancrit next opened the refrigerator, where he stored the adenovirus he used to carry and implant the modified DNA for their gene therapy. He skimmed his index finger along the racks of vials filled with green liquid, each emblazoned with a label bearing a number, a name, a time duration, and the words TRIAL TERMINATED stamped in red. All his glorious failures. He stopped at the rack with the designation #17-MARISA A. 52 HRS., 23 MIN.

He checked his watch. Maddox was due to reach the end of his gene therapy within the next three or four hours.

"Leave that for now," Pancrit told the Corps Security agents regarding their cleanup work. "I need your help with Clem."

The physician filled two syringes, one with a mild sedative and the other with a lethal dose of morphine, and set them beside the SoulScan on the cart, then pushed it out of the lab. Tackle and Block accompanied him to the observation room where they'd confined their current test subject. The moment they reached the room's locked entrance, Maddox threw himself against the window with a grating shriek.

Pancrit pulled the cart to one side and jerked his head toward the door. "You first."

Tackle glowered at him, but unlocked the room.

Clem Maddox tried to bolt through the door the moment they opened it, but the Corps Security agents each seized one of his arms and lifted him from the floor as they dragged him back inside.

"You lied to me!" Maddox screamed at Pancrit, kicking his dangling feet to twist himself free from the agents' grasp. *"You told me I could be with Amy!"*

"I didn't lie to you, Clem." Pancrit wheeled the cart through the door with the solicitousness of a garçon delivering room service. "We'll have you with her in no time."

Tackle and Block wrestled Maddox onto a table with a top upholstered in Naugahyde and outfitted with sinewy leather straps. Pancrit then jabbed the needle containing the sedative into the patient's arm. As it took effect, the drug weakened Maddox enough to enable the Corps Security agents to cinch the belts tight around his torso and limbs.

Clem's thrashing slowed, and he slurred his obscenities. "No ... no more shots," he muttered, mush-mouthed. 'Already got ... too many people in my head."

"Only one more, Clem. I promise." Pancrit smiled and readied the needle with the morphine.

When the tranquilizer had sufficiently pacified his test subject, Pancrit used the surgical tape to affix each of the SoulScan's twenty metal electrodes to its corresponding node point as marked in ink on Maddox's shaved scalp. With the sensors in place, he switched on the SoulScan monitor. As he expected, the three glowing green lines that scrolled across the top of the screen jiggled with the subdued brain waves of Clem's sedated thoughts. The bottom three lines alternately flattened and fuzzed with irregular bursts of scratchy static. This intermittent interference indicated that one or more souls—possibly several—were "knocking," attempting to access and control Maddox's mind and body.

If left to the faulty efficacy of Bartholomew Wax's latest DNA treatment, Maddox would most likely have remained in this inadequate intermediate state, neither able to permit the knocking souls to inhabit him completely nor to keep them from constantly impinging on his consciousness. The continuous assault would inevitably grind away at the man's sanity.

As soon as it became clear that he would have to dispense with this patient, anyway, Pancrit had decided to salvage some data from the abortive clinical trial by improvising an experiment. Treatment #17 had had the unfortunate side effect of dislodging the soul of the test subject Marisa Alvarez, from her body, leaving it vacant for any wandering spirit to usurp. Pancrit had found the result intriguing and wanted to evaluate it further. But, of course, the meddlesome Dr. Wax had precluded the possibility of additional study by killing the patient. Pancrit had therefore administered Treatment #17 to Clement Maddox two days ago, curious to see how soon it would remove the man's soul and how long the body could be maintained in a nominally "alive" but soul-free state.

The hydra of insulated electrode wires swayed as Clem shook his head and mumbled, adrift between the shores of waking and sleeping. "Amy …"

"Easy, my friend. It won't be long now." Pancrit patted Maddox's immobilized arm, then went to fetch a chair and a clipboard in order to record his observations as the carrier virus finished its transformation of the subject's brain.

Carl Pancrit was six years old when he first saw a human being die.

His parents had gone to Hawaii for a week for their anniversary and left him with his paternal grandmother, a morbidly obese widow who wheezed through her nose from the labor of walking. She'd been puffing harder than usual that afternoon as she shopped at the supermarket while trying to monitor Carl, who scampered up and down the aisles in his Lone Ranger outfit, clicking his empty cap gun at the other customers. By the time they got back to her house, she was wobbling dangerously on her thick heels as she carried the grocery sacks up the driveway from her Thunderbird.

Oblivious as only a boy of six could be, Carl ran ahead to the front door and turned back to fire his six-shooter at her. He didn't so much open the door for her as he left it ajar when he bounded into the kitchen. His grandmother tottered behind him, striving to breathe. She had almost made it to the counter when the paper bags slid from her embrace to spill on the floor, disgorging hot dogs and the chocolate-chip cookie ingredients he'd made her buy. With one hand massaging the cleft between her heavy breasts, she staggered backward to drop into one of the chairs at the breakfast table, but failed to center her weight on it. It clattered out from under her, dumping her into the puddle of leaking milk and shattered eggs on the linoleum.

Through the eyeholes cut in his black mask, little Carl watched her fibrillating at his feet. His arm drooped to his side, the cap gun forgotten. "Grandma?"

She lifted her head, her jowls slicked with yolk, and rotated her fluttering eyes up to look at him. Her lips plumped into an O as if to push out words like smoke rings, but no sound emerged.

Carl dropped the gun and took off his cowboy hat and Lone Ranger mask; he felt stupid for being in costume during a crisis. Fear frosted his skin. Grandma was sick, and it was up to him to help her. But what could he do? Run to the neighbors' house? He didn't even know them.

Nine-one-one did not exist during Carl's childhood, and he did not read well enough at that age to look up a number to call an ambulance. But his parents had told him that if there was ever an emergency, he should dial zero on the telephone and tell the operator what was wrong. He hurried to drag a chair over to the wall so he could climb up to the big black rotary phone mounted there.

When he had surmounted the chair and unhooked the receiver, however, he paused to check on his ailing grandmother again. He was scared to talk to strangers and hoped that she might be all right now so he wouldn't have to call.

Grandma was not all right. Her head had sunk back into the pooled food, and though her eyes were open, they didn't look at him ... or at anything. A tremor shivered her body like the aftershock of an earthquake, and she lay still.

Carl stood on the chair, his small hands sweating on the receiver, the dial tone deafening in his ear. He knew that he should be calling the operator for help, that he would get in serious trouble if he didn't, but the sight of his expiring grandmother spellbound him. He did not fully comprehend the significance of what he witnessed, yet sensed that it resided outside the prescribed boundaries of his protected innocence. It fascinated him *because* it was forbidden.

He hung the receiver back on its hook and climbed off the chair to crouch beside his grandmother's cooling corpse.

A fright that felt like excitement thrilled him as he knelt to peer into her open eyes and watch the vitreous fluid cloud behind the drying corneas. With one quivering forefinger, he poked the still-soft, still-warm flesh of her left cheek. Not so long before, he had learned how to use a magnifying glass to focus a pinpoint of sunlight on an ant to transform the skittering insect into a speck of smoking carbon. This was like that, making him wonder at what point something alive became not-alive. A few minutes ago, the mound of matter heaped before him had been Grandma. What had changed?

Almost an hour passed before he finally called the operator. He did not need to feign terror as he talked to her, for he knew that what he had done was wrong, that he would be punished severely for failing to help his grandmother—that everyone would discover the awful interest he had taken in her demise.

But none of that happened. On the contrary, the police and paramedics who responded to the scene said nothing but comforting things to him and did not challenge him when he said that he'd been watching TV in the living room and hadn't heard Grandma's fall in the kitchen. They took him to stay with his aunt and uncle, who showered him with sympathy, bought him presents, and offered to cook whatever he wanted for dinner. Even his parents did not blame him for forcing them to return from their vacation three days early. Far from it. They praised his bravery, and his father promised to take Carl on a fishing trip as soon as he felt up to it. When the local paper included a brief item on the "Boy, 6, Stranded with Dead Grandmother," his mother proudly clipped the article and pasted it in her scrapbook.

"What happened wasn't your fault, Carl," they all said. "You tried to save her."

Eventually, he began to believe them. The intervening hour between Grandma's collapse and his phone call to the operator shortened to seconds in his memory. Yet he could not efface the unhealthy fixation on death the event had aroused in him. It underlay all his waking thoughts, like profane graffiti beneath a wall's whitewash. Hungering to pose illicit questions, he grew guarded and sly in his pursuit of the answers.

"Where did Grandma go?" he asked his father during their eventual fishing trip.

His dad became preoccupied with casting his line back into the lake. "To Heaven, of course."

"How do you know?" Carl kept his tone plaintive, wistful, so he would not seem insolent.

"The Violets prove it." The glib response made it sound as if no further explanation were necessary. His father acted as if he'd rather be discussing the facts of life than the facts of death.

"Who are the Violets?"

"You'll find out when you're older." That assertion closed the conversation. Carl never raised the subject with his father again.

He chose to explore the undiscovered country on his own instead. When people asked why he became a doctor, he said, quite truthfully, "Because of what happened to my grandmother." They would nod in solemn admiration, assuming he had dedicated himself to preventing such tragedies. But that wasn't what he meant at all.

In order to observe the transition from this world to the next firsthand, he often had to precipitate the passing of his patients at a time and under conditions that he selected. He cultivated an avuncular bedside manner to put his elderly subjects at their ease, and impressed the next of kin by his steadfast attentiveness to his patients until the very end. Little did they realize that he was there to see the precise moment the light left the patients' eyes.

"What happened wasn't your fault," they always told him. "You tried to save them."

Dr. Pancrit not only tried to save them—he *did* save them. Saved them the pain and futility of the nub end of this life by delivering them to the next. Far from afflicting his conscience, the certainty of an afterlife exonerated him. What was murder when the soul never truly died? He merely eased his victims' inevitable transmigration with the blessed oblivion of morphine.

For his father had been right. When he got older, Carl found out all about the Violets. He read every account of them he could find, pored over every fragmentary description of the afterlife offered by the souls that they summoned. Here, at last, was a direct window into that unreachable, invisible existence that so captivated him.

The stories the dead told tantalized without satisfying, however. They spoke of an intangible realm of pure consciousness devoid of senses; there was no sight, no sound, no touch, no taste, no scent, only memory and thought. Legends also circulated about a life beyond this limbo, but since the Violets could not summon the souls who went there to report what it was like or if it even existed, the place remained a fabrication of myth and conjecture. From ancient times, the world's religions had each tailored their vision of the afterlife to accommodate the facts the Violets divulged, with no means of confirming or denying any of their suppositions.

For believers like Carl's father, no proof was needed, but an empiricist like Carl Pancrit needed certainty. If the soul was merely another form of electromagnetic energy—energy that Newton stated could be neither created nor destroyed—then its persistence after the body's death did not imply anything. Not God or Satan, not Heaven or Hell, not reward or punishment, not good or evil. The maddening inconclusiveness of the evidence only inflamed the lust for absolute knowledge engendered that day Carl watched his grandmother die. If he could experience the dead directly, the way the Violets did, instead of secondhand ... if he could *feel* for himself the "call" of the Place Beyond that some souls in limbo described ... then perhaps he could quell the obsession that had possessed him since the age of six.

His frustration led him to take greater risks in his research. His timid colleagues began to question his ethics, and the university at whose hospital he worked opened an investigation into his patients' deaths. Fortunately, the North American Afterlife Communications Corps spared him the indignity of prosecution, for it, too, wanted to grant others the Violets' necromantic gift. Conduits were far too useful to the NAACC for it to rely solely on the vagaries of Nature to supply them.

"I can tell you're the perfect man for the job," Delbert Sinclair, the head of Corps Security, had said when he selected Pancrit to head up Project Persephone.

"It's my life's ambition," he'd replied at the time. An ambition that he vowed he would soon realize.

The sedative Pancrit had administered to Clement Maddox wore off after the first couple of hours, after which the patient resumed his hostile outbursts. The leather restraints secured his thrashing body, however, so Pancrit only had to worry about plugging his ears against Maddox's caterwauling.

Checking the SoulScan readout and making notations on his clipboard at regular intervals, Pancrit became excited when, fifty-one hours, fifty-nine minutes, and eighteen seconds after he had initially given Maddox the Treatment #17 adenovirus, the patient began experiencing "dropouts": brief lapses when he fell silent and immobile as his brain waves flatlined on the SoulScan readout. These episodes grew longer over the next hour, coinciding with a growing amplitude and definition of the waves that spiked the bottom three lines of the monitor's display—the lines that signified the presence of knocking souls.

"No ... no, you can't stay," Maddox babbled to the ghosts during his infrequent periods of lucidity. *"She's coming, I tell you."*

Dr. Pancrit noted the precise time at which the top three lines of the SoulScan smoothed to straightness for the last time: 7:43 P.M. Its quantum energy no longer anchored to mortal matter, the sentience known as Clement Everett Maddox had departed. Pancrit was pleased to see, however, that the body's autonomic functions still operated, albeit with increasing feebleness.

He'd just jotted a measurement of the untenanted body's pulse when a flurry of zigzags on the SoulScan screen's lower three lines caught his attention. Concurrently, the body lashed to the padded table stirred, and Pancrit wondered if he had pronounced Maddox's passing prematurely.

Cleared of personality, Maddox's face had relaxed to an almost infantile softness. It retained that ingenuousness as it awoke, but a new persona sculpted a mature awareness into its expression.

"Clem?" the lips breathed with feminine delicacy. "I'm here, baby. Where are you?"

Carl Pancrit could barely contain his excitement. "Amy Maddox?" he asked.

The dead woman looked at him with her husband's half-blue, half-violet eyes. "Yes?"

"I'm afraid your husband isn't here anymore."

"I'm too late?" Her gaze wandered, frantic, distressed, as if she expected to see the man in whose body she resided. "He called and called me and I tried to come, but I could never get in."

"I know he longed to be with you," Pancrit agreed, savoring the pathos like bitter brandy. Poor Clem! He had successfully summoned his beloved wife at last but since he was not a true Violet, she could only inhabit his body after he had vacated it.

"I've got to find him," Amy said. She shut Clem's eyes, closing herself off from the world that had divided her from her lover for so long. On the bottom three lines of the SoulScan readout, the wavelengths stretched to tautness. Amy was dropping out.

"Wait! I can help you, Mrs. Maddox," Pancrit said quickly, hoping to persuade her to stay. "If you can answer a few questions—"

He did not get the chance to debrief her about the afterlife, however, for she had already returned to it. Perhaps she and Clem would finally enjoy their long-delayed reunion.

Nature evidently abhorred a vacuum, for in the next instant another spirit took up residence in the living corpse. Scribbles of consciousness skittered along the SoulScan readout, and Maddox's face hardened with cantankerous misanthropy.

"Where am I?" the body's new occupant snapped at Pancrit. It tried to sit up, discovered that its arms and legs were tied down. "This is that cursed Greener Pastures, ain't it?" it demanded, surveying the surroundings. "You people *killed* me with your incompetence. So help me, if I get in touch with my grandson, I'll make you pay, I swear I will."

Pancrit heaved a sigh and jammed the morphine-laden hypodermic into the body's forearm. As much as the Treatment #17 phenomenon intrigued him, he had neither the time nor the patience to transport a test subject who kept changing personalities every few minutes. Nevertheless, the experiment had proven promising and warranted further research.

Leaving the former Greener Pastures resident to rattle and gripe in the dying body, Pancrit ambled out into the hallway, tapping his pen on the clipboard as he mulled over his notes.

16

Two on a Couch

That night, as she huddled with Serena around her "office"—the small desk in the living room where she kept her computer—Natalie began to wonder if their entire undercover op at Greener Pastures had been a bust. According to her Web searches, no one in Seattle seemed to have noticed that Clement Maddox was missing, Evan Markham had kept himself underground, and the main thing that came up for the entry "Dr. Wax" were advertisements for Dr. Zog's Sex Wax, a surfboard coating.

The name "Pancrit" produced a few thousand results, most of them genealogical. When she entered "Carleton Pancrit," the search returned nothing.

Did you mean "Carl Anton Pancrit"? the search engine asked her.

"Maybe I did," she murmured aloud, pulse quickening as she clicked on the link.

This time, only a handful of results came on-screen, most of them articles archived from the *Philadelphia Inquirer* that dated back to the early eighties. Natalie selected the most promising title in the list, **"University Doctor Suspended for Possible Ethics Violations."**

She felt Serena squeeze her shoulder as the article came up. "Nat, I think we've found our man."

University Doctor Suspended for Possible Ethics Violations

King of Prussia, Pa.—Dr. Carl Anton Pancrit, a lead physician at the Pierpont University Center for Gerontology, has been put on indefinite, unpaid leave pending investigation of "certain unauthorized research activities," a university spokesperson said in a prepared statement yesterday.

The university refused to state the nature of the research in question, but sources close to the investigation, on condition of anonymity, stated that Dr. Pancrit, 42, had abused his professional relationship with terminal patients to further his study of the passing of the soul's quantum energy from the physical body at the time of death.

Specifically, these sources say, a colleague discovered Dr. Pancrit attending to a cancer victim to whom he had attached a SoulScan device. The SoulScan, a sophisticated instrument capable of registering a soul's electromagnetic fluctuations, is generally used only on licensed conduits of the North American Afterlife Communications Corps. These conduits, commonly known as Violets for their violet-coloured eyes, employ the device to confirm that a deceased individual's soul has inhabited them.

According to the colleague, whose name was withheld, Dr. Pancrit hoped the SoulScan would show precisely how long the patient's soul remained in the body after cessation of autonomic functions. Although Pancrit presented a signed form in which the unnamed cancer patient consented to the experiment, university officials believed the doctor's methodology to be a violation of prevailing medical ethics.

The revelation has also spurred the families of some of Dr. Pancrit's previous patients to press for a review of the physician's treatment of their deceased relations.

Dr. Pancrit could not be reached for comment.

Natalie and Serena skimmed the other relevant articles, but none of them revealed what became of the investigation, or of Dr. Carl Anton Pancrit. A terse, one-paragraph item merely stated that Dr. Pancrit had resigned his post at the university and that the Gerontology Center had settled all outstanding malpractice claims for an undisclosed amount.

"How do you suppose he wriggled out of that one?" Natalie wondered.

"Two words—*Corps Security*," Serena said. "Corps never has enough Violets to satisfy it. Pancrit must've cut a deal with 'em. If the N-double-A-C-C paid off the families and shut down the investigation before he went to jail, he'd churn out all the Violets they want." She snorted her contempt. "Crazy bastard might just do it, too."

"But he hasn't yet. He said the project wasn't working, and Maddox was ... screwed up somehow." Natalie didn't want to think about what that meant for Calvin. The foil didn't seem to protect him as well as it first had; by the time she and Serena got back to the condo that evening, he had begun hearing voice-echoes in his head again, "remembering" things that hadn't happened to him, feeling the spider-skitters in his extremities that indicated a knocking soul. At that moment, he was lying on her father's bed upstairs, muttering to himself.

This subject's going to end up like all the others.

No, Natalie told herself. Calvin would *not* end up like Maddox. There had to be some way of reversing the process.

"We need to talk to Wax," she declared.

"That'd be great if we knew how to get ahold of him." Serena rose from her chair to stretch her long acrobat's arms. She'd shed her grandma costume in favor of a khaki tank top and camo pants, but hadn't had a chance to wash the silver out of her wig, making her look like a geriatric commando. "You sure that was Evan's voice you heard talking to Pancrit?"

'Positive."

"So this Wax guy is dead. We could summon him ourselves if we had a touchstone for him. 'Course, that would entail finding out who the hell he was and where his stuff is."

"Maybe not. Maybe we can find the touchstone first." Natalie remembered the list of forgeries Pancrit wanted her to paint: *The Scream, Storm on the Sea of Galilee, Madonna of the Yarnwinder,* and the others. All of which had made headlines when the mysterious Arthur Maven returned the stolen works to their respective museums without apology or explanation.

I told you what would happen to your pretty pictures if you disappointed me, Pancrit had threatened Wax.

"Wax has some connection to those stolen paintings Pancrit asked Calvin and me to copy," she said, thinking aloud. "What if he came into contact with the originals? He might have touched them ... or at least the frames. We could use those as touch-stones."

Serena smacked her forehead. "Of course! It's so simple—all we have to do is lay our hands on a couple of Rembrandts. Why didn't *I* think of that?"

"No, I'm serious! *Sea of Galilee, Chez Tortoni,* and *The Concert* are all back at the Isabella Stewart Gardner Museum in Boston. We could be there in a day. I'd only need to touch one of the paintings long enough to summon Wax." She paused for her friend to insert a put-down. "Unless you've got a better idea."

Serena frowned but didn't reject the proposal out of hand. "Boston, huh? Long way to go for a wild-goose chase."

"It's closer than Oslo," Natalie smiled with goofy optimism.

"Can't argue with that." Serena mulled it over, then took out the wallet she carried in place of a purse. She produced her Corps credit card and handed it to Natalie. "Go ahead and book our flights. Give me a day's layover in Albuquerque."

The request unnerved Natalie. She didn't want to be without Serena's protection. "You're not coming to Boston?"

"I'll meet you there. Right now, I gotta go chat with Uncle Simon. This thing's even bigger and badder than the ol' paranoid thought it was."

"It's just ... I can't leave Dad and Callie here alone. And Calvin's a mess—I'll have to take him with us."

Freed from the brown contacts she'd worn that afternoon, Serena rolled her violet eyes upward, as if she could see through the living-room ceiling to the man who languished, sweating, in the bed upstairs. "I wouldn't get too attached to Calvin if I were you, Nat. Things don't look good for the boy."

*

As soon as Natalie had reserved a red-eye flight to New Mexico for her, Serena bid her farewell with a tight-lipped "Good luck." Nettled by Serena's cold-blooded pessimism, Natalie gave her an equally curt good-bye. No matter how grim the prognosis, she wasn't about to treat Calvin like a pet that needed to be put to sleep. The moment Serena's Harley rumbled off into the night, Natalie went up to see how he was doing.

She got the answer even before she entered the bedroom, for his broken, desperate mumbling leaked out the open door.

'A-B-C ... d-d-DEE ... E-F ... juh-juh-GEE—"

Calvin broke off, embarrassed, as she leaned through the door frame, as if she'd overheard him singing in the shower. He sat up on the bed and steadied himself, still wearing the foil beneath his baseball cap and folding his arms to keep from wrapping them around his head. "Oh. Hey."

He reminded Natalie of herself at five years old, when she was first practicing her protective mantra at the School. She, too, had been too scared to admit that she could not control her own mind, too proud to let others know how hard the mental discipline was for her. "Mind if I come in?" she asked.

"Please. It'll be nice to actually see the person who's talking to me for a change."

She seated herself beside him on the rumpled comforter. "How's it going?"

"I have plenty of company, if that's what you mean. How do you stand it? All those people talking to you, all the time? Most of them ticked off about something or other."

"You learn to tune them out." Natalie wondered if that would be true for Calvin, however. He seemed to be far more receptive to souls than any Violet she'd ever known, including herself.

"You find out anything about our mad-scientist friends?"

"Sort of. But we need to go to Boston to learn more."

"We?"

"I can't leave you here alone in your condition. Not with Evan and Pancrit out there looking for us."

Calvin nodded gamely. "Okay, Boston it is. When do we leave?"

"First thing in the morning, so we should get some sleep." Natalie glanced with chagrin at the bed she was going to ask him to vacate for her father. "I can let you have the couch tonight, if you want."

"No, you don't need to do that. Just give me a throw pillow, and I'll crash on the floor."

"C'mon, you need a good night's rest." Natalie nudged him in the ribs. "Tell you what—the sofa bed's wide enough. We can share." Raising a hand to cut off any prurient speculation, she added, "Fully clothed, of course."

He lifted his hand to pledge. "On my honor as a gentleman." His singular green-violet eyes went glassy, his expression going from comic to tragic so fast that she feared another soul might be trying to enter him. "I can't tell you what it means, Natalie— everything you've done for me. I know I'm nothing but a schmuck who showed up on your doorstep, but I swear, if I make it through this ..."

He grasped for something he could offer in repayment, but apparently couldn't come up with anything worthy.

Natalie smiled. "You'll make it. Now, let's go have a slumber party."

The sofa bed was big enough for both of them—barely. Calvin's feet jutted out over the edge of the mattress, and Natalie had to lie on her side to keep from brushing shoulders with him.

A light sleeper under the best of circumstances, Natalie found it impossible to doze off while fretting about Evan and Pancrit, dressed in her street clothes, and crammed next to a man she barely knew whose bulk made the flimsy springs of the couch cot screech every time he rolled over. The fact that he kept mumbling to himself didn't help, either.

Insomnia loves company, so it was only a matter of time before she said, "Calvin? You awake?"

"Of course." He flipped over to face her, the mattress cresting and dipping with his shifting weight. "Thought you'd never ask."

As was her custom, Natalie had left the lights on in the kitchen in case she needed to get up during the night. The dim illumination that stretched into the living room reflected off the crinkled foil on Calvin's head and whitened his smile, which she returned. "Mind if I pose a personal question?"

He sighed. "Anything's better than lying here listening to the whispering in my brain. Shoot."

"Your technique on that Rembrandt is astonishing. I think you're one of the most gifted painters I've ever met—even better than Hector Espinoza, though don't you dare tell him I said that."

Calvin grinned. "I'm liking this so far. What's the question?"

"With all that talent, why blow it by breaking the law and going to jail?"

His smile wilted. "Ouch. Talk about a backhanded compliment."

Natalie had anticipated that Calvin's past would be a sore spot for him. Perhaps infected by Serena's mistrust, she wanted to probe the depth of his remorse, to test whether he regretted committing the crime as much as getting caught for it. She could forgive him one ghastly mistake if he'd truly learned from it. After all, Natalie herself had become so desperate for money after leaving the Corps that she had gone to Peru to participate in an illegal hunt for Incan treasure. The lapse in moral judgment led her to kill two men, and though she had killed in self-defense, the memory of their dead faces served as an indelible emblem of her own past sins.

Calvin looked so morose, so utterly overcome by the awareness of his own failure, that Natalie felt guilty for bringing up the subject. "I'm sorry," she said, preparing to drop the matter. "It just seems like . . . such a waste."

"Not that much of a waste." His gaze wandered from her, and at first Natalie thought he wanted to avoid looking her in the eye. Then she followed his line of sight to the portrait she'd drawn of Callie embraced by Dan's spirit. The slanting light from the kitchen cast it in an even more ghostly aura.

"You want to know the truth? Why I copy the masters?" he asked. "Because I don't have what you have: a vision. I can look at one of your pictures, I can recognize its brilliance, understand how it works its magic. I can even replicate it in a mechanical, Xerox-machine way. But when I try to come up with something myself . . . Nada."

Natalie watched him, wary that he might be handing her a come-on line, but his dispirited, wistful tone convinced her of his sincerity. Calvin Criswell, the most gifted artist she'd ever met, envied her—and his envy flattered her more than his praise. "Thanks," she began, "but I don't think you give yourself enough credit."

"I don't think *you* give yourself enough credit, Natalie. If I could do what you do, I'd never mess with dead people."

Called upon to justify how she'd squandered her own gifts, Natalie didn't know what to say.

"I never had a choice," she whispered, doubting her own rationale. She'd always blamed the Corps for denying her admittance to its Art Division and railroading her into law enforcement. But wasn't that merely another excuse she'd used to postpone her artistic ambitions, to put off final judgment of her own creative worth? Even now, wasn't she doing exactly what Calvin had done—churning out the work of Dead White Guys instead of her own?

"Maybe you're right," she admitted. "But you don't need to mess with dead people, either. I know you have a vision of your own, Calvin. You just have to find it and have faith in it."

He let out a dry chuckle. "Something you believe in."

"What?"

"Nothing. Something your daughter told me." Before she could inquire what that was, he brought out his usual raffish grin, his shield against seriousness back in place. "Okay, you got to ask your personal question. Now it's my turn."

Equally eager to change the subject, Natalie propped herself on one elbow. "Yeah? And that would be?"

He fluffed a few locks of her black, pixie-cut hairdo. "Why this wig? I like the red one better."

Natalie didn't know whether to laugh or groan, remembering how Dan had charmed her by complimenting her hair, no matter which color she wore.

"For your information, a disguise is supposed to *divert* attention, not attract it," she said to explain why she'd picked her drabbest hairpiece for the undercover operation that afternoon. "And while we're on the subject of hair ... lose the billy-goat look." She indicated his would-be beard. "The Beat Generation ended in the fifties."

"Oh." He fingered the goatee as if he'd forgotten it was there. "Part of the whole image thing. To some of my customers, the beard's the only thing that separates an artist from a homeless person. Which isn't far off, actually."

Natalie laughed. "You know, you'd actually be kinda cute without that fuzz on your face."

"And you'd be gorgeous even with a goatee."

The earnest way he said it threw her. It took her a

moment to crack a grin. "Now I *know* you're just trying to butter me up."

"No, I'm serious. I couldn't believe it when you showed up at my apartment. Munch's drawing didn't do you justice."

Natalie ignored the fluttering acceleration of her pulse. "Oh, yeah, I'm beautiful, all right. But not when I have black hair." She tossed a few strands of her wig for emphasis.

"I didn't say that. I only said I liked the red one better." Calvin admired her with those green-violet eyes, which now seemed miraculous rather than misbegotten.

Natalie didn't know who moved closer first. Certainly not her. She hadn't kissed a man since Dan died, for her attempts at romance inevitably ended in disaster. Nevertheless, her face and Calvin's gravitated toward each other until his breath warmed her lips ...

... then jerked back from the brink the moment they heard the slap of her father's slippers on the stairs. Clad only in an old hotel bathrobe, Wade descended until he came in view of the living-room couch.

"Hey, kiddo, could I borrow some of your floss? I ran—Oh, gosh." Shading his eyes to emphasize that he wasn't watching, he did an about-face and hurried back the way he'd come.

"Sure, Dad. Help yourself!" Natalie called after him. She put a fist over her mouth to keep from laughing aloud.

Calvin lay back, with his hands behind his head,

whistling with exaggerated innocence. When a couple of minutes had passed without further interruption, he shot her a mischievous look. "Think it's safe to try again?"

"I guess we'll find out." She listed toward him, and his mouth rose to meet hers—

"Mom, I can't sleep."

Calvin and Natalie peeled away from each other again, and she craned her head around to face Callie, who stood at the foot of the stairs in her bare feet and flannel nightgown. "What is it, baby girl?"

The girl stiffened with den mother disapproval as her gaze shifted to Calvin. "I had a dream about Dad."

Natalie wondered if her face had turned as red as it felt. "Oh? What was it?"

"Never mind. It was only a dream. Didn't mean to *bother* you." She thumped up the stairs and out of sight.

"Callie! *Callie!*" Failing to draw her daughter back for an apology, Natalie turned to Calvin. "You'll have to forgive her. She—Hey, wait!" She caught hold of his T-shirt as he was about to climb out of bed.

He shook his head and tried to rise again. "I don't think this was such a good idea. You take the bed. I'm not gonna sleep much, anyway."

Natalie did not let go. "Don't take it personally. Callie was very close to her father ... she's done this to every guy I've seen since."

"Oh, that makes me feel better." Calvin rolled his eyes, but reclined beside her again.

"We could give it one more try ..."

"What? And have Serena barge in on us? I can't wait to see how passive-aggressive *she'll* be."

"Relax. Serena's gone." She prodded his side, a teasing lilt in her voice. "Third time's the charm."

"Or the jinx." He pushed himself onto his side again and gazed into her face, stroking her drab black locks with his fingertips as if it were her real hair and red, the way he liked it. "What the heck."

Calvin lowered his lips onto hers, and this time no interruption prevented the contact. Natalie curled her hand around the back of his neck to hold him there, pull him closer. Pressure, soft yet insistent, growing with the release of inhibition. Mouths widening as tongue-tips darted out to touch and dance ...

Then the giddy head-rush of the kiss ended with a sharp intake of breath as Natalie's lips drew air. Calvin pushed away from her, and Natalie almost growled in frustration.

This was no petty disturbance, however. Shock had bleached Calvin's face bone-white, and his entire body vibrated with the tremors of incipient seizure.

"Calvin! What is it?" She reached to comfort him, but the gesture only panicked him.

"Don't touch me!" He practically fell out of bed to get away from her, landing in a sitting position beside the couch in an embryonic crouch. "My God. I can feel your mom—and your stepmom—and Lucy—and Arthur and ..." He slapped his head as if it were a radio with poor reception. "... Ruskin? *Russell.* And more—too many. They're all here."

In awful comprehension, Natalie raised her fingertips to touch the deceptively tender contours of her lips. That kiss had been the first time that Calvin had come in contact with her bare skin. "Jesus, Calvin."

In the heat of the moment, she'd forgotten that she, too, could be a touchstone for all the dead people she'd known and loved: Nora Lindstrom, her mother, and Sheila Lindstrom, her stepmother, both butchered by Vincent Thresher, as well as Lucy Kamei, Arthur McCord, Russell Travers, and all the other friends Evan had eviscerated during the Violet Murders. Like Clement Maddox, Calvin apparently soaked souls up from the environment like a sponge, without a true Violet's ability to sift the knocking and select the inhabitation.

"Take slow, even breaths," Natalie instructed him. She took her own advice so that Calvin wouldn't see her own alarm at his condition. "You're going to be fine."

He did as she said, and his tremors subsided.

"That's it. Stay nice and calm. I'll be right back."

She scampered to the kitchen and pawed past the bottles of cleanser under the sink to grab a pair of rubber Playtex gloves from a box beneath the drainpipe. Natalie slid her hands into the gloves and pulled the cuffs of her long-sleeved knit sweater down over her wrists so that there would be no exposed skin. When she returned to the living room, she was gratified to hear Calvin reciting the alphabet again.

He won't end up like Maddox, she told herself.

Squatting beside Calvin's hunched form, Natalie displayed her insulated hands to get his attention. "I won't touch you again, I promise. See? These will protect you. And tomorrow we'll go to Boston, and Dr. Wax will tell us how to keep this from happening to you. But you've gotta hang in there, okay?"

His mumbling trailed off, and he lifted his head as if it were the weight of the earth. "I'm trying. *Please don't give up on me.*"

She avoided his weary, wanting gaze, and Serena's warning replayed in her head. *I wouldn't get too attached to Calvin if I were you, Nat. Things don't look good for the boy.*

Maybe her friend was right. Maybe that doomed kiss was an omen, a warning. Bad things befell the men Natalie became involved with. She couldn't do that to Calvin, too.

"I'm sorry," she said. "It's my fault. I shouldn't have—it won't happen again. Try to get some sleep."

With the passivity of the hopeless, Calvin got back into the sofa bed, and Natalie carefully arranged herself beside him so as not to brush against any part of his body. At some point during the molasses hours of early morning, however, Calvin slipped his bare hand into her gloved grasp, which he gripped the way an infant wrings comfort from a security blanket. They remained linked like that until dawn, united yet separated, the only boundary between them a thin layer of latex and the unresolved threat it represented.

17

Queen of the Wannabes

To the world at large, she was Amanda Bethany Pyne, an underachieving high-school senior notable only for her predilection for black lace clothing, heavy eyeliner, and a garish assortment of neon-colored wigs. But here, in the sanctum of her bedroom, with her wig off and her violet contacts on, she became Amalfia, world-famous conduit for the North American Afterlife Communications Corps.

The ecstatic chill she felt as she admired her gaunt reflection in the vanity mirror made it easy to imagine that a soul was knocking, eager to inhabit her. As always, she began by buzzing an electric razor over her bare scalp, which she shaved more assiduously than her legs. The pattern of dots she'd had tattooed there a couple weeks back had finally stopped hurting. They weren't actually node points since she didn't *have* node points, but there were twenty of them and the tattoo artist had distributed them in a realistic fashion. Amanda thrilled at the authenticity they gave her.

Her parents would doubtless freak if they ever found out that she'd spent two months' allowance to deface herself for life. She giggled at the thought. Maybe seeing her head spotted like an Easter egg would make Mom and Dad stop bugging her about the wigs she wore. Better purple or lime-green hair than no hair at all, from their point of view.

Amanda's violet lenses gleamed in the wavering light of the sandalwood-scented candles that burned in sconces at either side of the mirror, thickening the air with their musky incense. She leaned close to the mirror, her dull brown eyes staring through the stained glass of her contacts at the captivating irises of the Violet before her.

Amalfia.

Stroking her stubbly scalp until she raised goose bumps beneath the tatted black webbing of her top, Amanda rose from the chair at her vanity table and swayed to the music smoking from the speakers of her boom box: ambient trance laced with Gregorian chant. She shut her eyes, pretending that the lull of the melody and the scent of the candles were the sense-memories of a forlorn spirit seeping into her psyche.

From the world you know to the world you knew, she rhapsodized. *Come to me, come to me, come on through!*

Her spectator mantra. Unlike some of the Violet posers she knew, she had composed her own rather than cribbing Goth song lyrics or snatches of Poe and Baudelaire. So whom would she permit to possess her tonight? Chopin, possibly, eager to draft a new concerto with her hands? Or maybe Cleopatra would relate, with coquettish insouciance, how she intoxicated and subjugated the most powerful men of the ancient world—advice Amanda could use in her own love life. She had taken French and Latin classes for just such an occasion, garnering the only A's she'd received in high school.

Perhaps the knocking soul was simply some forgotten murder victim whose only hope for justice was to reveal her killer to Amalfia. Amanda had once aspired to be a homicide detective, having always loved murder mysteries and true-crime books. In fact, it was one such book that led to her infatuation with conduits: *Plucking the Violets* by Sidney Preston, the *New York Post* reporter who initially broke the story of the Violet Killer's murder spree. After that, Amanda collected every Violet tie-in item she could—DVDs and posters from the various movies and TV shows that featured conduit characters, art prints of posthumous collaborations painted by Violet artist Hector Espinoza, even CDs recorded by NAACC musician Lucinda Kamei before the Violet Killer got her. For a girl befogged by adolescence, the Violets shone like a lighthouse, a beacon leading her toward an existence of purpose and meaning. These people associated with the most famous and glamorous individuals of all time, solved crimes and captured killers, revealed the most coveted secrets of history and the afterlife—and got lifetime employment with full benefits from the NAACC, to boot. Amanda had found her dream job, her true vocation.

The fact that she had not been born with the necessary qualifications was further proof that reality sucked.

She was not alone in believing that Nature had cheated her of her true identity. Web pages and chat rooms devoted to "proto-Violets" mushroomed in

211

the metastasizing Internet, cloistered among sites for the aficionados of such arcana as cross-stitching, bass fishing, cannibalism, medieval religious iconography, celebrity nude photos, and Chihuahua breeding. Violetworld.com, SoulSong.net, Afterlifer.org— they all provided a venue for quasi-Violets to commune and commiserate about being denied their birthright in the genetic lottery. There, they could feed one another's fantasies, blogging accounts of their imagined inhabitations and role-playing the Corps camaraderie they would never know.

Amanda had spent time on all of these sites, usually instead of doing homework. On this night, when she tired of rolling on her bedspread in the throes of violent possession, she went over to her desktop computer to log on to Deadtalker.com. Her parents, husband-and-wife real-estate agents, were too busy to concern themselves overmuch with her private life, but they did care enough to give her DSL.

As soon as the Deadtalker home page loaded, she entered her user name and password in the blank fields below the enormous violet eyes on-screen. **"Welcome, Amalfia,"** the page replied. **"Please wait while we summon the site map."**

The map consisted of several bald heads, both male and female, complete with node points, each with a link such as "Soul Mate Personals" or "Inhabitation Info" beneath it. Amanda clicked on the "Deadtalk Chat" link, and the eyes of the Violet above it flashed. As the site redirected Amanda to the chat meeting page, she glanced at the clock in the monitor's lower right corner. It was early yet—only 11:22. Deathdreamer had promised to rendezvous with her at midnight, but she hoped that he was as impatient to get together as she was.

Deathdreamer was by far the coolest proto-Violet she'd met online—definitely *not* a poser. He knew stuff about the inner workings of the Corps—details of murder investigations, life at the Iris Semple Conduit Academy—that Amanda hadn't seen in *any* of her books or movies. He told her—in strictest confidence, of course—that he had actual connections inside the NAACC and that he could get her a job with them. She figured she'd only be fit for filing papers at Corps headquarters in D.C., but that would be better than working retail. And maybe it would give her a chance to meet some Violets in person ... as well as Deathdreamer himself.

Scanning the list of screen names in the chat room's dialogue box, Amanda was glad the other Deadtalkers couldn't see her disappointment. No Deathdreamer. Only MantraMan and Ghostess, two *major* posers, monopolizing the conversation as usual. MantraMan acted as if he'd summoned Louis XV, "the Sun King," emoting in misspelled Netspeak about how horrible it was to be guillotined during the French Revolution, while Ghostess lapped it up and flirted shamelessly in return.

Wrong Roman numeral, dude, Amanda thought with a *tsk-tsk* of contempt. *If you're gonna talk the talk, at least get the right Louis.* She could have ignited a flame-war over it, but the pretension so demoralized her that she let the others ignore her, only entering the discussion when someone asked her a direct question. After ten minutes of watching the inane chatter scroll past her, she was about to give up and check out another site when a new party popped up in the room.

Deathdreamer: amalfia? u here?

She grinned, her fingers doing a merry jig on the keyboard.

Amalfia: not 4 long! want 2 go private?

Deathdreamer: u bet! lead the way ...

She typed "c ya!" to the posers, then clicked the onscreen button that would open a one-on-one dialogue box, continuing her remarks only when she and Deathdreamer were electronically isolated from the Deadtalker clique.

Amalfia: thanx 4 saving me! mman makes me wish *he* was dead. then I could use my protective mantra & make him go away!!! lol

Deathdreamer: yeah ... that's y I'd rather deal w/dead people!:)

Amalfia: me 2! :) btw ... about that corps job u talked about. how old do I have 2 be 2 get it?

Deathdreamer: depends. r u ready?

Amalfia: am I!!! I'd take it in a 🖤 beat.

Deathdreamer: *now*????????????????

The eagerness of his query took her aback for a sec. She laughed aloud as she keyed in her reply.

Amalfia: heck yeah!!!!!!!!!!!!!!!!!! I'm packin my bags ...

Deathdreamer: I'm serious. It's y I wanted 2 meet u 2nite.

Amanda now wished she could see Deathdreamer's face, to see who he was and whether he was kidding.

Amalfia: lol great! swing by & pick me up in 10 minutes. :)

Deathdreamer: no need. I'm rt outside yr window.

She waited for him to punctuate the joke with a winking emoticon. He didn't. Though she felt as gullible as a kid falling for the *pull-my-finger* gag, Amanda couldn't keep herself from glancing behind her at the window across the bedroom. It remained as she had left it—closed, with black velvet draped over the curtain rod to blot out the external world. She resisted the urge to rip the cloth down and look outside. *Boy, what a dupe*, she thought, laughing at her own silliness.

Amalfia: LMAO!!! ok, u got me. I actually xpected to c u there. forgot 1 thing: u don't even know my real name.

Deathdreamer: o but i do. it's amanda bethany pyne, and u live at 1725 cedar ln, where I am rt now.

Now Amanda really did feel the stubble on her scalp stand straight up as if a soul were knocking, but the sensation was not so pleasant this time. Before tonight, she'd paid as much attention to the scare stories about Internet predators as she did to the preachy videos on drugs, sex, and smoking that they showed in Health class. But here she was, in the starring role of one of those stories, talking with some perv in cyberspace about whom she knew zip ... yet who knew who she was and where she lived.

Wait a minute. There was no way some random stranger could find out her name and address. Deathdreamer had to be one of her friends jerking her chain. Of course! No wonder he knew exactly how to snag her interest. Whoever it was had gone to a lot of trouble, researching those tantalizing tidbits about the NAACC as bait and then lying in wait for her online. Amanda was relieved, yet the prank also made her feel stupid and sad.

Amalfia: ok ... jig's up. is this kevin? or carla?

Deathdreamer: no. but i am yr friend.

Amalfia: who r u? & how'd u set this up?

Deathdreamer: the corps got yr name & address from yr isp. told u I had connections! ;)

Again, the frigid prickling of her skin. She whipped around to look at the window, but the black cloth still blocked her view. Amanda couldn't decide whether to yank the curtain down, bolt from the room, or scream for her parents. Instead, she hit CAPS LOCK and punched out an ultimatum.

Amalfia: STAY AWAY FROM ME, U PSYCHO!! OR I CALL THE COPS!!!!!!!!!!!!!!!!!!!!

She tensed, ready to spring from her chair, but he made no attempt to come through the window for her.

Deathdreamer: u don't need to do that, amanda. i'll go away, and u will never hear from me or the corps again.

Amanda's fingers hovered over the keyboard. What if this guy was legit, and she was blowing her only chance to be with the NAACC? The threat of never learning Deathdreamer's offer suddenly seemed worse than anything he might do to her tonight. She released CAPS LOCK.

Amalfia: how do i know u r 4 real?

Deathdreamer: cause i stopped by floral acres to visit yr uncle pete. he told me he misses the hikes up mt. baldy.

Amanda swallowed the breath that balled in her throat. Until last summer, her uncle Pete had lived in Claremont, and every time she went to visit him they would trek through the nature trails on and around the highest nearby mountain. He fell off a ladder in August while repainting his garage and currently resided in Floral Acres, the local cemetery.

Amalfia: u could have found that out from anyone.

Deathdreamer: maybe. but i found it out cause i'm a violet & u can be 2.

Her vision blurred so much it became hard to read. She thought it might be her contacts making her eyes water, but in fact she was tearing up. Amanda wanted to believe it was due to grief for Uncle Pete or fear of the man who might be lurking outside her window. In reality, another fear brought her to the verge of weeping: the dread of hopes raised only to be dashed.

Amalfia: u r soooooooooo full of it.

Deathdreamer: no, amalfia. the corps wants u. they can make u what u were always meant 2 be. open the window & I will prove it.

She swiveled her office chair toward the window. The black drape resembled a magician's cloak, waiting to be swept aside to unveil miracles.

This is so nuts, she thought, striving to be sensible. Blotting her eyes, she pivoted back toward the computer to dissuade herself.

Amalfia: i can't. my parents will miss me. & i have a chem test 2morrow.

The excuses sounded pathetic even to her. Deathdreamer did not relent.

Deathdreamer: aren't u tired of pretending? isn't it time u asked—r u a poser or a violet? r u amanda ... or amalfia????????????

Amanda spread her hands over her naked scalp, freckled with its ridiculous fake node points, unable to reply.

Deathdreamer: i can't come back after 2nite. yr decision???

Amalfia: |

The cursor blinked for her answer. Amanda stared at the blank space next to her Violet name, for it summed up her life—fantasy without follow-up, a persona with no identity behind it.

Without entering her choice, she got up from the computer, took one of the candle sconces from the

219

vanity table, and went to the window. As she flung the black cloth to the floor, the figure standing outside glanced up from the glowing display of his PDA. She raised the sash and unhooked the screen, which he slid out and set aside.

Amanda had always pictured Deathdreamer as being a boy little older than herself, but the man who smiled at her in the candle's glow was at least in his mid-thirties and did not look like the typical pseudo-Violet. His black clothing was functional, not aesthetic—a cat burglar's outfit. He had neatly styled blond hair and black brows, suggesting a dye job. And the eyes, set deep beneath those brows, needed no lenses to give them their violet fire.

"Hello, Amalfia," he said.

18

The Ash Field

Among the plains and mesas west of Albuquerque, New Mexico, a thorny fence of wooden posts and barbed wire hemmed in a twenty-acre sprawl of dusty earth and brittle brush. A few head of cattle listlessly ambled the land's perimeter, but they were for show, to make outsiders believe this compound was simply another ranch. For this patch of desert nurtured a far more precious commodity than livestock—one that had to be isolated and protected from the mass of common humanity.

A large, low, adobe-style building squatted at the center of the property, its brick walls a burnt umber in the stretching shafts of daybreak as Serena Mfume rumbled up the dirt road toward it in a rented Jeep. To Serena, who spent most of her late teens and early adulthood here, this was a sort of homecoming. Yet the sight of the stark pueblo structure—part bunkhouse, part temple—did not inspire smiles, but rather a reverential pensiveness, as if she were paying respects at a grave site. The burial mound where her youth was interred.

The severity of her mood only intensified when she arrived at the adobe complex, knowing that she had to confront the traumas of both the past and the future. The sound that greeted her as she got out of the Jeep drove the point home. The dry, brisk air of the desert morning quavered with the strangled groans and squeals of people in torment. Serena recognized the cries in an instant; she had made them herself on several occasions.

They could only have come from the Ash Field.

Serena sighed. She'd hoped that by arriving at dawn, she might meet with Simon before he began the day's training. Alas, Master McCord never was one for letting his acolytes sleep in.

Bypassing the main entrance to the pueblo, Serena went around the western face of the building, toward the place of pain. This ranch served as the private boot camp where Simon McCord indoctrinated his inner circle of handpicked disciples—conduits he believed had exceptional abilities worthy of his tutelage. To Simon, Violets had an obligation to consecrate their entire lives to the divine duty given them by God. Anything less was sacrilege, and Master McCord used his grueling practice regimen to weed out the weak of will. Among his hapless acolytes, the Ash Field had earned notoriety as the worst of all these exercises.

It resembled nothing more than a vacant square of dirt about twenty feet to a side, the soil distinguished from the surrounding desert by its color—darker in some spots, lighter in others. When not in use, the Field was covered by a broad canvas tarp, anchored in place by heavy metal rods and stakes to protect the sacred ground from the wind and infrequent rain. But today the cover had been drawn back to reveal the Ash Field's singular quintessence of dust: soot imported by the sackful from Auschwitz and Dachau, Hiroshima and Nagasaki, from napalmed villages in Vietnam and from Ground Zero in New York. Anywhere the human form had been reduced to its elemental carbon and pulverized to a fine powder.

Upon this bed of crematoria compost reposed a dozen figures robed in white linen. Tattooed node points pocked the sheen of their shaved heads like craters. A few knelt, hunched and mumbling in a kind of prayer, yet heaving as if about to retch. Others lay disarrayed like reaped wheat, torsos twisted and limbs awry. All but one squealed in anguish. Only the group's focal figure remained as silent and serene as a pyramid, his legs folded beneath him, head bowed, hands pressed together beneath his chin.

As she approached, Serena could only see the back of the man's egg-shaped head with its jutting moth-wing ears, but she would have known who it was even with her eyes closed. Only Master Simon McCord seemed impervious to the Ash Field.

For a Violet, the strongest possible touchstone for a soul was a piece of the dead individual's body, be it blood, bone, or flesh. Traversing a common cemetery could prove fatal for an untrained conduit, for a dozen souls might start knocking at once, and their battle for dominance of the Violet's brain could easily result in a lethal seizure. To set foot on the Ash Field was akin to walking through a hundred churchyards in a single step, for it contained microscopic particles from literally thousands of corpses—thousands of touchstones for thousands of souls, all of whom could try to inhabit a Violet simultaneously.

One of the acolytes, a pink-pale young man with barely visible Nordic-blond eyebrows who'd been grunting from the effort of maintaining control, abruptly shrieked and grabbed his head. He dropped into the dust, wriggling as if being devoured by worms, the gray grounds of skeletons sticking to his sweat-soaked face. When a froth of spittle foamed from his mouth, the student next to him, a waifish Vietnamese girl, darted worried glances at him even as she strived, whimpering, to defend herself from the onslaught of dispossessed spirits.

"Leave him," Simon commanded when she moved to aid her convulsing classmate. "He must learn."

Serena waited at the threshold of the Ash Field, partly out of deference for the lesson in progress but mostly from her own aversion to the ordeal. She watched as, one by one, the stricken students stilled the cacophony in their minds, mastering their bodies enough to return to a kneeling position, although some still shuddered with the struggle. After several minutes, only the pale young man remained cataleptic, yet Master McCord showed no indication that he would end the exercise anytime soon. Serena knew that Simon considered it an affront for anyone to tread on the Ash Field in shoes, so she commenced her own protective mantra and removed her steel-toed boots.

I've got peace like a river, she recited silently. *I've got peace like a river. I've got peace like a river in my soul . . .*

The instant the bare sole of her left foot imprinted the peppery dirt, the souls stampeded her, their immaterial essences clawing at and clinging to her consciousness like a horde of ravening beggars. Disjointed memories flooded her mind—visions of lost loves and searing death, happy children and sadistic soldiers, all blurring into incomprehensibility like a pack of riffled playing cards. Serena's legs deadened with a numbing paralysis, but she refused to allow them to collapse beneath her. As Simon had taught her, she let the rhythms of the old spiritual from her childhood soothe and sustain her, matching her breaths to their cadence.

I've got love like an ocean I've got love like an ocean.
I've got love like an ocean in my soul ...

The desperate dead continued to bombard her, but the shell of Serena's will held them at a remove, as if they were hailstones glancing off a roof. With only a coltish tremble to her stride, she walked forward to stand at attention at Simon's side.

"Ah, Serena." He rose to greet her, entirely at ease, as if refreshed from a pleasant nap. "I trust you've come with news of the Violet Killer."

"Yes, sir. But he is the least of our worries." She restrained the urge to breathe through her mouth as she spoke; Simon would no doubt view her huffing and puffing as a sign of weakness. But she did not cease chanting her mantra in her mind, even for a second. "I've discovered another matter that needs our immediate attention. One we should discuss ... privately."

"I see." He surveyed his prostrate disciples, still

quivering from the strain of the test they'd endured. "Very well—you are all dismissed. And take *him* with you."

He indicated the pallid young man, whose face had darkened to a grotesque shade of magenta as he gasped for air and coughed up spit. Simon clucked his tongue as a couple of the man's fellow students draped his limp arms around their shoulders and dragged him from the Ash Field. "You know, if he weren't William Wilkes's son, I wouldn't even bother," Master McCord remarked, loud enough for everyone present to hear. "Now, then, what is this new crisis?"

Serena withheld her answer until the last of the students departed for the pueblo. Some of them could only marshal the energy to crawl from the Ash Field on all fours. Serena herself wished she could have this conversation in a more relaxed location, but Simon didn't move. "It's the Corps," she said at last. "They're trying to make us obsolete."

Master McCord gave a chuckle of disdain. "Wishful thinking on their part!"

"They could succeed. They've isolated the gene responsible for conduit ability and they're implanting it in ordinary people. And Evan Markham's helping them."

Simon's amusement evaporated as quickly as a water droplet on a hot griddle. Although he was legendary for his incandescent temper, Serena had never seen him so furious.

"Tell me." Choked with rage, his voice barely rose above a whisper. "Tell me *everything*."

Serena related what little she knew about Carl Pancrit and Project Persephone, praying that Master McCord would not vent his wrath on the bearer of bad news.

"*Blasphemy.*" Simon's eyes flared with violet fire. "You were quite right to come to me about this matter, Serena. Tell no one else."

"No one," Serena agreed, but did not mention that Natalie Lindstrom and her family were already involved.

Her obedience mollified him. "You understand, don't you, Serena? Only God's chosen ones may serve as the emissaries of the Next World. For anyone else to usurp our ordained power is a *sin.*"

"Yes, sir. What do want me to do?"

"Destroy the project. Obliterate it so that it can never be resurrected."

Serena's frown lines calcified as she thought of Calvin Criswell and of Natalie's attraction to him. "What about the . . . test subjects? What do I do about them?"

Simon McCord bent to scoop a fistful of the Ash Field from the ground at his feet. "It is your duty to eliminate the unworthy."

He took hold of her left hand and let the dust of multitudes sift into her open palm.

19

Airport Insecurity

When she heard Calvin lightly snoring beside her in the morning, Natalie chose to slip out of bed without waking him. He needed the rest, and she had a to-do list that would have daunted even Hercules.

Callie did not make the travel preparations any easier. More sullen and snappish than usual, she griped about how early it was and refused to get out of bed. For his part, Wade merely seemed flustered and tongue-tied, as if unsure whether to acknowledge his daughter's dalliance or pretend that it hadn't happened. By the time Natalie helped both of them finish packing and returned to the living room, only a shallow depression remained in the sofa bed.

"He's in the bathroom," Callie grumbled as she descended the stairs, behind her mother. "And he takes for-*ev*-er."

"Callie!"

Her daughter trudged on into the kitchen and helped herself to a glass of orange juice. Natalie vowed that she would give that girl a good, long lecture about respect just as soon as they didn't have serial killers and evil doctors to worry about.

Although Natalie had removed the latex gloves after she got up that morning, she put them back on before climbing the stairs to check on Calvin. She had barely tapped on the bathroom door when he yanked it open and spread his arms wide with the flair of a gymnast landing his dismount.

"*Ta-da!*" His right hand still held one of the twin-blade razors Natalie used to shave her legs, and a dollop of shaving cream still foamed on his upper lip, but his chin was smooth and fuzzless. He rubbed it with his free hand for emphasis. "Well?"

Natalie laughed and clapped her gloved hands. "Told you you'd look cute without the facial fur. Cuter, I should say."

For the first time, she studied his features with the care of a portraitist. The slight upturn to the nose and the pointiness of the chin gave his face its whimsy, along with the endearing tendency of his broad, full cheeks to dimple when he grinned. But the corners of his large eyes had a downward slant, and bags had begun to puff beneath them, giving them a mournful cast. If the masks of Comedy and Tragedy ever mated, Natalie thought, Calvin would be their offspring. She could hardly wait to draw him.

It made her happy to see him in a joking mood again, but she could tell from the way his eyelids and mouth quivered that the souls were knocking louder than ever. The tattered remains of a doubled sheet of aluminum foil still covered his head, but it didn't fit well over the springy curls of his sandy hair. He would never make it through airport security that way.

"Losing the beard was a good start," Natalie said, strolling to the bathroom sink, "but we need to go a bit further." She opened a drawer and took out the electric clippers she used to shave her own head.

When she plugged in the shears and came at him, Calvin shied away. "Whoa there, Delilah! Leave me some hair."

She peeled off her wig to reveal her own bare scalp, striped with the white bands of double-sided tape still stuck to it. "You won't find any sympathy here, pal. Now, kneel."

She pointed imperiously to the floor at her feet. Whispering the Alphabet Mantra, Calvin got to his knees and removed the foil from his head. He seemed more afraid to lose its protection than his hair.

It only took a couple of minutes for Natalie to plow the locks from Calvin's head, leaving him a prickly lawn of stubble through which one could see the shiny skin of his scalp. When he stood and looked at their twin reflections in the mirror, she stroked his denuded crown with her gloved hand. "There! Now you look like a *real* Violet."

"Yeah," he said tonelessly. His grin did not return, and he immediately resumed muttering the alphabet.

He cheered up a bit when she plastered an even thicker layer of foil over his cranium, then covered the crinkly sheets with bandages and surgical tape from her first-aid kit to insulate and disguise the metal.

"Glad you survived that tumor operation," Natalie remarked as they examined the result, and Calvin laughed in spite of his anxiety.

To keep Sanjay Prashad from guessing their travel plans, Natalie sent Wade and Callie on ahead in her dad's car without any luggage, as if they were simply going to spend another day at the library. She and Calvin planned to meet them in the parking lot of Downtown Disney, the shopping center near Disneyland in Anaheim, once they'd had a chance to ditch the Corps Security agent. They waited about a quarter hour after her father drove off, then loaded the bags into her Volvo and prepared to leave, with Calvin hiding his bandaged head under the Padres cap.

When the garage door opened, though, they saw that Prashad wasn't the only person they needed to worry about.

A woman with wooden beads threaded into her long blond hair paced the gutter in front of the condo, hugging a fringed gypsy shawl around her shoulders to ward the early-morning chill off the bare arms and décolletage exposed by her low-cut corset top. As the Volvo emerged, the woman clopped up the driveway in her spike-heeled sandals to block the car.

Calvin let his head droop into his open palms. "Good God. Tranquillity ..."

Only after Natalie saw his mortification did she make the connection: the topless model dressed like a Greek muse that she'd seen in the painting on the easel in his apartment He'd done a good likeness. Indeed, the way the woman's heavy mascara had trickled streaks of black across the dark rose blush of her cheeks made her look like a portrait whose paint had started to run.

"Cal!" The Volvo's rolled-up windows dampened but could not seal out her screech. "Don't think I don't know it's you! That stupid disguise doesn't fool me for a second."

He heaved a sigh and lowered his window. "Trank, what're you doing here?"

She put her hands to her chest as if the shock would give her a heart attack. "Oh, puh-*leeease!* What am *I* doing here? You leave me at your place half-naked, without any explanation, without ever calling to let me know you're okay. Then I find out you've spent three whole nights with this ... this ... this *skank*, and you dare to ask me what *I'm* doing here?"

Calvin glanced at Natalie for her reaction, his face as red as the ace of hearts. "Trank, you don't understand—"

"No, I don't! If you want to go whoring around, at least have the courtesy to break up with me first."

Natalie's mouth fell open in amazement at the woman's sheer temerity. "Now, wait just a minute—"

Calvin cut her off by removing his baseball cap and indicating his bandages. "I have a *brain tumor,* Tranquillity. Natalie's taking me out of town for a few days to see a specialist."

Tranquillity coughed up a laugh. "Oh-ho-ho! That's the best one I've heard yet! Like *she's* some kind of brain surgeon. I know exactly what you're up to, Cal, and I am *so* going to *get* you for it. You hear me? You are *so* going to get it."

She sneered this prediction through teeth clenched in a bulldog underbite, turned with a sweep of her shawl, and stalked off.

Natalie clicked her fingernails against the steering wheel, waiting for Calvin to turn toward her, but he didn't seem able to. "You want to go talk to her?" she asked, making no attempt to conceal her dislike for the idea.

"No." He rolled up his window. "Drive."

Natalie maneuvered the Volvo out of the driveway. As they rode away from the condo, neither of them could keep from watching Tranquillity get into the red Mazda she'd parked across the street.

Natalie remembered the way Calvin had looked at her as they shared the sofa bed, the kiss they'd almost consummated. The sudden appearance of another woman threw a penumbra of mistrust over all the feelings of the previous night. Had Calvin simply been "whoring around," to use Tranquillity's choice phrase?

"So who was *that?*" she asked Calvin. Her tone cautioned him that his response would answer several unspoken questions, as well.

"A mistake." Despite the green contact lenses he wore, she could see the genuine shame and fear shining in his eyes. "I swear."

"I don't doubt it," Natalie said, her voice warm with arch amusement. She could hardly hold his past mistakes against him while they were still running from one of hers, could she?

Tranquillity had distracted Natalie so much that she'd forgotten to check whether Sanjay Prashad was tailing them. She was actually relieved when she saw the black Mitsubishi framed in her rear-view mirror, for she needed to monitor him in order to lose him.

As planned, she and Calvin arrived at Downtown Disney as the morning crowds awaited the opening of Disneyland. After parking the Volvo, they strolled together through the open-air mall between a tropical-themed restaurant styled as a fire-spewing stone temple and a four-colored cartoon edifice of specialty boutiques and souvenir shops. Out of the corner of her eye, Natalie caught a glimpse of Prashad's diminutive figure darting through the throng of milling tourists to keep pace with them.

She hitched the handle of her canvas tote onto her shoulder to cue Calvin, who veered off into a store that vended Disney-character clothing. When forced to choose whom to follow, Prashad stuck with Natalie, as she had hoped. She led him in and out of several establishments, pretending to window-shop, tarrying long enough to give Calvin time to change clothes and transfer their luggage from the Volvo into her dad's car, which Wade had parked in a lot adjacent to theirs. Then she ducked into a women's restroom, where Prashad could not follow her, and changed out of her T-shirt and jeans and into the sundress she'd folded into the tote bag. She also swapped her short, black wig for a brown, shoulder-length one, traded her boots for flip-flops, and donned a pair of Minnie Mouse sunglasses—as un-Natalie an outfit as she could cobble together.

Prashad did not follow her when she emerged. Instead, he lingered outside the ladies' room and goosenecked his head to peer inside every time the door swung open, attracting any number of affronted scowls from the women who passed in and out.

Natalie looped back to the parking lot where her father's Camry waited, employing her peripheral vision to make sure that she'd left the Corps Security agent behind. Calvin stood beside the car as she approached, but she would not have recognized him if she hadn't known whom to expect. He wore a pair of her dad's old Dockers, which were an inch too short for Cal, a Mickey Mouse sweatshirt that he'd bought in the store where she'd left him, wrap-around mirror shades, and, to cover his bandaged scalp, a cap with a pair of jumbo-size Mouse Ears.

"Whaddaya think?" he asked, modeling the outfit for her.

She chuckled. "Your own mother wouldn't recognize you."

"She tries not to." He jerked his head toward the car. "We should probably get moving. Your kid's already asking 'Are we there yet?'" He opened the front passenger door for her. Although he feigned nonchalance, Natalie could hear the constant whisper from his moving lips.

"I pledge allegiance to the flag of the United States of America, and to the Republic for which it stands ... "

Apparently, the Alphabet Mantra did not work as well as it had at first, so Calvin was experimenting with others. The revelation made Natalie uneasy.

With Callie and Wade in the car, she didn't have a chance to chat further with Calvin about Tranquillity. Indeed, little conversation of any kind occurred during the drive to LAX. Since Natalie still worried about her nine-year-old being smothered by an exploding airbag, she made Callie sit in the backseat, next to Calvin, which only made the girl sulk even more. Calvin was too preoccupied to mind, though, for a new wave of knocking souls inundated him. The Pledge of Allegiance failed him, so he switched to Beatles tunes, singing the lyrics to "Nowhere Man" and "Yesterday" in a baritone thin and reedy with desperation. Callie growled and covered her ears, while Wade ignored the proverbial elephant in the car by concentrating on his driving to the exclusion of all else. All Natalie could do was cast an anxious glance over her shoulder and tell Calvin, "It's going to be okay." She began to wonder if that were true, however.

The situation did not improve when they got to the airport. The tension increased even before they got out of the car, when Natalie insisted that her daughter wear dark glasses to cover her violet irises while they traveled.

"Why do I need to put on these lame glasses?" Callie flailed the shades, which, like Natalie's, featured Minnie Mouse on their plastic rims. "I don't care if people know I'm a Violet."

Natalie exhaled to calm herself, wondering if she'd gone too far in cultivating her child's self-esteem. She was glad that she'd raised Callie to be proud of who and what she was ... except when they needed to travel incognito. "Honey, we don't want to attract attention."

"Why not? Violets are cool. Even *he* wants to be one." The girl glared at Calvin, who still hummed Lennon and McCartney hits with frantic shrillness.

Her patrician disdain would have made Simon McCord proud.

"That's enough, young lady." Only later did it occur to Natalie that this was the first time she hadn't called Callie "baby girl." She unbuckled her seat belt and leaned over the seat back until her eyes were inches from her daughter's. "It's for your own safety. Now, you can either wear the glasses, or I can get you a pair of contacts like Calvin and I have. Would you like that better?"

"No." Callie pouted, but lost some of her nerve. She slid the shades on with a haughty air, as if it had been her idea to wear them all along.

Having subdued Callie for the moment, Natalie redirected her concern toward Calvin. Facial tics tried to distend and reshape his expression, and his failed mantras fragmented into gibberish. Occasionally, an exclamation such as *"Help"* or *"Don't"* burst from his mouth in a pitch and inflection that did not belong to Calvin. These abortive inhabitations became so frequent as Natalie escorted him into the terminal that she might as well have been taking him through a graveyard.

"Good thing we aren't attracting any attention," Callie murmured to her mother, as Calvin's mental-patient mumbling drew the stares of everyone they passed.

Wearing a pair of black leather gloves that she'd dug out from among her old teen-rebel wear, Natalie kept a tight hold on Calvin's hand and prayed they wouldn't have trouble getting through the security checkpoint. In anticipation, she'd taken off his Mouse

Ears so that the guards could see the gauze she'd wound around his scalp. She would have given him a pair of her Playtex gloves to wear, too, but she worried that his bizarre appearance already made him look like a fugitive from a sanitarium.

As she expected, the hidden layer of folded foil set off the metal detector when Calvin walked through it, causing the screener to stop him for a personal inspection.

"It's a plate in his head," Natalie hastened to explain. "He had a tumor removed."

"Uh-huh." The screener, a balding black man almost a foot shorter than her, grabbed his handheld metal detector. "Would you step over here, sir?"

He waved the wand over Calvin's torso and up and down his legs, but the detector only blared when the sensor swept over his scalp.

With impeccable timing, Calvin chose that moment to suffer another of his micro-inhabitations. He broke away from Natalie's side and gaped at her and the screener as if they'd materialized out of thin air. *"Who are you people? What are you doing to me?"*

Hearing the commotion, other security personnel tightened a circle around them. Calvin squeezed his eyes shut and wrapped his arms around his head.

Natalie lowered her voice to a confidential whisper. "He has these episodes. Brain damage."

Dubious, the screener called to Calvin. "Can you understand me, sir?"

Calvin's posture relaxed as he muttered to himself for a few seconds, then opened his eyes. "Yeah ... sorry about that."

"You with this lady?"

Calvin returned to Natalie's side, took her hand. "Yes."

The screener frowned at Natalie. "You sure he's gonna be okay?"

"Oh, yeah," she lied. "I'll give him a tranquilizer before we board."

The man evaluated both Calvin and the line of irate passengers building up behind him, and evidently decided that Calvin wasn't worth the hassle. "Make sure you ask a staff member if you need assistance," he told Natalie. "If he has any more problems, they won't let him on the plane."

"Yes, sir."

The screener waved them on through the checkpoint. When they were out of his hearing, Natalie whispered in Calvin's ear. "You hear that? You've *got* to keep control."

"I'm trying, believe me." He kept his face bowed to the floor, mouthing the words to "Ticket to Ride" as they hurried to the gate.

If Calvin's ostensible illness had a plus side, it enabled their party to board the plane first along with the handicapped passengers. To Natalie's relief, Calvin remained cocooned in a state of nearly catatonic concentration while they awaited takeoff. Because she'd summoned air-crash victims for the National Travel Safety Board, Natalie had suffered a phobia of flying for most of her adult life, so it felt weirdly gratifying to be the calm one for a change, offering comfort to someone else during a plane trip. She slipped her gloved hand into Calvin's, entwining her fingers with his and squeezing, remembering how Dan had eased her fear with the same gesture during their flights together.

Wade and Callie sat across the aisle from Natalie so they could share the window, for they actually enjoyed the view from twenty thousand feet. Her father even talked like the whole trip was one big family vacation, although that may have been simply his attempt to brighten the mood.

"You know, Boston's where I met Grandma Nora," he remarked to Callie as the jet rose into the clouds. "She was fresh out of the School, working the Strangler case, and I was trying to sell a new heating system to the Boston Police. Grandma Nora always complained about the cold, so I think she helped me close the deal."

Natalie couldn't help but eavesdrop, for she had never heard this story. Her father had seldom spoken of his first marriage after Nora went insane when Natalie was only five years old.

Callie favored Wade with her only smile of the day. "Was it love at first sight?"

"Yeah, pretty much." He chuckled. "Like Romeo and Juliet, only worse. All her Violet friends hated me, and my whole family thought I was throwing my life away."

"But you were happy, right?" Callie cast a sidelong glance at Calvin and her mother.

"For a while, yeah." The years seemed to settle upon Wade as he gazed into the blue abyss outside the window. "It'll be good to get back to New England. I miss it."

"Me, too," Callie said, although she'd only visited the East Coast during a couple of summer vacations. She pulled the plastic shopping sack of activity books she'd brought with her onto her lap. "I'm thinking about going to school in New Hampshire."

She wouldn't, Natalie thought, aghast. But she did. From her bag, Callie pulled out a full-color, glossy brochure, heavily creased in the middle, its cover dominated by a pillared Victorian mansion that might have seemed majestic or stately to one who did not know what went on inside it.

The Iris Semple Conduit Academy: An Introduction, declared the florid script beneath the picture.

"Where did you get that?" Natalie snapped.

"From the trash, where you always throw it." Callie leafed through the pages with deliberate languor, admiring photos of happy Violet children sharing hijinks in the dormitories, playing soccer among trees fiery with orange-and-red autumn leaves, and mastering arcane arts in classrooms over-seen by shaven-headed Violet sages. "It doesn't look like such a bad place."

Natalie cursed the Corps's direct-marketing program, whose slick propaganda littered her mailbox with relentless regularity. She'd bet every dime she had that not a single actual Violet posed for those photos, only a bunch of pretty people rented from a modeling agency, the color of their eyes digi-tally shifted to purple with a photo-editing program.

Letting go of Calvin's hand, Natalie dodged a passing flight attendant to lean across the aisle and snatch the brochure from her daughter's grasp. She crumpled the booklet in her fist. "Don't you *ever* let me catch you with this again."

"That's not fair!" Callie shrilled. "I just wanted to *look* at it. *I* don't mess with *your* stupid decisions."

Natalie understood which decisions Callie meant, and she might have shouted if the surrounding passengers hadn't already begun to glare at the two of them. "We'll talk about this later, young lady," she hissed. "You have no idea the trouble I've gone through to keep you from—"

"Natalie."

She twisted around in her seat to find Calvin with his arms wrapped around his shoulders, shivering as if in a subzero chill. "He ... he was sitting here," he stammered. "In the seat pocket ... somebody planted a gun for him ... but an air marshal shot him ..."

He lost the ability to speak then, but he'd said enough. Natalie scrambled to unfasten both her own seat belt and his. "Fight him, Calvin," she urged. "Don't let him in."

Never in her life had Natalie so wished for a SoulScan unit and its hated Panic Button. Ordinarily, she wouldn't subject her worst enemy to the nerve-searing electroshock, but she feared that Calvin didn't have the experience or training to cast out an inhabiting soul on his own. Although a good jolt from Serena's stun gun would have done the job, too, Natalie hadn't brought it because she knew security would never have let her take it on the plane. She'd have to find some other way of driving the spirit out of Calvin's brain. But what?

She slung her purse over her shoulder in the

unlikely event it contained anything that would help her, then grabbed Calvin's hands. Leveraging what weight she had in her thin frame, she got him onto his feet and yoked his arm around her neck. Semiconscious now, he listed heavily against her, dragging his feet as she tugged him toward the aft lavatories.

A flight attendant hastened up the aisle to intercept them, her expression of alarm made melodramatic by her excessive rouge and eye shadow. "Is something wrong?"

Natalie forced a smile. "Oh, no. Just a little airsickness."

Calvin lifted his drowsing head, and murmured what sounded like a prayer in foreign syllables of an exotic, lyrical cadence.

Arabic.

The flight attendant's apprehension became bewilderment, and Natalie slapped a hand over Calvin's mouth. "Hold it in, honey," she told him in a cheery but pointed tone." "'Scuse us!"

She kept Calvin muffled as she pushed her way past the attendant and lurched on toward the rear of the plane. *Please, no*, she silently begged when she saw a paunchy businessman bouncing on the balls of his dress shoes in front of the lavatories, indicating that they were all occupied.

One of the restrooms opened and an elderly woman shuffled out, planting her cane as cautiously as if walking on stilts. "Sorry!" Natalie chirped to the businessman as she shoved Calvin through the door ahead of him. "It's an emergency."

She slammed the door and slid the lock shut, ignoring the businessman's angry thumping as she propped Calvin against the lavatory's tiny basin. There, beneath the paper-towel dispenser, the wall offered a 110-volt outlet for passengers who wanted to touch up their appearance with an electric razor or curling iron before touching down at their destination. If she could get Calvin to jam some metal in there ... but not for too long ...

Natalie dumped the contents of her purse into the bowl of the washbasin and pawed through them. When she uncovered Calvin's mouth, he keened the music of a muezzin calling the faithful in Mecca. His eyes nearly white as the irises rolled up underneath the lids, he abruptly switched to Middle Eastern-accented English.

"I failed Him," he wailed. "I failed in my martyrdom, and God did not let me into Heaven ..."

From the jumble of breath mints, loose change, makeup accessories, and wadded tissues that tumbled into the sink, Natalie fished out a pair of tweezers that she occasionally used to pluck her eyebrows. She bent the branches of the stainless-steel wishbone outward until the tips lined up with the slots of the outlet, then wrapped Calvin's flaccid fingers around the tweezers' closed end, cupping her gloved hands over his right hand to hold and maneuver it.

"I failed." Calvin's limp hand clenched in her grasp. *"But I will not fail again."*

Natalie tugged on his hand until the tips of the tweezers quivered in front of the socket, but the crook of Calvin's left arm wrapped around her neck like a python, constricting her breath and holding her at bay.

Struggling to retain her hold on his right fist, she stamped as hard as she could on his foot. The pain was enough to make him cry out and hunch forward, giving her enough slack in his arm to drive the tweezers into the outlet.

Although the gloves insulated her hands, Natalie fancied she could feel the current jangling her flesh like a struck tuning fork, but that may have been her own memories of the Panic Button. The lights in the lavatory barely flickered and the connection didn't spark or crackle. Even Calvin made no sound, for electrocution causes the diaphragm to contract, forbidding breath. The only indication of the agony he endured was the board-stiff posture of his body, which vibrated with strain as all of his muscles tightened at once.

How long was enough? How long was too much?

Natalie had no way of knowing. After a few seconds, she hammered her fists down on his clenched hand to loosen it from the tweezers and break the connection.

Freed from the paralyzing voltage, Calvin's muscles all relaxed at once. His arm slipped away from Natalie's throat, and his body folded like a deck chair, slumping him into a heap in front of the toilet. Crouching, Natalie removed one of her gloves and palpated his neck, and only when she detected a reviving pulse did she become aware of the frantic rapping on the door.

"Ma'am? Sir?" the flight attendant shouted from outside. "Do you need help? I can unlock this—"

"No, we're fine," Natalie called out, even though they weren't. "We'll be out in a minute," she added, even though they wouldn't.

Calvin rotated onto his side and drew his knees up to his chest. He either couldn't get up yet or didn't think it was worth the effort.

"Oh, God, Natalie," he croaked. "What am I gonna do?" Trapped tears fused his eyelashes together. Whether they were from pain or despair, she couldn't tell.

"You're going to get through this. We both will." And, since it was all she could do for him now, she put her glove back on and held his hand.

20

One for Practice

It took much of the morning for Evan to transfer custody of Amanda Bethany Pyne to Tackle and Block for transport to the White Sands facility along with the lab equipment. He didn't get to Boo's condo until almost nine and immediately sensed that something had changed. All the cars had disappeared from along the curb, including Sanjay Prashad's, and drawn shades closed the eyes of the windows.

Evan parked his rented Ford Taurus across the street and snatched his field glasses off the passenger seat, cursing Pancrit for making him his errand boy. If Evan had been watching Boo last night instead of sweet-talking that witless teenager, he would have known what was going on now.

Scanning the condo's façade with the binoculars, he could see no light filtering through the lace curtains in the living room or bedrooms. Ordinarily, either Boo or her father would be home-schooling Callie at that hour. Evan couldn't accept that they were gone, however, and he trained his attention so thoroughly on the empty residence that the loud rapping behind him startled him so much he nearly dropped the field glasses.

He turned to see a blond woman in a corset top

and peasant skirt knocking on the passenger-side window. She mimed cranking a handle, and he rolled the window down.

"If you're looking for Calvin Criswell, you're wasting your time." She exhaled spiced smoke into his car from the clove cigarette that still smoldered in her right hand. "He left a couple hours ago with his new girlfriend."

The news that Boo might be romantically involved with Criswell bored deep into Evan's chest. Nevertheless, he played coy, unsure whether this informant would turn out to be an asset or a liability, "What makes you think I'm looking for someone named Calvin ... Crispin, was it?"

The woman laughed and shook her head. "Oh, *puh-lease.* Calvin's a crook and you're a cop, right? I want to help you bust him. I saw the Indian guy staking out the place and waited for him to come back, but I guess he's still tailing Cal."

"Ah, yes—Detective Prashad." Despite years of experience in dissembling, Evan had difficulty maintaining a straight face as he became insta-cop. Good thing he'd put in his brown contacts before he came. "You're very perceptive, Ms. ...?"

"Moon. Tranquillity Moon."

"A pleasure, Ms. Moon." Setting aside the binoculars, he got out of the car and went around to shake her hand. "Detective Prashad and I would be grateful for any assistance you can offer our investigation."

"The pleasure is mine." She threw her cigarette butt on the sidewalk and ground it under her spike-heeled sandal. "From what I've seen, Cal's back in the forgery business, big-time."

"More than that, Ms. Moon. You're fortunate he didn't threaten your life." He nodded toward the condo with taciturn professionalism. "You say there's no one there now?"

"No. Cal said they had to go away for a few days."

"You know where?"

She smirked with sarcasm. "Like he's really going to tell his ex."

"Yes ... I see what you mean. Excuse me." Evan opened the car again and took a small, zippered pouch from the glove compartment "Would you mind accompanying me for a minute?"

"You want to take a statement?"

"Not yet. I want you to help me secure the crime scene."

A frown of misgiving crossed her face, but she toddled to keep up with him as he stalked across the street. "Don't you need a warrant for that?"

"No, ma'am. Thanks to you, we now have probable cause." When they reached the condo's door, Evan indicated the front step. "Wait here. I'll go around and let you in."

"If you say so." She glanced around at the adjacent condos, self-conscious.

She needn't have worried. Evan knew that, over the years, Boo's neighbors had become so inured to Corps Security agents harassing her that they wouldn't call the police even if they saw a stranger entering her home, as he was about to do.

He went around the garage to the end unit's

security gate, where he paused to unzip the pouch he'd brought from the car. Making sure that he was hidden from Tranquillity's sight, he took out a pair of surgical gloves that thinned like stretched taffy as he pulled them over his fingers. He then jimmied the gate's lock with a small screwdriver from the pouch.

Once inside the complex, Evan circled around to the condo's back door, which faced the community's pool and recreational center. Having cased the place many times during the past few weeks, he knew that, unlike the one on the front entrance, this door contained a large, four-paned window. Although it was broad daylight and anyone in the surrounding buildings might witness him, Evan sauntered up to the door without hesitation. Infiltration, after all, depends on attitude. Act guilty, and you arouse people's suspicions; behave like you belong there, and they assume you do.

Standing with his back to the courtyard to block a clear view of what he did, Evan pretended he actually possessed a key and was simply having trouble turning it in the lock. In reality, he took a diamond-edged glass cutter from his pouch and etched a small triangle from the corner of the pane closest to the doorknob. He punched the loose shard of glass inside and snaked his hand through the hole to flip the dead bolt and the lock on the knob. Barely a minute after he had left the front step, Evan entered Boo's home.

The back door opened into the kitchen, where it stood at a right angle to the door that connected with the garage. Although Evan had a switchblade in his pouch, he pulled a small, sharp paring knife from a butcher's block on Boo's counter and stuck it beneath the waistband of his jeans, tugging the tail of his black turtleneck down to cover the handle. He then passed through the dining area and living room to let Tranquillity in at the front door.

"Don't touch anything," he said, raising a hand to show her the gloves he wore. "Have to preserve the integrity of the crime scene."

"Whatever you say." She edged inside, wrapping her arms around her to make herself smaller and treading as if every step she took destroyed vital evidence. "You sure you don't want me to wait outside?"

"It's not safe." Evan shut the door and locked it. "You're a material witness now."

Her glum nod showed that she did not appreciate the distinction.

"You say Criswell and his ... *girlfriend* were taking a trip. They say how they were traveling?"

Tranquillity shook her head.

"Let's see if we can find out. He crossed to the desk he'd noted when passing through the living room and booted up Boo's computer. Tapping keys with his rubber fingers, he called up her Internet access software and opened the file of e-mail saved on her hard drive. At the top of the list of subject lines and e-mail addresses was an "E-Ticket Confirmation" from Southwest Airlines.

Tranquillity peered over his shoulder as he brought up the Lindstrom family's itinerary. "Find anything?"

"Possibly." Intrigued, Evan could not resist a slight smile. "LAX to BOS," the booking read. Boston: Bartholomew Wax's hometown. During the hours he had spent in Evan's head, trying to look busy as he wasted time in Pancrit's laboratory, Dr. Wax had often daydreamed nostalgically of Beantown in general ... and one museum in particular. Now, why do you suppose Boo would want to go there?

"Ms. Moon ... do you recognize this name?" He stepped to the left of the computer and pointed to Wade Lindstrom's ticket reservation at the bottom of the screen as he slid his right hand underneath his shirttail.

She bent forward to read the name. "I don't know. Looks the same as Cal's girl—"

Evan smothered her mouth with one latex-covered hand, tilting her head back and anchoring her against his body while his other hand swept the knife up to slash her throat. Tranquillity bugged out her eyes, as much from disbelief as from pain, while her arterial blood jetted out to spatter the computer monitor and keyboard.

Evan hugged her against him. "You've been a great help," he murmured as she squirmed. "Could you do me one more favor?" His lips brushed her ear. *"Say hi to Dan Atwater."*

The strength melted from Tranquillity's limbs, and Evan found himself supporting her weight. The spray from the wound drooped to a drizzle with the falling blood pressure, and her head lolled back upon Evan's shoulder, widening the gash across her neck. When he was reasonably certain that she wouldn't bleed all over his clothes, Evan arranged her cadaver in the center of the living-room floor, pushed up the sleeves of his turtleneck, and set to work. *"One times one is one,"* he murmured to protect himself from the dead woman's soul. *"One times two is two ... "*

Evan had never killed for his own sake before. His previous victims had all been Violets, all of them his friends. He'd delivered them to death as an act of mercy, relieving them of the daily onslaught of agonized souls vying to inhabit them. After putting them out of their misery as quickly and painlessly as he could, he defiled their corpses after the fact, dressing up the murders with the trappings of sadism in order to disguise his motivation—to create the fictional psychopath known as the Violet Killer.

He now repeated the M.O. he had invented, gouging out Tranquillity's eyes and slitting open her belly to draw the worm of her small intestine out to form a talismanic circle around her body. But on this occasion, he did it solely for his own benefit. To vent ten years of fury at languishing in Corps headquarters' soul-cage oubliette. To protest how Boo had betrayed him, scorning his gold in favor of dross like Atwater and Criswell. To poison the haven she had created for herself and Atwater's bastard by making this clean, cozy home a touchstone for the pitiful soul of this petty, stupid woman whose entrails he spread over the carpet.

And, most important, to practice for the next time.

21

The Doctor and the Gardner

The Lindstrom family made it through the rest of the flight to Boston by trading seats so that Calvin did not have to contend with the touchstone for a terrorist. When they finally landed around five o'clock, Eastern Time, none of them possessed energy for anything more than checking into their hotel and eating a dispirited meal of burgers and fries. If this really had been a family vacation, Natalie might have reserved the adjacent room in addition to the one in which they were staying, since a sandwiched pair of locked doors could be opened to connect the two rooms. That way, each of them could have had his or her own bed. Because this was not an ordinary trip, however, Natalie decided they should stay together for greater safety, so she and Calvin ended up sharing one queen-size bed while Wade and Callie took the other. Needless to say, this arrangement meant Natalie and Calvin again had to try to doze off fully dressed.

Calvin continued to fade in and out, fleetingly possessed by unpredictable spirits. When bedtime came, Natalie did not take any chances. She gave him twice the recommended dose of some over-the-counter sleeping pills and lashed his wrists and ankles together with pairs of panty hose that she bought at the pharmacy where she got the drug.

Deciding what to do with Calvin the following morning was far more difficult. His condition would surely draw attention if he accompanied them out in public, and Natalie didn't know how she would handle another inhabitation like the one he'd endured on the plane. With Carl Pancrit and Evan both hunting for them, however, Natalie refused to leave any member of her group alone and unguarded. After a hasty continental breakfast, she chose to risk taking Calvin with her when she, Callie, and Wade caught a cab to 2 Palace Road in Boston's Back Bay district.

The Isabella Stewart Gardner Museum had once been the "summer palace" of its eponymous owner, the indomitable society matron known as Mrs. Jack after the late husband from whom she inherited her millions. Modeled upon a fifteenth-century Venetian palazzo, the rectangular, four-story manse had remained, by Mrs. Jack's decree, virtually unchanged since her death in 1924. Shaded by trees that had grown to maturity over the past eight decades, the unimposing walls of gray stone and roof of red tile barely hinted at the glories they embraced. Only the baroque sculpting of the arched windows promised the kind of beauty that could be called "art."

When Natalie had conceived the idea of using *Storm on the Sea of Galilee* or one of the other stolen paintings as a touchstone to summon the elusive Dr. Wax, she imagined doing so in a sleepy, sparsely attended gallery patronized only by cognoscenti. She had not considered the sensation created by the largest unsolved art heist in modern history, nor the phenomenon of the missing paintings' equally mysterious return. Tourists of seemingly every nationality and ethnicity lined the queue that snaked out the entrance and down the sidewalk in front of the museum, and the Lindstrom party had to wait almost an hour to get inside, with Callie constantly grousing about having to stand still for so long.

The Gardner had milked the publicity for all it was worth, touting the restored collection as the "Reunion Exhibition." A banner as big as a Times Square advertisement hung in the foyer with the jubilant greeting WELCOME HOME, REMBRANDT! beside a blow-up of the Dutch master's miniature self-portrait. Placards posted on stainless-steel stands related how, at 1:20 A.M. in the black morning of March 18, 1990, two men armed with pistols and disguised with fake mustaches gained entry to the museum by posing as police officers investigating a disturbance. Once they'd overpowered and incapacitated the guards on duty, they set about slashing canvases from their frames. The works they selected to steal seemed idiosyncratic to the point of being arbitrary, for they passed over invaluable pieces by Titian and Raphael in favor of some minor sketches by Degas.

It bore all the hallmarks of a Corps Security operation, Natalie thought—crude, brutal, yet effective. But what did these purloined masterpieces have to do with Project Persephone? Perhaps Dr. Wax could tell her … if she ever got the chance to speak with him.

There was one advantage to the spectacle the museum created around the recovered paintings: it made them easy to find. Signs pointed the way to each of the star attractions, saving Natalie the trouble of searching three floors of cavernous galleries for a single picture. Nevertheless, it took another half hour for her to reach *Storm on the Sea of Galilee*, in part because she had to tug Calvin through the museum's shifting throngs as if leading a blind man. Ever babbling under his breath, he'd taken to shutting his eyes while he walked, inching his feet forward as if each step might tumble him over a precipice. Hardly anyone took notice of him amidst the honeycomb buzz of activity in the halls, however, for Natalie had covered his bandages with the Padres baseball cap again.

Wade followed the two of them, keeping a tight hold of Callie's hand so she didn't get separated from them in the crowds. Eventually, they made it to a large room whose walls bore the metallic sheen of green satin embroidered with gold fleur-de-lis.

"Well, there it is," Wade said when he saw the mob of spectators encircling one of the room's paintings. "Now what do we do?"

An excellent question, Natalie thought. She had assumed she'd be able to get close enough to touch the painting in an unobtrusive fashion to summon Wax. She now saw how impossible that would be. Red velvet rope fenced in the Rembrandt, holding people at a distance of two feet from the canvas. A docent stood to one side of the picture, lecturing a group of more than a dozen visitors, while a portly guard attended a short distance away, resting a hand on the pistol in his hip-holster as if daring any thief to challenge his machismo. The Gardner was clearly determined that its stolen masterpieces would never disappear again.

Natalie peered at the Rembrandt in helpless vexation. Because Mrs. Gardner's will had forbidden any alteration in the arrangement of the museum's display, the three-foot-high gilt frame had stayed in place, enclosing a barren patch of wallpaper, for more than fifteen years. The art-restoration experts who'd replaced the canvas in its frame had incorporated a narrow matte border to cover the frayed fringe of the painting where the thieves had cut the centuries-old canvas from its original stretcher. Seeing the original, Natalie marveled again at how Calvin had created an uncanny copy working only from the flat, dull reproductions printed in books. Barely three yards away, the picture seemed close enough for her to press her palm against, yet a moat of humanity isolated it from her.

"Maybe we can create a distraction," she suggested to her father because she had no better ideas. "You and Callie could make some kind of commotion to catch people's attention. I should only need a few seconds ..." Trying to be optimistic, Natalie understated the time usually required to summon a soul. If it took several minutes, as it often did, that trigger-happy guard would have them all up against a wall with their legs and arms spread before Wax showed up.

"You don't have to do that," Calvin interjected.

"This whole place is a touchstone for Wax."

His pained whisper startled her. Although she still gripped his hand in her gloved fist, he'd become so withdrawn that she had ceased to think of him as an active participant in the conversation, talking *past* him the way people do in front of vegetative patients. When she saw the pinched intensity of his face, the eyes and mouth squeezed shut as if to deny access to demons, Natalie realized the irony of their situation. While she had been seeking a way to draw Wax inside her mind, Calvin had been trying to keep him out of his.

Natalie understood the hazards of permitting the artist to be possessed by the soul of a man about whom they knew next to nothing. With Calvin's condition deteriorating daily, however, she believed the danger of *not* speaking to Wax outweighed the other threats.

"Let him in," she whispered.

Ground down by the unremitting assault of the dead, Calvin welcomed her permission to give in and give up. The inhabitation was gentle—an abdication, not an overthrow. Calvin draped one arm around Natalie's shoulders and relaxed against her, and all the weariness and fear etched into his brow and eyes were wiped clean. A look of cerebral, apprehensive naïveté took their place, such as might belong to a shy child prodigy.

The heaviness on Natalie's shoulder lightened as he began to support his own weight again. When he became aware of how close he was to her, he fluttered backward in embarrassed agitation, as if he'd accidentally violated her personal space. Then he noticed his surroundings, and he slowly panned the room, his eyes and mouth O's of wonder as he saw the antique mahogany furnishings, the silken walls, the dark, chocolaty lacquer of the oil portraits.

"Am I dreaming?" he said in a voice hushed with awe.

He stopped, transfixed by *Storm on the Sea of Galilee*.

"Dr. Wax?" Natalie asked.

He wheeled around to face her, frightening her with the sudden ferocity that contorted Calvin's features. "Did Carl put you up to this? Is this his idea of a joke?"

She shook her head. "We're not with Dr. Pancrit—"

"Mr. Pancrit." Wax pointed to the Rembrandt. "He said he'd taken all my children prisoner."

It took Natalie a moment to make sense of the bizarre assertion. "The stolen paintings? No ... they all returned safely."

Wax seized her shoulders, trembling. "Are you sure? The da Vinci *Madonna* ... I saw it burn."

"That was a forgery."

"How do you know?"

Natalie frowned. "Because it was painted by the man whose body you're in."

Wax put his hands to what had been Calvin's face a few minutes earlier. "You mean this isn't that other conduit? The lunatic—the one Carl calls 'Markham'?"

A seismic quiver trilled through her at the mention of Evan's name. "No. His name's Calvin and his life's in danger. That's why we need to talk to you about Project Persephone."

"I see." The subject obviously distressed him as much as Evan bothered her, and his attention wandered back to the Rembrandt. "You ... you say they're all safe? Carl had *The Scream*—"

"Another forgery." She allowed herself a small smile of mischief. "I did that one myself."

Calvin's eyes glistened with a joy that wanted to weep, and his voice became hoarse with Wax's emotion. *"Thank you"*

He roved the gallery with his gaze. "I've thought of this place so often over the years. Could ... could we go out into the garden?"

Given the fact that some of the surrounding tourists had begun to gape at them, Natalie thought that was an excellent suggestion.

"Cool!" Callie exclaimed as they stepped out into the portico that bordered the garden. "It looks like the School."

Natalie shared her opinion if not her enthusiasm. Bounded as it was on all sides by the four wings of the museum, the Gardner's central courtyard reminded her a great deal of the one at the Iris Semple Conduit Academy. With four stories of flat stone surrounding you, the sky receded to an impossible, inaccessible height, as if you were peering up from the bottom of a deep, sheer pit. Unlike the School, however, the Gardner sheltered its seasonal flowers and manicured sod with a glass roof, permitting the formal garden to remain green even in the bleakness of a Boston winter. Greco-Roman statues watched over the paved pathways with the blank eyes of cemetery angels, giving the enclosure an aura of funereal peace.

While Wade took Callie for a stroll to keep her occupied, Natalie stayed with Wax as he seated himself on a concrete bench between two Doric columns. The doctor clasped Calvin's hands in delight as he reveled in the clipped, orderly beauty before him—Eden in miniature.

"I used to eat my lunch here every day," he reminisced, inhaling a long draft of the floral-fragrant air that the skylight bottled in the courtyard like perfume. "I could sit here for hours. Simply sit and look and think."

Natalie did not have the patience to watch him sit and look and think for hours. "Pancrit gave Calvin the Project Persephone treatment," she said, "but something's gone wrong."

"Of course," Wax replied. "It doesn't work."

"Why not?"

He sighed and puzzled for a bit, confounded by the struggle to simplify his genius for an ordinary person. "When we first conceived of using gene therapy to create new Violets," he began, "it naturally occurred to us that the mutated DNA responsible for conduit ability would be contained in the same gene that determined eye color, given the positive correlation between the two characteristics.

"But we were only partly correct. The gene that turns the conduit's eyes their distinctive violet color merely creates the node points in the brain through which dead souls can impinge upon and even subdue the Violet's consciousness. When we tried changing this gene alone in our test subjects' DNA structure, the results were ... unpleasant."

The grimness of his tone tightened the knot in Natalie's gut. She thought of Clement Maddox ... and Calvin. "What happened to those test subjects?"

"The treatment created node points in their brains, as we'd hoped. The dead could enter their minds, but the subjects lacked the ability to *regulate* that access. Souls could come and go as they pleased, and our quasi-Violets could do nothing to filter them out.

"That led us to suspect that another gene entirely contributed the filtering mechanism that natural conduits possess. It took considerable trial-and-error to discover it." Again, Wax's expression conveyed how "unpleasant" the results of those errors had been.

Natalie cleared her throat, for the next question stuck there like a bone. "What ... what's going to happen to Calvin?"

"There are several possibilities. Some subjects became what we call 'whisper-ridden.' They could not keep souls from knocking, but the souls could never achieve full inhabitation. Although they were never in danger of complete possession, the patients found the constant intrusion of the dead to be rather trying psychologically."

Natalie found the doctor's clinical detachment to be *quite* trying, psychologically. "And the other subjects?"

"Well, at the opposite end of the spectrum were the 'empty vessels.' The treatment somehow severed the quantum connection that lodged their own souls inside their bodies. With the body left uninhabited, any knocking soul could occupy it for a short time, only to be displaced by another and another, in endless succession."

"And how do I know which will happen to Calvin?"

Natalie's voice had become so soft, she could barely hear herself.

"Hmm. He won't be merely whisper-ridden, since full inhabitation is obviously possible." Wax spread Calvin's hand over his chest to underscore the observation. "Yet his consciousness retains its linkage to the body and returns to prominence between inhabitations. Is that correct?"

"Yes."

Wax nodded. "Then I'm afraid your friend will most likely degenerate into a 'captive audience'— fully conscious and aware, yet never the dominant inhabitant. Worst of both worlds, I'm afraid."

The fact that he delivered this nihilistic diagnosis with Calvin's face and Calvin's voice only made it more hideous. "There must be something you can do," Natalie insisted. "Reverse the process."

He shook Calvin's head. "I tried. Once the node points become part of the brain's neural structure, they cannot be eliminated without destroying the neurons themselves."

"No ... there *has* to be a way." Horrid images from Natalie's childhood erupted from her subconscious, memories of the time before she attended the School and mastered her mantras, when she spent hours or even days as the unwilling receptacle for whatever desolate spirit commandeered her. A "captive audience," indeed. She could see, hear, feel, but was

264

powerless to stop her body from shouting obscenities at her parents as if they were total strangers or from running away in a vain attempt to return to someone else's abbreviated life. She hardly dared to imagine what it would be like if the waking nightmare never ended, if she could never reclaim her own existence. Was that the curse awaiting Calvin Criswell, the only man since Dan that she felt she could love?

"*I can't believe that,*" she said aloud. Her mind groped at solutions that popped like soap bubbles in her grasp. "You said you found the gene that creates the ... what did you call it? The filtering mechanism?"

"Yes. Eventually."

"What if you could treat Calvin with that? *Finish* making him a complete Violet?"

Wax chuckled. The novelty of the idea evidently amused him. "You know, I hadn't considered that. I suppose it might—" His expression became suddenly severe. "No, that's impossible."

"But you said you hadn't even considered it!"

He shook Calvin's head, more vehemently this time. "I'm sorry, I can't help you." His gaze flicked back toward the galleries. "Carl tempted me with those paintings, and I succumbed. I see now how wrong that was. I mustn't be that weak again."

Natalie was on the verge of grabbing *Storm on the Sea of Galilee* off the wall and smashing it in front of Wax to change his mind. "It's *your* fault Calvin's the way he is," she accused. "How can you leave him to a fate worse than death if there's a chance he can be saved?"

"You dont understand." Wax appeared to listen to a cry no one else could hear. "Carl loves death. He thinks we'd be better off if we could all commune with the departed. The Corps only wanted a steady supply of conduits, but Carl's plans were much bigger than that. He intended to create a carrier virus that would open the doors of Hades to everyone on the planet.

"I realized the enormity of the horror I was helping to create the first time I saw *The Scream* up close. That skeletal creature with its eyes agape in awful comprehension, unable to silence the piercing shriek of the Abyss. I'd stare at that picture every night, and every day I'd go to work and see the same expression on my patients ..." He looked at the empty air as if the painting hung, invisible, before him. "Are—are you telling the truth about doing a forgery for Carl? I could have sworn it was the real thing."

"In some sense, it was," Natalie admitted. "I had Munch's help."

He regarded her with new understanding, as if he could see past her brown contact lenses. *"You're a Violet.* Then you know what it's like—the perpetual call of the dead. Do you think humanity is ready for that? Do you think that child out there would be so carefree if she had the specter of mortality perched on her shoulder every day of her life?" He peered out over the courtyard, where Callie made a game of jumping in and out of the shadows of the clouds that drifted over the glass roof. Natalie wondered what Wax would say if she told him that the happy little girl to whom he referred had been *born* with Death at her cradle.

"If you won't help Calvin," she threatened, "I'll go to Pancrit himself."

"All the more reason why I can't oblige you." Wax cast another wistful glance around at the sanctuary of the Gardner as if it would be all he'd ever see of Paradise. "I can't tell you how grateful I am that you brought me back here. I only wish there was some way I could repay you."

"So do I." Natalie watched Dr. Wax's expression dissolve from Calvin's face ... or perhaps that was only the shifting refraction of the liquid in her eyes. She resisted the impulse to cry, however, for she refused to let Calvin see her despair. He had enough of his own to bear, and the instant he resumed command of his eyes, he wept enough for both of them.

"You heard him, Natalie. I'm doomed. I might as well end it now, while I still can."

She put her arms around him, making sure that her bare skin did not come in contact with his. "I won't let that happen to you."

She left the phrase ambiguous. Calvin looked at her, sniffed to quiet himself. "Would you ...?"

"I'll do whatever it takes. But you have to trust me, Calvin. You can't give up yet."

He rubbed the rest of the moisture from the hollows around his eyes and bobbed his head. "Okay." He managed a shaky smile. "It's funny. I always had people call me 'Cal' 'cause I hated my name. Until you said it."

Natalie smiled, blinking to imprison her own tears. "I can't believe that! 'Calvin' is *so* much better than 'Cal.'"

They laughed so brightly that Wade mistook their commiseration for levity.

"You two seem happy!" he said as he led Callie to rejoin them. "What did you find out?"

Natalie was trying to come up with a way to convey the bad news to him when a flash of movement made her look at the arched window closest to them. There, she noticed the four of them reflected in the glass, grouped as if for a family portrait yet shadowed by the overhanging colonnade. Submerged beneath their image lay the outline of a man inside the museum who peered out at them, creating the impression that there was a spectral fifth member of their party. Their reflection obscured his facial features except for the golden crescent of his short blond hair, yet his brooding posture gave Natalie the same eerie sense of familiarity that she'd felt when she'd seen the bearded derelict outside the grocery store. She saw him for only an instant before he withdrew into the unseen depths of the gallery, like a sea creature sinking back into the trenches of the ocean floor.

"We still have problems," she told her father in a tired voice, staring at the black cavity in the glass where the blond man had stood.

22

The Monster Under the Bed

Evan Markham cursed himself as he rushed out of the Gardner to his rented Nissan. Boo had seen him; he felt sure of it. He'd stared at her too long—he always stared too long—and she'd recognized him.

She'd always been his greatest weakness, the habit he couldn't quit, and he hated her for it. If he hadn't wanted to spare her ungrateful hide during the Violet Murders, he wouldn't have ended up in that white plastic hellhole beneath Corps headquarters. Boo hadn't even had the decency to kill him, to set him free into the afterlife of the True Life that Simon McCord promised them all. So he would show her no mercy, either. Although he'd fantasized often about gutting her innards and plucking out her gorgeous violet eyes as keepsakes, he refused to let her off that easy. Death was far too kind for her.

Before Boo and the others emerged from the museum, Evan made it to his car and put on a hasty disguise. Mirrored sunglasses, a coarse fake mustache, a tightly permed brown toupee, an unbuttoned bowling shirt thrown over his black tee. The getup made him look like a seventies porn star, but it enabled him to remain unnoticed as he tailed the

Lindstrom family to the Patriot's Pride hotel near Logan Airport.

To avoid attracting their attention, he went around the block before entering the parking lot, then circled the building until he spotted Boo helping her brain-damaged boyfriend through a side entrance in the hotel's westernmost wing. She darted a glance toward Evan's car, but he drove by without appearing to notice her. As soon as Boo herded Criswell inside, however, Evan parked the Nissan and ran to watch them through the pane of glass in the door that had shut behind them. He counted the number of doors they passed so he could calculate which room they entered when they caught up with Old Man Lindstrom and Atwater's brat, who had walked on ahead of them.

Evan smiled. How like Boo! Maybe she wasn't afraid to ride in an elevator anymore, but after a lifetime of acrophobia, she habitually reserved a room on the ground floor. That suited him just fine.

He sauntered around the hotel until he came to the front entrance and strode through the lobby to the reservations desk. Whipping off his sunglasses to reveal his blue contact lenses, he smiled at the pretty receptionist. "Hey, there!"

She looked barely old enough to be out of high school and squirmed in humiliation at the stiff Revolutionary War tailcoat and tricornered hat the hotel made her wear. "Yes, sir? Can I help you?"

"Yeah. See, my wife and I are celebrating our anniversary tonight, and, well ..." He gave a bashful chuckle, pawed the floor with his foot. "Okay, you might think this is silly, but we spent our wedding night here, and I was wondering if we could get the same room for old time's sake."

She shrugged and tapped a couple of keys on her computer terminal. "I can see if it's available. What was the number?"

"One-nineteen." The room next to Boo's.

The receptionist's face lighted with mild surprise as she watched the monitor. "Yeah, looks like it's free. What's the name for the reservation?"

"Daniel Atwater." He almost snickered as he handed her the fake Visa card Pancrit had obtained for him through the Corps. Evan had personally requested the alias.

"And your wife's name?"

"Natalie." A toothy grin. "I want to surprise her."

He wished he could have claimed credit for planning the connecting door with Boo's room, but that was a serendipitous gift. The mechanical locks on the parallel doors would be so much easier to pick than the electronic card-key lock on the door that faced the hotel hallway.

Although Evan proceeded with caution when he carried his suitcase of supplies into Room 119, he needn't have worried. Boo's own paranoia kept her holed up in her room, so she never had the opportunity to see him in the hallway. Evan listened through the thin dividing wall with amusement as she forbade her daughter to go to the hotel pool and forced the pizza delivery man who brought their dinner to produce I.D. before she'd unlatch the door to receive her order. Her fear flattered him.

Still, there were considerable drawbacks in stalking a quarry who expected a trap. Evan knew that Boo never slept deeply, and when something worried her, she didn't sleep at all. He'd never be able to break into that room tonight unseen as long as she was inside it, yet he also could not flush her out of there as long as she thought he might be lurking outside ... unless he presented her with a more immediate danger.

Evar opened the first of the doors between the two rooms—the one whose lock he controlled—and placed a chair beside it, where he stayed for several hours, remaining virtually motionless. When he overheard Boo tell her kid that it was time to brush her teeth, he silently rose and lifted the lid of the large suitcase he'd placed on the bed. Nestled inside, a five-gallon plastic can of gasoline polluted the air with its stench. Next to it rested a padded nylon camera case with a shoulder strap. Evan unzipped its main compartment and took from it a compact set of locksmith's tools and a tranquilizer dart gun—a standard-issue NAACC weapon that Corps Security agents often used to take fugitive Violets into "protective custody." He loaded six darts, although he only needed four, and set the gun and the lock picks on the floor beside the connecting door. The camera case's remaining contents—a switchblade and a box of matches—he shoved into the pockets of his jeans.

When he'd stashed the suitcase beneath his bed, Evan stepped out of Room 119 and strolled down the hallway until he came across the flat red handle of a fire alarm mounted on the wall. Before he could pull it, however, a skinny septuagenarian emerged from an alcove down the hall, wearing nothing but Bermuda shorts, a bathrobe, and a hearing aid, with a full ice bucket in his hands. Evan continued along the corridor to the niche that contained the ice and soda machines and pretended to waffle between Coke and Dr Pepper while waiting for the senior to trudge back to his room. With the hallway clear, Evan stalked back to the fire alarm and slammed the handle down, breaking the glass rod that secured it.

A *wah-wah-wah* blare resounded in the hallway with the grating persistence of a hangover headache, followed by a chorus of curses from behind every numbered door. As the clamor of evacuation began, Evan hurried back to the seclusion of Room 119, where he inclined his ear to the adjoining room.

"I don't smell smoke," he heard Old Man Lindstrom say. "Think it's a false alarm?"

"I hope so," Boo replied. "Give me a second to get Calvin loose and we'll go."

Crouched beside the connecting door, Evan waited until the chatter of the Lindstrom family meandered out to meld with the grumbling crowd in the corridor. When the door to their room clicked shut on silence, Evan set to work on the lock.

Within minutes, he'd opened the connecting door and crept into Boo's room, the dart gun in his hand. He made sure to close and relock the door behind him, then scanned the interior for a place to hide. They were far too likely to look in the bathroom, and the "closet" was nothing more than a wooden rod lined with hangers dangling from notched rings. That left the two queen beds. Although neither had its sheets turned down for the night, the spreads on both bore the indentations of body weight. Old Man Lindstrom's street clothes lay dumped on one bed, while a couple pairs of stretched-out panty hose littered the other like shed snakeskins.

Evan flattened himself on the floor beside the first bed and slid beneath its frame, then pulled the hem of the spread down in place to shade him from the light of the room. The space created a coffinlike confinement. With every breath, his chest touched the metal of the box springs, and the smell of dust from the mattress infected his nostrils. But a decade of imprisonment at Corps headquarters had taught him how to tolerate close quarters.

It had also taught him how to remain absolutely still and silent. Even his heart barely beat as he lay there with the gun at his side for over half an hour, occupying his mind with recollections of life before he left the School, when the future still held promise and Boo still loved him. When they were teenagers, she would make him chase her through the surrounding maple orchards, glancing behind to laugh at him, her cheeks pink from autumn chill. But she'd always let him catch and kiss her. Back then.

His pulse quickened a bit when he heard Boo's father bluster into the room.

"... probably some stupid schoolkids," he said. "The firefighters searched everywhere and couldn't find any sign of a blaze."

Turning his head to the right, Evan saw, in the narrow line of light between the bedspread and the carpet, the soles of leather slippers moving around the bed. The box-spring creaked and sagged, compressing his chest so that he had to breathe even more shallowly.

"Maybe so," Boo replied, "but if Calvin weren't in such a state, I'd move to another place right now."

Evan caressed the trigger of the gun at the mention of Criswell's name. In the background, the artist kept up an unceasing, frantic patter.

"*All the King's horses and all the King's men ...*"

No doubt his pathetic attempt at a mantra. Both Wax and Pancrit had told Evan how futile that was. The knocking souls would eventually break through, and Criswell could do nothing to stop them.

The bed next to Evan's groaned. "Hold still, Calvin," Boo said.

"*... couldn't put Humpty together—*"

Criswell choked on the words, and the bedsprings squealed with the violence of his movement. With a harpy's shriek, his voice became shrill and hysterical. "I wish to God I'd never seen you, Cal! He killed me 'cause of you."

The Moon woman. Evan tensed. He hadn't considered that Criswell would be a touchstone for her. If she told Boo about the murder, Boo would know for certain that Evan had followed her to Boston ...

"Come on, Calvin," Boo urged. "Say your mantra. Get a grip."

Her calm exhortations only whipped Tranquillity into a frenzy. "This is *your* fault, you slut! *You* put him up to it!"

An angry neighbor thumped loudly, his yell muted by the wall. *"Keep it down! Some of us want to sleep!"*

"Forgive me, Calvin," Boo said.

"So help me, if I get my hands on—" The rest of Tranquillity's threat slurred into a cotton-mouthed mumble.

Patient as a stone, Evan bided his time. He heard Boo triple-check the locks and latches on all the doors and windows while her father and daughter settled into the bed above him. The Moon woman either left Criswell's body or tired of trying to talk through whatever Boo had used to gag her. Finally, the lights went off.

Even then, Evan did not move. Only when a liquid snoring wafted down from Old Man Lindstrom's side of the bed did he begin to edge out from under the box spring, taking great pains not to tug on the bedspread as he did so.

His limbs stiff from immobility, he raised himself to his feet with agonizing slowness. No sudden movements, in case Boo's eyes were open. The key was speed: neutralize as many of the targets as quickly as possible. Any two of them might be able to overpower him if they ganged up on him. Even the kid.

He leveled the barrel of the dart gun at Old Man Lindstrom's neck. *Pop!*

Boo's father jerked once, lay still. At the puff of the CO_2 cartridge, a silhouette in the far bed sprang upright, looking straight at him. *"Callie!"* she cried.

But Evan had already swung his gun toward Atwater's brat. *Pop!* The nail point of a thimble-size dart pierced her shoulder. A brief yelp of pain escaped the waking girl before she plunged back into sleep.

Boo lunged toward him, but that only made her a bigger target. *Pop!* Evan landed a shot in her midriff and she dropped onto the foot of the bed shared by her unconscious father and child.

He aimed the gun toward the fourth target, expecting it to come for him or to run for help. When it merely wriggled and grunted on the far bed, Evan held his fire and sidled around for a closer look. Squinting in the darkness, he discerned the prone figure of Criswell, lying on his side, his arms tied behind his back, his ankles trussed up with knotted panty hose. The tongue of a white washcloth stuck out of his gagged mouth.

Evan grinned and stuck the gun under the waistband of his jeans, concealing it with his shirttail. He would leave Calvin Criswell awake for the big finale.

With quick efficiency, he reopened the connecting door and returned to Room 119 to retrieve the gas can from his suitcase. He unscrewed the cap and liberally doused the periphery of the room with the fuel, but left a clear path from the beds to the exit into the hallway. He unlatched this door and stuffed a hand towel from the bathroom at the foot of the jamb to keep it from shutting and locking him out.

Ordinarily, a man could not carry a full-grown, unconscious woman out of a building without arousing suspicion. Unless, of course, he was rescuing her from a fire.

As the combustible reek of the gasoline permeated

the room, Criswell floundered more furiously. Doubled up, he had worked his bound hands over the hump of his rear and was sliding them down his thighs to try to loop them over his feet and get them out from behind his back. Evan smiled at his contortionist routine and started striking matches.

With flames climbing two walls of the room and the smoke detector screeching, Evan took off his bowling shirt and tied it around his nose and mouth like a mask, then heaved Atwater's brat onto his shoulder. Pancrit wanted her for leverage. The room's sprinkler system began to squirt as he carried the kid out.

In the corridor, the *wah-wah-wah* of the fire alarm droned again, but the boy-who-cried-wolf effect made people slow to leave their rooms. "Christ, not again!" the irate neighbor shouted, unaware that a real fire roared next door to him. Evan had taken the kid to his car and come back for Boo before the first irritable guests leaned out into the hall to see what was going on.

The cloth over his face could not strain out the stifling smoke as he stormed back into the burning room. The drapes on the window opposite the door had become a shimmering curtain of translucent yellow and orange, flickering firelight over the bed on which Boo and her father slumbered in oblivion. The sprinkler still rained down on them in a token effort to extinguish the surging blaze. Drawn into a ball, Criswell strained to nudge his bound wrists past his heels.

With the flames' illumination, Evan could now

savor the impotent rage on the artist's face. He especially wanted to see his rival's expression as he went around to stand over Natalie's dad. With the heat of the fire bathing his back and the spray of the sprinkler cooling his face, Evan drew the switchblade from his pocket, flicked out the blade, and drove it like a spike into Old Man Lindstrom's heart. Wade may have been too drugged to feel the impalement, but the reflexive muscles of his body spasmed in pain for him.

The cloth in Criswell's mouth reduced his howl to a whimper. Evan yanked the knife from Wade's chest, the sheen of blood still on the blade, and gently tossed it toward the helpless artist. It flopped onto the bed a few inches from Criswell, the blade leaving a dark stain on the white sheet.

Evan laughed. Nothing would have pleased him more than for Criswell to use the murder weapon to cut himself loose and escape from the burning room, only to be blamed for Wade Lindstrom's death.

Scooping Boo's limp body into his arms, Evan hefted her out the door. Several people now stood in the hallway, gawking at the room that exhaled white smoke yet too timid to look inside.

"Oh, my!" exclaimed a woman in a flannel nightgown with her graying curls in a hairnet. She stared at Boo, whose left arm slipped off her lap to dangle down past Evan's waist.

"Run for it!" he shouted. "It's an inferno in there!"

Cradling Boo to his chest he charged out of the hotel amongst the stampede of guests, who all took his advice. During the ensuing pandemonium in the parking lot, no one took much notice of him as he carried Boo to the Nissan and laid her on the back-seat. He got in the car, pulled the bowling shirt off his face, and sped away from the Patriot's Pride just as the fire engines arrived at the hotel for the second time that night. At the first red light he came to, Evan grabbed the cell phone that lay beside the sleeping girl on the passenger seat and hit a button to dial a preprogrammed number.

"I've got them," he told the person at the other end.

23

A Captive Audience

If Calvin could find anything good about being hog-tied next to a bleeding man in a room engulfed with fire, it was that even the dead found their lot preferable to his. Tranquillity had departed with the promise to persecute him further, either in this life or the next, and the few souls who'd flitted through his mind since then fled to the netherworld the moment they got a look through his eyes. Maybe they feared they'd ended up in Hell. It would've been an understandable mistake.

Whatever prompted them to leave him alone, Calvin was grateful to have his brain all to himself as he tried to think of what to do. If it were only his own worthless life at stake, he might have let himself burn, but the man who'd butchered Tranquillity now held Natalie and Callie captive and had left Wade to die in front of Calvin's eyes. Only the quixotic hope that he might somehow save them kept him struggling to escape, even as the smoke crept down his throat.

The terry cloth that clotted his mouth like a gigantic hair ball prevented him from coughing when he choked, causing his chest and abdomen to heave without relief. Although it seemed to take hours,

Calvin edged his bound wrists past the toes of his stocking feet mere seconds after Evan Markham carried his kidnap victims out of the hotel. With his hands finally in front of him, Calvin plucked the towel from his mouth and hacked ash from his lungs until vomit crested on his tongue.

He hesitated only an instant before snatching up the switchblade to sever the nylons around his ankles. Freeing his wrists required a more awkward maneuver and he didn't have the time. Instead, he jumped up and braved the flames and smoke lapping at the other bed to press a hand to the welling puncture wound in Wade Lindstrom's chest.

He didn't hold it there long enough to feel for a heartbeat. He didn't need to. For, as the blood slicked Calvin's fingers, Wade began to knock.

A hospital maternity ward. A pretty, if prematurely aged, young woman in a wheelchair, smiling even as the newborn in her arms bawled as if she could see the future that awaited her parents. And when the baby girl calmed enough to open her eyes, they gleamed with the same violet hue as her mother's . . .

The implication of the memories Wade bequeathed to him made Calvin want to wail, but his grief came out as another fit of coughing. Reflex caused him to recoil from the body, wiping the wet redness from his fingers onto his shirt. The fire flowed up the bedspread to consume Wade Lindstrom in a de facto funeral pyre. Sickened, Calvin would have hurled away the knife that had killed Natalie's father, but he held on to it, determined to use it on the man to whom it belonged.

Hunching over to shield himself from the heat of the flames and to distract attention from his tied hands, he dashed out of the room and into the tide of hotel guests surging toward the exit. A few stared at him as if they couldn't believe anyone had still been in that room, but most only cared about getting themselves outside. A couple of firefighters fought to drag a hose through the flow of evacuees.

In the parking lot around the hotel, the same people who'd pushed and shoved to escape the fire turned around to watch and gossip about it. A couple of them pointed out Calvin as one of the survivors, but he walked away from them without turning around. Thank God he and Natalie had gone to bed fully dressed; Calvin wished now that he'd worn his shoes as well, for the asphalt felt as frigid and hard as a glacier under his stockinged feet.

When he reached the edge of the hotel's property, he stretched his hands as far apart as he could and angled the knife to saw the nylons wrapped around his wrists. Calvin left them on the ground where they fell, closed the switchblade, and slipped it in the front pocket of his jeans. He needed to find a phone—there had to be *someone* he could call for help—but before he could go in search of one, a numbness deeper than the Boston cold penetrated his limbs. He wanted to run, to yell, to *move*, but instead he stood there and folded his arms, smiling a smile that he did not feel and that was not his.

"Don't even *think* I'll let you save her, Cal," he heard himself say. "That psycho can cut her to ribbons, for all I care. Just like he did me."

Humpty Dumpty sat on a wall, he babbled, buried in the back of his own head. *Humpty Dumpty had a great fall* …

But Calvin knew that all the nursery rhymes and all the Beatles songs in the world couldn't put him together again.

It was a small consolation to him that, although he could not retain control of his body, neither could Tranquillity. She wanted to march him straight to the police and concoct a "confession" to give them, but she barely made it half a block before she was displaced by the forlorn spirit of a bag lady who froze to death while sleeping in a doorway during a snowstorm. She went wandering in search of the mongrel puppy that had been her only companion in life, only to be supplanted by a drug dealer vowing vengeance on the rival hoods who shot him. He gave way to a Minuteman who fought as part of a Continental Army that was too poor to afford snappy uniforms like those worn by the staff at the Patriot's Pride. He simply goggled in awe at the wonderland of excess wrought by the democracy he'd sacrificed himself to help found. A parade of others followed, each hijacking Calvin's form for a brief time in futile pursuit of objectives that no longer mattered.

Pedestrians went out of their way to clear the sidewalk for the man who shambled among them with only socks on his feet, muttering in one voice, then shouting with an entirely different accent and intonation. No doubt the bandages on his head contributed to the assumption that he was mentally ill. If they noticed the stains on his shirt, they must have presumed that the blood was his own. A few cop cars passed him during his peregrinations through the streets, but every metropolis has more homeless weirdos than it knows what to do with, and the police had more pressing emergencies to address.

Calvin witnessed it all as a hapless observer, with no more power over his own destiny than a piece of scrap paper tossed by the wind. He tried every possible mantra he could think of, to no avail. Meanwhile, he was forced to watch the inhabiting souls squander the precious minutes he needed to find Natalie. Tranquillity taunted him with the utter negation of his current existence when she reclaimed his body as it wandered along Commercial Street near the Callahan Tunnel to Logan Airport.

"You know, Cal, I could just throw you in front of the next bus that rolls by here." She did a precarious tap dance on the curb as traffic thundered past only a foot away. "But I want you to feel how worthless you are. Do you suppose he's cut her open yet? You oughta know, Cal—you're a deadtalker now, after all. Of course, maybe she doesn't *want* to come and talk to you, because you got her killed." She chuckled. "Maybe she hates you even more than I do. Wouldn't *that* be a laugh!"

No, Calvin thought. *Let me die, let me be a walking puppet—just don't let Natalie hate me.*

If he'd had control of his eyes, he would have wept, and the inability to let out the emotion felt worse than choking on smoke with a cloth stuffed in his mouth. He couldn't accept that Wax and

Tranquillity were right. There *had* to be some way he could fend off the dead, to recover his autonomy. What was it Callie had told him?

Your mantra has to be special. Something you believe in.

What did he believe in? Calvin once lacked an answer to that question, but now he had one: Natalie. She was the only thing to come into his life in which he had absolute faith. She had believed in him more than he'd ever believed in himself, and now his belief in her would save him. For her sake as well as his, he would find a way to be himself again.

I believe in Natalie, he thought, the words strengthening his resolve like a good, stiff drink. *I believe in Natalie.*

In the midst of doing a merry, mocking jig with his blistered feet, Tranquillity wobbled and frowned.

Calvin sensed that the balance of wills had tilted in his favor. *I believe in Natalie,* he thought, his repetition accelerating with his eagerness. *I believe in Natalie I believe in Natalie I believe in Natalie . . .*

Tranquillity pressed his hands to his temples. "No! I won't, I won't, I won't," she bleated, as if refusing to say uncle.

And yet, though she pursed his lips in spite, the next words out of his mouth were his. "I . . . believe . . . in *Natalie!*"

You can't get rid of me, Cal, Tranquillity spat into his consciousness. *Not ever.*

But he did.

"*I believe in Natalie!*" he shouted to the passing traffic and the filthy street and the starless darkness of the overcast night sky. "*I BELIEVE IN NATALIE!*"

Calvin ripped the skullcap of bandages and foil from his bald head, flung it on the pavement, and stomped on it with his sore feet, chanting the only protection he'd ever need against fear and death.

The ice water of urgency quickly cooled his initial euphoria. He had no car, no money, no shoes, and no idea how long he would be able to retain his hard-won freedom. Despite what Tranquillity had said, the fact that Natalie hadn't knocked gave him hope that she might still be alive, but he had no way to locate her in time.

Or did he?

Calvin looked down at the finger streaks of blood he'd rubbed on his shirt, now dried to a rusty brown. *The dead travel fast,* he remembered reading in some book back during his college days.

Although he did not have a spectator mantra and knew nothing about how to summon a specific soul, he balled his fist around the stained cloth and called to Wade Lindstrom with his mind. To open himself to inhabitation again, he stopped reciting his newfound protective mantra, risking that the touchstone of blood would draw Wade to him before any stranger's soul could knock.

Calvin shuddered as the all-too-familiar prickling sensation stiffened the stubble on his scalp. His brain again absorbed images of Natalie's mother, young and glowing with the first light of marriage and motherhood, but thoughts of another woman collided with them. A somewhat older woman, with a timid smile and pale blue eyes, her brown hair pinned up with Puritan restraint. A name accompanied the memory: "Sunny."

"Kiddo?" he heard himself say. Wade glanced around, perplexed to find himself alone on a dreary Boston thoroughfare.

It's Calvin, sir. It took a moment for him to adjust to communicating by thought rather than speech. *I need your help.*

"Oh." His shoulders sagged with Wade's disappointment. "I thought it would be Natalie or Callie calling me."

That's why I need to talk to you. The man who killed you has them—

The news of his own demise appeared to shock Wade. "Wait! *Killed* me? I thought my heart gave out."

No. I think it was the bad man your granddaughter talked about—the guy named "Evan." He also killed my ex, and now he's kidnapped Callie and Natalie. You've got to help me find them.

"Evan ... " Natalie's father spoke the name. as if it were the only thing left that could frighten him." Tell me what to do."

Go to Natalie. See if she can tell you where she is. Then come back and knock and tell me what you've found out.

"Of course. I would have gone to her before now, but ... I've been renewing some old acquaintances."

Natalie's mom? Calvin guessed. *And ... Sunny?*

Wade shook Calvin's head and took a sudden interest in the holes forming in his threadbare socks; "I got lonely all those years Nora was in the hospital. Then I met Sunny and my life seemed complete again. They've both waited for me to join them ... and I still love them both. It's ... strange."

As Wade Lindstrom pondered the dilemma of his transcendental polygamy, Calvin couldn't help but recall the paternal shade embracing Callie in the portrait Natalie had drawn. Dan Atwater, absent yet omnipresent. When the time came, with whom would Natalie choose to spend eternity—the F.B.I. agent hero and father of her child, or the failed artiste and ex-con forger?

Calvin decided not to worry about that until they were all dead. God willing, that might not be for a long time ... if he got moving.

Have you ever touched Serena? he asked Wade. *Shaken hands or whatever?*

"Yeah, I think so. Why?"

She was supposed to meet us here in Boston. I only pray she made it. Calvin checked his location, sighted a service station about a block away. *After you find Natalie, go tell Serena to meet me at the Exxon on Commercial Street, okay?*

"I'll do my best." Wade smiled. "Good luck, son. Save our girls."

I will.

As Wade flew off into the ether like Mercury to deliver his messages, Calvin trudged toward the gas station, whispering his mantra to ward off not only the dead but also pain and cold and worry: *"I believe in Natalie. I believe in Natalie. I believe in Natalie ..."*

24

The Ex

Awareness returned to Natalie in the form of a pulsing headache, an aftereffect of her drug-induced sleep. She opened her eyes to find herself looking sideways at the gray vinyl of car upholstery. She tried to call out to Callie, but a strip of duct tape sealed her mouth. When she attempted to sit up, she discovered that while she was passed out Evan had taken the precaution of roping her wrists to her ankles behind her back to immobilize her, as if trussing up the legs of a rodeo calf. She knew Evan had done it, for he'd tied her up the same way the last time they'd been together, when he'd abducted her a decade ago.

If she had any remaining doubts about the identity of her captor, Evan ended them when she started to writhe. "Take it easy," he said, guessing what she wanted. "She's right here next to me. She's smaller than you are, so it might take her longer to snap out of it."

Natalie angled her face upward until she could see Evan peering down at her over the back of his car seat like a castle guard on a parapet. He no longer wore a disguise other than the blond of his hair, and she recognized the covetous longing in his expression even in the bluish predawn light inside the car. Age lines, colored contacts, and hair dye could not keep her from distinguishing a face that had once been as familiar to her as her own, yet he had never looked as much like a stranger to her as he did now.

She tried to pry her lips apart beneath the sticky polymer of the tape, but Evan shook his head. "No, I won't let you talk quite yet. I want you to feel how I felt at Corps headquarters. Trapped and silent."

He stretched an arm out over the back of his seat to play with the strands of her wig. "Except you can't really know what it was like. A soul cage gives a whole new meaning to the word *solitary*. For ten years, I had no one to talk to—not even the dead." His voice became as brittle as thin ice. "Maybe I should put *you* in a soul cage for ten years. Maybe then you'd understand."

Natalie breathed harder, imagining herself imprisoned in a makeshift soul cage of Evan's construction, without the comfort of a single soul, living or dead. A black room worse than death.

"And yet, Boo, even after everything you've done to me, I still find it hard to hate you." Evan quivered with emotion—whether from anger or love or self-loathing or frustrated lust, it was impossible to tell. "All that time, I tried. I didn't say a word to anyone, because I was practicing all the vicious, hurtful things I wanted to say the next time I saw you. But here we are, and I can't remember any of it."

He glanced out the windshield of the parked car at the lightening sky. "Pancrit's boys will be here soon. The doc wants to know what Bartholomew Wax said to you, and he'll do stuff to your kid until you tell him what it was."

Reaching over to the seat beside him, Evan cupped Callie's chin in the claw of his hand and pulled her face forward until Natalie could see how he pinched the girl's slack cheeks. "It's a shame, because she's a pretty thing." He cast a withering look at his former lover. *"She should have been mine."*

Natalie convulsed with fury, so livid that she mistook the tingling of her skin as the rush of blood to her head.

"But I can forgive and let live." Evan pushed Callie back against the headrest. "I have no loyalty to Pancrit. We can drive away from here right now and never see him again. We'll all be a family, and I'll raise Callie as my own."

He smiled. "I can see you're already thinking of all kinds of objections to my generous offer. That's why I'm not going to take the tape off until you've had a chance to calm down a bit. I suggest you consider my proposition carefully before you give me your answer."

The pricking sensation in her fingers and toes, which Natalie had blamed on the rope cutting off her circulation, grew stronger. *Not now,* she thought, exasperated that some dead nuisance had chosen that moment to knock. She was about to shoo it away with her protective mantra when it spoke to her.

Hey, kiddo.

She was glad that Evan had left the tape over her mouth or she might have screamed then. Instead, she strived to suppress the sudden anguish so that Evan would not see it on her face, while she silently commenced her spectator mantra.

Dad, what did he do to you? she asked as he settled into her consciousness.

That doesn't matter, Wade said. *What matters is what he hasn't done to you. Is Callie okay?*

So far. But Evan's going to give us to Pancrit. What about Calvin?

He sent me. You know where we are?

In a car. I was knocked out until a minute ago, and all I can see through the windows from this angle is the sky. Can you stay a few minutes? Maybe I can find out more.

I guess I'll have to. Calvin told me to find Serena, but unless I have some info to give them ...

The whoosh of a jet engine, like a conch shell's roar amplified a thousandfold, descended upon them. Wheels screeched on a runway.

"Oops," Evan murmured. "The boys got here sooner than I thought. I guess I need your answer now." He tore the tape from Natalie's mouth.

Although it burned as if he'd ripped off the bottom half of her face, Natalie refused to flinch. "I'd sooner date the Devil," she said.

Evan chuckled. "Apparently you misunderstood me. We aren't negotiating what happens to you; Pancrit has already promised I can have you when he's done. I'm giving you the chance to save your daughter."

Natalie's gaze flicked to the seat where Callie remained comatose, but she barely paused before responding. "She'd be better off with her real father."

If Evan had any problem hating her before, the

reference to Dan eliminated it. "Your choice," he said.

He took a box cutter from the glove compartment and cut the rope from her ankles but left her hands tied behind her back. Natalie barely had a chance to straighten her stiff legs before Evan got out of the car and dragged her from the backseat.

As he set her on her feet she saw that she stood on the grassy fringe of a tiny airfield whose two landing strips formed a Maltese cross of asphalt. Off to one side rose a single small white tower with a flagpole in front of it, while several hangars for light aircraft clustered near the ends of each runway, including the one beside which Evan had parked his Nissan. On the tarmac about twenty yards away, a corporate Lear jet had come to rest, the fin of a gangway lowered from its side. The thread of orange dawn on the horizon illuminated the figures of Block and Tackle as they descended the plane's gangway steps. They had ditched their white medical uniforms in favor of military fatigues, and now carried both stun guns and sidearms on their belts.

Natalie tamped down her fear in order to give clear, firm instructions to her father. *Get an eyeful, Dad*, she told him, surveying the airport. *Tell Calvin and Serena everything you can. And hurry.*

I will, Wade promised. *Hang tough, kiddo.*

His soul fluttered off like a carrier pigeon as Evan prodded Natalie with his dart gun. "Time to fly," he said.

25

Message Received

I believe in Natalie. I believe in Natalie. I believe in Natalie ...

Calvin squatted on the concrete bumper of a parking space outside the Exxon station on Commercial Street, shivering as the morning sun peeked above Boston Harbor. He pathologically repeated his mantra, not only to stave off inhabitation but also to keep himself from contemplating all the worst-case scenarios he could imagine. What if Wade couldn't reach Natalie? What if she and Callie were already dead? Worst of all, what if they were still alive, but Calvin could do nothing to help them?

I believe in Natalie ...

Although he believed passionately in those words, he couldn't repeat them forever. He had to sleep sometime. Yet if he let down his mental shield for even a minute, the souls started knocking again. Without the genetic "filtering mechanism" that real Violets possessed, the node points in his brain would remain ghost magnets, sucking souls into his head twenty-four/seven. When Natalie asked whether it would be possible to give him that filtering mechanism, Dr. Wax told her no ... but Calvin, who had eavesdropped on his thoughts, knew he was lying. If he could only get Wax to help him ...

I believe in Nat—

Calvin smacked his forehead. Wade may have been trying to knock all this time, and Calvin was unintentionally keeping him out with his protective mantra. Why couldn't the dead use call waiting?

He broke off his protective mantra and grabbed the bloodstain on his shirt again, concentrating on Natalie's father. Wade inhabited him almost immediately, skipping the formality of a greeting in order to brief Calvin as quickly as possible.

"They're at a little municipal airport," he said aloud, "but I couldn't tell where."

At least they're alive, Calvin thought in reply.

"For now. Some guys were about to fly them away on a plane when I left."

Great. What about Serena?

"Here comes your answer now."

With a rather prissy, alto purr, a blue Yamaha motorcycle decelerated into the service station's parking lot to idle in front of Calvin. The leather-jacketed rider who straddled the bike's saddle raised the tinted visor of her helmet to reveal Serena's violet eyes.

"Heard you need a ride," she said.

Using Calvin's voice, Wade described the airport he'd seen to Serena to see if she could identify it. She took a wireless Internet-equipped PDA from a pocket inside her jacket and called up maps of the Boston vicinity to narrow the possibilities.

"You say the place looked provincial, so they must

have left the city," she deduced, "but they probably wouldn't go more than an hour's drive away. Did you see or smell the ocean?"

Wade shook Calvin's head. "Definitely not."

"That rules out the landing fields on Nantucket and Martha's Vineyard. They must've gone inland. Somewhere nice and private for Mr. Pancrit to do his dirty work. Hmmm ... let's try Fitchburg." Serena tapped her stylus on the PDA screen to call up the airport's Web page, then showed the site's thumbnail photos to Wade. "Look familiar?"

Wade shook a finger at the airfield as if picking it out of a police lineup. "That's it! I'm sure of it!"

Serena looked even grimmer than usual as she shut off the PDA and tucked it back in its pocket. "I was afraid of that. Fitchburg's over fifty miles away."

"B-but it can't be," Wade stammered. "The plane—they were going to take off any minute ... "

"I don't suppose Evan said where they were flying?"

"No." He grasped for hope the way a falling man claws the empty air. "M-maybe I could go back—stay with Natalie until they land?"

"On the other side of the country?" Serena asked, her tone heavy with fatalism. "We'd never make it in time."

I can think of one person who probably knows where they're going, Calvin interjected. When Serena didn't react, he remembered that he couldn't be heard.

"Wait! Calvin has an idea," Wade said on his behalf. "What is it, Cal?"

Bartholomew Wax. He must be familiar with every rat hole Pancrit's ever crawled out of.

Wade brightened with excitement. "Yes! Yes! But can you get him to talk?"

I'm not sure. He inhabited me at the museum, so I guess that makes me a touchstone for him. You'll have to leave before I can summon him, though.

"Of course. Right away."

"Care to let me in on this conversation?" Serena said. "I'm a Violet, not a mind reader."

"Oh! Right ... Actually, I'll let Calvin tell you. I've got to go."

The cottony numbness in his limbs ebbed as Natalie's father ceded control. *Godspeed, son*, he said. *Take care of my babies.*

"I will, sir," Calvin answered aloud. "Whatever it takes."

Serena grew testy. "If this is Calvin I'm talking to, will you please tell me what you have in mind?"

"I'm making a collect call to Dr. Wax," he told her. "But let me do the talking." And, since he did not yet have a spectator mantra, Calvin concentrated on the one thing that he and Bartholomew Wax had in common, the image that bound them together: Edvard Munch's *The Scream*.

The anesthetic tingling returned to his extremities, and the wraithlike countenance of the figure in Munch's painting morphed in his mind into a series of spectral faces, all with shaved heads and violet irises. Beings that screamed and scratched and bit him before he shut their staring eyes with the deliverance of death ...

His head and shoulders drooped as Wax settled into his bones like a cold dew. "Why can't you leave me in peace?" the scientist lamented when he reluctantly assumed the ability to speak.

Calvin thought of the murders he'd witnessed in Wax's memory and decided to be blunt. *Because you're going to have even more blood on your hands if you don't finish the project.*

"I did what had to be done." Because he could not address Calvin directly, Wax pleaded his case to Serena, who watched him with the stone face of a juror. "Don't you see that? It was for the greater good."

Oh, yeah? Calvin shot back, the inner voice of conscience. *And when Pancrit kills a nine-year-old girl and her mother, will that be for the greater good too?*

"I can't keep Carl from committing his crimes," Wax said, "but I can stop him from perpetrating an atrocity on all of humanity."

You say that now, but until Natalie told you that your precious "children" were safe and sound, you were ready to sell out the whole human race for a few pieces of cloth covered in old paint.

Wax wrung Calvin's hands, flustered in his haste to rationalize. "Y-you of all people should understand. You're an artist—I've seen it in your thoughts. You know those masterpieces are irreplaceable."

And a person isn't? You spoke to Natalie at the museum. You've seen the replica of The Scream *she made with Munch, but you haven't seen what a brilliant artist she is in her own right. And you never will if Carl Pancrit murders her. Think of how many artworks will be destroyed if she dies. A lifetime's worth …*

Wax touched trembling fingers to Calvin's open mouth. "My God."

Sensing that an avalanche of guilt threatened to crush the doctor, Calvin softened his tone. *You get it now, don't you? Everyone* is a masterpiece.

"Yes. Yes, you're right." Bartholomew Wax glanced around at the service station with a frantic eagerness. "What can I do?" he asked Serena in a plaintive tone.

"Tell us where Pancrit took the girls." She nodded toward the back of the cycle's seat. "Then hop on and hold tight. We got a plane to catch."

26

Treatment #17

No one seemed happy to arrive at the windowless bunker of a building that crouched among the gypsum dunes of White Sands Missile Range. Even Tackle and Block appeared to dread the structure, probably because they were aware of its history. Natalie and Callie didn't need to know about the place to fear it, for they could see Carl Pancrit's gold BMW parked in the lot out front.

It was after noon when they got to the compound. Tackle had piloted the Lear jet during the five-hour flight from Massachusetts to Texas, and Block had driven them the ninety miles from the El Paso Airport to Las Cruces, New Mexico, in a Humvee. An actual U.S. Army Humvee, not a steroid-enhanced SUV for testosterone-challenged weekend warriors. Although Callie awoke from her drug-induced doze during the plane flight, she and her mother passed the entire trip in almost total silence. Neither one had had anything to eat that day, and both still had their hands tied behind their backs.

The intuitive revulsion Natalie felt for the White Sands facility only increased when they descended from the Hummer, for Evan began to mumble to himself as they approached the front security door.

Usually too macho to let anyone hear him saying his protective mantra, he whispered with furious speed.

"... *five times three is fifteen, five times four is twenty, five times five is twenty-five ...*"

Natalie tensed, her presentiment confirmed. This was not a laboratory. It was a mausoleum.

As they stood before the entrance, she whispered to Callie, "Say your mantra, honey."

Her daughter must have sensed the same danger, for she obeyed immediately. Natalie then took her own advice, thinking, *The Lord is my shepherd; I shall not want ...*

Block apparently did not possess either the identity card or thumbprint necessary to unlock the security door, so he punched in a number on the alphanumeric keypad beside the door and spoke into the intercom above it. "It's us," he said, staring into the lens of the surveillance camera mounted above the entrance. "Tell the boss we're here."

"Check," a female voice barked from the speaker.

A minute or more passed before the portal finally disengaged from its jamb with an electronic buzz. Tackle pulled the door open, and they stepped into the minimalist institutional foyer to find Carl Pancrit waiting to welcome them.

"Ah, the two Ms. Lindstroms! At last, we have the pleasure of working together." He smiled. Pancrit could smile because he was not a Violet, and so could not feel the crush of angry spirits pressing in on him.

But Callie did. Despite repeating her mantra with breathless insistence, she shrieked and crumpled to the floor the instant they crossed the threshold.

Natalie felt the souls, too, their lust for rebirth trilling through her teeth like foil on a bad filling. As they vied to occupy her brain, she glimpsed flashes of their past: captives in Hades, like Persephone, their minds caught between life and death, until Bartholomew Wax had pushed them completely into the darkness with the poison in his vaccination gun. Although she had never been here before, Natalie knew exactly what the ward beyond the next security door looked like, for she could see it in her mind, littered with the bodies of the doctor's previous patients.

She could not even respond to Pancrit's crass greeting, for she was overwhelmed by the same nauseating dizziness she experienced in a graveyard. The risk here was the same: inhabitation by more than one soul could incite a fatal epileptic fit.

Teetering drunkenly, Natalie braced herself against the nearest wall. *"Yea, though I walk through the valley of the shadow of death, I will fear no evil,"* she prayed aloud, for both herself and her child.

The corporal at the front desk rose from her chair, alarmed. "Sir ... should I call for med support?"

Carl Pancrit dismissed her concern. "No, they'll be all right in a minute. We're going to the auxiliary wing. See that we're not disturbed." He turned to the Corps Security agents and gestured to Natalie and Callie. "Bring them along."

With the Twenty-third Psalm circling in her mind, Natalie recovered enough to check on her daughter, who had fallen silent. She soon discovered, with

303

more than a little pride, that Callie seemed to be in complete control. Hunched in a fetal posture, she'd withdrawn into herself to concentrate on her protective mantra, like a turtle retreating into its shell. When Tackle tried to take hold of her arm, however, Callie got to her feet and reproached him with an imperious scowl. "Don't touch me. I can handle myself."

He muttered something with the word *brat* in it, but let her walk ahead of him as Carl Pancrit conducted them all down the corridor to the left of the reception desk. Evan followed them like an unpaid debt.

The auxiliary wing ran parallel to the test subjects' ward and could easily have been mistaken for the offices of a common medical clinic. Only the security door at the end of the hallway, marked with the thorny, interlocking crescents of the biohazard warning emblem, hinted that health care was not the facility's primary concern.

Pancrit took them only halfway down the corridor, leading them into an examination room furnished with what appeared to be three modified dentist's chairs, each outfitted with heavy leather belts and padded cuffs. Natalie noted that two of the chairs had all their surfaces wrapped in latex.

"As you can see, ladies, I prepared for your arrival." Pancrit patted the rubber sheet on one of the seat backs. 'I've added a fresh layer of insulation to prevent any unwanted ... disturbances, shall we say?"

The implication made Natalie redouble the recitation of her mantra. These chairs ... they were touch-stones for Pancrit's past patients—the mad souls murdered in the ward.

"We're not going to sit there," she declared.

"Actually, you are. Your only decision is whether to do so voluntarily." Pancrit cupped a hand around his mouth and said in a mock whisper, "Between you and me, I wouldn't make a fuss. After what you put the boys through at the old folks' home, they're itching to give you and your girl a taste of the same." He indicated Block and Tackle, who'd both drawn stun guns from their belts. "Now, if I could have the younger Ms. Lindstrom take a seat here—"

"Leave her alone. Use me instead."

When she stepped toward the chair, Callie blocked her. "*No*, Mom. I can do it—whatever it is."

"Honey, whatever it is, you *don't* want to do it." Natalie ached with helplessness. Several times that day, she'd thought of throwing herself in their captors' line of fire to give Callie a chance to escape. But with her and her daughter's arms still bound and with Evan, Tackle, and Block all armed and guarding them, Natalie knew it would be a futile gesture that would only get them both killed. She'd chosen to stall instead, hoping that somehow her father would be able to lead Calvin to them, but she watched that possibility become ever more remote, like a castaway who sees a potential rescue ship sail from view.

Having passed through the denial and anger phases, Natalie tried bargaining with Pancrit. "If you let Callie go, I'll do whatever you say," she offered. "Just tell me what you want."

"What do I want?" he replied. "For you to *stop wasting my time.*"

Pancrit gave a nod, and Natalie shuddered with involuntary tremors as the darts from Block's stun gun lashed her with its voltage. Her body, rigid with contracting muscles, took a step forward without her consent and toppled over like a malfunctioning robot. The pain, as searing as the bolt from a SoulScan Panic Button, was not the worst part, however. Worse by far was hearing her daughter drop to the floor beside her, both of them wriggling like eels yet unable to draw enough breath to do more than gasp.

Natalie did not black out when they cut off the juice from the stun gun, although it might have been better if she had. With the nightmarish passivity of the incapacitated, she felt her slack body hefted into one of the chairs like a medschool cadaver laid out for dissection, and saw Tackle and Block fasten the belt around her waist and the cuffs around her ankles and wrists. They then rotated the chair so she would have a prime view as they strapped Callie to the seat next to her. Meanwhile, Pancrit maneuvered a pushcart with a SoulScan unit and his attaché case into place beside Callie's chair.

"The wonderful thing about science," he said, "is that even a failed experiment has something to teach us." He brushed his fingers through Callie's shoulder-length brown curls and flicked the switch to start the electric hair clipper in his right hand. The resonance of the room's acoustics amplified the buzz until it sounded like a nest of hornets.

Held fast to the examination chair, Callie remained semiconscious from the stun-gun shot, mercifully unaware of Pancrit's intentions. All too alert now, Natalie could only dread what Pancrit would do. Block and Tackle stood guard at either side of her in case she caused trouble, although she would've had to be Houdini to move an inch.

Pancrit peered at her across her captive child. "Mr. Markham tells me you visited the Gardner Museum. Did you by any chance chat with our mutual friend Bartholomew Wax while you were there?"

"Yes." Still deadened from the electric current, Natalie's teeth and tongue were slow to form words. "But ... Wax didn't tell us anything. He s-said ... the project was a bust and there was no hope for Calvin."

"I see. Well, at least the last statement is accurate."

Lowering the clippers to Callie's hairline, Pancrit sheared the locks from her scalp in ugly swaths.

Natalie let out a yelp. Though she knew the haircut wouldn't hurt—she'd had ones like it many times in her life—Natalie couldn't bear to have Callie look like a Corps Violet. It was like seeing her seared with a slave brand.

Pancrit continued to lecture while he worked. "I suppose Barty—Dr. Wax, that is—described some of the fascinating side effects we observed in our less successful trials. Mr. Criswell's case is, of course, one example."

"You *knew* the gene therapy didn't work when you gave it to him," Natalie said.

Pancrit smiled like a humble family practitioner.

"In medicine, the threat of treatment can often prove motivational for the patient to become proactive in achieving the physician's goals. Which brings me to your daughter."

He snapped off the shears and set them aside, then dusted Callie's shorn scalp of the loose clippings, which drifted to the floor like down feathers. "One of the most interesting results we encountered in our research derived from Treatment #17. The recipient was an unfortunate girl named Marisa Alvarez, who ... well, by any chance did Dr. Wax tell you about the phenomenon of the 'empty vessel'?"

Natalie's face went cold as the blood drained from it. "Yes."

"Good. Then I can spare you a rehash. In every previous instance of the empty-vessel effect, the test subject's body, although vacant, could not retain a single soul for any great length of time before another soul supplanted it. My theory is that the underdeveloped node points of our pseudoViolets could not *hold on to* a given soul indefinitely. But, I wondered, what if I could remove the soul of a *real* Violet?" He laid his palm on Callie's forehead. "Then, perhaps, I could *transplant* the soul of one dead individual into an empty vessel capable of supporting it. A dead individual, say, like Dr. Wax himself."

He picked a plastic sandwich bag off the pushcart. Sealed inside it was a carefully preserved bread-bag twist-tie.

"*No!*" Natalie's examination chair rocked as she squirmed in its restraints. "It won't do any good to bring him back. I told Wax that all the paintings are safe. You can't threaten them anymore, because he'll think you're only destroying forgeries."

For a second, Pancrit's patina of gentility disappeared. "You *really* shouldn't have done that. Fortunately, I'll have other means of persuading Dr. Wax to cooperate—once I have him in the body of a nine-year-old girl." Callie moaned and opened her eyes, and Pancrit restored his genial smile. "Ah! Our Sleeping Beauty awakes!"

"Callie!"

Still groggy from the stun-gun shock, she turned her bare head in the direction of her mother's cry, struggling to make sense of the situation. "Mom? What's going on? I hurt all over."

"Just … stay calm, honey," Natalie said, although she was on the verge of tears herself. *Please, Dad*, she thought. *Help us—and hurry.*

Callie attempted to sit up, but the bonds held her fast. Pancrit patted her shoulder, as if he were her pediatrician instead of her inquisitor. "We're going to find out where your node points are, pretty lady. You want to be an official Violet, don't you? I only wish we didn't have to crop your lovely curls to do it."

"It doesn't bother my mom; it won't bother me." The revelation that she had no hair seemed to terrify Callie even more than being immobilized in front of a madman, but she glowered at Pancrit defiantly. "You're the bad man, aren't you? The one named Evan."

"No, that would be *me*." Leaning against the nearby wall, Evan frowned at Natalie, obviously assuming she'd defamed him in front of the child.

Pancrit chuckled. "I'm not the bad man, child. I'm a doctor. I'm here to help." He took the twist-tie from the plastic bag and placed it in her right hand. "Hold this touchstone for me for a few minutes. A soul will start knocking, but you don't have to let him in. Yet,"

"*Callie, don't!*" Natalie yelled. "Throw it away!"

Pancrit switched on the SoulScan and uncoiled its electrode wires. "Now, now, there's no need to frighten the girl. This will go far more easily if she behaves."

Callie scrunched her eyes shut the way she did at the dentist and began to wail.

Watching the SoulScan, Pancrit took one of the electrodes and glided it over the surface of the child's scalp. When he saw the monitor's green inhabitation lines spike, he fixed the electrode in place with surgical tape and took up the next one.

Desperate to stop or at least stall him, Natalie babbled about the gene for the filtering mechanism and everything else that Dr. Wax had told her, not caring what Pancrit did with the information as long as it saved her daughter. Pancrit did not even slow down, however, but continued to pinpoint Callie's node points until he had attached all twenty electrodes. The hydra of insulated white cables emanating from the girl's head looked like tubes ready to extract her essence.

Callie abruptly quieted, her eyes like melting amethysts. "It's okay, kiddo," she murmured to herself. "Don't be sad."

Natalie's heart quickened with apprehension. That wasn't Wax inhabiting her daughter—it was Wade

Lindstrom. Natalie had not had a chance to tell Callie that her grandfather was dead, and this was not the way she wanted to break the news. While she was glad that Dad had come back to be with his grandchild, Natalie knew he could do little to prevent Treatment #17 from separating Callie's soul from her body.

Absorbed in preparations for his experiment, Carl Pancrit did not catch the significance of what Callie had said. "That's a good girl," he murmured, and opened his attaché case. "Just relax. This may sting a bit."

He brought out his vaccination gun and fed it a vial of green liquid. Natalie shrieked as he lowered the tip to Callie's arm.

At that instant, the corporal from the reception desk opened the door and leaned inside. "Sir?"

"My life is nothing but a series of interruptions." Pancrit heaved a sigh, the vaccine gun still poised to inject. "I thought I told you I didn't want to be disturbed."

"Yes, sir—sorry, sir. But ... I thought you might want to talk to these people."

"And why on earth would I want to talk to whomever you've got out there?"

"To make a deal," Calvin's voice replied.

The corporal opened the door wide, and Calvin limped into the examination room behind Serena. Trapped in her chair, Natalie almost gave herself whiplash as she swung her head around to see him. He wore a pair of borrowed sneakers two sizes too big for him, five-o'clock shadow roughed both his

311

jaw and his bare scalp, and the hollows of his eyes were bruised with fatigue, but he had never looked more beautiful to her.

Evan bristled like a tomcat claiming his territory.

"Mr. Criswell," Pancrit muttered, "why on earth would I make a deal with *you?*"

"Because, *Mr.* Pancrit, I'm not Calvin Criswell. I'm Bartholomew Wax"

All the air seemed to leave the room, and no one was able to speak.

Then Evan stalked forward to stare Calvin down. "He's bluffing. Boo said it herself—Wax knows the paintings were frauds. He'd never bargain with you."

The corporal, who stood at attention by the door, cleared her throat. "Sir ... he knew the intercom code for the front entrance. It's why I let them in—why I thought you'd want to see them." Whether she mentioned this for Calvin's benefit or to defend her own actions was unclear.

Whoever looked out through Calvin's eyes remained unruffled. "What do you think, Carl? Are you curious to hear my offer?"

Pancrit scrutinized the man's expression. "Yes, Barty," he said at last. "Very curious."

"You can start by putting that injection away." Wax indicated Callie, who softly wept. "If anything happens to that child or her mother, you can forget about the project."

Pancrit grimaced, but set the vaccination gun back in his attaché case. "And?"

"When the treatment has been perfected, you will

use it to complete Calvin Criswell's course of therapy. Then you will let him and Ms. Lindstrom and her daughter go unharmed."

"And if I refuse?"

"That's where I come in," Serena said, unfolding her arms to reveal the .45 automatic in her right hand. She directed it at Pancrit's head.

Tackle, Block, and the corporal all reached for their weapons, but Pancrit raised his hands. "Easy, everyone." He kept his gray eyes trained on Calvin. "So, Barty ... no more tricks?"

"No more tricks, Carl?" Wax parroted to challenge him.

Pancrit frowned and began peeling the electrodes off Callie's head. "Then let's get to work."

Natalie exhaled, tears finally escaping the corners of her eyes. Tears of grief for the father she'd lost, and tears of gratitude for the family she still had. As soon as Tackle set them both free, she rushed to embrace Callie, to cry with her.

"*Grandpa*." The word itself was an accusation.

"I know, honey," Natalie said. "I'm sorry."

Callie pulled back from the hug, glared at her. "Why didn't you tell me?"

"I didn't know how, baby girl. But Grandpa's still with us. He helped save us."

Her daughter's gaze froze to ice. "Who did that to him?"

Natalie didn't know how to tell her child that, either, but her eyes spoke for her as they glanced over to see the fearsome bitterness graven into Evan Markham's face.

313

Carl Pancrit guided the group through an open archway near the end of the corridor and into a small lounge, which contained a table and chairs, a couch, soda and snack machines, and a rack of outdated copies of *Time* and *Newsweek*. White head-to-toe sterilization suits hung from a series of metal hooks on the wall, each complete with a plastic faceplate and breath filter that resembled a gas mask.

"The rest of you can wait here," Pancrit told the group as he and Bartholomew Wax each grabbed one of the uniforms. "This shouldn't take long."

They both put the suits on over their street clothes, although Wax found that his old outfit did not fit on Calvin's elongated frame and had to trade it for a larger one. When the two of them were finally ready, they passed through the security door at the end of the hall that bore the biohazard symbol and disappeared from view.

Carl Pancrit's idea of a short wait differed from that of a normal person. He possessed an Edison-like monomania that apparently enabled him to work without food or sleep. The rest of them idled in the lounge with all the vivacity of lobotomy patients, sustaining themselves on dry sandwiches and potato chips from the snack machine. Hours passed, and Natalie's watch told her that the sun must have set by now, although the facility's constant fluorescent lighting made it impossible to say when. At least here they could languish in relative peace, sheltered a bit from the ghosts of the ward.

Impatient for Calvin to become himself again, she

paced to and from the laboratory to monitor the scientists' progress through the door's square, thick-glassed window. Natalie found it odd to see the formidable Carl Pancrit become the sorcerer's apprentice. He took orders and scribbled notes on a clipboard, acting as a glorified lab assistant, while Bartholomew Wax moved about the lab in Calvin's body, programming instructions into the computers and automated genetic sequencing and engineering equipment. The machines did most of the actual work. Contrary to what Natalie had imagined, gene splicing did not involve microscopic forceps and scalpels, for the cutting and pasting of DNA sequences was all performed chemically with care-fully selected enzymes. Wax merely told the comput-ers what to do and moved the resulting genetic soup from one machine to another. The process of injecting the recombinant DNA into the adenovirus that would carry it through the body to the tissue targeted for genetic alteration appeared to be equally mechanical and equally tedious.

At last, the portal to the lab shushed open with a release of sterilized air and the two men emerged, lifting the masks from their sweat-moistened faces.

"How did it go?" Natalie asked, walking beside them as they returned to the staff lounge.

"Hell if I know," Calvin said. "I flunked bio in high school."

She grinned in delight and nearly threw her arms around him. However, as soon as he plunked down in a chair and began massaging his temples with the heels of his palms, mumbling, she remembered what happened the last time she'd touched his bare skin. Now that Wax no longer inhabited him, Calvin was exposed to the facility's former patients. He said his mantra louder and louder as if increasing the volume could amplify its defense. *"I believe in Natalie ... I believe in Natalie ... I believe in Natalie ..."*

Calvin blushed, aware that she could hear him. "It works better than anything else," he explained.

"I'm glad." She smiled. "I believe in Calvin."

But she secretly fretted about him. Despite all her Violet training, she would not have been able to withstand for long the constant barrage of knocking souls Calvin now endured. No one could. The dead don't sleep: they could hound you to exhaustion, then grind your sanity to dust, the way Vincent Thresher had destroyed Natalie's mother. If Calvin didn't acquire the filtering mechanism soon, he might end up like Nora Lindstrom ... or worse.

Natalie did not know whether to be heartened or worried by Carl Pancrit's enthusiasm as he stripped off his sterilization suit. "The new treatment seems promising—*very* promising," he announced. "Now all we need is our test subject."

Natalie glanced at Calvin, who slumped semi-conscious in his chair. "But I thought—"

Pancrit anticipated her objection. "Oh, by all means, we'll treat Mr. Criswell, too. But because he participated in a previous, unsuccessful trial, he's rather tainted as a control case. Not to worry, though—I have the perfect candidate."

He hung up his uniform and hurried from the auxiliary wing, leaving Natalie to trade quizzical looks with Calvin and Serena. Tackle, Block, and Evan did not display the slightest trace of surprise, however.

Pancrit returned a few minutes later, accompanied by a petite teenage girl in a black camisole and skirt. Shaved clean, her head bore what appeared to be tattooed node points, but her eyes were brown, not violet. She hugged a battered paperback to her chest as if drawing biblical courage from it.

Smiling with fatherly pride, Pancrit put a hand on her shoulder. "Allow me to introduce Amanda—"

"Amalfia," she corrected him. She beamed when she saw Natalie and held out the book, which turned out to be Sid Preston's noxious tell-all about the Violet Killer case. "It's such an honor to meet you, Ms. Lindstrom. You've always been my inspiration. Would you sign this for me?"

27

The Initiation of Amalfia

Natalie had never expected to receive rock-star adulation, and the fact that she got it here, in a secret government compound, with the lives of her family at stake, struck her as so surreal that it left it her speechless.

"I have a pen," the girl added when Natalie didn't respond. She proffered a blue ballpoint topped by a grinning rubber skeleton with teeth marks chewed into his skull.

Sure, I'll autograph your book, Natalie was tempted to say. *And you'll also want that blond guy leaning up against the wall there to sign it. He's the Violet Killer!*

Instead, she pleaded with Pancrit. "You can't do this to her."

He scoffed at her concern. "Oh, and I suppose if I were testing some new antidepressant or ADHD pill, that would be okay. Possible side effects: brain aneurysm and suicide. At least she stands to *gain* something from this treatment. Something she wants. Isn't that right, Amanda—or should I say *Amalfia?*"

The girl trembled with a virgin's nervousness. "Yes. I want it more than anything."

She spoke as fervently as a religious-cult convert.

It unnerved Natalie to see how this naive adolescent craved the ability of which Natalie had so often wished to rid herself. "Amalfia ... I don't think you understand what it means to be a conduit. You have to guard against dead souls, day and night. Some of them are angry, violent. Your life is never your own—"

"I know all that." She embraced the true crime book again, holding it over her heart like a shield. "I *am* a Violet. I should have been born one."

"There's still time to change your mind," Natalie insisted. "Don't let them bully you—the choice is yours."

"That's right. It is." With frosty resolve, the teen sealed herself off from further discussion.

Natalie gave up on trying to dissuade her and resorted to legal technicalities. "What about her parents?" she asked Pancrit. "She's not old enough to give consent."

"She'll be eighteen in ... how soon?"

"Seven months," Amalfia said.

Pancrit grinned. "Close enough."

Natalie shook her head. "I can't allow this."

Block and Tackle hemmed Natalie in on either side to prevent any interference.

"The question is not whether Ms. Pyne will receive the treatment," Pancrit said. "The question is, will Mr. Criswell?"

She glanced back at Calvin, who still muttered in misery on the couch. He needed the gene therapy if he wanted any hope of peace in the future.

"At least ... at least let us help her through the

transition," she suggested. "In case she needs any coaching."

Pancrit bowed his head. "Your experience will be most welcome. Shall we proceed?"

Natalie had assumed that the gene therapy would require multiple doses over several weeks as it had with Calvin's original treatment, and she didn't know whether to be thankful or apprehensive when Pancrit told them that the adenovirus he was going to use would take effect within a couple of days— "About the length of time it takes to catch the common cold," he said.

"I deliberately gave Mr. Criswell a more gradual, slow-acting retrovirus in delivering his previous therapy," the physician explained as he prepped his vaccination gun for the injections. "If I'd administered this adenovirus to him before, he wouldn't be with us now."

They had returned to the auxiliary wing's examination room, where Calvin and Amalfia (as she preferred to be called) currently occupied the latex-covered chairs, although in their case Pancrit had deemed the restraints unnecessary. The rest of the group watched from chairs at the room's periphery, except for Natalie, who stayed at Calvin's side.

"You think I'm ready for this?" he asked her as Pancrit fitted his gun with a fresh needle.

"It's not so bad." Natalie squeezed his shoulder. "As long as you're not alone."

Carl Pancrit nudged her aside. "Not to intrude, but ... "

He stapled the gun's tip into Calvin's bicep, then went back to his attaché case to change the needle and vial for Amalfia. It happened so fast that Natalie could hardly believe that that single, fleeting second had irrevocably altered Calvin's life.

Another second, another prick of a needle, and Pancrit forever changed Amalfia's life. "Well, that's it for now," he declared as he packed the vaccine gun back in its case. "Pick a room in the ward and make yourselves comfortable. I'll have Corporal Johnston bring you some food and fresh bedsheets—"

Natalie glowered at him. "You're kidding, right? We can't even go *near* the ward."

The physician chuckled at his own thoughtlessness. "You're right, of course. How silly of me. But we'll find a place for you. It's only a couple of days, after all."

He hustled from the room with the attaché case in hand, leaving them in the charming company of the Violet Killer and the Corps Security goons.

Natalie gazed into Calvin's strange and wondrous green-and-violet eyes and felt a jarring sense of unreality. The injection seemed so anticlimactic, such a nonevent—as brusque and routine as a flu inoculation—that she found it hard to believe it could precipitate the transformation it promised.

Only a couple of days . . .

At least they wouldn't have long to wait.

20

Sleepover Party

Only a couple of hours had passed since Amalfia had received the injection, but she was already ogling her eyes in the mirror of a compact from her handbag.

"I think I see some violet!" She pulled the eyelids away from her corneas to examine each iris. "There's, like, little tiny specks of it."

"Yay." Callie made no effort to disguise the sarcasm in her cheer. Here they were, prisoners of a bunch of killer bad guys, and Amalfia acted like it was a girls' sleepover party. All she wanted to do was talk, and since Callie happened to be closest to her in age, she had to put up with most of the teen's blather.

At the moment, they were alone in the staff lounge, which Callie's mom had decided was the safest room in the facility for them to stay. Before the treatment, Amalfia had lodged in one of the cells formerly occupied by Dr. Wax's test subjects. She would have returned to the ward to wait for the shot to take effect, but Callie's mom thought that would be a very bad idea. If the gene therapy was a success, Amalfia would not want to be sleeping in a tomb when she began her life as a Violet.

The girls lay on the floor on Army bedrolls that Corporal Johnston, the uniformed woman from the

322

front desk, had brought for them. The adults had gone off into the hallway to talk amongst themselves, leaving Callie and Amalfia to get ready for "bedtime," although both of them were too keyed up by the day's events to sleep. It didn't help that the fluorescent lights in the facility stayed on twenty-four hours a day. Amalfia had changed out of her camisole and skirt into an oversized black T-shirt with a skull decal on it and a pair of black biker pants. Callie still wore a pink flannel nightgown with little cartoon penguins on it—the only clothes she had to wear, since they'd lost all their luggage in the burning hotel back in Boston. She plumped up the throw pillow under her head, but couldn't get used to the feeling of cloth against the skin of her scalp, where her hair used to be.

"Your mom is so cool." Amalfia sat up, propping her elbows on her knees. "It must be exciting to be around her all the time."

Callie thought of all the times she'd been captured and almost killed by crazy men because of her mother's work. "Yeah, I guess."

"I want to be just like her," the teen said, still checking her eyes in the mirror occasionally to see if she'd missed any new developments. "Dr. Pancrit and Deathdreamer have promised I can go to the Conduit Academy right away. I *so* can't wait! What's it like?"

"I wouldn't know." Scrunched down inside her sleeping bag, Callie rolled onto her side with her back to Amalfia.

The teen didn't get the hint. "But I thought *all*

Violets went to the School, like, as soon as they could talk."

"Not this one."

"How do you get your training?"

"My mom teaches me."

Amalfia set aside the compact. "Yeah, and I'm sure she's great and all, but what about your job training? Like me—I want to work with the police. Murder cases and stuff."

"I want to be a veterinarian," Callie lied, envy turning her stomach. After more than four years, she still had nightmares about Vincent Thresher, dreams in which she caught ghastly glimpses of the terrible things the killer had made her do when he took control of her body—and even worse things he would have done if he'd been allowed to stay. The bad man her mother called "Evan" had just murdered Grandpa Wade, and he kept giving the rest of them dark, angry looks. Because of Thresher and Evan, Callie had secretly aspired to police work; she wanted to help F.B.I. agents like her father put bad men away where they could never hurt anyone again. She *wanted* to be like her mother, but couldn't. She was born a Violet, but was denied the use of the one thing that made her special. And now this stupid girl who'd never been inhabited by a soul in her life was going to go to the School and become a conduit for the police, just like Callie's mom had been. It wasn't fair.

"You want to be a *vet?*" Amalfia said, as if to rub it in. "That seems like a total waste, if you ask me."

Callie snapped upright. "Yeah? Well, no one asked you, did they?"

Amalfia looked as hurt as if Callie had hit her. "Sor-*ry*! Gee, what's wrong with you?"

My grandpa was just murdered, she could have answered, or *Dr. Pancrit tried to kill me today*. But Callie didn't feel like sharing such personal details with Amalfia. She'd even excused herself several times to go to the women's restroom to cry for Grandpa Wade in private.

"You don't know anything about me," she taunted Amalfia. "You don't know anything about being a Violet. You don't know anything about anything."

The teen stiffened like a teacher with an insolent pupil. "Hey! I've read every book there is—"

"It's not the same."

"Oh, yeah? I bet I know more about your mom's Violet work than *you* do."

"Think so, huh?" Callie gave a spiteful smile. "That just proves how dumb you are. You don't even know who your boyfriend, Deathdreamer, is."

Amalfia's supreme confidence wavered into uncertainty. "What do you know about him?"

"Mom told me that his real name's Evan and he's a bad man. He killed my grandpa and kidnapped my mom and me to bring us here."

The teenager shook her head. "No, you're wrong. Deathdreamer wouldn't—" Her eyes widened as a thought unsettled her. "*Evan?*"

She snatched up that paperback book she always kept within arm's reach—the one about the

Violet Murders. Callie hadn't learned anything about the Violet Murders—it was one of many subjects her mom avoided—but she relished the growing panic with which Amalfia thumbed through the pages.

She came to rest on one of the black-and-white photo pages at the center of the book, trembling as she stared at it. *"Deathdreamer ..."*

"Did somebody call?"

Amalfia gasped and dropped the book as she glanced up at the speaker. Callie went from smug to fearful when she turned to see Evan standing in the open archway of the lounge entrance. She hadn't heard him approach and didn't know how long he'd been listening to their conversation.

"My ears were burning," Evan murmured, striding over to them. From Callie's vantage point on the floor, he seemed about ten feet tall. "I hope you ladies know it's not nice to talk about someone behind his back."

Amalfia yelped and skittered back as he shot a hand down to seize her book.

Evan thrust the paperback toward her, shaking it in accusation. "I especially don't like people who believe lies about me. You wouldn't do that, would you, Amalfia? 'Cause that might make me really, really *mad*."

A metallic snap drew Callie's attention back to the lounge's archway, and she was overjoyed to see Serena standing there, locking the slide of her automatic pistol into place to chamber a bullet.

"Speaking of getting mad, I'm gonna be real

steamed if you don't get out of here in about two seconds," she told Evan.

As he turned to face her, his hand moved toward the butt of the tranquilizer gun stuck under the waistband of his black jeans.

"Oh, please." Serena leveled the .45 at him. "*Give* me a reason."

Radiating rage, Evan did not draw the dart gun. Instead, he tore Amalfia's book asunder, first ripping it in half along the spine, then shredding the pages into clumps of crumpled paper. He stalked from the room, strewing the confetti of text behind him like the feathers of a plucked hen.

"You girls get some sleep," Serena said when he was gone. "I'll make sure he doesn't bother you again."

Callie nodded as if sleep were really possible, and Serena left. When the girls were alone, Amalfia uncurled from the shivering ball she'd become and reached out to touch the cast-off pages in front of her. As she began to cry, Callie lowered her head in shame. If she hadn't tried to goad Amalfia by telling her about Evan, he wouldn't have exploded. They were lucky that the paperback was the only thing he destroyed.

"I'm sorry about your book," Callie said quietly. "We can get you a new one. I could even get Mom to sign it for you ... if you want."

Amalfia raised her tear-streaked face, her look expressing both gratitude for the gesture of friendship and surprise at its source. "That's ... that's very sweet of you ..." She gave an embarrassed chuckle, wiping her cheeks with the back of her hand. "I'm sorry. I forgot your name."

"Callie." She let the implied slight go, and extended her hand to Amalfia with a smile. "Callie Lindstrom."

29

A Promised Bond

The pinpoint specks of violet that Amalfia fancied she could see in her brown irises in the hours after the injection actually began to appear after about a day. The remaining flecks of green in Calvin's eyes also disappeared, supplanted by the rich violet color that bled into them with imperceptible slowness. Natalie had grown so accustomed to the two-tone beauty of those hybrid irises that she was almost disappointed when they became homogenized like hers.

For both Amalfia and Calvin, the change was accompanied by a mild sore throat and runny nose—the reaction of their immune systems to the infecting adenovirus, Pancrit told them. He checked on them at regular intervals during every waking hour, examining the progress of their eyes with a penlight and questioning them about their sensitivity to the facility's knocking souls. Each time, Calvin reported that he was still ridden with whispers, to which Amalfia was still deaf. Pancrit would note the observations on his clipboard then withdraw to the seclusion of his office, where he'd apparently spent the night.

Although Natalie felt it was best for all of them to stay together in the staff lounge, it made for cramped quarters. The foot of her and Calvin's bedrolls lay only a yard away from those of Amalfia and Callie. Corporal Johnston brought them frozen meals to heat in the room's microwave and a pack of playing cards to keep the girls occupied. Callie taught Amalfia how to play Crazy Eights, Amalfia taught Callie how to play Kings Corners, and they played Gin Rummy and Go Fish and Concentration, and were both bored stiff inside of three hours. Natalie and Calvin chatted about art and read all the outdated magazines cover to cover.

As if the tedium were not enough to deal with, they also had to suffer the constant intrusion of either Block or Tackle, who took shifts patrolling the corridor. Evan, too, lurked in the hallway, and though he had not dared to reenter the lounge since Serena forced him out at gunpoint, he hovered around it like a circling buzzard. For her part, Serena never let him out of her sight. She always kept her back to the wall, never lay down, and hardly seemed to blink. Natalie knew why, too. If Serena let down her guard for one second, someone would try to disarm her.

"This is like old times for me," Calvin quipped about their confinement as he scraped the last of his mac-and-cheese dinner from its tray with a plastic spoon. "Except the food is better, and there's more privacy."

He kept his voice hushed, for the girls had already bedded down for the night in their sleeping bags at the end of the staff lounge, opposite the table where they sat. It was close to midnight of their second day at the facility, and Natalie and Calvin had deliberately waited to dine until late so they could talk undisturbed.

The reference to his term in prison jarred her. Natalie had grown so comfortable with him that she'd let his past slip her mind.

"It ... must have been hard for you," she said, trying to be broad-minded, sympathetic. "I've heard such terrible things about those places—the things they do to you there ..." Natalie imagined that a handsome, sensitive guy like Calvin would be a prime target for the hard-core prisoners to push around—or worse.

Calvin seemed as horrified by the notion as she was and shook his head as if trying to dislodge the image from his mind. "Oh! *No* ... it wasn't like that. I went to Club Fed. Minimum-security camp in Englewood. No murderers or rapists, only non-violent short-timers like me and middle-aged, white-collar wusses who'd get the crap beat out of them in the Big House. I bunked in a cubicle with a CFO busted for insider trading. Nice guy. We used to play foosball together, and he'd share the brownies his wife brought him."

Despite the almost nostalgic tone with which Calvin reminisced, Natalie could see his eyes turn glassy, could hear his voice become reedy with desolation. "Must have been something bad about the place," she said softly, not wanting to pry.

"It wasn't the place. Worst they ever did was make us pick up trash along the freeway." His mouth twitched but failed to smile. "The bad part is finding out exactly how worthless you are. All those

331

beautiful people in the art world. All the girls I used to hang with. All my so-called friends. Even my folks ..." He rubbed his watering eye as if it actually itched, then hacked up a laugh. "Nobody brought this boy any brownies."

Natalie ached for him. She remembered that Dan had once described how his family welcomed him back into their fold, even after he had accidentally shot and killed an innocent man in the line of duty. He said that was when he realized that no matter what you did, no matter how badly you screwed up, the people who loved you would always take you back. That had certainly been the case with Natalie's own loved ones, who had forgiven her time and again for the countless mistakes she'd made and continued to make. But Calvin had no one to forgive him.

"You're not worthless, Calvin," she said. "You're priceless."

He hid his face behind his hands. "If I could only believe you meant that."

She smiled. "Believe in Natalie."

"I do." He looked at her, his almost-violet eyes reddened with inflamed capillaries. "You're the only one who's ever stuck with me, and if I could get you and Callie out of here, I'll at least have done one good thing in my life."

The hope and anxiety that had been brewing within Natalie over the past week roiled in her stomach. "And ... what happens after that? What happens when *you* get out of here?"

"You mean *if*," he said.

"I know you will," she insisted. "We all will. What then?" He stared at her, and Natalie became afraid that she sounded pushy, needy, perhaps desperate. She backed away from the question, shrugged as if it were simply a casual inquiry. "I mean ... did you have any plans? Pancrit promised you a place in the Corps's Art Division—that's a pretty sweet deal."

Disappointment dimmed the light in Calvin's eyes, as if he'd expected her to say something else. "Yeah, that. I haven't given it much thought. You know, about what it'll be like ...'

To be a Violet, she finished for him silently.

"You should go for it. You'll be perfect." She hoped she sounded encouraging, not jealous. "You deserve a fresh start."

"A fresh start." He drew a deep breath and slowly exhaled, the way she often did when trying to work up courage for something. "That's what I really want, Natalie. I want to try again."

"You mean your own art? That's an awesome idea—"

"No, I mean with you. Like on the couch."

The fact that she had secretly longed for this moment only made its actuality more terrifying.

Be careful what you wish for, she thought, her emotions on the edge of a precipice over which she could not see. Yes, Calvin was attractive, he was funny, and he was smart. He was the best artist she'd ever known, and he'd risked his life to save her and Callie. In many ways, he felt like the twin from whom she'd been separated at birth ... but she'd only known him for a handful of days, less time than she'd spent with Dan. What if it didn't work out? What if he hurt her? Or, perhaps worse, what if she hurt him? He'd already been hurt so much ...

"I want that." Natalie reached over to him, nearly touched his cheek, her trembling fingers hovering over the stubbly skin as if pushing against a force field. "I want another chance with you. Maybe when we get back—"

"What if we don't get back?"

The possibility that this might be their only time together left her stunned and silent, and she withdrew her hand. Desire clashed with caution. Was it better to give in to her feelings, even if it meant only one night of happiness and a lifetime of lingering heartbreak afterward? Her brief relationship with Dan had brought her years of sadness, yet she would not have forgone that love for all the world. Would the agony of never knowing what she might have had with Calvin be even worse than the pain of allowing him into her heart only to lose him forever?

Steeped in ambivalence, neither of them could look at the other. Calvin picked at a hangnail he didn't have. "I'm sorry. You've done so much for me already—I don't have the right to ask anything more than that. I only wanted to let you know that ... no matter what happens tomorrow ... you're more than a friend to me, Natalie."

"You're so much more than a friend to me, Calvin," she admitted, her voice barely audible. "That's why I'm so scared. But I'm willing to try again."

And she leaned toward him, brought her face within an inch of his. He quivered as she drew close, opened his mouth for hers, but turned his head aside before their lips touched.

Natalie flinched back, mortified. "My fault. I shouldn't—"

"No, no, no! I want to," Calvin hastened to say. "I just wondered ... could you give me a little head start?"

His adolescent embarrassment alleviated her own. "Sure."

"I believe in Natalie," he whispered. *"I believe in Natalie ... I believe in Natalie ... "*

She touched her mouth to his moving lips in the most delicate of kisses, and though he could not speak, she knew he continued the mantra in his mind. Natalie cupped a hand to his face as they drew out the kiss, and Calvin did not pull away, and not a soul, either living or dead, interrupted them.

It was the only kiss—the only contact—they braved that night, but it was enough. As they lay down side by side on their bedrolls to sleep, they rested with the promised bond of a future together ... no matter how long or short that future might be.

Her mind racing with the implications of that bond, Natalie lay awake for more than an hour before finally nodding off. She had not been asleep long when she felt someone shaking her shoulder.

"Ms. Lindstrom? Ms. Lindstrom?"

Natalie awoke to find Amalfia bending over her.

"I … I think I *feel* them." The teen tapped her shaven temples, her mouth quivering in an uncertain smile. "I think they're knocking."

Not a trace of brown remained in her violet eyes.

30

Violets in Bloom

As soon as he heard the news, Carl Pancrit sent Tackle and Block to escort them all to the examination room, even though it was past three in the morning. Serena frowned as they emerged from the lounge into the hallway.

Natalie had never seen her friend look so tired or so old, even when she'd worn the makeup to go undercover at the convalescent home. "How long has it been since you slept?" she asked.

"Four days," Serena said. "I'm working on a personal best."

"How can you do that to yourself?"

Serena regarded her with eyes suddenly sad. "It's easy when you got problems to keep you awake."

As always, she brought up the rear of the procession to make sure that no one got behind her. That included Evan, who waited for Serena to go first, then grudgingly preceded her when she prodded him with her .45.

Pancrit greeted his patients like a solicitous barber, inviting Calvin and Amalfia to seat themselves in the latex-covered chairs. This time, however, he took the precaution of fastening the straps and cuffs once they were seated.

"Seeing as how you're good friends with Dr. Wax," Pancrit said as he secured Calvin's restraints, "perhaps you could summon him long enough for me to check how your node points are shaping up."

Calvin did as he suggested, holding Wax in his mind until Pancrit could affix the electrodes of a SoulScan to his bare cranium. Bursts of scribbling fuzzed the three green lines that ran along the bottom of the monitor's screen.

"Looks good," Pancrit remarked. "Now . . . can you get rid of him?"

Calvin initiated his protective mantra, although Natalie noted with a smile that he didn't say it loud enough for Pancrit to hear. She watched the SoulScan readout and saw that the inhabitation lines flattened to inactivity.

"How do you feel?" she asked Calvin.

He paused in the repetition of his mantra, listening for whispers. "Better, I think."

Carl Pancrit exhibited little interest in Calvin's cure. Once he saw that the gene therapy had evidently endowed Calvin with the filtering mechanism he'd lacked, the physician quickly moved on to his true test subject.

Even though her wrists were cuffed to the arms of the chair, Amalfia still held her compact mirror in her right hand, angling it to see her reflection.

Pancrit grinned. "Well? What do you think?"

Her newly violet eyes became dewy with elation. "They're even more beautiful than I thought they'd be."

"Those are merely the cosmetic improvements, my

338

dear," he told her. "It's time to determine if you're a Violet within as well as without."

"Sure she is!" Callie rooted from the sidelines. "You show him, Amalfia! You're one of the team now."

Pancrit took the mirror from Amalfia and set it on his supply table, then picked up a folded hospital gown.

Natalie realized what he was about to do. "Wait! Is that a touchstone? You shouldn't—"

"I can handle it," the teen declared. "I *have* a spectator mantra." She turned her palms upward and shut her eyes, chanting, *"From the world you know to the world you knew! Come to me, come to me, come—"*

The couplet never reached its rhyme. As soon as Pancrit draped the dressing gown across her open hands, Amalfia stiffened and jittered as if struck by lightning, eyes popping wide. Her trapped breath coughed out in great, heaving retches, and her twisting arms and legs threatened to wrench her joints from their sockets as they strained against the cuffs that held them.

Natalie rushed to her side, afraid Amalfia might choke on her tongue, but Amalfia's fit did not faze Pancrit.

"She'll be fine." He picked up the first of the nearby SoulScan's electrodes and pressed it to her head as if testing the ripeness of a cantaloupe. "See, she's settling down already."

Amalfia stopped convulsing, although she did not look in the least settled. The baby-fat sweetness of her adolescent features hardened into an anthracite ferocity when she saw the man beside her. *"Pancrit."*

He smiled. "Harold? We've missed you around here."

"Lying bastard!" Amalfia snapped forward like a Doberman at the end of its leash. "You conned me into that cursed experiment. If Wax hadn't got me first, I would've killed *both* of you—"

"Look, Harold, I'd love to catch up on old times, but I'm a little busy right now." Pancrit signaled Block, who grabbed Amalfia's head and pried her jaws apart so that Tackle could stuff the wadded hospital gown in her mouth. Together, they managed to hold her still long enough for Pancrit to continue locating her node points.

"Blast these silly tattoos!" He peeled off an electrode that he'd mistakenly taped to one of the black spots on her scalp. "Don't I have enough distractions to deal with?"

His querulous mood did not improve until he finished hooking Amalfia up to the SoulScan and looked at the dancing inhabitation lines on the green monitor. "Ah! That's better."

He nodded to his assistants. They let go of her, leaving red pressure fingerprints on her chin and cheeks.

"The node points seem to be in place. Let's see how the filtering mechanism works." Before Natalie could say anything, Pancrit smacked the large red disk of the SoulScan's Panic Button.

The jolt caused Amalfia's body to buck, and blanked Harold's hostility from her expression like a DELETE key. When the voltage finally dropped her back into her seat, she sat rigid, mewling, fearful that any movement might increase her pain. Pancrit tugged the dressing gown from her mouth, uncorking the sob behind it.

"Yes. *Yes.*" An unwholesome eagerness crept into his reaction as he watched the SoulScan's inhabitation lines, which remained flat. "The filtering mechanism seems to be protecting the node points from immediate reoccupation. Congratulations, Amalfia! You are officially a Violet."

The news only made her cry more, as if he'd pronounced sentence on her.

"Haven't you done enough to her—to all of us?" Natalie asked. "You've got what you want. Let us go."

"Not quite yet." Pancrit took off his blue blazer, unbuttoned the cuff of his left sleeve, and rolled it up past his elbow. With dreamlike fascination, he affixed a fresh needle to his vaccine gun and plugged in another vial of green fluid. "No more interruptions."

He jammed the injection into his arm, head bowed in reverence, as if accepting the Eucharist.

"Very well." Pancrit set the gun back into its niche in the attaché case and snapped the lid shut. "I'm done with you."

Natalie took that as permission to unbind Calvin. She only got his right hand loose before she saw the figures in her peripheral vision begin to move, like a flock of crows about to take flight. Block. Tackle. Serena. Evan.

It all happened with the simultaneity of disaster. Upon hearing Pancrit's cue, Tackle and Block quick-drew their side-arms. Serena anticipated their treachery and raised her .45 before their handguns even cleared their leather holsters. Still strapped to her chair, Amalfia shrieked at the crack of the shot that zoomed over her head to explode into Block's heart, while Natalie dived to shield Callie. Block fell back against the wall, leaving a crimson streak on the paint as he slid to the floor.

Serena swung the gun around to his partner. She would have killed Tackle, too, but she hadn't counted on the appearance of Corporal Johnston. Perhaps Pancrit had stationed her outside the room, for at the first sound of gunshots, the soldier shouldered the door open and began firing her own .45.

Bullets slammed into Serena's right shoulder and chest, throwing her off balance and causing her gun-hand to slacken and drop the pistol. As she fell to the floor, weaponless, both Tackle and the corporal sighted their guns at the only other mobile enemy targets: Natalie and her daughter.

Then came two consecutive puffs—*pop pop*—like the spitting of an Amazonian blowgun. Evan's tranquilizer darts. As if stung by insects, Johnston slapped her neck, Tackle grabbed his arm, and both collapsed, unconscious.

Recognizing that the battle had inexplicably turned against him, Carl Pancrit lifted his attaché case to cover his face just in time, for another *pop* lodged a dart in the case's leather lid. He held the case up to deflect further fire as he ran to the door.

Before he could make it out of the room, Serena rolled onto her right side, her shoulder shattered and bleeding, and with her left arm took something that resembled a grenade from the pocket of her leather jacket. She pulled the pin with her teeth and lobbed it toward Pancrit, but when it landed ahead of him in the corridor outside the room, it did not explode. Rather, a cloud of gray smoke like tear gas burst from it, causing Pancrit to cough and rasp as he inhaled the strange fog while fleeing down the hall.

"I knew he'd try and welsh on me," Evan Markham commented, calmly watching his former boss escape. He chucked the empty tranquilizer dart gun aside and snatched Tackle's 9mm automatic off the floor, smiling at Natalie and Callie. "But I couldn't let him kill you. Especially now that you're mine."

31

Deathdreamer

The whole debacle had taken less than a minute. The brimstone aroma of gunpowder saturated the air, and Natalie's ears still rang from the shots. Evan had saved her and Callie from being exterminated by Pancrit's goons, but only for something worse.

The fallen corporal's gun lay a couple yards from Natalie, and she considered making a grab for it.

Evan saw the object of her gaze and directed the barrel of Tackle's 9mm at Callie. "Uh-uh."

Keeping the gun trained on the girl, he sidled over to stomp on Serena's good hand as she reached across the floor to retrieve her .45. She bellowed in agony, and he kicked the automatic out of her reach.

Desperate for rescue, Natalie glanced at Calvin, who was still strapped to his chair, except for the one hand she'd managed to free. He made a *shush* sign with his lips and slipped his fingers into his right hip pocket.

Still lashed to her chair, Amalfia hiccoughed sobs as she tried to plead with Evan. "Deathdreamer ... you don't want to hurt us. Let us go, and we'll help you get away. We won't tell anyone about you."

"Oh, I'll get away, all right," he replied, "but I'm not going alone. So, Boo ... about the offer I made earlier. Because I'm feeling generous, I'm prepared to increase it."

"And how is that?" Natalie asked in a hoarse voice. If she could keep him talking long enough to give Calvin time to do whatever he had planned ...

"Not only will I be a good father to Callie," Evan said, "but I'll also refrain from shooting everyone in this room."

Afraid to speak for fear of triggering his threat, Natalie cringed when Callie raised her voice.

"I *have* a father."

"Had," Evan corrected her. "You need a new one."

"I'd rather die," Callie jeered.

"Oh? You mean like this?" Evan pointed the 9mm at the passed-out corporal and fired. Johnston's body jiggled as the bullet tore through her forehead, the exit wound spraying scarlet on the linoleum behind her head. Callie yelped and pressed closer against Natalie's back, her defiance quashed.

"Who's next, Boo? Your fearless protector here?" He sauntered over to where Serena moaned and bled. "Seems like a waste of a good bullet. Or maybe my charming Amalfia?"

She squealed as he aimed the gun at her.

"Leave them alone, Evan," Natalie said quietly. "I'll go with you."

Callie tightened her grip. *"Mom, no!"*

"I've got a better idea, *Deathdreamer,*" Calvin said. "Why don't you leave us *all* alone?"

Evan strutted to stand over Calvin's chair. "Ah! Our brave artist finally speaks up. Being the gentle-man you are, I thought you were going to let me kill all the ladies first. But now that you've reminded me ... you *are* the perfect choice."

As he raised his gun to Calvin's head, a small metallic *click* sounded, and Calvin lunged his free fist toward Evan's solar plexus. The blow seemed to knock the wind out of the Violet Killer, so much so that his shot went wide, grazing Calvin's ear. Evan doubled over, eyes wide in bewilderment, and flinched as Calvin jerked his balled hand upward.

Thrusting Calvin away from him, Evan gaped, uncomprehending, at the handle of the switchblade that protruded from his slashed abdomen. Natalie barely had time to wonder where Calvin had gotten the knife before Evan began to heave, as if unable to vomit some poison he'd swallowed.

The fit subsided a bit, and Evan drew himself up to his full height, turned his violet gaze upon Natalie. "Kiddo?"

She got to her feet. "Dad?"

He still held the gun, arm quavering. *"Run."*

That was all her father was able to say, but Natalie got the message. Wade had managed to inhabit Evan, but could not control such a powerful Violet for long.

As proof, the next halting words to come from Evan's mouth were the multiplication tables—his protective mantra. "... two ... t-times three ... is s-six ..."

Natalie went for the dead corporal's gun, while Calvin hurried to undo the buckled cuffs on his arm and legs.

"... *two times four is eight, two times five is ten—*" Evan grabbed the switchblade and yanked it from his

346

midsection with a shudder. A line of red spittle trickled from his lips as he let the knife fall to the floor.

Natalie got the corporal's .45, but when she spun around to shoot, Evan already had the 9mm aimed at Calvin, who'd failed to unbuckle the cuff on his left foot.

"—*TWO TIMES SIX IS TWELVE! TWO TIMES SEVEN IS—*"

The bang wrenched Natalie's heart. But it was Evan's violet eye that exploded from its socket. As his body collapsed, Natalie saw that Serena had dragged herself over to her .45, which she held, quivering, in her bruised left hand.

"Good thing that bullet didn't go to waste," she said, lowering the gun.

He's dead, Natalie thought with both relief and trepidation. Ten years ago, she had chosen not to kill Evan Markham because she knew he could and would come back to plague her. This time, she had no choice.

"Say your protective mantras, everyone," she advised the others, and commenced her own.

Thou preparest a table for me in the presence of mine enemies, she recited in her mind as she went to release Amalfia from her chair.

The girl's face glistened with tears and mucus, and she vacillated between self-pity and self-loathing. "It *hurt*," she sniveled. "I didn't know it was going to hurt so much. And why didn't my mantra work?"

"The first time is always hard." Once she'd unfastened the cuffs, Natalie peeled the electrodes off the teen's scalp as gently yet as quickly as she could.

"You get used to it with practice."

"And how could I let myself trust that psycho?" Amalfia covered her violet eyes with her unbound hands. *"God*, I'm nothing but a poser."

"No, Amanda, you're the real thing now. That's the problem." Natalie laid a hand on the girl's bare scalp, pitying her. "Come on. Let's get out of here."

"Uh ... we may have a little problem with that," she heard Calvin say from behind her.

Natalie turned to see that, through a superhuman mastery of mind over pain, Serena had risen to her feet and lurched to the door, where she braced herself against the wall, her right arm folded across her wounded chest like a broken wing. Her left hand held out the .45, pointed at them.

"I can't let you leave," she croaked.

32

Eliminating the Unworthy

Teetering on the edge of unconsciousness, Serena could not lift her eyelids more than halfway, but the eyes beneath them still burned with a fanatic determination. Her left hand had started to swell since Evan had stepped on it, but it did not lower the gun it held.

Natalie could not believe that the old friend who'd saved her life more than once would now end it. "Serena . . . what are you doing?"

"Only God can grant us our gifts, Nat. You know that." Serena threw disparaging glances at Calvin and Amalfia. "Promised Uncle Simon I'd eliminate the unworthy."

"Unworthy?" Natalie darted an accusing finger at the room's exit. "What . . . you let Carl Pancrit just walk out of here, but you're gonna 'eliminate' a scared teenager and a struggling artist?"

"I didn't let Pancrit walk," Serena said. "That wasn't tear gas coming out of the grenade. It was dust from the Ash Field. It was supposed to be a test for Calvin—trial by fire, and all that."

Alarmed, Calvin waited for someone to explain. "Natalie, what is she talking about?"

She stared at Serena and started to quake, for she knew what the Ash Field did to even the strongest

Violets. "That's not a test—it's murder. You planned to kill him all along, yet you pretended to help him. Why?"

'To find this place. I needed to see Project Persephone for myself ... so I could destroy it."

"And what about me and Callie?" Natalie crossed the room to kneel beside her daughter. "Are you going to kill us, too?"

"No one can know this thing ever existed." Serena drew a deep breath, her face cramped by a pain more intense than that caused by her splintered shoulder and pierced breast. "Sorry, Nat."

Her finger tightened on the trigger, but the shots didn't come. If they had been Corps Security stooges, she would have snuffed them all by then.

"Serena?" Callie looked up at her godmother with liquid, uncomprehending eyes. "Did we do something wrong?"

Serena's face rippled with warring loyalties, her finger frozen on the trigger of the quivering gun. Then she dropped her head and let the arm that held the .45 fall to her side. With capitulation came total exhaustion, and she slid down the wall into a sitting position, shuddering as the sobs that shook her rib cage squeezed her wounds.

"Aw, hell. With any luck, I'll be dead before Simon can give me grief." She gave a woeful laugh. "Not that that'll stop him."

Natalie inched toward her friend and crouched beside her. "Thank you." She gingerly lifted the .45 out of Serena's slack hand and set it aside. "I owe you. Again."

Serena couldn't even lift her brow from her knees; she merely pivoted a half-peeled eye toward Natalie. "Then you can do me a favor."

Natalie nodded. "We'll get you out of here—"

"No. Forget about me. I want you to get back in that lab." With agonizing slowness, she unzipped her leather jacket and opened its left flap for Natalie to see the lining. "Wherever you see something that might have those genetic doohickeys in it, stick one of these on it."

Duct-taped to the coat's lining were more than a dozen small, crude bricks of a gray claylike substance, each of which bore a numbered label and had a black oblong electronic device attached to one end. Natalie did not need to be a demolitions expert to recognize them as plastic explosives.

When she acted skittish about touching the stuff, Serena chuckled. "Don't be shy. C-4 don't bite."

She coughed, and the phlegm in her mouth lined the teeth of her smile with red.

Natalie gently tore the bomb packages free from Serena's jacket. "Okay, but how do I get back in the lab? Pancrit had a security card."

Serena shifted her eyes toward the dead corporal. "She probably has one."

'You need a thumbprint—"

"She has one of those, too. There's a knife over there."

She indicated the switchblade that Evan had dropped beside Calvin's chair.

Natalie whitened with disgust but fetched the knife. She then hunched over the soldier's corpse and searched her pockets and was almost disappointed when she found the security card.

"Don't look, Callie." Repeating the Twenty-third Psalm faster and faster in her mind, Natalie sawed at the flesh between the thumb and index finger of the corporal's right hand.

He restoreth my soul; He leadeth me in the paths of righteousness for His name's sake ...

She could feel the numbness in her extremities as the touchstones of cooling skin and congealing blood funneled the quantum energy of the soldier's spirit into her, but the mantra kept the soul from gaining ascendance.

Calvin came up beside her when she'd finally torn the digit free from the hand. "Need some help?"

"No. I won't be gone long. Stay here and watch them." *In case Serena changes her mind*, she wanted to add, but from the look Calvin gave her, Natalie knew that he was already thinking the same thing.

She draped the explosive devices, which were still joined by the strips of duct tape, over her left forearm, stuck the switchblade under the waistband of her jeans, and cupped the severed thumb and security card in her right hand. Wanting to dispense with this chore as quickly as possible, she dashed out of the examination room and down to the door at the end of the corridor.

As much as she would have loved to hurl the thumb away once she'd pressed it on the security door's touchpad, Natalie shoved it and the security card in her pocket in case she needed them to get out of the facility. Once she'd gained access to the lab, she used the bloody switchblade to slice off the bombs one by one, taping one to each of Carl Pancrit's computers, thermal cyclers, gene sequencers, and centrifuges.

... Thy rod and Thy staff, they comfort me ...

Never ceasing to repeat her mantra, she placed the explosives and ran back to Serena's side in the examination room. "They're all set. How do we detonate 'em?"

Serena blinked, as groggy as if she'd awakened from a nap. She snaked her left hand into the inside pocket of her jacket that lay over her heart. "Good thing they only shot my right half."

She pulled out her PDA and set it on the floor beside her. Squinting to focus, she steadied her palsied hand and touched the stylus to the screen to page through several menus. Two rows of white numbered boxes appeared on the display. As Serena scraped the stylus over them, the boxes turned black.

From down the hall came a fusillade of sequential blasts, like the finale, of a fireworks display. Fire alarms rang throughout the complex, and the noise actually drowned out Amalfia's continuous wailing.

Serena shut her eyes and grinned. "Sweet music to my ears ..."

She slumped sideways.

"Serena." Natalie palpated her friend's neck. The pulse barely registered. She turned to Calvin. "Can you carry her?"

He gave her an incredulous look. *"Carry her?* She was going to kill us!"

"But she didn't."

Calvin put up his hands. "All right. Anything to get us out of this place." He squatted, hooked one of Serena's slack arms around his neck, and thrust his arms under her back and thighs like the tines of a forklift, raising her from the floor with a grunt.

"By the way ... how did you and Serena get here? Did you bring a car?"

He snorted. "Serena? A car? You know better than that."

Natalie sighed. "Never mind. I've got another idea."

Calvin groaned under Serena's dead weight. "If I only come out of this with a hernia, I'll be ecstatic," he groused as he lurched into the corridor.

Natalie herded Callie and Amalfia out of the examination room ahead of her, then frisked Block's corpse until she located his car keys. A mumble from behind her reminded her that Tackle was only unconscious, so she snatched up Serena's .45 for protection before following the others to the front entrance. The smoke of burning plastic in the laboratory had already polluted the foyer with an acrid mist, and Natalie took huge gulps of the fresh desert air when they exited the facility into the night outside.

Having passed through the final security door, she rid herself of the severed thumb. Serena's latest rented motorcycle—a red Kawasaki—still sat out front, but Carl Pancrit's BMW was gone. They needed a vehicle that would carry them all, so Natalie went to commandeer the Hummer with Block's keys. Compared to the Volvo, it felt like steering a tank, but she didn't care about its maneuverability, only its mobility.

Calvin rested on his knees with Serena in his lap until Natalie pulled up. After he hoisted Serena into the rear of the vehicle, he took the front passenger seat, while Amalfia and Callie piled into the back.

Surely goodness and mercy shall follow me all the days of my life, Natalie thought as she gunned the engine and set them rumbling down the road through the moonscape of white dunes. *And I will dwell in the house of the Lord forever.*

Whenever she glanced over at Calvin, she could see his lips moving as he, too, kept repeating his mantra. From the backseat, she heard Callie murmur, *"Now I lay me down to sleep . . . "*

Only Amalfia was silent.

Finally, she let out a plaintive whimper. *"Please, Deathdreamer, leave me alone."*

Natalie stomped on the Hummer's brake, and the momentum of the huge vehicle caused it to skid for several yards along the gravel lane, nearly dragging them over the side of a dune. Twisting around to look at the seat behind her, Natalie saw that Amalfia had gripped Callie in a headlock, choking off the child's mantra.

"Hey, Boo." The teen grinned wickedly in the ominous light from the dashboard. "I know Amanda isn't exactly made of muscle, but you think I can still snap your kid's neck?"

By reflex, Natalie grabbed and aimed the .45, which she'd stuck barrel-down into the vehicle's cup holder.

"Go ahead, Boo," Evan said with Amalfia's voice.

"Blow this idiot kid away. Better than letting your daughter die, right?"

Natalie angled the gun upward but kept it ready. "Amanda? I know you can hear me. You don't have to let him control you."

Evan laughed. "You're talking to her like she's one of us."

He had a point. How could Natalie imbue Amalfia with the mental discipline she needed to reclaim control of her body?

Answer: the same way Natalie had first learned to force out an unwanted soul. The Alphabet Mantra. Even kids who weren't Violets had practiced the alphabet countless times during their life, concentrating on it until it became a part of them.

"Listen to me, Amanda. *Sing the Alphabet Song.*" She cleared her throat to wipe the fear from her voice and sang. "*A-B-C-D-E-F-G . . .*"

Calvin got the drift and joined in. "*H-I-J-K-L-M-N-O-P . . .*"

Evan laughed again, but then his grin became a grimace. As Amalfia's lips moved in time with the music, Evan's cruelty faded from her features.

"That's it, Amanda!" Natalie got to the end of the alphabet and started over. "*A-B-C-D . . .*"

Amalfia's singing became audible, thin and halting, but becoming stronger with each refrain. "*. . . W, X, Y, and Z.*"

She let go of Callie, who added her hoarse voice to the chorus. "*Now I know my ABC's! Won't you sing along with me?*"

More tears coursed down Amalfia's cheeks, but

these were joyful ones. Natalie put the gun away.

The four of them continued to belt out the Alphabet Song, with ever greater gusto, all the way back to Las Cruces.

33

Late Arrival

In retrospect, Jase Bedlow should have known there was something wrong about a sixty-some-year-old guy in a business suit wearing dark glasses at three in the morning. He just assumed the dude had snorted some coke to keep awake on the highway and didn't want everyone to see his pupils dilated as big as quarters. If Jase had realized what a hassle the whole thing would turn out to be, he would've told the freak "Sorry, no vacancy," even though the place was practically empty.

Usually, manning the front desk at the Cactus Catnap Lodge was a kick-back job. Located in the no-man's-land along I-10 between Blythe and Indio, the low-rent motel didn't see much business in the middle of the day, much less the middle of the night. That's why Jase took the graveyard shift: he got paid to study for his classes at UC Riverside (he'd switched majors five times in twelve years) or to watch DVDs and play games on the motel's computer. He didn't have to do squat except check in the occasional guest, which took about five minutes.

Except for the dude with the shades, damn him.

The guy did not look like he normally stayed in flea traps like the Cactus Catnap. For starters, he rolled into the motel's breezeway in a gold Beemer. Yet he didn't seem to have any luggage other than a leather briefcase that he wrapped his arms around as if it was his firstborn son or something. Jase began to think maybe the dude didn't just take drugs—he might actually be a dealer.

"I need a single for the night," the guy said, sponging sweat off his forehead with a handkerchief.

Jase gave a lopsided grin. "Night's almost over. And we charge for another night if you stay past noon."

"Fine, whatever. Just hurry it up."

With sluggard slowness, Jase drew a registration form from a notch in the desk and started to fill it out. "What's the name?"

"Carleton Amis."

The dude handed him a driver's license and a platinum Visa. *Definitely* a dealer, Jase decided. "Las Cruces, huh?" he asked, transcribing the address on the license. "You've come quite a ways. How long you been on the road?"

"Two days." The length of time seemed to have great significance for him, and he repeated it. "Almost exactly two days."

"Where you headed?"

"Orange County. I've got business with some people in Fullerton." Amis swiveled his head as if someone had come up behind him. "You have a lot of guests tonight?"

"Hardly any. Why?"

The dude cocked his ear, listening. "I heard voices . . ."

I'll bet you did, Jase thought. "Let me run this card. Back in a sec."

He stepped into the tiny office behind the front desk and swiped the Visa through the credit-card reader. While waiting for the receipt to print, he surveyed the pegboard where the lodge hung the keys of the available rooms. "You want smoking or non?"

Amis didn't answer.

Jase raised his voice. "I said, you want smoking or non?"

The only response was a strangled rasp, followed by a thump and a clatter.

"Mister?" Jase glanced back through the office door, but the dude had disappeared. The clerk returned to peer over the front desk and finally saw the source of that hissing, gurgling sound he heard. "Holy crap."

The dude in the business suit flailed and gibbered on the floor as if a horde of maggots were gestating in his chest. He hacked, trying to cry out, but all that spewed from his mouth was a froth of churned saliva.

"Aw, hell!" Jase muttered. "Why'd you have to O.D. on my shift?"

Panicking for his job security, he snatched up the phone receiver and punched in nine-one-one. Before the call could connect however, Amis ceased wriggling and lay heaped there like a beached jellyfish. That was when Jase noticed that the guy's convulsions had knocked his sunglasses askew, revealing blank eyes blooming with a deep violet color.

"Jesus," the clerk exclaimed, as the perplexed emergency operator peppered his ear with questions.

It would have. been impossible to determine from Carl Pancrit's expression whether, in his first moments as a Violet, he gained the insight into the afterworld for which he'd yearned. Thousands of souls poured into him through the Ash Field dust specks that had settled in his lungs, but if they finally whispered to him the secrets he so longed to share, the knowledge did not appear to please him. And it was unlikely that anyone would ever summon him to learn his final revelation.

34

The Forgotten Adversary

The remnants of the Lindstrom family returned to California like veterans retreating from the front—no banners, no parades, only battle fatigue and shell shock.

They had any number of reminders of what they'd lost in the fight. Serena had not regained consciousness when they'd last seen her at the hospital in Las Cruces, and although the doctors predicted that she would eventually recover, she needed a titanium ball joint to replace her shattered shoulder. Amanda had gone back to her parents, who were so flummoxed by her inability to handle her new gift that they were already contemplating sending her to the School for Violet training. Natalie had had to ask Hector Espinoza to wire her traveling money since all their luggage had gone up in flames at the hotel in Boston, and she, Calvin, and Callie had to take a taxi back from the airport because when they got to the parking garage at LAX, they realized that only Wade had had keys for the Camry.

Wade Lindstrom's charred remains still lay in a drawer at a morgue in Boston, pending delivery to the cemetery of his daughter's choice. Natalie didn't know if he wanted to be buried with her mother in

Pasadena or with Sheila in New Hampshire, and she hadn't had either the time or the heart to summon him to ask his wishes.

Ill omens at home told her that the war was not over. Yellow POLICE LINE DO NOT CROSS ribbons zigzagged over the front door and Sanjay Prashad leaned against his Mitsubishi at the curb, looking far too pleased with himself. He grinned at them as they got out of the cab.

"I do not think that you will want to go in there," he said, indicating the condo. "The stains on the carpet—it would be most unpleasant for the child . . . particularly given her unique attributes."

Calvin paled. "Oh, God . . . Tranquillity."

With gathering gloom, Natalie looked at the haven she'd created for herself and her child. It was the kind of cookie-cutter construction she hated, but she'd bought it because it was new, with no taint of death, and over the past decade it had become the citadel that defended them against enemies of both this world and the next. She wanted nothing more than to hole up behind its walls right now, raise the drawbridge, and lower the portcullis. How could it be that they would never set foot inside it again?

"The authorities are most anxious to speak with Mr. Criswell regarding Ms. Moon's death," Prashad continued, his smile like an ivory scythe. "I must confess that I had to inform them that I witnessed a very bitter argument between the two of them shortly before her murder."

"Calvin had nothing to do with that, and you know it," Natalie seethed.

"Oh, I have little doubt of Mr. Criswell's innocence. Of course, with his past criminal record, and the fact that many people saw him leave the hotel room in Boston where your father was stabbed to death ... well, a jury may not agree with me."

His audacity smothered her, left her clamoring for words strong enough to denounce him.

Pushing ahead of her mother, Callie spoke up instead. "Calvin didn't kill Grandpa Wade. It was the bad man. Evan."

The Corps Security agent beamed at the child's precocity. "I am certain you are correct, young lady. And that is why I am prepared to use all the influence of the N-double-A-C-C on Mr. Criswell's behalf."

Uh-oh. Here it comes, Natalie thought. "What do you want?" she asked Prashad, although she already knew.

He pressed his palms together. "Due to recent *setbacks* in our research-and-development program, the Corps will not have as many conduits at its disposal as it had planned. Any influx of new members to make up this deficit would be most appreciated."

"Leave Natalie out of this," Calvin said. "I'm the one in trouble. *I'll* go to work for the Corps. I can do that now. See?" He opened his eyes wide so Prashad could admire his new violet irises.

"While the Corps would be most grateful for your services, Mr. Criswell, I am afraid that they alone will not be sufficient to secure your freedom."

Prashad awaited a counteroffer from Natalie. She stared at him, unwilling to accept that, after all they had survived, this unctuous little bureaucrat would prove their undoing. It was like being checkmated by a pawn, trumped by a deuce.

She clasped Calvin's hand in hers. "I'll go back to the Corps."

The agent bowed his head courteously, but he had not finished pressing his advantage. "Again, your renewed membership will be most welcome. But there is a significant monetary incentive contingent upon your daughter's enrollment in the Conduit Academy."

Not Callie, Natalie thought. *Not the School ... I'll do anything but that.*

"Forget it, Pee Wee." Calvin presented his wrists. "Slap the cuffs on. I can so do prison."

"No," Callie said. "I'll go."

The answer took all three adults by surprise. Even Prashad did not seem to expect Callie's cooperation.

Natalie crouched beside her. "Honey, you don't have to do this."

"Mom, he saved our lives." Her eyes shone with the same worrisome excitement Natalie had seen in them while Callie thumbed through the School brochure on the plane. "Besides, I *want* to go."

Calvin shook his head. "I can't let you do this. *Either* of you."

Callie lifted her chin with an obstinacy that made Natalie think of herself at that age. "I'm going to the School no matter what you do, so if you go to jail, you'll only make my mom miserable."

Calvin's gaze dropped to the toes of his shoes. He still wore the oversize sneakers that Serena had procured for him in Boston.

Natalie grasped her daughter's shoulders. "Please, baby girl. For *my* sake, don't do this."

"As gratifying as I find the child's enthusiasm, it is not really her decision," Prashad broke in. "In the unfortunate event that the authorities discover Mr. Criswell is guilty of murder, I am sure that they will also conclude that you have endangered your daughter by exposing her to such a violent individual. Naturally, Child Protective Services will have to obtain custody of the girl for her own safety."

He paused to permit Natalie to realize that she had no hope. Whether she cooperated or not, she would still lose Callie to the Corps.

"I recommend that you encourage your girl's admirable ambition to serve her country in the N-double-A-C-C," Prashad advised. "At least then you will retain the right to see her at the Academy during prescribed visitation opportunities."

Natalie couldn't speak. How had her existence fallen to pieces in less than five minutes?

Callie put her arms around her mother's neck, the child comforting the parent. "I'll be fine, Mom. Just like you."

"I hope so, honey," Natalie whispered. "I hope I'm fine. I hope we'll all be."

As they hugged, she peered over the shoulder of her growing girl at the home they had been denied. The sight of the condo wavered as her eyes turned watery, but Natalie knew the regret would not last. They would always have a home, she, Callie, and Calvin, wherever they were, as long as they had one another.

THROUGH VIOLET EYES

*In a world where the dead can testify against the living,
someone is getting away with murder.*

To every generation a select few souls are born with
violet-coloured eyes – and the ability to channel the
dead. Both rare and precious, and rigidly controlled
by a society that craves their services, these Violets
perform a number of different social duties.

But now the Violets themselves have become the
target of a brutal serial murderer – a murderer who
has learned how to mask his or her identity even
from the victims. Can FBI agent Dan Atwater, aided
by Violet Natalie Lindstrom, uncover the criminal in
time? Or will more of Natalie's race be dispatched
to the realm that has haunted them all since
childhood?

978-0-7499-4127-7

WITH RED HANDS

She can connect the living with the dead and help bring justice to the murdered. But now a killer is out to stop her ... with his own red hands.

Once part of an elite group of investigators with the power to interview the dead victims of violent crime, Natalie Lindstrom's had enough of the violence. Yet, as she tries to build a new life and protect her five-year-old daughter, Natalie still recognises injustice when she sees it, and knows a young man is getting away with murder.

The case against Prescott Hyland Jr is airtight – until a corrupt Violet delivers devastating testimony against another man. Now Natalie is being drawn back into her former career and a danger far worse than she can imagine. Because, in the world of the Violets, sometimes your past can literally come back to haunt you.

978-0-7499-4132-1

IN GOLDEN BLOOD

She's running from her past ... but the voices of the dead can never be silenced.

Natalie Lindstrom has a gift: the power to speak to the dead, to solve crimes by interviewing murder victims. But now Natalie wants to escape, from the voices that fill her head, and from the organisation that has used her as a crime-solving tool – and who now wants to recruit her daughter. So Natalie takes a job with an archaeologist in the mountains of Peru. Her job: to find a trove of priceless artifacts – by channelling those who lived and died at an ancient Incan site.

But in the towering Andes, Natalie enters a 500-year-old storm of betrayal, murder, greed, and rage. The slaughtered reach out to her. The slaughterers boast of their crimes. Alone, cut off from her family, Natalie faces a chilling realisation: every truth she uncovers is leading her one step closer to a terror beyond imagining.

978-0-7499-4137-6